cutting the night in two

Evelyn Conlon, born 1952 in County Monaghan. She lived for a number of years in Australia and has travelled extensively in Asia. Her short stories have appeared in many publications and anthologies. She was editor of *An Cloigeann is a Luach* while writer-in-residence in Limerick. Her novels are *Stars in the Daytime* (1989) and *A Glassful of Letters* (1998), her short story collections, *My Head is Opening* (1987), *Taking Scarlet as a Real Colour*, (1993), the title story of which was performed at the Edinburgh Theatre Festival, and *Telling: New and Selected Stories* (2000).

Hans-Christian Oeser, born 1950 in Wiesbaden, taught German literature and language at UCD and at the Goethe Institute Dublin. An Irish resident since 1980, he works as a literary translator, travel writer, editor and critic. Among his numerous translations are novels, short story and poetry collections by Irish authors such as Brendan Behan, Dermot Healy, Jennifer Johnston, John McGahern, Eoin McNamee and Christopher Nolan. In 1997 he won the Aristeion European Translation Prize for his translation of *The Butcher Boy* by Patrick McCabe.

cutting the night in two

SHORT STORIES BY IRISH WOMEN WRITERS

ED. EVELYN CONLON
& HANS-CHRISTIAN OESER

**NEW
ISLAND**

CUTTING THE NIGHT IN TWO
SHORT STORIES BY IRISH WOMEN WRITERS
First published June 2001 by
New Island
2 Brookside
Dundrum Road
Dublin 14

British Library Cataloguing in Publication Data
A catalogue record for this book is available
from the British Library

The Arts Council
An Chomhairle Ealaíon

New Island receives financial assistance from The Arts Council
(An Chomhairle Ealaíon), Dublin, Ireland.

Cover design: Artmark
Printed in Ireland by Colour Books Ltd.

Contents

Introduction

This anthology brings together a large number of stories by Irish women, some of whom are well known, some less widely read. It began as a portrait of work not always brought to the notice of readers, but quickly became a surprising upturning of the view sometimes given in the literary ledger.

It is believed by some that we have reached a stage where it is counterproductive to have an all-women anthology but we feel that this is far from true. If fiction really is the tuning into the communal unconscious, then we need, as readers, to have a complete history of that. Despite some improvement in anthological representation there has been an unfortunate fragmentation of the female voice coming from Ireland, leading indeed to an internal exile. We get some of these writers, some of the time, at the party. Next time we get a different few. This continuous scattering dilutes the overall voice and ensures that we cannot compare the work of the individuals who contribute so uniquely to the whole.

As a means of rectifying that fragmentation, this anthology takes its place alongside such collections as *The Female Line: Northern Irish Women Writers* (edited by Ruth Hooley, published by The Northern Ireland Women's Rights Movement in 1985), *Wildish Things: An Anthology of New Irish Women's Writing* (edited by Ailbhe Smyth, published by Attic Press in 1989), and *Territories of the Voice* (edited by Louise De Salvo, Katherine Hogan and Kathleen Walsh D'Arcy, published by Beacon Press and Virago Press in 1990). It is the first such enterprise in a decade and a good opportunity to look back over an entire century.

INTRODUCTION

Other notable compatriots are *Other Fires: Short Fiction by Latin American Women* (edited by Alberto Manguel, published by Picador in 1986), *America and I: Short Stories by American Jewish Women Writers* (edited by Joyce Antler, published by Beacon Press 1990), and *Cabbage and Bones: An Anthology of Irish American Women's Fiction* (edited by Caledonia Kearns, published by Henry Holt in 1997). We are lucky to have five writers from across the border, women writers from there having been particularly neglected. The final three stories are by authors of Irish descent, living in the US, Australia and England: further evidence of the vast wealth of Irish writing, in all its guises.

The prose of the writers assembled here is imaginative and often tough, shrewd about the subconscious negotiations that take place between people and between writers and the world. While we do not want to highlight any specific work, we had particular joy in finding Nora Hoult's story, with which our anthology begins, a comparatively early work that is shocking because we do not expect an apparently 'respectable married woman' to be so blasé about her life as an occasional prostitute, nor do we expect her husband to be so lazily complacent. Edna O'Brien's story, full of the uncertainty of new passion, combines a subtle realisation of class difference with a poignantly worldly view of the hopelessness of the illicit affair, which 'life the gaffer' will control. There is love in some of the work, but it is not innocent nor gauche. It is informed by an underground banter that in lesser hands than those of the writers presented here could be viewed as bleakly cynical but which in fact becomes gratifyingly illuminating.

The geographical locations vary greatly — Dublin, Belfast, Kerry, Scotland, Wales, New York, Australia, Greece, Germany. The concerns differ — a young bride becomes horrified by the day after the honeymoon, a woman steals a baby, a man is queasily rollercoasted into marriage by the illness of his girlfriend, Mary Lavin's wife and daughters hover on the economic knife edge between the possibility of lilacs and the reality of dung, an Irish American accounts for the lives of the Kennedys, an Irish Australian writer creates a menacing scene as a father urges his daughter to scream, and Mr Edelman, of the good vocabulary, gets ready to rescue her. The entire collection re-introduces us to some well-loved voices and introduces some new ones.

That these thirty-four stories were all written by women does not, of course, mean that there is a unified voice; on the contrary, the styles and points of view are so varied that the best reason for them to appear in the same book is that the reader will want to read stories of such diversity and of such a high calibre. We feel that this is a volume worth cherishing because of the success of the imaginative pact created between the writers and their world.

Evelyn Conlon
Hans-Christian Oeser
March 2001

NORA HOULT

Nine Years Is A Long Time

It wasn't until October was well under way that she began to wonder that she had had no word from him. Even then she didn't actually worry. He had probably gone on some business trip. Men in a good position, like he certainly was, often went away on business looking after their affairs. He might have gone to London: he was a member of some swell club there. That she did know, for he'd let out one day something about an important call being put through to his club in town, and he had had to return to Rotherfield sooner than he had expected.

All the same she found herself watching the posts, watching for the appearance of the telegraph boy — he usually wired. All the time she was watching. When she dusted the front room, or went to fetch anything from the cupboard, she would find herself come to a standstill in front of the window, and staring up and down the road. By the end of the month she admitted that it was a good piece over his usual absence.

Her husband thought it funny too. They had a talk about it one evening when their daughter, Irene, was out at her shorthand class.

She started the subject herself. She said: "What do you think about it, Harry? What's your real opinion? You can say right out what's in your mind, you know?"

They were sitting in the kitchen over the fire. He took up the poker, and knocked the coal about with it making a better blaze, before he answered. Then he said in a very thoughtful voice: "Well, of course, he might be dead."

She nodded her head. "I've thought of that myself."

So she had. But to have it put into words from him made it more real. Like hearing a thunder-clap when before you had just wondered if there mightn't be a storm about.

He added, leaning back in his chair, and looking at her out of small eyes blinking over their comfortable creases: "He could die sudden and you not a penny the wiser, seeing that you don't know his name or address or anything about him."

"I'll tell you this much," she said a little sharply, "if he did die, there'd probably be half a column at the least about him in the *Rotherfield Telegraph*. He'd be one of their leading citizens; there's no doubt about that. I wouldn't mind betting that he's the director of several companies."

"Well, what of it? You'd be none the wiser, since you don't know his name. There's several leading Rotherfield men died lately; about his age, too. I don't know that you'd do much good if you went over to Rotherfield, and looked up the papers. You wouldn't know, see, would you?"

She looked into the fire. "I suppose I wouldn't." She thought a little, then she said: "Tell you what. I wouldn't be surprised if his name started with a 'Mac'. He had a Scotch accent all right. Though he wasn't mean."

No, he wasn't mean. Three pounds a time came in very useful to help out. She was going to miss it, if it stopped. And so would Irene, and Mr Scott. Mr Scott was how she always thought of her husband.

He agreed with her this time. "Oh, no. I wouldn't say that he was mean. But reserved. Scotch people, of course, are like that. That was why he never let out a word about himself or his occupation."

The flames from the fire were beginning to scorch the front of her legs. She rubbed her hands up and down them. Then, crossing one leg over the other, she hazarded: "I often had the idea that ship-building was his line. Else, what brought him to

Merseyhead so regular? I mean he came here before he met me."

"Very likely," said Mr Scott. "Quite likely, I'd say." He took out his pipe and his pouch, and began to press tobacco into the bowl.

She watched his red face bent forward with some hostility. If her Rotherfield friend didn't turn up soon, he'd feel it. He'd have to go without tobacco. All she had now was Irene's pound a week and about a pound profit on Miss Halpin, their paying guest, who had a good post as manageress of Bailey's, the big drapers. Two pounds a week didn't go far towards keeping them well fed, and with good fires. Seeing as he was the one who was out of a job, who didn't contribute nothing, it was only fair he should give up things.

"So that's what you think, that he's dead?" she asked, resuming the conversation, but as if she were attacking him.

He took a draw at his pipe, before answering. He was always one like that, one to take his time over things. It would annoy you if you didn't know him. It annoyed you when you did know him, too.

"I didn't say that he *was* dead, for I don't know. What I said was that he might he dead, for all you know, or that I know, or for all that we *would* know."

He stopped and looked at her, as if hoping that at last she had got the position clear. Deciding to take no risk he added patiently, "Because, you see, you are not in possession of his name, or of his address, or anything about him except that he lives, or lived, at Rotherfield. So that you can't find him, or satisfy your mind."

"I know that. I don't need you to tell me that ."

"Well, then …"

"And I tell you, Mr Scott, you'll find it no bloody joke us losing three quid a month."

"I know that." His mouth pursed into lines of bitter resignation. "How long is this going on, I wonder?"

What he meant was, how long before his father kicked the bucket? Before their two minds was a picture of an old paralysed man. Just sitting in a big chair holding on grimly to life. When he died there'd be money coming to Mr Scott as his only son. *When* he died. All over the world there were people waiting for other people to die, and settle their financial problems for them. And it seemed like that the longer you waited, the longer you had to wait.

Mr Scott said what they'd each of them said many a time: "You'd think that with nothing to do, nothing to live for as you might say, he'd be glad to go. I'm sure I should in his place."

She nodded her head. But that topic was threadbare. Her mind went back to her own problem. Why didn't her Rotherfield friend wire? Wasn't she going to see him again ever?

The fire was too hot on her other leg now. So she reversed her position. Then she held out both legs in front of her. She used to have good legs; they were a little on the fat side now. She'd put on eight pounds this last year. Eleven stone ten was her weight.

"Do you think I've got to look much fatter lately?" she asked him.

Mr Scott looked at her indifferently, "I don't know. Maybe you have."

"My legs are fatter, aren't they?"

"You always had a good calf."

"Yes, but my ankles were slim. I used to be able to get my thumb and middle finger to meet round. Now I can't."

She showed him. There was a good inch of flesh-coloured stocking to spare over the squeezed flesh.

"Hmmm." He stared. Then he said: "Thinking of slimming or what?"

14

"Doctors say it's very bad for you. Besides, it wasn't as if I was a big eater. And heaven knows I get my share of exercise with all the housework."

"I'd leave it. I don't think it makes much difference. Nature intended there to be two kinds of women, big and small. I like the modern slim woman myself."

She had heard him say this till she was tired of hearing him. Whenever he came in from the pictures, he'd go on talking about some lovely slim little girl till you'd think he was daft. Getting into his dotage he was. Pinning pictures of girls up on his bedroom walls; just legs and scraps of lingerie. Sixty! An old man really. She could ask him, why he married her then? Of course she'd been slimmer then, but she'd always had a figure.

She said: "My Rotherfield friend said he always liked a woman with a figure. Something to get hold of."

"Some men do," he agreed, nodding his head in deep assent, so that you could see the thin hair brushed neatly across the top. "There was a time, I remember it well, when most men liked them big. Fashions change in women like they do in everything else. I think Edward liked them on the full-figured side. But I believe the Prince of Wales likes them skinny."

"Go on with you! What do you know about what the Prince of Wales likes in the way of women?"

"As much as anybody else, I suppose. Why, only the other day I walked back from the library with a man who knew someone who knew …"

"You told me that bit before. Anyone can pretend they know anything, can't they? Well, I'd better get Irene's supper."

She got up from her seat with a jerk. Anyhow it was no good worrying. Worrying never did any good. She might hear from him tomorrow.

But she didn't hear. Nor the day after. Nor the day after that …

A depression settled slowly and abidingly on her spirit. It was a bad time in the garden. You couldn't do anything with it just now, but prop up the chrysanthemums against the wind. And the daily housekeeping round, making the list for Mr Scott to go to the shops, cooking meals, washing clothes, ironing, dusting, and for diversion talking to Miss Halpin — who was as dull as ditchwater, and had probably never had a man in her life — hung heavily. When she lay down after clearing up from the one o'clock dinner, she didn't go to sleep, but her thoughts went round in a dull painful question. It seemed to rain every day, so that you had no heart in you to go for a bit of a walk or up to see the shops. It was a pity, because they said there was nothing like a walk or a change to take your mind off things — and walking reduced the weight too.

What she was really missing was the change her Rotherfield friend made, she decided. It had been a sort of holiday when she got his wire or letter. Then Mr Scott knew that he'd have to manage everything himself. She'd be the rest of the morning having a bath, and dressing herself with special care. The last touch was a drop or two of Coty's *Chypre,* that was too expensive to use for any but very special occasions. Then after a light lunch — no steak and onions — off to the Queen's where they always met. She liked sitting in the lounge of the Queen's, with well-dressed people about her, and having a drink and a chat, and then another drink before they went off to the hotel.

They were nearly always able to have the same bedroom, with the red curtains and the alabaster vases on the mantelpiece, so that it was really homelike in its familiarity. Mrs Weston always had the gas-fire lit for them ready.

It wasn't that her Rotherfield friend really attracted her in the way one or two men — no, really only one man in her life — had attracted her. But still a woman wanted to get into bed with a man now and then. It was only natural. She had always felt better in herself afterwards. Mrs Weston sent them tea up, or if they preferred they had it downstairs in the lounge. You'd see quite a good class of people having their tea, too; you'd be surprised. Mrs Weston knew some really famous theatrical people like the time when Daisy Allen had stayed with her. Handy, the place was. And central. Well Mrs Weston would be wondering what on earth had happened to her.

Almost every month — he'd missed now and again, of course — as regular as regular for nine solid years.

It *had* been a change. He went off pretty soon afterwards. Had some dinner engagement usually, he said. And she'd meet Irene coming out from the office, and they'd go off to the pictures, and have a little bit of supper somewhere afterwards. It always seemed to her that when she went into Spinetti's with Irene men used to look at her with increased attention. They looked at her a damn sight more than they did at Irene, pretty and slim and young as she was. Anyhow she always felt pleased with herself and warm and comfortable inside.

Now, if he never came to see her again, or if she never saw him again, life would just go on as if it were a wet November all the time.

She began to spend more time in front of her looking-glass. One morning she went out, and recklessly bought a special pot of expensive skin food. Irene saw it when she came back from the office.

"What's that? Is that yours?"

"Yes. I treated myself for a change. Mrs Rosenbaum was telling me that it's terribly good for the skin. Works marvels. So it should at the price."

"Well, I just hope to goodness, mother, you are not going to start making yourself up the way Mrs Rosenbaum goes on. I think it's disgusting. An old woman like that."

"She's not an old woman. She's only about fifty."

"Well, I do think there's nothing more repulsive than to see a woman of that age trying to make herself look young. They never do; they just look repulsive, revolting. Why should a woman when she's past forty go on fussing about herself?"

"I suppose you'd like me not to use powder or lipstick, even?"

"Well, I don't say I mind a little powder, but ..."

She stopped, and shrugged her shoulders. Standing there scornful and young, with her smooth skin and hard eyes. She was always bossing her now. Last time they'd gone out together, she'd said: "Mother, you've got too much rouge and lipstick on," rubbed it off herself. And she wouldn't let her smoke on top of trams: when once she had wanted to light up — "Please don't, mother. If any of the girls at the office should get on!"

The whole thing was that she was beginning to put on airs and graces, to fancy herself. But Irene wasn't a bit like an ordinary girl, like she'd been when she was eighteen. She said she hated men. Once she had told her straight: "Well, if it hadn't been for some of my men friends, *you'd* have had a thin time when you were a kid, I can tell you. It wasn't your father supported you and him at the war."

Did her good to be told straight out. Of course, young people were like that, very intolerant. They thought no one should look nice but themselves. She said, and now there was anger in her voice: "Well, if you think I'm going to look dowdy just to please you."

"I don't want you to look dowdy. But if you have a lot of stuff on your face with your red hair — and honestly, mother, it suits you better if you'd stop henna-ing it so much — if you put on a thick cream and lipstick with your hair and big figure, it makes you look conspicuous, that's all."

"You're jealous. Because when we're out together more men look at me than they do at you."

"I'm not at all jealous ..." Irene looked at her mother as if she were going to say hard words, then she went out of the room with her lips tightly pressed together.

Mrs Scott sat down in front of the fire, holding the skin food in her hand. There was a pain in her heart which she tried to banish by getting up quickly and putting a record on the gramophone:

"There's a lovely lake in London … "

"Pom pom pom-pom pom pom pom-pom," she hummed to herself defiantly, but her thoughts went on all the same. So Irene thought she was too old to bother about herself, that she looked fast when she took a bit of trouble with her appearance. She wasn't too old. She tried to cheer herself up thinking of the story her Rotherfield friend had told her about the old man who was asked at what age sexual desire had left him. But the smile faded, because it took her thoughts back to him again. Why *hadn't* she heard from him?

Had he got tired? Might as well face it. Irene thought of her as old and fast-looking. Had he come to think that about her? She got up and took down the oval mirror that hung over the mantelpiece and examined her face intently; then she held it farther away, so that it included the reflection of part of her figure as well.

She couldn't see that she looked so old. There was something cheeky and attractive about her face, especially when she made her eyes laugh. Experienced, of course. Well, why not? Well, wouldn't she be a fool at her age if she didn't look as if she had had something to do with men? Withering on the virgin thorn — somebody, not her Rotherfield friend, somebody else had used the phrase once, and she remembered it with satisfaction. That wasn't her line. Though it just about suited her lady lodger.

Of course she was on the plump side. That was upstairs. Her hips were still slim, and, thank God, she didn't stick out behind. And her friend had always said …

She heard Irene's steps in the hall. and replaced the mirror quickly. The hall door banged. She had gone back to work without saying "good-bye". Bad tempered. Not got over her buying something for herself. What she was going to do

19

straight off was to go upstairs, and give her face a good massage with the skin food.

She came down to the afternoon cup of tea in a good temper. Her skin felt as soft as velvet to her touch, and the lines from nostrils to the corners of her mouth showed a lot less. Even Mr Scott noticed it. He said: "You do look smart."

He said that because she had on her best satin blouse, and men always liked satin. Satin or velvet. But he wouldn't have said anything, if she hadn't done her face up. They chatted amiably, and when he said: "Do you know Bessy Morris is on at the Palace: I wouldn't mind seeing her," she surprised herself by saying: "Let's go."

"But what about her ladyship's supper?"

"Let her have it cold for once. I'll do her up a nice salad and leave the coffee, so that it only wants heating."

"And Irene?"

"It just won't do that girl any harm to get her own eats for once. She's getting above herself."

"Haven't I said she puts on too many airs? Ever since she went to that office she's been a changed girl. And you always stick up for her."

"Well, I did stick up for her. But as a matter of fact you're right for once. She's getting to think there's no one in the world but herself."

"That's just what I've often said."

"I know that, and I'm agreeing with you. See?"

Pleasantly they set off for the Palace. It wasn't often that she went out with her husband. Not likely. It was treat enough for her to give him the money to go to the pictures. But he didn't look so bad when he was dressed nicely, with his hat brushed and everything. Irene would think she'd gone off her chump going out with him. It would show Miss Scott that she wasn't everybody.

She did it in style, too. At the interval, she slipped him half a dollar, and they went into the saloon, and had a Scotch and splash. He passed her back the change, and it warmed you up, so that you enjoyed the second half better.

Still, wasn't it funny, even in the Palace, a place he'd never be likely to go to, unless compelled by some business function, she found herself looking for her Rotherfield friend. Once she really thought she saw him, looked a bit like at the back, and her hand stiffened, ready to clutch Mr Scott's arm. But when the man turned, it wasn't a bit like him really.

Bessy Morris sang one of her old songs. She sang: *"I don't want to get old; I don't want to get old; I want to stay just as I am ..."* Running furiously up and down the stage, and making everyone die laughing. *"I want to come home at half-past four and have a row with the woman next door; I don't want to get old ..."*

She laughed a lot; and she also laughed loudly at the jokes of the comedian who followed. Thank God, she had a sense of humour and could enjoy a saucy story. A man in front, a very nice-looking, well-dressed fellow, too, kept looking round and trying to catch her eye. She didn't take any special notice: after all it wasn't playing the game to give a man encouragement when you were out with another — even if it happened to be only her husband, and she was paying for him.

All the same it just showed that she wasn't quite on the shelf whatever Irene thought. When they stood up for *God Save The King*, he just stared and stared at her. Mr Scott noticed it. He whispered: "Would you like me to slip away quietly?" but she shook her head. No, she didn't feel like it, and after all she had given all that up.

When they were sitting in the tram, she slipped out the mirror attached to her hand-bag, and was satisfied. There was a green light in her grey eyes that beckoned. Putting it back she hummed: *"I don't want to get old; I don't want to get old ..."*

The next day wasn't so good. To begin with she had found herself with the definite expectation that she would hear from her friend that morning, and by twelve o'clock, when nothing had come — he was considerate; he always let her know before

21

twelve — her spirits went down, plop, and she as definitely decided that it was the finish, and that she might as well face the fact. She stood at the window, and told herself so in good round language. Then she stared up and down.

It was one of those not infrequent days when without actually raining, it looked as if it were going to rain, that it would rain if the weather wasn't too indifferent and spiritless to be able to do anything so positive. It *should* rain. A grocer's van passed; the woman from two houses up went by on her morning's shopping. Mrs Scott's eyes followed her critically. What a way to go out, shoes all muddy, old mackintosh ... oh, who cared! An errand boy wheeled by on a bicycle, whistling cheerfully. Let him whistle. He knew damn all about life.

Yes, he must be dead, and if he was dead, that was that, she couldn't do anything about it. Or he'd found another woman, younger and better-looking than she was. But that didn't seem reasonable. After all if he'd stuck to her for nine years, when he could have any girl he wanted, as any rich man could, why should he change now? Nine years showed that he was the faithful sort. Or he'd made it up with his wife; of course there was a wife somewhere; she knew that though he kept his mouth close. Perhaps she'd been in a lunatic asylum, and been let out cured. And he was sticking to her. That was another thing about married men. They might be ever so bitter about their wives, say they'd spoilt their lives, and all that stuff. And the very next thing, for the sake of his children, or for the sake of his home, or for the sake of his bloody position, or his bloody conscience, he'd turn you down as if you weren't flesh and blood at all.

Still, nine years was a long time, and she'd have thought he'd have done it before if he were going to do it.

Well, everything went in time, and it was no good moping about it. "The best of friends must part," as the old saying was. It wasn't as if she'd actually been in love with him, still you got used to having a man. At this very moment, she wouldn't mind

... it was last night's outing, and being near her period. That was why she felt so depressed, too.

Depression or not, no good standing there, Mr Scott would be wondering when he was going to get his dinner: Dinnertime was what he spent all *his* morning waiting for. Like his blasted cheek, but there it was.

When they were sitting over a cup of coffee and Irene had gone back to work, Mr Scott said suddenly: "Do you know when I was coming back I saw a telegraph boy cycling up the road this morning, and I made sure he was going to turn in here. He just went a few doors on: I think it would be for Tilson's."

"Who the hell would be sending us a wire? The Sweep isn't on now. Did you think your father had died at last?"

"Not likely!" Mr Scott sniffed contemptuously through his nose. "No, *he'll* never die. I thought it was from your friend, of course."

"Well, you can give up thinking about him. It's over three months now." She put her cup on the table, and then turning towards him, raised her voice emphatically. "I shan't hear from him again. Not never. See?"

"I don't know. Christmas is coming. That might bring you something. Why are you so sure of a sudden?"

"I couldn't tell you why I'm so sure. I just know it today. I feel it in my bones. Somebody has been making mischief, saying that I'm a married woman, not a widow, like I told him, and my friend is so straight that he wouldn't go with a married woman. He told me that once, and I remember it now. Somebody might easily have seen me and him at the Queen's, and known us both. Or else he's dead. Or else ... anyhow I just know I shan't see him again. So that's enough about that."

Mr Scott looked at her face. She was getting quite worked up about it. He sought for sympathetic words. "Well, no wonder you're upset. It must be — I was working it out in bed last night — must be a good nine years since you first ran into

23

him — just by the Arcade, wasn't it? — and he turned out so lucky. Ah well, no use crying over spilt milk." He waited for her to speak, but as she said nothing he went on tentatively: "Dare say you could easily pick up someone else if you fancied?"

She gave him a hard look. "Could I? Well, I might. But you know damn well that having Irene going to an office, I can't do what I please. Besides, after being so regular with just the one man ..." She stopped and her lips began to be unsteady. Horrified, she comprehended in a lightning flash that she had got the habit of being faithful. Why, if that chap last night had spoken to her, and she'd been on her own, she would have behaved like a silly kid and rushed away. She had just got out of the way of all that ... pretty awful to think that she, Sally Scott, had dwindled into a Miss Prim and Steady for the rest of her life. Not a single man in her life, for you wouldn't count Mr Scott. Past work and past everything he was. She choked back a sob. That's what her Rotherfield friend had done to her. That's what a woman got for being so blasted loyal. She took out her handkerchief.

"Don't take on about it," said Mr Scott, rising uncomfortably. "'Course I can understand your feeling sore. Nine years is a long time."

"Oh, shut up, can't you? Don't you know any other words? Shut up, can't you?"

The tears were coming. She couldn't stop them. Aghast at herself, she got up, and turned her back, trying for self-control.

Mr Scott stood a few seconds contemplating her back, her downcast head. Her hair looked pretty when it caught the sun. It wasn't like Mrs Scott to give way. If it were Irene it would be different. She often threw fits about nothing at all. But, whatever her faults, Mrs Scott was generally a sensible cheerful woman. Why couldn't she see that she'd been lucky to keep her friend as long as she had done? Should he pat her shoulder? Better not. She might only fly out at him.

Mrs Scott put an end to his dilemma by saying: "Hadn't you better put the kettle on for washing up?"

"Right you are," said Mr Scott, and shuffled rapidly away into the scullery.

Mrs Scott replaced her handkerchief, and took out her flap-jack. She dabbed her nose with powder, saying under her breath: "That's that." Then, moving briskly, she started to collect the dishes and bring them into the scullery.

ELIZABETH BOWEN

Unwelcome Idea

Along Dublin bay, on a sunny July morning, the public gardens along the Dalkey tramline look bright as a series of parasols. Chalk-blue sea appears at the ends of the roads of villas turning downhill — but these are still the suburbs, not the seaside. In the distance, floating across the bay, buildings glitter out of the heat-haze on the neck to Howth, and Howth Head looks higher veiled. After inland Ballsbridge, the tram from Dublin speeds up; it zooms through the residential reaches with the gathering steadiness of a launched ship. Its red velvet seating accommodation is seldom crowded — its rival, the quicker bus, lurches ahead of it down the same road.

After Ballsbridge, the ozone smell of the bay sifts more and more through the smell of chimneys and pollen and the July-darkened garden trees as the bay and line converge. Then at a point you see the whole bay open — there are nothing but flats of grass and the sunk railway between the running tram and the still sea. An immense glaring reflection floods through the tram. When high terraces, backs to the tramline, shut out the view again, even their backs have a salted, marine air: their cotton window-blinds are pulled half down, crooked; here and there an inner door left open lets you see a flash of sea through a house. The weathered lions on gate posts ought to be dolphins. Red, low-lying villas have been fitted between earlier terraces, ornate, shabby, glassy hotels, bow-fronted mansions all built in the first place to stand up over spaces of grass. Looks from trams and voices from public gardens invade the old walled lawns with their grottos and weeping willows. Spit-and-polish alternates with decay. But stucco, slate and slate-fronts, blotched Italian pink-wash, dusty windows, lace curtains and dolphin-lions seem to be the eternity of this tram route. Quite soon the modern will sag, chip, fade. Change leaves everything at the same level. Nothing stays bright but mornings.

The tram slides to stop for its not many passengers. The Blackrock bottleneck checks it, then the Dun Laoghaire. These are the shopping centres strung on the line: their animation congests them. Housewives with burnt bare arms out of their cotton dresses mass blinking and talking among the halted traffic, knocking their shopping-bags on each other's thighs. Forgotten Protestant ladies from 'rooms' near the esplanade stand squeezed between the kerb and the shops. A file of booted children threads its way through the crush, a nun at the head like a needle. Children by themselves curl their toes in their plimsoles and suck sweets and disregard everything. The goods stacked in the shops look very static and hot. Out from the tops of the shops on brackets stand a number of clocks. As though wrought up by the clocks the tram-driver smites his bell again and again, till the checked tram noses its way through.

By half-past eleven this morning one tram to Dalkey is not far on its way. All the time it approaches the Ballsbridge stop Mrs Kearney looks undecided, but when it does pull up she steps aboard because she has seen no bus. In a slither of rather ungirt parcels, including a dress-box, with a magazine held firmly between her teeth, she clutches her way up the stairs to the top. She settles herself on a velvet seat: she is hot. But the doors at each end and the windows are half-open, and as the tram moves air rushes smoothly through. There are only four other people and no man smokes a pipe. Mrs Kearney has finished wedging her parcels between her hip and the side of the tram and is intending to look at her magazine when she stares hard ahead and shows interest in someone's back. She moves herself and everything three seats up, leans forward and gives a poke at the back. 'Isn't that you?' she says.

Miss Kevin jumps round so wholeheartedly that the brims of the two hats almost clash. 'Why, for goodness' sake! ... Are you on the tram?' She settled round in her seat with her elbow hooked over the back — it is bare and sharp, with a rubbed joint: she and Mrs Kearney are of an age, and the age is about thirty-five. They both wear printed dresses that in this weather stick close to their backs; they are enthusiastic, not close friends but as close as they are ever likely to be. They both have high, fresh, pink colouring; Mrs Kearney could do with a little less weight and Miss Kevin could do with a little more.

They agree they are out early. Miss Kevin has been in town for the July sales but is now due home to let her mother go out. She has parcels with her but they are compact and shiny, having been made up at the counters of shops. 'They all say, buy now. You never know.' She cannot help looking at Mrs Kearney's parcels, bursting out from their string. 'And aren't you very laden, also,' she says.

'I tell you what I've been doing,' says Mrs Kearney. 'I've been saying goodbye to my sister Maureen in Ballsbridge, and who knows how long it's to be for! My sister's off to County Cavan this morning with the whole of her family and the maid.'

'For goodness' sake,' says Miss Kevin. 'Has she relatives there?'

'She has, but it's not that. She's evacuating. For the holidays they always go to Tramore, but this year she says she should evacuate.' This brings Mrs Kearney's parcels into the picture. 'So she asked me to keep a few other things for her.' She does not add that Maureen has given her these old things, including the month-old magazine.

'Isn't it well for her,' says Miss Kevin politely. 'But won't she find it terribly slow down there?'

'She will, I tell you,' says Mrs Kearney. 'However, they're all driving down in the car. She's full of it. She says we should all go somewhere where we don't live. It's nothing to her to shift when she has the motor. But the latest thing I hear they say now in the paper is that we'll be shot if we don't stay where we are. They say now we're all to keep off the roads — and there's my sister this morning with her car at the door. Do you think they'll halt her, Miss Kevin?'

'They might,' says Miss Kevin. 'I hear they're very suspicious. I declare, with the instructions changing so quickly it's better to take no notice. You'd be upside down if you tried to follow them all. It's of the first importance to keep calm, they say, and however would we keep calm doing this, then that? Still, we don't get half the instructions they get in England. I should think they'd really pity themselves ... Have you earth in your house, Mrs Kearney? We have, we have three buckets. The warden's delighted with us: he says we're models. We haven't a refuge, though. Have you one?'

'We have a kind of pump, but I don't know it is much good. And nothing would satisfy Fergus till he turned out the cellar.'

'Well, you're very fashionable!'

'The contents are on the lawn, and the lawn's ruined. He's crazy,' she says glumly, 'with A.R.P.'

'Aren't men very thorough,' says Miss Kevin with a virgin detachment that is rather annoying. She has kept thumbing her sales parcels, and now she cannot resist undoing one. 'Listen,' she says, 'isn't this a pretty delaine?' She runs the end of a fold between her finger and thumb. 'It drapes sweetly. I've enough for a dress and a bolero. It's French: they say we won't get any more now.'

'And that Coty scent — isn't that French?'

Their faces flood with the glare struck from the sea as the tram zooms smoothly along the open reach — wall and trees on its inland side, grass and bay on the other. The tips of their shingles and the thoughts in their heads are for the minute blown about and refreshed. Mrs Kearney flutters in the holiday breeze, but Miss Kevin is looking inside her purse. Mrs Kearney thinks she will take the kids to the strand. 'Are you a great swimmer, Miss Kevin?'

'I don't care for it: I've a bad circulation. It's a fright to see me go blue. They say now the sea's full of mines,' she says, with a look at the great, innocent bay.

'Ah, they're tethered; they'd never bump you.'

'I'm not nervous at any time, but I take a terrible chill.'

'My sister Maureen's nervous. At Tramore she'll never approach the water: it's the plage she enjoys. I wonder what will she do if they stop the car — she has all her plate with her in the back with the maid. And her kiddies are very nervous: they'd never stand it. I wish now I'd asked her to send me a telegram. Or should I telegraph her to know did she arrive? ... Wasn't it you said we had to keep off the roads?'

'That's in the event of invasion, Mrs Kearney. In the event of not it's correct to evacuate.'

'She's correct all right, then,' says Mrs Kearney, with a momentary return to gloom. 'And if nothing's up by the finish she'll say she went for the holiday, and I shouldn't wonder if she still went to Tramore. Still, I'm sure I'm greatly relieved to hear what you say ... 'Is that your father's opinion?'

Miss Kevin becomes rather pettish. 'Him?' she says, 'oh gracious, I'd never ask him. He has a great contempt for the whole war. My mother and I daren't refer to it — isn't it very mean of him? He does nothing but read the papers and roar away to himself. And will he let my mother or me near him when he has the news on? You'd think,' Miss Kevin says with a clear laugh, 'that the two of us originated the war to spite him: he doesn't seem to blame Hitler at all. He's really very unreasonable when he's not well. We'd a great fight to get in the buckets of earth, and now he makes out they're only there for the cat. And to hear the warden praising us makes him sour. Isn't it very mean to want us out of it all, when they say the whole country is drawn together? He doesn't take any pleasure in A.R.P.'

'To tell you the truth I don't either,' says Mrs Kearney. 'Isn't it that stopped the Horse Show? Wouldn't that take the heart out of you — isn't that a great blow to national life? I never yet missed a Horse Show — Sheila was nearly born there. And isn't that a terrible blow to trade? I haven't the heart to look for a new hat. To my mind this war's getting very monotonous: all the interest of it is confined to a few ... Did you go to the Red Cross Fête?'

The tram grinds to a halt in Dun Laoghaire Street. Simultaneously Miss Kevin and Mrs Kearney move up to the window ends of their seats and look closely down on the shop windows and shoppers. Town heat comes off the street in a quiver and begins to pervade the immobile tram. 'I declare to goodness,' exclaims Miss Kevin, 'there's my same delaine! French, indeed! And watch the figure it's on — it would sicken you.'

But with parallel indignation Mrs Kearney has just noticed a clock. 'Will you look at the time!' she says, plaintively. 'Isn't this an awfully slow tram! There's my morning gone, and not a thing touched at home, from attending evacuations. It's well for her! She expected me on her step by ten — "It's a terrible parting," she says on the p.c. But all she does at the last is to chuck the parcels at me, then keep me running to see had they the luncheon basket and what had they done with her fur coat ... I'll be off at the next stop, Miss Kevin dear. Will you tell your father and mother I was inquiring for them?' Crimson again at the very notion of moving, she begins to scrape her parcels under her wing. 'Well,' she says, 'I'm off with the *objets d'art*.' The heels of a pair of evening slippers protrude from a gap at the end of the dress box. The tram-driver, by smiting his bell, drowns any remark Miss Kevin could put out: the tram clears the crowd and moves down Dun Laoghaire Street,

31

between high flights of steps, lace curtains, gardens with round beds. 'Bye-bye, now,' says Mrs Kearney, rising and swaying.

'Bye-bye to you,' said Miss Kevin. 'Happy days to us all.'

Mrs Kearney, near the top of the stairs, is preparing to bite on the magazine. 'Go on!' she says. 'I'll be seeing you before then.'

MARY LAVIN

Lilacs

'That dunghill isn't doing anyone any harm, and it's not going out of where it is as long as I'm in this house,' Phelim Mulloy said to his wife Ros, but he threw an angry look at his elder daughter Kate who was standing by the kitchen window with her back turned to them both.

'Oh Phelim,' Ros said softly. 'If only it could be moved somewhere else besides under the window of the room where we eat our bit of food.'

'Didn't you just say a minute ago people can smell it from the other end of the town? If that's the case I don't see what would be the good in shifting it from one side of the yard to the other.'

Kate could stand no more. 'What I don't see is the need in us dealing in dung at all!'

'There you are! What did I tell you!' Phelim said, 'I knew all along that was what was in the back of your minds, both of you! And the one inside there too,' he added, nodding his head at the closed door of one of the rooms off the kitchen. 'All you want, the three of you, is to get rid of the dung altogether. Why on earth can't women speak out — and say what they mean. That's a thing always puzzled me.'

'Leave Stacy out of this, Phelim,' said Ros, but she spoke quietly. 'Stacy has one of her headaches.'

'I know she has,' said Phelim. 'And I know something else. I know I'm supposed to think it's the smell of the dung gave it to her. Isn't that so?'

'Ah Phelim, that's not what I meant at all. I only thought you might wake her with your shouting. She could be asleep.'

'Asleep is it? It's a real miracle any of you can get a wink of sleep, day or night, with the smell of that poor harmless heap of dung out there, that's bringing good money to this house week after week.' He had lowered his voice, but when he turned and looked at Kate it rose again without his noticing. 'It paid for your education at a fancy boarding school — and for your sister's too. It paid for your notions of learning to play the piano, and the violin, both of which instruments are rotting away inside in the parlour and not a squeak of a tune ever I heard out of the one or the other of them since the day they came into the house.'

'We may as well spare our breath, Mother,' Kate said. 'He won't give in, now or ever. That's my belief.'

'That's the truest word that's ever come out of your mouth,' Phelim said to her, and stomping across the kitchen he opened the door that led into the yard and went out, leaving the door wide open. Immediately the faint odour of stale manure that hung in the air was enriched by a smell from a load of hot steaming manure that had just been tipped into a huge dunghill from a farm cart that was the first of a line of carts waiting their turn to unload. Ros sighed and went to close the door, but Kate got ahead of her and banged it shut, before going back to the window and taking up her stand there. After a nervous glance at the door of the bedroom that her daughters shared, Ros, too, went over to the window and both women stared out.

An empty cart was clattering out of the yard and Phelim was leading in another from which, as it went over the spud-stone of the gate, a clod or two of dung fell out on the cobbles. The dunghill was nearly filled, and liquid from it was running down the sides of the trough to form pools through which Phelim waded unconcernedly as he forked back the stuff on top to make room for more.

'That's the last load,' Ros said.

'For this week, you mean,' Kate said. 'Your trouble is you're too soft with him, Mother. You'll have to be harder on him. You'll have to keep at him night and day. That is to say if you care anything at all about me and Stacy.'

'Ah Kate. Can't you see there's no use? Can't you see he's set in his ways?'

'All I can see is the way we're being disgraced,' Kate said angrily. 'Last night, at the concert in the Parish Hall, just before the curtain went up I heard the wife of that man who bought the bakehouse telling the person beside her that they couldn't open a window since they came here with a queer smell that was coming from somewhere, and asking the other person if she knew what it would be. I nearly died of shame, Mother. I really did. I couldn't catch what answer she got, but after the first item was over, and I could glance back, I saw it was Mamie Murtagh she was sitting beside. And you can guess what that one would be likely to have said! My whole pleasure in the evening was spoiled.'

'You take things too much to heart, Kate,' Ros said sadly. 'There's Stacy inside there, and it's my belief she wouldn't mind us dealing in dung at all if it wasn't for the smell of it. Only the other day she was remarking that if he'd even clear a small space under the windows we might plant something there that would smell nice. "Just think, Mother," she said. "Just think if it was a smell of lilac that was coming in to us every time we opened a door or a window." '

'Don't talk to me about Stacy,' Kate said crossly. 'She has lilac on the brain, if you ask me. She never stops talking about it. What did she ever do to try and improve our situation?'

'Ah now Kate, as you know, Stacy is very timid.'

'All the more reason Father would listen to her, if she'd speak to him. He may not let on to it, but he'd do anything for her.'

Ros nodded.

'All the same she'd never speak to him. Stacy would never have the heart to cross anyone.'

'She wouldn't need to say much. Didn't you hear him, today, saying he supposed it was the smell of the dung was giving her her headaches? You let that pass, but I wouldn't — only I know he won't take any more from me, although it's me has to listen to her moaning and groaning from the minute the first cart rattles into the yard. How is it that it's always on a Wednesday she has a headache? And it's been the same since the first Wednesday we came home from the convent.' With that last thrust Kate ran into the bedroom and came out with a raincoat. 'I'm going out for a walk,' she said, 'and I won't come back until the smell of that stuff has died down a bit. You can tell my father that, too, if he's looking for me.'

'Wait a minute, Kate. Was Stacy asleep?' Ros asked.

'I don't know and I don't care. She was lying with her face pressed to the wall, like always.'

When Kate went out, Ros took down the tea-caddy from the dresser and put a few pinches of tea from it into an earthenware pot on the hob of the big open fire. Then, tilting the kettle that hung from a crane over the flames, she wet the tea, and pouring out a cup she carried it over to the window and set it to cool on the sill while she went on watching Phelim.

He was a hard man when you went against him, she thought, a man who'd never let himself be thwarted. He was always the same. That being so, there wasn't much sense in nagging him, she thought, but Kate would never be made see that. Kate was stubborn too.

The last of the carts had gone, and after shutting the gate Phelim had taken a yard-brush and was sweeping up the dung that had been spilled. When he'd made a heap of it, he got a shovel and gathered it up and flung it up on the dunghill. But whether he did it to tidy the yard or not to waste the dung, Ros didn't know. The loose bits of dung he'd flung up on the top of the trough had dried out, and the bits of straw that were stuck to it had dried out too. They gleamed bright and yellow in a ray of watery sunlight that had suddenly shone forth.

Now that Kate was gone, Ros began to feel less bitter against Phelim. Like herself, he was getting old. She was sorry they had upset him. And while she was looking at him, he laid the yard-brush against the wall of one of the sheds and put his hand to his back. He'd been doing that a lot lately. She didn't like to see him doing it. She went across to the door and opened it.

'There's hot tea in the pot on the hob, Phelim,' she called out. 'Come in and have a cup.' Then seeing he was coming, she went over and gently opened the bedroom door. 'Stacy, would you be able for a cup of tea?' she asked, leaning in over the big feather-bed.

Stacy sat up at once.

'What did he say? Is it going to be moved?' she asked eagerly.

'Ssh, Stacy,' Ros whispered, and then as Stacy heard her father's steps in the kitchen she looked startled.

'Did he hear me?' she asked anxiously.

'No,' said Ros, and she went over and drew the curtains to let in the daylight. 'How is your poor head, Stacy?'

Stacy leaned toward Ros so she could be heard when she whispered.

'Did you have a word with him, Mother?'

'Yes,' said Ros.

'Did he agree?' Stacy whispered.

'No.'

Stacy closed her eyes. 'I hope he wasn't upset?' she said.

Ros stroked her daughter's limp hair. 'Don't you worry anyway, Stacy,' she said. 'He'll get over it. He's been outside sweeping the yard and I think maybe he has forgotten we raised the matter at all. Anyway, Kate has gone for a walk and I called him in for a cup of tea. Are you sure you won't let me bring you in a nice hot cup to sip here in the bed?'

'I think I'd prefer to get up and have it outside, as long as you're really sure Father is not upset.'

Ros drew a strand of Stacy's hair back from her damp forehead. 'You're a good girl, Stacy, a good, kind creature,' she said. 'You may feel better when you're on your feet. I can promise you there will be no more arguing for the time being anyway. I'm sorry I crossed him at all.'

It was to Stacy Ros turned, a few weeks later, when Phelim was taken bad in the middle of the night with a sharp pain in the small of his back that the women weren't able to ease, and after the doctor came and stayed with him until the early hours of the morning, the doctor didn't seem able to do much either. Before Phelim could be got to hospital, he died.

'Oh Stacy, Stacy,' Ros cried, throwing herself into her younger daughter's arms. 'Why did I cross him over that old dunghill?'

'Don't fret, Mother,' Stacy begged. 'I never heard you cross him over anything else as long as I can remember. You were always good and kind to him, calling him in out of the yard every other minute for a cup of tea. Morning, noon and night I'd hear your voice, and the mornings the carts came with the dung you'd call him in oftener than ever. I used to hear you when I'd be lying inside with one of my headaches.'

Ros was not to be so easily consoled.

'What thanks is due to a woman for giving a man a cup of hot tea on a bitter cold day? He was the best man ever lived. Oh why did I cross him?'

'Ah Mother, it wasn't only on cold days you were good to him but on summer days too — on every and all kind of days. Isn't that so, Kate?' Stacy said, appealing to Kate.

'You did everything you could to please him, Mother,' Kate said, but seeing this made no impression on her mother she turned to Stacy. 'That's more than could be said about him,' she muttered.

But Ros heard her.

'Say no more, you,' she said. 'You were the one was always at me to torment him. Oh why did I listen to you? Why did I cross him?'

'Because you were in the right. That's why!' Kate said.

'Was I?' Ros said.

Phelim was laid out in the parlour, and all through the night Ros and her daughters sat up in the room with the corpse. The neighbours that came to the house stayed up all night too, but they sat in the kitchen, and kept the fire going and made tea from time to time. Kate and Stacy stared sadly at their dead father stretched out in his shroud, and they mourned him as the man they had known all their lives, a heavy man with a red face whom they had seldom seen out of his big rubber boots caked with muck.

Ros mourned that Phelim too. But she mourned many another Phelim besides. She mourned the Phelim who, up to a little while before, never put a coat on him going out in the raw, cold air, nor covered his head even in the rain. Of course his hair was as thick as thatch! But most of all, she mourned the Phelim whose hair had not yet grown coarse but was soft and smooth as silk, like it was the time he led her in off the road and up a little lane near the chapel one Sunday when he was walking her home from Mass. That was the time when he used to call her by the old name. When, she wondered, when did he stop calling her Rose? Or was it herself gave herself the new name? Perhaps it was someone else altogether, someone outside the family? Just a neighbour maybe? No matter! Ros was a good name anyway, wherever it came from. It was a good name and a suitable name for an old woman. It would have been only foolishness to go on calling her Rose after she faded and dried up like an old twig. Ros looked down at her bony hands and her tears fell on them. But they were tears for

Phelim. 'Rose,' he said that day in the lane. 'Rose, I've been thinking about ways to make money. And do you know what I found out? There's a pile of money to be made out of dung.' Rose thought he was joking. 'It's true,' he said. 'The people in the town — especially women — would give any money for a bagful of it for their gardens. And only a few miles out from the town there are farmers going mad to get rid of it, with it piling up day after day and cluttering up their farmyards until they can hardly get in and out their own doors! Now, I was thinking, if I got hold of a horse and cart and went out and brought back a few loads of that dung, and if my father would let me store it for a while in our yard, I could maybe sell it to the people in the town.'

'Like the doctor's wife,' Rose said, knowing the doctor's wife was mad about roses. The doctor's wife had been seen going out into the street with a shovel to bring back a shovelful of horse manure.

'That's right. People like her! And after a while the farmers might deliver the loads to me. I might even pay them a few shillings a load, if I was getting a good price for it. Then if I made as much money as I think I might, maybe soon I'd be able to get a place of my own where I'd have room to store enough to make it a worthwhile business.' To Rose it seemed an odd sort of way to make money, but Phelim was only eighteen then and probably he wanted to have a few pounds in his pocket while he was waiting for something better. 'I'm going to ask my father about the storage today,' he said, 'and in the afternoon I'm going to get hold of a cart and go out the country and see how I get on.'

'Is that so?' Rose said, for want of knowing what else to say.

'It is,' said Phelim. 'And do you know the place I have in mind to buy if I make enough money? I'd buy that place we often looked at, you and me when we were out walking, that place on the outskirts of the town, with a big yard and two big sheds that only need a bit of fixing, to be ideal for my purposes.'

'I think so,' Rose said. 'Isn't there an old cottage there all smothered with ivy?'

'That's the very place. Do you remember we peeped in the windows one day last summer. There's no one living there.'

'No wonder,' Rose said.

'Listen to me. Rose. After I'd done up the sheds,' Phelim said, 'I could fix up the cottage too, and make a nice job of it. That's another thing I wanted to ask you, Rose. How would you like to live in that cottage — after I'd done it up, I mean — with me, I mean?' he added when he saw he'd startled her. 'Well Rose, what have you to say to that?'

She bent her head to hide her blushes, and looked down at her small thin-soled shoes that she only wore on a Sunday. Rose didn't know what to say.

'Well?' said Phelim.

'There's a very dirty smell off dung,' she said at last in a whisper.

'It only smells strong when it's fresh,' Phelim said. 'And maybe you could plant flowers to take away the smell?'

She kept looking down at her shoes.

'They'd have to be flowers with a strong scent out of them!' she said — but already she was thinking of how strongly sweet rocket and mignonette perfumed the air of an evening after rain.

'You could plant all the flowers you liked, you'd have nothing else to do the day long,' he said. How innocent he was, for all that he was thinking of making big money, and taking a wife. She looked up at him. His skin was as fair and smooth as her own. He was the best looking fellow for miles around. Girls far prettier than her would have been glad to be led up a lane by him, just for a bit of a lark, let alone a proposal — a proposal of marriage. 'Well, Rose?' he said, and now there were blushes coming and going in his cheeks too, blotching his face the way the wind blotches a lake when there's a storm coming. And she knew him well enough, even in those days, to be sure he wouldn't stand for anyone putting between him and what he was bent on doing. 'You must know, Rose Magarry, that there's a lot in the way people look at a thing. When I was a young lad, driving along the country roads in my father's trap, I used to love looking down at the gold rings of dung dried out by the sun, as they flashed past underneath the horses' hooves.'

Rose felt like laughing, but she knew he was deadly serious. He wasn't like anybody else in the world she'd ever known. Who else would say a thing like that? It was like poetry. The sun was spilling down on them and in the hedges little pink dog roses were swaying in a soft breeze.

'Alright, so,' she said. 'I will.'

'You will? Oh, Rose! Kiss me so!' he said.

'Not here Phelim!' she cried. People were still coming out of the chapel yard and some of them were looking up the lane.

'Rose Magarry, if you're going to marry me, you must face up to people and never be ashamed of anything I do,' he said, and when she still hung back he put out his hand and tilted up her chin. 'If you don't kiss me right here and now, Rose, I'll have no more to do with you.'

She kissed him then.

And now, at his wake, the candle flames were wavering around his coffin the way the dog roses wavered that day in the summer breeze.

Ros shed tears for those little dog roses. She shed tears for the roses in her own cheeks in those days. And she shed tears for the soft young kissing lips of Phelim. Her tears fell quietly, but it seemed to Kate and Stacy that, like rain in windless weather, they would never cease.

When the white light of morning came at last, the neighbours got up and went home to do a few chores of their own and be ready for the funeral. Kate and Stacy got ready too. and made Ros ready. Ros didn't look much different in black from what she always looked. Neither did Stacy. But Kate looked well in black. It toned down her high colour.

After the funeral Kate led her mother home. Stacy had already been taken home by neighbours, because she fainted when the coffin was being lowered into the ground. She was lying down when they came home. The women who brought Stacy home and one or two other women who had stayed behind after the coffin was carried out, to put the furniture back in place, gave a meal to the family, but these women made sure to leave as soon as possible to let the Mulloys get used to their loss. When the women had gone Stacy got up and came out to join Ros and Kate. A strong smell of guttered-out candles hung in the air and a faint scent of lilies lingered on too.

'Oh Kate! Smell!' Stacy cried, drawing in as deep a breath as her thin chest allowed.

'For Heaven's sake, don't talk about smells or you'll have our mother wailing again and going on about having crossed him over the dunghill,' Kate said in a sharp whisper.

But Ros didn't need any reminders to make her wail.

'Oh Phelim, Phelim, why did I cross you?' she wailed. 'Wasn't I the bad old woman to go against you over a heap of dung that, if I looked at things rightly, wasn't bad at all after it dried out a bit. It was mostly only yellow straw.'

'Take no heed of her,' Kate counselled Stacy. 'Go inside you with our new hats and coats, and hang them up in our room with a sheet draped over them. Black nap is a caution for collecting dust.' To Ros she spoke kindly, but firmly. 'You've got to give over this moaning, Mother,' she said. 'You're only tormenting yourself. Why wouldn't you let him see how we felt about the dung?'

Ros stopped moaning long enough to look sadly out the window.

'It was out of the dung he made his first few shillings,' she said.

'That may be! But how long ago was that? He made plenty of money other ways as time went on. There was no need in keeping on the dung and humiliating us. He only did it out of obstinacy.' As Stacy came back after hanging up their black clothes, Kate appealed to her. 'Isn't that so, Stacy?'

Stacy drew another thin breath.

'It doesn't smell too bad today, does it?' she said. 'I suppose the scent of the flowers drove it out.'

'Well, the house won't always be filled with lilies,' Kate said irritably. 'In any case, Stacy, it's not the smell concerns me. What concerns me is the way people look at us when they hear how our money is made.'

Ros stopped moaning again for another minute. 'It's no cause for shame. It's honest dealing, and that's more than can be said for the dealings of others in this town. You shouldn't heed people's talk, Kate.'

'Well, I like that!' she said. 'May I ask what you know, Mother, about how people talk. Certain kinds of people I mean. Good class people! It's easily seen you were never away at boarding school like Stacy and me, or else you'd know what it feels like to have to admit our money was made out of horse manure and cow dung!'

'I don't see what great call there was on you to tell them!' Ros said.

'Stacy! Stacy! Did you hear that?' Kate cried.

Stacy put her hand to her head. She was getting confused. There was some truth in what Kate had said, and she felt obliged to side with her, but first she ran over and threw herself down at her mother's knees.

'We didn't tell them at first. Mother,' she said, hoping to make Ros feel better. 'We told them our father dealt in fertiliser, but one of the girls looked up the word in a dictionary and found out it was only a fancy name for manure.'

It was astonishing to Kate and Stacy how Ros took that. She not only stopped wailing but she began to laugh.

'Your father would have been amused to hear that,' she said.

'Well, it wasn't funny for us,' Kate said.

Ros stopped laughing, but the trace of a small black smile remained on her face.

'It wasn't everyone had your father's sense of humour,' she said.

'It wasn't everyone had his obstinacy either!' Kate said.

'You're right there, Kate,' Ros said simply. 'Isn't that why I feel so bad? When we knew how stubborn he was, weren't we the stupid women to be always trying to best him? We only succeeded in making him miserable.'

Kate and Stacy looked at each other.

'How about another cup of tea, Mother? I'll bring it over here to you beside the fire,' Stacy said, and although her mother made no reply she made the tea and brought over a cup. Ros took the cup but handed back the saucer.

'Leave that back on the table,' she said, and holding the cup in her two hands she went over to the window, although the light was fading fast.

'It only smells bad on hot muggy days,' she said.

Kate gave a loud sniff. 'Don't forget summer is coming,' she said.

For a moment it seemed Ros had not heard, then she gave a sigh.

'It is and it isn't,' she said. 'I often think that in the January of the year it's as true to say we have put the summer behind us as it is to say it's ahead!' Then she glanced at a calendar on the wall. 'Is tomorrow Wednesday?' she asked, and an anxious expression overcame the sorrowful look on her face. Wednesday was the day the farmers delivered the dung.

'Mother! You don't think the farmers will be unmannerly enough to come banging on the gate tomorrow, and us after having a death in the family?' Kate said in a shocked voice.

'Death never interfered with business yet, as far as I know,' Ros said coldly. 'And the farmers are kind folk. I saw a lot of them at the funeral. They might think it all the more reason to come. Knowing my man is taken from me.'

'Mother!' This time Kate was more than shocked, she was outraged. 'You're not thinking, by any chance of keeping on dealing with them — of keeping on dealing in dung?'

Ros looked her daughter straight in the face.

'I'm thinking of one thing and one thing only,' she said. 'I'm thinking of your father and him young one day, and the next day, you might say, him stretched on the bed inside with the neighbours washing him for his burial.' Then she began to moan again.

'If you keep this up you'll be laid alongside him one of these days,' Kate said.

'Leave me be!' Ros said. 'I'm not doing any harm to myself by thinking about him. I like thinking about him.'

'He lived to a good age, Mother. Don't forget that,' Kate said.

'I suppose that's what you'll be saying about me one of these days,' Ros said, but she didn't seem as upset as she had been. She turned to Stacy. 'It seems only like yesterday, Stacy, that I was sitting up beside him on the cart, right behind the horse's tail, with my white blouse on me and my gold chain that he gave me bouncing about on my front, and us both watching the road flashing past under the horse's hooves, bright with gold rings of dung.'

Kate raised her eyebrows. But Stacy gave a sob. And that night, when she and Kate were in bed, just before she faced in to the wall, Stacy gave another sob.

'Oh Kate, it's not a good sign when people begin to go back over the past, is it?'

'Are you speaking about Mother?'

'I am. And did you see how bad she looked when you brought her home from the grave?'

'I did,' said Kate. 'It may be true what I said to her. If she isn't careful we may be laying her alongside poor Father before long.'

'Oh Kate. How could you say such a thing?' Stacy burst into tears. 'Oh Kate. Oh Kate, why did we make her cross Father about the dunghill? I know how she feels. I keep reproaching myself for all the hard things I used to think about him when I'd be lying here in bed with one of my headaches.'

'Well, you certainly never came out with them!' Kate said. 'You left it to me to say them for you! Not that I'm going to reproach myself about anything! There was no need in him keeping that dunghill. He only did it out of pig-headedness. And now, if you'll only let me, I'm going to sleep.'

Kate was just dropping off when Stacy leant up on her elbow.

'You don't really think they will come in the morning, do you Kate — the carts I mean — like our mother said?'

'Of course not,' Kate said.

'But if they do?'

'Oh go to sleep Stacy, for Heaven's sake. There's no need facing things until they happen. And stop fidgeting! You're twitching the blankets off me. Move over.'

Stacy faced back to the wall and lay still. She didn't think she'd be able to sleep, but when she did, it seemed as if she'd only been asleep one minute when she woke to find the night had ended. The hard, white light of day was pressing on her eyelids. It's a new day for them, she thought, but not for their poor father. Father laid away in the cold clay. Stacy shivered and drew up her feet that were touching the icy iron rail at the foot of the bed. It must have been the cold wakened her. Opening her eyes she saw, through a chink between the curtains, that the crinkled edges of the big corrugated sheds glittered with frost. If only — she thought — if only it was summer. She longed for the time when warm winds would go daffing through the trees, and when in the gardens to which they delivered fertiliser, the tight hard beads of lilac buds would soon loop out into soft pear-shaped bosoms of blossoms. And then, gentle as those thoughts, another thought came into Stacy's mind, and she wondered whether their father, sleeping under the close, green sods, might mind now if they got rid of the dunghill. Indeed it seemed the dunghill was as good as gone, now that Father himself was gone. Curling up in the warm blankets Stacy was preparing to sleep again, when there was a loud knocking on the yard-gates and the sound of a horse shaking its harness. She raised her head off the pillow, and as she did, she heard the gate in the yard slap back against the wall and there was a rattle of iron-shod wheels travelling in across the cobbles.

'Kate! Kate!' she screamed, shaking her. 'I thought Father was leading in a load of manure.'

'Oh shut up, Stacy. You're dreaming — or else raving,' Kate muttered from the depths of the blankets that she had pulled closer around her. But suddenly she sat up. And then, to Stacy's astonishment, she threw back the bedclothes altogether, right across the footrail of the bed, and ran across the floor and pressed her face to the window pane. 'I might have known this would happen!' she cried. 'For all her lamenting and wailing, she knows what she's doing. Come and look!' Out in the yard Ros was leading in the first of the carts, and calling out to the drivers of the other carts waiting their turn to come in. She was not wearing her black clothes, but her ordinary everyday coat, the colour of the earth and the earth's decaying refuse. In the raw cold air, the manure in the cart she was leading was still giving off, unevenly, the fog of its hot breath.

'Get dressed, Stacy. We'll go down together!' Kate ordered and grabbed her clothes and dressed.

When they were both dressed, with Kate leading, the sisters went into the kitchen. The yard door was open and a powerful stench was making its way inside. The last cart was by then unloaded, and Ros soon came back into the kitchen and began to warm her hands by the big fire already roaring up the chimney. She had left the door open but Kate went over and banged it shut.

'Well?' said Ros.

'Well?' Kate said after her, only louder.

Stacy sat down at once and began to cry. The other two women took no notice of her, as they faced each other across the kitchen.

'Say whatever it is you have to say, Kate,' Ros said.

'You know what I have to say,' said Kate.

'Don't say it so! Save your breath!' Ros said, and she went as if to go out into the yard again, but Stacy got up and ran and put her arms around her.

'Mother, you always agreed with us! You always said it would be nice if —'

Ros put up a hand and silenced her.

'Listen to me, both of you,' she said. 'I had no right agreeing with anyone but your father,' she said. 'It was to him I gave my word. It was him I had a right to stand behind. He always said there was no shame in making money any way it could be made, as long as it was made honestly. And another thing he said was that money was money, whether it was in gold coins or in dung. And that was true for him. Did you, either of you, hear what the priest said yesterday in the cemetery? "God help all poor widows." That's what he said. And he set me thinking. Did it never occur to you that it might not be easy for us, three women with no man about the place, to keep going, to put food on the table and keep a fire on the hearth, to say nothing at all about finery and fal-lals.'

'That last remark is meant for me I suppose,' Kate said, but the frown that came on her face seemed to come more from worry than anger. 'By the way Mother,' she said. 'You never told us whether you had a word with the solicitor when he came with his condolences? Did you by any chance find out how Father's affairs stood?'

'I did,' Ros said. But that was all she said as she went out into the yard again and took up the yard-brush. She had left the door open but Stacy ran over and closed it gently.

'She's twice as stubborn as ever Father was,' Kate said. 'There's going to be no change around here as long as she's alive.'

Stacy's face clouded. 'All the same, Kate, she's sure to let us clear a small corner and put in a few shrubs and things?' she said timidly.

'Lilacs, I suppose!' Kate said, with an unmistakable sneer, which however Stacy did not see.

'Think of the scent of them coming in the window,' she said.

'Stacy, you are a fool!' Kate cried. 'At least I can see that our mother has more important things on her mind than lilac bushes. I wonder what information she got from Jasper Kane? I thought her very secretive. I would have thought he'd have had a word with me, as the eldest daughter.'

'Oh, Kate.' Stacy's eyes filled with tears again. 'I never thought about it before, but when poor Mother —' she hesitated, then after a gulp she went on — 'when poor Mother goes to join Father, you and I will be all alone in the world with no one to look after us.'

'Stop whimpering, Stacy,' Kate said sharply. 'We've got to start living our own lives, sooner or later.' Going over to a small ornamental mirror on the wall over the fireplace, she looked into it and patted her hair. Stacy stared at her in surprise, because unless you stood well back from it you could only see the tip of your nose in that little mirror. But Kate was not looking at herself. She was looking out into the yard, which was reflected in the mirror, in which she could see their mother going around sweeping up stray bits of straw and dirt to bring them over and throw them on top of the dunghill. Then Kate turned around. 'We don't need to worry too much about that woman. She'll hardly follow Father for many a long day! That woman is as strong as a tree.'

But Ros was not cut out to be a widow. If Phelim had been taken from her before the dog roses had faded in the hedges that first summer of their lives together, she could hardly have mourned him more bitterly than she did when an old woman, tossing and turning sleeplessly in their big brass bed.

Kate and Stacy did their best to ease her work in the house. But there was one thing Kate was determined they would not do, and that was give any help on the Wednesday mornings when the farm carts arrived with their load. Nor would they help her to bag it for the townspeople, although as Phelim had long ago foreseen, the townspeople were often glad enough to bag it for themselves, or wheel it away in barrowfuls. On Wednesday morning when the rapping came at the gates at dawn, Kate and Stacy stayed in bed and did not get up, but Stacy was wide awake and lay listening to the noises outside. And sometimes she scrambled out of bed across Kate and went to the window.

'Kate?' Stacy would say almost every day.

'What?'

'Perhaps I ought to step out to the kitchen and see the fire is kept up. She'll be very cold when she comes in.'

'You'll do nothing of the kind I hope! We must stick to our agreement. Get back into bed.'

'She has only her old coat on her and it's very thin, Kate.'

Before answering her, Kate might raise herself up on one elbow and hump the blankets up with her so that when she sank back they were pegged down.

'By all the noise she's making out there I'd say she'd keep up her circulation no matter if she was in nothing but her shift.'

'That work is too heavy for her, Kate. She shouldn't be doing it at all.'

'And who is to blame for that? Get back to bed, like I told you, and don't let her see you're looking out. She'd like nothing better than that.'

'But she's not looking this way Kate. She couldn't see me.'

'That's what you think! Let me tell you, that woman has eyes in the back of her head.' Stacy giggled nervously at that. It was what their mother herself used to tell them when they were small.

Then suddenly she stopped giggling and ran back and threw herself across the foot of the bed and began to sob.

After moving her feet to one side, Kate listened for a few seconds to the sobbing. Then she humped up her other shoulder and pegged the blankets under her on the other side.

'What ails you now?' she asked then.

'Oh Kate, you made me think of when we were children, and she used to stand up so tall and straight and with her gold chain and locket bobbing about on her chest.' Stacy gave another sob. 'Now she's so thin and bent the chain is dangling down to her waist.'

Kate sat up with a start. 'She's not wearing that chain and locket now, out in the yard, is she? Gold is worth a lot more now than it was when Father bought her that.'

Stacy went over to the window and looked out again. 'No, she's not wearing it.'

'I should hope not!' Kate said. 'I saw it on her at the funeral but I forgot about it afterwards in the commotion.'

'She took it off when we came back,' Stacy said. 'She put it away in father's black box and locked the box.'

'Well, that's one good thing she did anyway,' Kate said. 'She oughtn't to wear it at all.'

'Oh Kate!' Stacy looked at her.

'What?' Kate asked, staring back.

Stacy didn't know what she wanted to say. She couldn't put it into words. She had always thought Kate and herself were alike, that they had the same way of looking at things, but lately she was not so sure of this. They were both getting older of course, and some people were not as even-tempered as others. Not that she thought herself a paragon, but being so prone to headaches she had to let a lot of things pass that she didn't agree with — like a thing Kate said recently about the time when they were away at school. Their mother had asked how many years ago it was, and while Stacy was trying to count up the years, Kate answered at once.

'Only a few years ago,' she said. That wasn't true but perhaps it only seemed like that to Kate.

Gradually, as time passed, Stacy too, like Kate, used to put the blankets over her head so as not to hear the knocking at the gate, and the rattle of the cart wheels, or at least to deaden the noise of it. She just lay thinking. Kate had once asked her what went through her head when she'd be lying saying nothing.

'This and that,' she'd said. She really didn't think about anything in particular. Sometimes she'd imagine what it would be like if they cleared a small space in the yard and planted things. She knew of course that if they put in a lilac bush it would be small for a long time and would not bear flowers for ages. It would be mostly leaves, and leaves only, for years, or so she'd read somewhere. Yet she always imagined it would be a fully grown lilac they'd have outside the window. Once she imagined something absolutely ridiculous. She was lying half awake and half asleep, and she thought they had transplanted a large full grown lilac, a lilac that had more flowers than leaves, something you never see. And then, as she was half-dozing, the tree got so big and strong its roots pushed under the wall and pushed up through the floorboards — bending the nails and sending splinters of wood flying in all directions. And its branches were so laden down with blossom, so weighted down, that one big pointed bosom of bloom almost touched her face. But suddenly the branch broke with a crack and Stacy was wide awake again. Then the sound that woke her came again, only now she knew what it was — a knocking on the gate outside, only louder than usual, and after it came a voice calling out. She gave Kate a shake.

'Do you hear that, Kate? Mother must have slept it out.'

'Let's hope she did,' Kate said. 'It might teach her a lesson — it might make her see she's not as fit and able as she thinks.'

'But what about the farmers?'

'Who cares about them,' Kate said. '*I* don't! Do you?' When the knocking came again a third time, and a fourth time, Stacy shook Kate again.

'Kate! I wouldn't mind going down and opening the gate,' she said.

'You? In your nightdress?' Kate needed to say no more. Stacy cowered down under the blankets in her shame. All of a sudden she sat up again.

'There wouldn't be anything wrong with Mother, would there?' she cried. This time, without heeding Kate, Stacy climbed out over her to get to the floor. 'I won't go out to the yard, I promise, I'll just go and wake Mother,' she cried. She ran out of the room.

'Come back and shut that door,' Kate called after her. Stacy mustn't have heard. 'Stacy! Come back and shut this door,' Kate shouted.

Stacy still didn't come back.

'Stacy!' Kate yelled. 'Stacy?'

Then she sat up.

'Is there something wrong?' she asked. Getting no answer now either, she got up herself.

Stacy was in their mother's room, lying in a heap on the floor. As Kate said afterwards, she hardly needed to look to know their mother was dead, because Stacy always flopped down in a faint the moment she came up against something unpleasant. And the next day, in the cemetery, when the prayers were over and the gravediggers took up their shovels, Stacy passed out again and had to be brought home by two of the neighbours, leaving Kate to stand and listen to the stones and the clay rumbling down on the coffin.

'You're a nice one, Stacy! Leaving me to stand listening to that awful sound.'

'But I heard it, Kate,' Stacy protested. 'I did! Then my head began to reel, and I got confused. The next thing I knew I was on the ground looking up at the blue sky and thinking the noise was the sound of the horses going clipclap along the road.' Kate stared at her.

'Are you mad? What horses?'

'Oh Kate, don't you remember? The horses Mother was always talking about. She was always telling us how, when she and Father were young, she used to sit beside him on a plank across the cart and watch the road flashing by under the horses' hooves, glittering with bright gold rings of dung?'

Kate, however, wasn't listening.

'That reminds me. Isn't tomorrow Wednesday?' she said. 'Which of us is going to get up and let in the farm carts?' When Stacy stared vacantly, Kate stamped her foot. 'Don't look so stupid, Stacy! They came the day after Father was buried, why wouldn't they come tomorrow? Mother herself said it was their way of showing — showing that as far as they were concerned the death wouldn't make any difference.'

'Oh Kate. How do you think they'll take it when you tell them —'

'Tell them what? Really Stacy, you *are* a fool. Tomorrow is no day to tell them anything. We'll have to take it easy — wait and see how we stand, before we talk about making changes.'

Kate was so capable. Stacy was filled with admiration for her. She would not have minded in the least getting up to open the gate, but she never would be able to face a discussion of the future. Kate was able for everything, and realising this, Stacy permitted herself a small feeling of excitement at the thought of them making their own plans and standing on their own two feet.

'I'll get up and light the fire and bring you a cup of tea in bed before you have to get up, Kate,' she said.

Kate shrugged her shoulders. 'If I know you, Stacy, you'll have one of your headaches,' Kate said.

Stacy said nothing. She was resolved to get up, headache or no headache. On the quiet she set an old alarm clock she found in the kitchen. But the alarm bell was broken, and the first thing Stacy heard next morning was the rapping on the gate. When she went to scramble out, to her surprise Kate was already gone from the room. And when Stacy threw her clothes on and ran out to the kitchen, the fire was roaring up the chimney, and a cup with a trace of sugar and tea leaves in the bottom of it was on the windowsill. The teapot was on the hob but it had been made a long time and it was cold. She made herself another pot and took it over to sip it by the window, looking out.

Kate was in the yard, directing the carts and laughing and talking with the men. Kate certainly had a way with her and no mistake. When it would come to telling the farmers that they needn't deliver any more dung, they wouldn't be offended.

One big tall farmer, with red hair and whiskers, was the last to leave, and he and Kate stood talking at the gate so long Stacy wondered if, after all, Kate mightn't be discussing their future dealings with him. She hoped she wouldn't catch cold. She put a few more sods of turf on the fire.

'Do you want to set the chimney on fire?' Kate asked when she came in. Stacy didn't let herself get upset though. Kate was carrying all the responsibility now, and it was bound to make her edgy.

'I saw you talking to one of the men,' said she. 'I was wondering if perhaps you were giving him a hint of our plans and sounding him out?'

'I was sounding him out alright,' Kate said, and she smiled. 'You see, Stacy. I've been thinking that we might come up with a new plan. You mightn't like it at first, but you may come round when I make you see it in the right light. Sit down and I'll tell you.' Stacy sat down. Kate stayed standing. 'I've been looking into the ledgers, and I would never have believed there was so much money coming in from the dung. So, I've been thinking that, instead of getting rid of it, we ought to try and take in more, twice or three times more, and make twice or three times as much money. No! No! Sit down again, Stacy. Hear me out. My plan would be that we'd move out of here, and use this cottage for storage — the sheds are not big enough. We could move into a more suitable house, larger and with a garden maybe —'

When Stacy said nothing Kate looked sharply at her. It wouldn't have surprised her if Stacy had flopped off in another faint, but she was only sitting dumbly looking into the fire. 'It's only a suggestion,' Kate said, feeling her way more carefully. 'You never heed anything, Stacy, but when I go out for my walks I take note of things I see — and there's a plot of ground for sale out a bit the road, but not too far from here all the same, and it's for sale — I've made enquiries. Now if we were to try and buy that it wouldn't cost much to build a bungalow. I've made enquiries about the cost of that too, and it seems —'

But Stacy had found her tongue. 'I don't want to move out of here, Kate,' she cried. 'This is where we were born, where my mother and father —' She began to cry. 'Oh Kate! I never want to leave here. Never! Never!'

Kate could hardly speak with fury.

'Stay here so!' she said. 'But don't expect me to stay with you. I'm getting out of here at the first chance I get to go. And let me tell you something else. That dunghill isn't stirring out of where it is until I've a decent dowry out of it. Cry away now to your heart's content for all I care.' Going over to their bedroom Kate went in and banged the door behind her.

Stacy stopped crying and stared at the closed door. Her head had begun to throb and she would have liked to lie down, but after the early hour Kate had risen she had probably gone back to bed. No. Kate was up and moving about the room. There was great activity going on. Stacy felt so much better. She knew Kate. Kate had never been one to say she was sorry for anything she said or did, but that need not mean she didn't feel sorry. She was giving their room a good turn-out? Perhaps this was her way of working off her annoyance and at the same time show she was sorry for losing her temper. Stacy sat back, thinking her thoughts, and waited for Kate to come out. She didn't have long to wait. In about five minutes the knob of the bedroom door rattled. 'Open this door for me, Stacy! My arms are full. I can't turn the handle,' Kate called and Stacy was glad to see she sounded in excellent form, and as if all was forgotten. For the second time in twenty-four hours Stacy felt a small surge of excitement, as Kate came out her arms piled sky high with dresses and hats and a couple of cardboard boxes, covered with wallpaper, in which they kept their gloves and handkerchiefs. It was to be a real spring cleaning! They hadn't done one in years. She hadn't noticed it before but the wallpaper on the boxes was yellowed with age and the flowery pattern faded. They might paste on new wallpaper? And seeing that Kate, naturally, had only her own things she went to run and get hers, but first she ran back to clear a space on the table so Kate could put her things down.

But Kate was heading across the kitchen to their mother's room.

'There's no sense in having a room idle, is there?' she said, disappearing into it. 'I'm moving in here.'

There was no further mention of the dunghill that day, nor indeed that week. Stacy felt a bit lonely at first in the room they had shared since childhood. But it had its advantages. It had been a bit stuffy sleeping on the inside. And she didn't have so many headaches, but that could possibly be attributed to Kate's suggestion that she ignore them.

LILACS

Every Wednesday Kate was up at the crack of dawn to let the carts unload. As their father had also foreseen, they were now paying the farmers for the manure, but only a small sum, because they were still glad to get rid of it. And the townspeople on the other hand were paying five times more. Kate had made no bones about raising her prices. The only time there was a reference to the future was when Kate announced that she didn't like keeping cash in the house, and that she was going to start banking some of their takings. The rest could be put as usual in the black box, which was almost the only thing that had never been taken out of their mother's room. A lot of other things were thrown out.

Kate and Stacy got on as well as ever, it seemed to Stacy, but there were often long stretches of silence in the house because Kate was never as talkative as their mother. After nightfall they often sat by a dying fire, only waiting for it to go out, before getting up and going to bed. All things considered, Kate was right to have moved into the other room, and Stacy began to enjoy having a room of her own. She had salvaged a few of her mother's things that Kate had thrown out and she liked looking at them. If Kate knew she never said anything. Kate never came into their room anymore.

Then one evening when Con O'Toole — the big whiskery farmer with whom Kate had been talking the first day she took over the running of things — when Con started dropping in to see how they were getting on, Stacy was particularly glad to have a room of her own. She liked Con. She really did. But the smell of his pipe brought on her headaches again. The smell of his tobacco never quite left the house, and it even pursued her in through the keyhole after she had left him and Kate together, because of course it was Kate Con came to see.

'Can you stand the smell of his pipe?' she asked Kate one morning. 'It's worse than the smell of the dung!' She only said it by way of a joke, but Kate, who had taken out the black box and was going through the papers in it, a thing she did regularly now, shut the lid of the box and frowned.

'I thought we agreed on saying fertiliser instead of that word you just used.'

'Oh but that was long ago, when we were in boarding school,' Stacy stammered.

'I beg your pardon! It was agreed we'd be more particular about how we referred to our business when we were in the company of other people — or at least that was my understanding! Take Con O'Toole for instance. He may deliver dung here but he never gives it that name — at least not in front of me. The house he lives in may be thatched and have a mud wall, but that's because his old mother is alive and he can't get her to agree to knocking it down and building a new house, which of course they can afford — I was astonished at the amount of land he owns. Come Stacy, you must understand that I am not urging him to make any changes. So please don't mention this conversation to him. I'll tell him myself when I judge the time to be right. Then I'll make him see the need for building a new house. He needn't knock the old one either. He can leave the old woman in it for what time is left her. But as I say, I'll bide my time. I might even wait until after we are married.'

That was the first Stacy heard of Kate's intended marriage, but after that first reference there was talk of nothing else, right up to the fine blowy morning when Kate was hoisted up into Con O'Toole's new motor-car, in a peacock blue outfit, with their mother's gold chain bumping up and down on her bosom.

Stacy was almost squeezed to death in the doorway as the guests all stood there to wave goodbye to the happy couple. There had been far more guests than either she or Kate had bargained on because the O'Tooles had so many relations, and they all brought their children, and — to boot — Kate's old mother-in-law brought along a few of her own cronies as well. But there was enough food, and plenty of port wine.

It was a fine wedding. And Stacy didn't mind the mess that was made of the house. Such a mess! Crumbs scattered over the carpet in the parlour and driven into it by people's feet! Bottle tops all over the kitchen floor! Port wine and lemonade stains soaked into the tablecloth! It was going to take time to get the place to rights again. Stacy was almost looking forward to getting it to rights again because she had decided to make a few changes in the arrangement of the furniture — small changes, only involving chairs and ornaments. But she intended attacking it that evening after the guests left. However, when the bridal couple drove off with a hiss of steam rising out of the radiator of the car, the guests flocked back into the house and didn't go until there wasn't a morsel left to eat, or a single drop left to refill the decanters. One thing did upset Stacy and that was when she saw the way the beautiful wedding cake on which the icing had been as hard and white as plaster had been attacked by someone who didn't know how to cut a cake. The cake had been laid waste, and the children that hadn't already fallen asleep on the sofas were stuffing themselves with the last crumbs. Stacy herself hadn't as much as a taste of that cake, and she'd intended keeping at least one tier aside for some future time. Ah well. It was nice to think everyone had had a good time, she thought, as she closed the door on the last of the OTooles, who had greatly outnumbered their own friends. Jasper Kane, their father's solicitor, had been their principal guest. He had not in fact left yet, but he was getting ready to leave.

'It will be very lonely for you now, Miss Stacy,' he said. 'You ought to get some person in to keep you company — at least for the nights.'

It was very kind of him to be so concerned. Stacy expressed her gratitude freely, and reassured him that she was quite looking forward to being, as it were, her own mistress. She felt obliged to add, hastily, that she'd miss Kate, although to be strictly truthful, she didn't think she'd miss her as much as she would have thought before Con O'Toole had put in his appearance.

'Well, well. I'm glad to hear you say that, Miss Stacy,' Jasper Kane said, as he prepared to leave. 'I expect you'll drop in to my office at your convenience. I understand your sister took care of the business, but I'm sure you'll be just as competent when you get the hang of things.' Then for a staid man like him, he got almost playful. 'I'll be very curious to see what changes you'll make,' he said, and she saw his eye fall on a red plush sofa that Kate had bought after Con started calling, and which Stacy thought was hideous. She gave him a conspiratorial smile. But she didn't want him to think she wasn't serious.

'I intend to make changes outside as well, Mr Kane,' she said, gravely. 'And the very first thing I'm going to do is plant a few lilac trees.'

Jasper Kane looked surprised.

'Oh? Where?' he asked and although it was dark outside, he went to the window and tried to see out.

'Where else but where the dunghill has always been,' Stacy said, and just to hear herself speaking with such authority made her almost lightheaded.

Jasper Kane remained staring out into the darkness. Then he turned around and asked a simple question.

'But what will you live on, Miss Stacy?'

LILIAN ROBERTS FINLAY
A Bona Fide Husband

The honeymoon was over. Tom had gone back to work. The new life had begun.

Eily snuggled down deeper into their brand-new double bed. She knew very well why she was not jumping out of bed, and facing this New Life. The honeymoon is over, Tom had said last night, back to the Job in the morning. His enthusiasm was unmistakable.

Eily had experienced a sense of disillusion that a honeymoon could not go on for a lifetime. She was awaiting more out of the week of honeymoon; more of joy, less of pain. There was a dim feeling of disappointment in the honeymoon but perhaps it was disloyal to feel like that.

In bed last night, Eily had begun to explain to Tom how saying the honeymoon is over was like giving no one a second chance. Tom was sleepy, and Eily would learn that "debating in bed was not one of his habits". He always used the identical phrase for the identical need, and "not one of his habits" was a favourite. In the middle of her struggle to communicate her feeling about honeymoons, without revealing her sense of disappointment, he yawned loudly.

"Tell you what," he mumbled, "we'll go over and see Mam and the family after tea tomorrow, tell them about London, and the air-raid shelters going up in Hyde Park … they won't believe a word of it …"

And then this morning, he was the one to rise promptly, full of high spirits, insisting that she stay in bed, bringing her a cup of tea. He was fussy and concerned about the sit of his tie and the contents of his brief-case. Laughingly feigning dramatic passion, he kissed her goodbye, then ruined it all by shouting back from the hall door, "Don't forget we are going over to Mam's tonight!"

Eily drew the eiderdown up to her chin. She would not begin the new life on a day that was going to end with a visit to Tom's mother. That visit could easily be postponed for a week, or a month. Or a year as far as Eily was concerned.

On this first day, she wanted to anticipate Tom's home-coming as the prelude to a long cosy evening of lingering over the meal, of talking heart-to-heart for endless hours. This very first night of the new life in their own home must be a night of total intimacy. Yes, Eily dreamed, a first night — if last night had to be the last night of the honeymoon, then tonight would be the romantic scene Eily loved, perhaps making love on the fireside rug with only the firelight for a lantern. But would Tom be likely to make love on the rug in front of the fire? She could imagine him saying another of his favourites, "A time and a place for everything" and, at the proper moment, marching her across the hall into the bedroom.

To quell the slight feeling of disloyalty, Eily defended him to herself. Tom might be self-conscious, this gave him a sense of his own dignity. Also he accorded dignity to others, which maybe was why he was so popular. Eily smiled when she reflected how popular Tom was; he had so many friends. She felt she had won a prize in Tom. Her faint disappointment merely marked her as lacking in appreciation. If only he had not said that the honeymoon was over, so jubilantly, failing to understand that she thought the honeymoon should be just beginning and that each moment of this present time would be spent in a secret exploration of its as-yet-unfulfilled delights.

But tonight Tom had to visit his mother. The thought brought her back to the proposed evening visit with a surge of such distaste that she leaped from the bed, and fled through the kitchen into the garden.

Eily loved the garden. Because of the garden, she had cajoled Tom into renting the cottage. He considered it too far from town but the rent was low. The front of the cottage gave onto a quiet road, the back and sides were all greenery. There was a hundred years of unplanned planting gone into this garden. Flowering trees were mixed in with apple trees; there were roses everywhere. Someone had made quaint garden seats with odds and ends of wood, all worn now and in need of a coat of paint, but comfortable and placed to catch the sun.

Eily sat down and tucked her feet under her. No one, she thought, could feel unhappy in this old garden. Tom had grumbled about all the work to be done in a big garden. He had, in fact, referred to the garden as a bit of a wilderness. But she would help him, and after all, what else was there to do with all the time they would have for spending together.

Eily's eyes were closed luxuriously against the sun … she pictured Tom digging and planting while she gathered great baskets of apples for all the apple-pies she would bake for him. Adam and Eve in Eden, never banished — living there for ever and ever.

Eily heard the side-gate click. Before she could move, a little boy came running around the path. He had a kitten clutched into his jersey.

"Mammy said would you like a cat?"

Eily took the white kitten. Too small to purr, it nestled contentedly against her flimsy nightdress.

"What's your name?" she asked the little boy.

"It's Francis, but me daddy calls me Franko."

"Franko is nice," smiled Eily, "it's different."

"And will you take the cat?" asked Franko pleadingly, "I mean the kitten. Our cat has six, and Mammy can only get homes for two … please take it … Mammy says if they don't get homes, she will have to send them to America and then we will never see them again. Please, will you? Mammy says Fuzz has too many too often but that's not her fault, only thirty a year is more people than Mammy knows to ask ... will you?"

Eily stroked the little kitten. "Are all the kittens white?"

"That is the only white one. Mammy said you would like a white one because you are, because you are ..." He had forgotten what his Mammy said.

"Because I am new?" Eily offered.

"Something like that," he was relieved, "there's another one, blacky-whitey and two all black."

"Do you think your Mammy would give me the blacky-whitey one as well?" Eily asked.

His eyes opened wide, "Do you mean you'd take two?"

"Why not," Eily smiled at his wonder, "I am sure Tom, my husband, loves kittens."

"Come with me, so!" shouted the little boy, not noticing that Eily was wearing a nightdress.

Eily had him point out his house and she promised to follow in a few minutes.

Eily enjoyed talking with Franko's Mammy. She and her husband, whose families had lived for generations in this area, had a market garden.

With the other kitten, instantly named "Clogs" for his four white feet, Eily was given a cabbage and a little bag of tomatoes. She felt very pleased and proud and immeasurably more mature. All shadowy doubt dispersed, the new life was beginning beautifully ... nice neighbours, two adorable kittens, and a cabbage for Tom's dinner.

Eily had never cooked a cabbage but she had a wedding present of a huge cookery book and lots of brand-new pots and tins. There were some apples on the cottage trees quite big enough to pick. Why not a scrumptious apple-pie to start the new life? Eily counted her money. Now she wished she had not spent all her savings in London but things in the big stores there had looked so glamorous and almost for nothing — but four hats? Eily loved hats and there would be years to wear them. She made a list with the help of the cookery book: six potatoes, six slices of cooked corn-beef, four ounces of margarine, six ounces of flour, some sugar, some bread-soda for the cabbage (the book said "a pinch" but could one buy a pinch?) — Eily wished she had taken Domestic Economy in school instead of French but then Sister Theresa had said only duds took cookery, so it must be easy. Yesterday, Tom had thought of stocking up with bread and tea and butter and milk, and even marmalade — this last a stroke of genius in Eily's eyes. Imagine remembering marmalade!

Eily made a place for the kittens in the shed, and took out her bicycle. Franko's Mammy had told her that the village was known as "The Cross", a few small shops and a Church, at a cross-roads. Eily was smiling to herself as she cycled along. She knew very well that anything more important than "The Cross" would intimidate a first-time housekeeper like herself.

Eily's parents were dead since she was a small child. All her years of growing up were passed in a boarding-school, and since then as a filing-clerk in a busy office in the town. Living in lodgings, she had shared (with other girls like herself) the slap-dash attentions of the landlady, Mrs Stakelum. This lady's pride, and claim to fame, was the great girth of her bosom which she was careful not to diminish by an over-indulgence in active domestic chores. The girls found her comforting and kind. They accepted the bosom and forgave her other inadequacies. Four years of Mrs Stakelum's "digs" had left Eily with a very sketchy idea of regular well-cooked meals, and a very easy-going attitude to household routine.

Tom was not too impressed with "Snowhite" and "Clogs". And, Eily thought, he was even less impressed with her cooking. The cabbage was stalky, the pastry was like cardboard, and his share of the corn-beef disappeared in one bite. He praised the new neighbour's tomatoes, making two sandwiches of them which he polished off with a cup of tea.

Tom, Eily was to learn, could at times be lavish with praise if the results were worth it. He saw no need for reassurance for efforts made. That would be "talk for talk's sake"—a motto of his with useful variations. His main concern this evening was to get going over to his Mam's.

So Eily hurried. She had piled the dishes in a basin. She was putting on her coat.

"Surely you are going to wash these things?" Tom queried. She smiled at him, "Sure I'll have nothing to do tomorrow when you are gone to work!"

Tom was aghast. "Every day brings its own work," he said sternly, "and no one leaves dirty dishes overnight. You had better do them now. Tomorrow is another day."

Taking off her coat, Eily thought of something Mrs Stakelum used to say each evening, as she took pride of place among the girls gathered around her kitchen after tea, "A good fire and enough to eat is half feeding!" Eily never knew exactly what it meant but it seemed very well-intentioned. It was fine for Mrs Stakelum, and Tom, to have all these sayings for her betterment — it was like living in a Vere Foster Headline Copy, the one in which she had first learned to write. She never could remember the ends of these lines — wasn't there one about "Woman's work?" There's another disloyal feeling, thought Eily, glimpsing Tom in the little parlour. He was stretched out on the couch with a newspaper. There are more ways of beginning a new life than sharing it.

Tom's father greeted them at the door. He had a completely different type of personality from Tom's mother. Eily thought he was out of a different class, a different age and maybe a different world. He was big and grizzled and rumpled. He enfolded Eily in a bear-hug lasting a little too long for comfort and he held her firmly against him as he asked her non-stop questions about her health and her happiness. Leaving no time for answers, he disappeared up the stairs. Eily gazed after him, she rather liked the nuzzling warmth of him — when it was over.

Tom said dismissively, "He's doing door-porter tonight. You haven't forgotten Mam's at-home night — this is Friday!"

In the dining-room, a family crowd had gathered around the table for the Friday night game of cards. There were the two married daughters and their husbands, the younger son and his girlfriend, the widower from next door, a neighbour and his wife. On the table, glasses and bottles and ash-trays gave an air of conviviality.

Tom's mother was seated at the top of the table near the fire. In studied deliberation, she removed her concentrated gaze from her hand of cards, giving the newcomers a surprised acknowledgement.

"We were not expecting you," she said shortly. "Batt and the wife have joined us. Twelve would be rather too many."

If Tom found anything wrong with this strange welcome, he gave no sign.

"We are just back from our honeymoon," he said loudly and jovially, "I'm sure you are all dying to hear all about it!"

"Absolutely dying!" chortled a brother-in-law, "All!" The younger brother's girlfriend giggled. Eily was painfully aware of many pairs of eyes fixed on her face. Tom put an arm around her shoulder lightly. She felt he was quite at home, this atmosphere was his natural element.

"Did you know," began Tom, "that the English are building air-raid shelters under Hyde Park? It's serious, you know. We had a strange ..." But this was too much for the brother-in-law.

"Strange?" he shouted, "Begin at the beginning. First night! Scene One!"

Through the guffaws that followed this hilarious innuendo, Eily heard Tom's mother banging the table with her heavy rings. Her voice pierced the cigarette haze, "We will return to the cards, if you please. Tom can get something to do until the second game. Maybe the supper. Good practice for the new wife."

Eily turned away from the card-players. Tom was rummaging on the side-board. He was examining the envelopes on a letter-rack. To her surprise, he opened and read all the correspondence, some bank statements, and electricity bills.

"They are not yours!" Eily whispered agitatedly.

Tom looked amused. "Course they are," he said, "I always read them." He opened a few drawers in case he had missed anything. He smiled fondly, "The same old junk! Come out to the kitchen."

There were plates of sandwiches neatly ranged beside the second-best tea-cups and saucers. Tom helped himself to a sandwich, and then to another sandwich.

"Have one," he offered. Eily demurred; she felt sure the sandwiches were counted. "I'm not hungry, maybe we could just tip-toe out and leave them to their cards?" She was almost begging.

"And miss the supper! Are you mad! No, we'll join the second game. We'll get the last bus easily. Stop worrying! You put the kettle on — put the gas low. I'll carry in the trays. I can put them on the side-table. They must be nearly ready soon."

If Eily had remembered about the card-game, and the at-home night, she thought she would have refused to come. It would have taken a bit of courage; Tom could be so adamant. His family were all card-mad experts, and she was not. There would be the usual inquest after the second game. Tom's mother would not hesitate to call Eily "a little silly", "a little dreamer", in a voice that clearly said "dunderhead", "stupid fool", "imbecile". Eily could not, and never would, understand how people remembered what cards had "gone before". Sometimes she forgot which suit was trumps or even if it was a no-trump game. In school, the only card-game was "Happy Families" but she did not care to excuse herself to Tom's mother with so paltry an excuse … best, really, to try harder to please.

Tom's mother made a big effort to be pleasant during the supper, detaching her mind from the first rubber to ask Eily a question or two.

"And how is the cooking coming along?"

"Aha!" laughed Tom, "Eily made an apple-pie today."

"An apple-pie bed?" put in the brother-in-law quickly.

The neighbour's wife choked and spluttered and was soundly thumped on the back by her husband.

"The price of a stone of flour is disgraceful in an agricultural country," enunciated Tom's mother from the top of the table.

The stone of flour! Eily now remembered the little grocer's surprised face when she had asked for six ounces of flour and four ounces of margarine. "I am new here," she had smiled at him, "we have the cottage with the mimosa tree." So one should buy flour by the stone? The little grocer had measured out the flour into a paper-twist, and cut a small piece of margarine in half. "Will there be anything else, Missus?" he had responded gallantly and Eily knew her face went pink from the unaccustomed "missus". And of course, six ounces of flour had not left any flour over for rolling out the pastry which, presumably, was the reason it was so tacky. Eily wondered at herself … how a girl who had earned her own living in an office could be such a ninny … mooning over kittens and not knowing how to buy flour.

Eily had plenty of time to think her own thoughts. It had been decided that there was no place for her in the second game. She sat in a corner with a newspaper. It was cold so far from the fire, she would have liked to get her coat but that would look rude. Also there was a danger of meeting Tom's father out in the hall. It wasn't that she disliked him: it was that it was odd the way no one ever mentioned him.

Eily was allowed to wash up the supper dishes. She was instructed to take extreme care of the good ware.

Going home in the bus, Tom was in a state of elation. The brother-in-law had told him, he said, that they were expecting him back at the club for the championships, and Mam had said that he could have lunch there with her on Saturdays to save him from trekking out to the cottage and, as Mam and he agreed, wasting time when he could be knocking a ball around.

"It's bad enough," said Tom, "to have to work half-days on Saturdays. The bigwigs don't go in on Saturday — it should be done away with: no one ever does a stroke on a Saturday. I'll go straight to Mam's from the office, and I'll probably have a few 'jars' with the lads after the game. I should be back in the cottage about nine or it could be a bit later if we are playing away, and then …"

Eily was not listening. The dim disappointment of the morning had returned. Its edges were sharper now and threatened to cut into the fabric of her life. She struggled with a thought too difficult to come clear. Was marriage for two people or only for a woman? The two people entering into the holy bond of matrimony, did that not set them apart? Both of them or only the woman? Did the man lay himself open to ribaldry, exposing himself for the gratification of fun-makers? Vaguely Eily had thought of marriage as a sacred place, a secret cell into which two people walked hand-in-hand. No one else ever came there, no one knocked on the door. If Tom was totally unaware of this lovely, solemn cell, then she must be in there by herself. She wondered if marriage could be a trap with steel teeth, ready to snap on her.

"So that's all settled then?" Tom was saying as he tucked his arm through hers, to walk up from the bus-stop to the cottage. Eily liked the warm feel of his arm, it was comforting. Did his arm feel her heart beating? She looked up at him. Tom was so handsome, even when he yawned, as he did now, "Our last long lie-in tomorrow! It's a good job I had this Saturday off! Saturdays after this are going to be murder!" His voice was younger than she had noticed before, teasing, tempting, "You will have to do without me on a Friday night in future!"

"Won't you be coming home?" Eily asked.

"Oh sure!" Tom replied very airily, "but only for my dinner and a sound sleep — and not for any hanky-panky, mind! Not on a Friday night!"

Eily remembered that at their wedding service the old priest had given a little talk about four things to have in a good marriage. A sense of humour was one of them. Did that mean you had to smile when you felt affronted? She did not smile.

Tom was first into the bedroom, and into bed.

"Hurry up!" he called to her, "it's lovely in here!"

"Coming," she replied. Now she was in no hurry. She brought in the kittens to give them milk; she was stroking them and whispering to them, hesitating about putting them back out in the shed. They were part of an earlier, carefree mood ...

"Eily!" There was no doubt he was getting impatient.

She had left her nightdress in the bathroom cupboard when she was hurrying out to Franko and his Mammy early that morning. It seemed a long time since morning, almost as if a lot of her life had slipped by today. She undressed slowly and put on the wedding nightdress. In the mirror, she looked the very same as always. Not desolate. Not abandoned.

"Eily!"

In the bedroom, she stood looking at Tom in bed. She had a question to ask him, but should she?

"Eily, you certainly know how to get a fellow worked up. Come on, what's keeping you?"

The question trembled on her tongue: what about the garden on Saturdays?

"Tom ..." but how not to spoil his pleasure in his Saturday sport?

"Eily, you look gorgeous! Will you come into bed, before I have to get out and drag you in!" His handsome features were set in a look of pleading adoration.

To Eily, Tom was irresistible. With the strange feeling of passing by a milestone in her life, she let the question fall. It would never be asked; and if it had, Eily was to learn that it would never have been answered.

EITHNE STRONG

Thursday to Wednesday

Like a fever in the blood, this wanting to go further. What were
the territories behind the frontiers of eyes and conversational
gambit? The routine demands of noses to be wiped, shoelaces
tied, chores organised, squabbles broken up, were not enough
to hold her steady. Like a thirst. Like an appetite hungry since
yesterday. New ground for questing.

Nora came into the room and threw herself on to her
mother's bed, her dark eyes watchful, aware. She knew.

"It's all a big plot, isn't it Mummy?"

"What is, my darling?"

No answer. Her face showed its knowing. The mother
turned her disconcertion to the mirror and saw there her
daughter still watchful. Oh for an unbetraying pale skin:
flushing conveys unsureness, guilt. She should not have to feel
guilty. What wrong was there in wanting to go out with him?
Spend a few hours in his company? "It is ridiculous that I
shouldn't feel free to do so," she was telling herself. "Why is
she so jealous and watchful of me still and all the latitude she
has been allowed to work out her own things?" She resented
the unspoken censure from her daughter and also,
immediately, was self-critical because of this resentment.

Rubbing make-up on to her face, she observed Nora in the
mirror, while trying to find inside herself a balance, trying to
surmount the troubling urgency; wondering was this, after all,
another instance like so many other countless instances where
she must submerge herself for the good of the general. Would

she be harming Nora, her half-formed standards of values? Was she not accountable for many troubles and puzzlements in the girl's so-far journey into adolescence? True maybe. True very likely. But her own journey into ever expanding life was often over uncharted areas. She was often confused and troubled herself but always convinced that she should go on.

As she stood there before the mirror her stomach went heavy in sudden sickness. She went on fixing up her eyes, thinking, as she drew a pencil around their careful blankness, that she was a silly woman. She was really like anyone else who went in for hole-and-corner only she was giving what she did a pretentious build-up: the ultimate good of human inter-relationship; advancement through understanding in the man-woman field and such-like. It was presumptuous to assume she was progressing beyond Mrs Suburban-married who steadily kept to the humdrum limits of social acceptability. Yes, I am a self-engrossed woman, giving myself airs.

"Where are you going Mummy?" Katherine came to jog on the edge of the bed.

"But you, *all* of you, knew I was going out tonight. I had asked Nora, two days ago, to be free for baby-sitting."

"But where?" Katherine insisted.

Nora said: "You are not going to the play — I know there were no bookings left. Then well … ?"

"I'm still going out," she heard the strain in her voice. In spite of the bothering thoughts and heavy stomach, she had decided to go.

"But where?" Katherine was not letting up.

"I'm not quite sure really. Just out. Out for the evening."

Nora got off the bed and went downstairs. Through the curtains her mother could see her sitting beside him on the garden seat. She was lengthened out seductively, a show of creamy flesh between short skinny rib sweater and jeans. He was noticing her. The mother thought: there she is, acting my rival — in spite of her thing with Greg, she is deliberately displaying her potential to a man who, she knows, likes me. It has all happened before. The old pattern. Any man interested in me will be made particularly aware of her lusciousness.

Nora's face was secret, unhappy, as she gave him a speculative sideways glance.

The mother, finally ready, went downstairs. The two small ones ran from the kitchen.

"Mummy, Mummy. I don't want you to go out."

"Nora will put you to bed tonight."

"No no. I want you to put us to bed. I want you to read us the story."

"Katherine will read the story."

"No no no. *You* must read the story."

"If you come straight to bed then, this minute, I'll read you a story."

"I don't want to go to bed now."

"But sweethearts, you can't have it every way. I'll put you to bed now and read you a story or else I go out immediately and Nora will put you to bed later — with a story then."

"Where are you going?"

"Oh — just — out. Out for the beginning, later there is a party I have been asked to."

She hugged and kissed them. They made small attempts at crying, wanting to keep her longer, but she went out into the garden.

He got up from the seat and followed her to the car. Nora came to the gate looking slantways from her mother, a small cynical smile shaping her mouth. The mother was very unhappy. She wished that as she was there in the car ready to go, with him beside her, they would all wave and smile at her, as they always did when every thing was in tune. Nora shouldered the gate-post and, when her mother, with mustered courage, looked full at her, met the look with a glassiness. She was her mother's child. She was also someone who, the mother felt, was at that moment seeing her through the remembered perspective of difficulties she had hoped were resolved between them.

He was looking at Nora; the girl's eyes moved to him. Was that a flicker of conspiracy in her look? In the lightning instant it took to think such a thing, the mother wondered was there something between them. Were they leagued in mockery against her? She let her hair fall over to hide whatever the horrible feeling in her chest was doing to her face and turned away to twist down the car-window. Katherine stood by it.

"Where are you going Mummy?"

"I'm not sure darling — out — just —" She did not want to keep on trying to give a truthful answer; she was afraid to use her voice any more. She bent her head sideways through the window for the usual goodbye kiss from Katherine. The car moved off and she noticed how he looked back at Nora.

Suddenly she felt like stopping, getting out, letting him move from now entirely on his own impetus. The outing was partly her engineering but she had gone to the trouble of fixing it because of some indications that he would like it.

In silence she drove for several minutes, aware that he was studying her. The earlier urgency to be alone with him had sunk right down beneath a weight of confusion.

Old troubled stuff between Nora and me. I had hoped all that fester lanced, cleanly healed. Wrong of me to start off her memory of the wound. Hostility of daughter towards mother is only abeyant, not resolved ... this driving-out with him can stir it, cause it to threaten what I had hoped was surer understanding. A stupid business, this making off with him, especially if what I fancied just now ... that look he gave her, she gave him ... or maybe I'm suspicious because I'm jealous of my own blossoming daughter. Natural enough that he might feel drawn to both of us ... we complement one another, different qualities. If things could only be more openly said and done. Anyway Nora is so greatly preoccupied with Greg, this present thing probably touches her only as another lightly taken for granted acclaim to her power of youth.

The mother, nevertheless, felt at this moment a dismal feebleness against such power. She was very still in her body while her mind churned over. Automatically she watched the road and shifted gears.

"Hello," he suddenly leaned forwards and towards her, the better to see her face. "How are you?"

Earlier in the day, or on any of the previous days since they had met, she would have answered such inquiry lightly, flippantly. Now she said:

"At the moment a bit involved …"

"So."

He had known it anyway. He sat back and did not speak any more until they passed someone he recognised from Brompton. With the easy light surprise of the well-travelled, much removed from the exclamatory astonishment of the insular Irishman, he said,

"It's that face from The Three Bells. Many a day I have watched him eating veal and ham pie." As if it were the most natural transition for that face now to be parading along Sandycove. She asked,

"Do you want to say hello? I'll pull in if you wish."

"No no. Not at this moment." He put a hand on her knee. In the lounge overlooking Coliemore Harbour, while they each sipped something, he said, "Your nervousness at leaving home was very apparent."

"Nervousness is too simple a description. It was much more than that."

"Tension then?"

"Yes, tension, and yet more." She looked across the harbour where one solitary motor-boat and its attendant skier ripped through the calm surface. A picture of Nora's face came before her mind's eye and this time, surprisingly, there came with it the first ease that evening. The heaviness lightened in her stomach. She looked back at him. "You see I put the children before everything else, that is after Brian. I hate hugger-mugger if you know — well, I hate deceiving. I couldn't explain to the children about you and this evening — having a drink out and that — Brian, of course, knows anyway. But the children, with them it's more complicated. There have been issues before, decisions to be made about — many things. I have found in trying to work them out as honestly as I know, that, well, that I have had to face up to much bother about personal wholeness — integrity is the usual word, I suppose. There has been much pain involved you know, and a — well — anything that comes near to stirring that sort of hurt into remembrance — it's not so easy you see. So therefore, nervousness is not exactly the word. You saw the outer side of — maybe covered trouble, if you like."

He was listening and looking, it seemed, with all attention, and then he turned towards the water-skier. That made her wonder had she been boring him. What *was* really behind the frontiers of eyes? But he looked away again from the skier and back to her, saying,

"Yes I hear. I think I have understood."

She felt perhaps he had. She also felt that, if need be, she could say out to him about her feeling involving Nora, himself and herself.

Afterwards, going to the car, he said, "I love your family you know."

"It always surprises me, but people seem to, in spite of the rows ... not *all* people of course. We are too chaotic."

"I have seen no rows."

"You haven't been with us long enough. The rows are bloody. I never believe in families that are just so *nice* all the time — some fur and feather flying is healthier; anyway I have to say that to console myself for lack of control ..." They were in the front seat and she stopped abruptly because he was not listening, only watching her. She was not proof against this; a kiss after that kind of looking was as natural as one breath after another. Gently she pulled at his tie.

"I know it's for the party later but I would prefer …" she began to undo the knot. He ripped the tie from his neck. She opened the buttons at the top of his shirt. He began also, impatiently, to undo them himself but she said, "Please let me. I want to." His chest was dark-skinned and thickly hairy. "A jungle," she put her face down to the dark hairiness. The last button about the trouser-belt. "All the way," she said.

"No no. I would be cold." He joked all the time covering up feeling. "You are very passionate," he was keeping her hands.

"I hardly think more than you."

"No no. I am not passionate." Another joke. Who had searched in the kissing? A small doubt moved in her.

"So you are not passionate? All right. Suits me fine." She would play his game a little.

"Women frighten me."

"Poor little thing." She remembered he had also said it the first day they had spoken together: a rather laboured sort of fun. "So they frighten poor little boy." She would continue in this way for a while. It could become less laboured. "And why do they?"

"Because I am impotent."

"Oh poor boy. Well neither can I make love."

Silence.

He bent his head low, nuzzling over the summer dress. The windows of the car were fogged over but some light shone from the harbour wall. Cars flashed all the time as people drove in and out of the parking space.

"We'll move out of here," she said. They drove to a place over the city, silence continuing between them. She watched the lights all around the bay. In her quietness an unhappiness was vaguely settling back on her. They did not touch. She said, "What do you want with me?" She was already detaching herself from an expectation of the promise she felt might have been contained in him. Why should she have needed anything really, who had had so much? And what of that earlier pounding fever?

Very quickly there blurred through her mind thoughts about the degrees in which they had circled nearer to one another over the few days since they had met. Her first reaction to him had been that his face told of great suffering. Yet when he spoke it was nearly always in drollery. She had felt a certain pity but nothing animal had stirred in her towards him. Later in the day, he went with their large family party on a picnic. She had come suddenly upon him lying in swarthy hairiness, sunning himself. The unexpectedness of so much hair repelled her. As she knelt on the grass and he moved easily, good-humouredly submitting to the tugs of children, she knew a query in herself: could she ever be drawn to caress this body? At that time she felt that she could not.

Through the first evening he ragged all the time. Most things he said had some bearing on her; motherhood, fertility, good management. Mocking but harmless; no barbs. Any time she looked towards him, his eyes were already on her. She remained reserved, trying to add him up.

Later that night a party of them were to meet in a Dublin pub. When she got there he had already had a few. He started on the compliments game but she was determined to get him off trivialities. She managed; his coherence on more consequential matters, his way of thinking, pleased her. His odd fatuous remark on her shape or looks did not bother her; they were part of the tune most men in the place had for the women with them, by this time of the evening. The other things he had to say made her feel there was much to him she wanted to know about.

As they tried to stand their ground on the crowded floor, his hand, steadying, gripped hers. She felt herself answering with tightened fingers. On the way home in a packed car she found herself squashed on to his lap. He kissed her hair and neck and even though she made no response, she liked it.

She was staking gladioli next day when he appeared; he fiddled about and did a few small helpful things. She was quiet, wondering about the night before and his extra drinks. And he spoke hearing her thoughts, maybe.

"It's a pity, not much talk today. No booze?"

"So that's what you think?"

"Well it's the essential oil, isn't it?"

"Not for me."

"Good. Actually I don't like pubs; my friends go there and so — sometimes I go."

The whole of the day some quality was in the air between them. All the time they were with other people, but it was there. A sliding look, a hand brushing in the traffic of meals, silences, part-said things, and always the drollery which sometimes baffled her. Once in a doorway he held a match to her cigarette and at such close quarters, she found all of herself answering him. All of her stirred then.

In a carful they went down the country. She held a lolling child in her lap; beside her he sat, controlled and removed in his corner of the seat. Once or twice in the longish trip she felt his fingers on her arm. He could as easily have taken her hand. She wondered why he hadn't. Nervous of being seen by Brian in the driving-mirror? He would not know, of course, that already she had told Brian she was drawn to him, was curious about him. People are so conditioned to the idea of deceiving husbands and wives. Why deceive? Because openness might suggest commitment? It is easier to have surreptitious indulgences. Pleasure living. She was already judging him to be in the category of pleasure takers and she knew nothing of him. Why the devil, she started to ask herself, should *I* judge? Even I, in my imagined emancipation, find myself still tuned to self-righteousness.

The sleeping child stirred restlessly in her lap. She wrapped him closer in her arms thinking: one absolute thing this, anyhow, over which there need be no doubt, no scrutiny — the caring for child by mother. And even with this clear thought she knew simultaneously a retrograde wish to be, at that moment, free of the child and his undoubted need of her, so that she might herself turn in enticement to the man beside her.

When they got home he said he was going into the town. Natural; his other friends from the London group were there. "If you, of course," he said, backing, "care to join us later — that would, needless to say, be our great pleasure."

What verbal flourish when he so chooses! Immediately she decided against going. She felt depressed now. How unaccountable the compound of a make-up, she self-assessed in some contempt for her own fluctuations. There was much to be done; she had three callers in the house that evening needing her attention. There were a hundred and one things to be seen to over a meal and general family doings. She put depression away behind a determined activity. Later when the house was quiet and Brian had gone to write some letters, she played a gloomy Scandinavian record. Nora came in.

"Why are you playing that awful ghostly music?"

Why indeed.

It was getting late, on for midnight. He will have gone to some party; will, very likely, be out until all hours. She had just finished making a list for the next day's supplies when he came back. Nora had said goodnight twice by this time and gone upstairs; she now returned downstairs and stayed around for one small contrived reason or another. Her mother felt she was keeping guard and although she understood the necessity in the girl, it irked her, this watchfulness. Some hardness in her resolved to outstay Nora; determined to see for once something she willed occur. So often the things she willed were thwarted, sometimes because she saw that what she initially willed, if carried out, would not be for the general best; sometimes through sheer crassness of circumstance. Just now her will was hard and clear, she would not this night yield to the censure which emanated from Nora. Her child was judging her from a remembered battleground which, at times, still seemed to space between them.

The mother went out to the garden where, in the light from the house, she began to collect littered odd toys. He followed her, helping.

"I'm going up now Mum, goodnight."

Nora's call through the open door was in her most usual voice, easy, non-measuring.

"Goodnight Nora." The third goodnight they had said to one another. Did I sound a nuance too casual with this one?

When they returned inside the house he stood there, waiting, while she put toys away and bolted the door for the night. Then they closed towards one another briefly, silently. After, she went to bed where Brian was already asleep.

All the next day she was busy; children, food, people, organising this and that, becoming vague, absent-minded in the pile-up of events. But at the back of it all was this distant fever beating in some recess of her. Time was short. Soon he would be gone. She could have just the one evening with him.

"Would you like it?" she had asked him.

"Of course, of course."

"We could link up with the others later ..." she put tentatively, not wanting to seem as if taking possession of the evening.

"We'll see — perhaps — but — we'll see."

And that was how it had been. So here they now were, looking down at the city while she asked him, "What do you want with me?"

And he was answering, "I like you. I like to be with you."

She was afraid to ask the question she really wanted to put, so she went around it.

"When you are close to somebody what do you want?"

He considered.

"I am like you maybe, this feline quality — you like to stroke. I too, I like to touch. This nearness is necessary."

But he did not stroke nor touch any more.

"Women frighten me."

It was the third time he had said it.

She started the car and began to drive down towards the city.

"We'll go and find the others," she said, "this party should be beginning by now."

"Please, not the party. I don't want it. I'd rather stay with you. But you — perhaps you want to go?"

"No, I don't especially want to."

"Then please — with you."

She turned into a deserted hedged lane and switched off the engine.

"Shall we go in the back?" she asked, surprising herself.

"The back is very nice," was all he had to say. She had always hated "very nice".

"I love your enthusiasm," she said and he met that with a sudden return of drollery, shouting in pseudo-élan,

"Fo' Chrissake, the back is *lovely*!"

"Shh." Mostly something jarred in her when people called on Christ that way. He will find me impossible to please.

"You see," he said, "I don't like cars. Cars are awful. I hate cars."

"So a car is what we have."

"Yes and it is no good."

When his flesh was bared she bent to kiss. And again the question rose in her. This time she asked it.

"You *were* joking, weren't you?"

"Actually I have not had much success this way."

She kissed again the soft limp place, knowing great pity. Poor fellow. All that joking.

"I told you women frighten me."

"Yes, now I believe you. But all the time you fooled so much about everything —"

"I am so sorry to disappoint you."

"Shh, please do not be. I really only wish to know you. This — does not — matter."

"I am always guilty, fearful."

"I surely cannot be frightening to you?"

"I know, but it is always this way."

"Maybe if you thought more about the other person —" she ventured, "if you could *give* yourself —"

He was silent and then said, "It's right of course, what you say. I know it but I cannot do it." And after a minute he went on, "Also, a car is awful. One must have time and space. I hate a car."

"I agree entirely. Don't worry. It is cold; cover yourself."

They drove back to the city, searching without much interest for the place where the party was to be. Many times he put a hand on her knee, an excusing, pleading hand.

"It's all right," she said, "I like you very much even so."

"Please, please, not *even so*."

"Indeed it was not a good way to say it. I *like* you. Don't worry."

"Tonight, I'll stay in town — my plane is so early to-morrow."

"I know. You might as well book in somewhere soon. I can't find this party place."

"The party, the party, I never wanted to go to it."

They stopped near the bridge.

"I have a feeling," she said, "we were so near to something and we missed. I don't mean just — bodies."

"It was the car," he said and laughed a short unhappy laugh. His last joke. "No, not true. Not all true anyway. And I did — believe me — come closer to you than to most."

He touched her mouth, "Goodbye then," and he was out on the pavement, walking away. He looked sad in the empty street. She drove the other way.

JUANITA CASEY

One Word

I am not a cruel woman, cried Miss Judith Dannaher. I love God's animals! But if I catch one of those bloody asses in my garden again I'll break all their bloody legs, Lord save us, like sticks for me fire.

Miss Dannaher kicked her own ass in the chest, and felt some measure of relief.

It was all his fault, that whoring Jimmy, roaring off at all hours of the day and night and attracting the rest of his outlaw band off the sand dunes and into her domains.

The times she had to go after the limb of Satan too, looking all over the place and up the roads for him when he broke his hobbles and was away with the nine others of his unspeakable tribe.

The nine belonged to various neighbours around, but having either broken out or been turned away, the nine lived off their wits and other people's gardens and occasionally would be caught up and press-ganged into work again for a few hours.

The long ears of them would scissor together at Miss Judith Dannaher's approach, the rain dropping off their thick pelts and pearling their whiskers as they hunched beneath the few shrubs and thorns around the Maiden's Tower, and she dare not utter the murder within her lest the whole lot take fright and whisk off up the road again. Only when it rained could she catch the wretched Jimmy with any ease, as all the asses were loth to move out from the shelter of the bushes.

Once she had him though. O once she had him. I'll knock shite out of yez, she'd choke hoarsely and mentally murder him all over in various delightful ways until she got him home, when knock shite out of him she did.

Sunshine on the other hand meant that long, soul-destroying saunter behind them all, pretending she didn't really want Jimmy at all and was just out for her health. Apoplexy quietly swelled within her as they moved step to her step, just in front, just out of grab, with their black tricorne eyes looking back at her and their tails demurely switching. By the Holy God, she would clench. By the Holy God ...

Two or three interesting hours could pass thus in gentle ambulation, while bees visited clover and cinquefoil and campion, and the breeze curled the frills of the asses' manes and caressed her hissing brow.

But if there was a wind, then goodbye to the asses and goodbye to Jimmy as they carolled and brayed, bucked and buffeted each other in a mad race to the sea, an ancient, disturbing spirit under their matted hides, and the wildness of swift Asia in their changed eyes. They became, for a short day, the inheritors of ruined Nineveh, the swift ones of Nimrod, the fierce runners of the deserts. Along the strand, matching strides with the waves, wheeling to confront the walker on the sands with the long, burning stare over the civilisations to their green time before men.

When the sea-grasses hummed and whistled and when the winds came, they lifted their scarred and heavy heads. They were the inheritors of the Khamsin and the Sirrocco. They were the Seers.

On these days, the wind also got into Miss Judith Dannaher's head, and she gave up and went to bed with a fierce migraine, which pounded and drummed as though all Jimmy's four hooves were, for once, kicking hell out of her.

With the occasional and begrudging help of the ever-reluctant Jimmy, Miss Judith Dannaher tilled the soil of her few acres, saved a little frantic hay, moved her hens' houses around her own cabin in an uproar of hens, oaths, and the total disarray of both herself and Jimmy, carted a variety of useful and useless agricultural products about, buried the cart and Jimmy at intervals beneath vast, steaming dollops of cow manure, and the same trio went shopping with the odour of sanctity adhering with the bits of straw to all three.

On these expeditions, Miss Judith Dannaher tugged, beat, swore, kicked, and wished the most interesting amendments upon the creeping Jimmy, but on the return journey nothing could hold him as he tore for home and freedom with his mouth pulled back to his ears and the cart and Miss Judith Dannaher yawing and gybing behind him like a boat in a following sea. Whoa, whoa, ye whore, I'll knock shite out of yez was the battle-cry of this ill-assorted equipage as it shaved corners, the village bus, slow children and old Mr Fintan Maloney on his crutches, and joyous dogs pursued its course with hopes of receiving a flight of sausages from one of its better rebounds.

Upon unharnessing the now demure and extinguished Jimmy, Miss Judith Dannaher would apply her arm, voice, and boots to him, and a fury of dust would erupt as she beat and whacked his hide like a carpet.

Miss Judith Dannaher lived on one side of the Maiden's Tower, and the brothers Johnny and Jimmy O'Neill lived on the other. Between their cabins ran a stream, and over the stream a plank bridge, and behind them a tangled patchwork of small fields and miniature forests of scrubby oaks, thorns and ash. In front lay the Burrows, mile upon mile of sand dunes, and in front of these a swish down on to the white miles of strand and the moody sea.

Miss Judith Dannaher's fields contained, as well as the occasional Jimmy, three old cows and three young heifers, her hens, some geese and a few ducks, and a tethered community of nanny goats, all spinsters like Miss Judith Dannaher and with therefore not a drop of milk between them.

The fields of Johnny and Jimmy O'Neill contained but themselves, some blackberries and fungi at the right seasons, and the brothers O'Neill let them get on with it.

The Maiden's Tower was a long pinnacle of stone, mushroom-capped with small square inlets to keep arrows out of spying eyes and was a fair example of the old round tower of Irish history. Legend and history however ran a race with truth, and all deadheated.

The Maiden had watched her Captain sail away on the tides of spring and whiled away the time and her heart's desire by building the Tower to his memory and to his return. Which he never did. That the Maiden chose to erect a peculiarly phallic edifice did not go unnoticed among the unsophisticated of the region, and private additions and ramifications to the Maiden's tale abounded in every family.

Every morning the brothers O'Neill arose and breakfasted without one word between them, and they both stalked down to their boat and its nets on the estuary shore. With long, deliberate strides they heroned down the shingle together, each one to his own task in the boat, moving together and each other like pieces in a jig-saw.

All day they rowed and netted at the river mouth close by, slow yet deft, unhurried yet quick enough, and without one word between them.

A lorry came out from the town each day to buy whatever catch they and the other scattered fishermen of the area might bring in, but on days of wind and white water the day began as usual with their Trappist breakfast, but no fishing could be attempted, and so Johnny and Jimmy O'Neill would stare at the sea from either side of the plank bridge, and without one word between them. Then Johnny would take the track over the Burrows, and Jimmy would follow the frothy tideline beside the sea, and a few hundred yards apart they would stalk the three miles into Coneytown village and bend into Barney Hagan's within a bootfall of each other. Seated on opposite sides of the Vandyke interior, they would drink time and the sea into an opacity of oblivion without one word between them and return under the moon and the flying clouds and the spit of the rain, Johnny taking the track over the black Burrows, and Jimmy following the luminous tideline beside the sea, a few hundred yards apart and so blind, so deaf, and so dumb that they could not, had they wanted to, have uttered one word between them. At the cabin, at which they arrived within each other's shadows, they unbooted and undressed to their combinations and, turning their backs to each other, fell asleep to the thunder of the surf and of their own snores.

Their lives, in this manner, had creaked apart and together down the same rut like the hub of a loosening wheel since the year of 1916 when Johnny joined the British Navy and Jimmy remained at home at his nets. In those days Miss Judith Dannaher had been as a lily in her fields, a shy wild violet of the Burrows. She and Johnny were to marry on his return from the wars. But one day she thought of the other bereft and languishing Maiden, decided a bird in the hand was better than an absent heart, and settled in its absence for Jimmy.

There was no haste, as Miss Judith had her farm and Jimmy his fish, and the rain and the sun and the winds rolled the seasons around them. Until, suddenly, there was Johnny. And from that one day the brothers O'Neill rethreaded the hole in their lives and went on with their netting as before, but now without one word between them. Miss Judith, after a suitable period of furious lament, rethatched her cabin, made herself a new apron, shot her father's old donkey, and bought a new one, a black jack she named Johnny, and out of which, for the next twenty-three years, she knocked shite.

Over the years she lost both her beauty and her old father and gained very little else but a whetstone of a temper upon which she honed her tongue.

CUTTING THE NIGHT IN TWO

On the day of the Second World War, Miss Judith lost her asinine fiancé in a plot of cabbages behind Michael Murphy's shed, ballooned with the bloat and upturned like a small, black currach with his four legs as stiff at each corner as bedposts.

A few days later Miss Judith, advertising, became engaged to the equally black-hearted Jimmy, then a winsome three-year-old with a shiny coat, and they settled into their mutual years of deadlock and checkmate, with Miss Judith knocking shite out of Jimmy as she had out of the late Johnny.

Thus the ordered years passed. They rolled by the brothers O'Neill with the porpoises of summer and the westerlies of winter, their wordless days punctuated by the flap of soles and bass, mullet and pollock on the boards of the boat at their feet. Their years of snapping congers, of turbot heavy as anchors, of fatuous skate and of quicksilver sprats, and of the rainbow leap of the salmon and the strange ungodliness of the huge angler fish with its mantrap jaws and its ventral parody of hands.

The years bloomed and seeded and withered too for Miss Judith Dannaher, with the harebells and the froggy marsh flowers, the mossy gates which opened her days into one field from another, and the faded finality of the grained back door shutting out the night's black paw. The days of unborn calves and ice on buckets, of geese on the high wind of Christmas, and of a striped snail on summer's rosetted wall.

The years of thistledown and blown spindthrift, the years of mustardseed.

The years changed, and to those who say there is no change their changeling lives must suffer the strangest of them all.

Like leaves, one falls on a bright day of frost, and the other is left for the night wind. One drifts to the wet grass, and one remains to tap in the sunlight.

It is a slow pavane, and yet those that are left say how swift is the end, how unexpected, how terrible. They cannot see the unravelling of the net, the break in the web, the turning of the inexorable kaleidoscope to bring about a new pattern, the new enigma.

On a December day, Miss Judith Dannaher closed all her windows and wedged the doors, fed her stock, and made up her fire. There could be no work until the sheeting rain and savage wind eased.

The hens peered out of their houses at the roar, and the tucked cows shivered at the closed door of their byre.

The wind flung the sand off the beach, and the sea ran against the sullen river's push, and they fought each other into a great, toothed, lionheaded wall of grey water.

The brothers O'Neill were caught up as their boat scraped ashore, and they were rolled in their black oilskins under its sucking arch like peas down a drain. The wind caught the ghosts of two words and tore them into infinity.

O Judith, cried Johnny.

O Judith, cried Jimmy.

In the dim cabin Miss Judith Dannaher had fallen asleep by her bright fire.

In a hollow of the whistling Burrows nine grey asses and one black with a broken hobble sheltered against the driving sand, patiently enduring the stinging fury of the wind with the humble acceptance of martyrs.

On the strand the whirling paper shell of a sea-urchin blew against a white branch of driftwood and disintegrated in a puff of fragments.

Her head settling further down on to her chest, Miss Judith Dannaher exhaled a strangled snore, and the light ashes of her dead fire stirred and fluttered on the cold hearth.

VAL MULKERNS

Away From It All

'It's a public beach,' she said, amused at his annoyance.

'It's ours,' he insisted, stubbornly. '*They* are Trá na Fuinseoige people. They should go there and stay there.'

They were, of course, though it was no argument. It was a stiff climb over the rocks to get to this particular place and people with small children did not come here as a rule. You would sometimes find the odd lone camper here, like the French boy last year, but mostly only lovers came. If you found people in one sandy cove, you simply climbed over to the next one, and there you might have been at the world's end. It was she who had first shown him this remote western peninsula, her place of childhood summers. Now his air of outraged ownership both touched and irritated her.

'I know him by sight,' she said suddenly, raising herself on one elbow to peer through sunglasses at the fat father. The man was loud as well as large in an orange-striped T-shirt, and going bald like Timothy himself. It seemed strange for somebody of his years to have small children. Then suddenly she blushed to find herself putting words on that random impression. If Timothy and she married, Timothy and anybody for that matter, his children would be equally small playing on just such a beach.

'He's one of the O'Donnells,' she offered. 'Spent years over in Bradford or somewhere and learned all about wool. He's manager of the new factory now.'

'With an English wife,' Timothy said disapprovingly, as a sharp voice called to the children. Younger than her husband, she was fair-haired and passive, fully dressed still and knitting in the sun. The small boy and girl, already in swimsuits, were kicking a red ball to one another at the waves' edge.

'She looks nice,' Sarah said firmly. 'Happy.'

He turned restlessly over on the rug and grunted. 'Since *they* won't go away, why don't we? Over those rocks there's a beautiful empty beach just waiting for us. Come on, love. Have our swim there.'

He was already on his feet, tugging at the rug, but Sarah felt stubborn and she did not approve of his disapproval.

'I'm staying here,' she said. 'You go over there for your swim if you like.'

'Alone?' His dependent eyes, the first of his features she had ever noticed, were full of sun and reproach. The thin top of his head was beginning to look angry so she rummaged out her sun cream.

'Bend down.' He did this obediently and she rubbed in the cream. Then he kissed her, mollified, and they lay back peacefully in the sun, but not for long.

'I must write to my mother,' he said. He searched in her straw bag where he had put a writing case among the sun oil and apples and togs. She knew he had been writing to his mother for all of the twenty years since the Department of Local Government had posted him to Dublin.

'What do you tell her every week?' she had often asked him, and lazily again now.

'Same old serviceable things,' he muttered, writing busily.

'She doesn't know about me, I suppose?'

'Good heavens, no.'

He had a selection of old-fashioned expressions — 'Goodness', 'My dear girl', 'Great Scott'. Two years ago when she had first taken him home, her own young sister had described him as 'Rather sweet really, but *un peu démodé*.'

Perfect. It described the stuffy clothes, obstinately clung to when everybody else had long since abandoned good grey suits, the style of speech, the verbal courtesies, the dated blond charm of his face which reminded her of a British film star her mother had often enthused over. You saw other faces like that in Sunday night movies on Irish television. She never remembered the actors' names, but they mostly had faces like Timothy's and it always happened that ample nineteen fortyish brunettes fought one another bitterly for their favours. Sometimes she wondered if Timothy's resemblance to the heroes of her mother's youth was the reason why he had been welcomed so warmly right from the beginning — to family meals, to parties, even to Christmas dinners. Timothy's mother and sister went for Christmas to relatives in Cork, but Timothy had always preferred to stay in Dublin. Formerly he had treated himself to a hotel meal on Christmas Day; now for two years he had come to them. She found it odd to be remembering Christmas during a July heatwave.

'As I write,' she mocked him suddenly, 'the sun beats down on this jolly little beach and I wish you were here.'

'Wrong,' he said. 'Why should I wish she was here? I'd much prefer you.'

It was a glib compliment, and she had even asked for it, but it made her extraordinarily happy, as on the night when they were sitting in his flat before a decidedly dull television screen, with terrible reception. When he complained she said, 'You *might* have been at the office stag party. Why didn't you go?'

'Because I much prefer spending an evening with you.'

There were compensations, of course, when at last the talk died out and the pretence of watching television was mercifully over. But occasionally she would have preferred an evening out at the theatre, a restaurant, anywhere where they could be alone in a crowd. Timothy however didn't like crowds and hated the theatre. He said restaurants were dangerous places where one was likely to be poisoned unless exceptional luck prevailed.

'Yet I *did* see you one night at the St Laurence Hotel in Howth,' she remembered, and said it aloud. 'That time Daddy suddenly took us all out to celebrate his Prize Bond.'

'Look,' Timothy said, alert, his letter laid unfinished in the breast pocket of his jacket. 'Sir Tycoon over there is about to sunbathe. Watch. Golly, he's fat.'

'You were with your sister,' Sarah remembered gently. 'I would have liked to know her.' For a second she brooded about the reason for this positive ache to know his family, his mother, his sisters, the people surrounding the unknown small boy who had been at school twenty years before she was born. He had made the introduction briefly, dutifully — 'Some good friends of mine' — but had shown no inclination for them to linger. They did not. He and his frowning oldish sister had left soon afterwards.

'Look,' Timothy said again. 'Where's the betting Mr Man will not be left in peace for long?'

On the ebbing tide the red ball had bobbed a little out of reach of the two children, who apparently had no intention of getting too wet. The boy waded out once to his knees but the ball drifted just beyond him and he waded back, whereupon his sister whacked him with her spade. Immediately afterwards she screamed for her father, and her brother screamed at her.

'Told you so,' Timothy said. 'Now let's see what he'll do.'

'For somebody who resented the arrival of people, you're very interested in them.'

She didn't know why she felt mildly irritated with him until, made lazy by the sun, she forced herself to back-track into their exchanges, but slowly. Yes. This was something Timothy did very often. Distracted your attention when he didn't want you to question him. You might just think of asking why, if he could take his sister out to a meal, he couldn't take you too occasionally.

'Poor fellow,' he was saying now. 'Bad luck, sir.' She raised herself on one elbow again and Timothy patted her knee. She moved away, but went on watching the father and his children. The small boy and girl were frantically hopping about now, urging him on.

He had apparently been interrupted in the course of undressing because he still wore his T-shirt on top and a huge overstretched swimsuit below. He stood uncertainly for a moment at the water's edge. His daughter tried to launch him, but without success. Timothy laughed delightedly.

'The ball's much further out now,' he said.

Quite suddenly Sarah found herself on the father's side. The water in the cove was icy, straight in from the Atlantic. The poor man probably had no intention of doing anything but sunbathe. She watched sympathetically as he waded out gingerly, pausing after every few steps to grip his hands under his arms. The children shrieked encouragement as he made a sudden grab at the ball, but it bobbed out of reach and he waded further in the direction of the rocky arm that divided this cove from the next. Quite suddenly, as they watched, he pulled the orange T-shirt over his head and emerged pale and pear-shaped. He turned to throw the shirt to his daughter, who didn't catch it. It floated at her feet but neither child paid any attention. Their father's movements had become crablike now in thigh-high water. He seemed at any moment about to wobble over.

'His feet are on the sharp stones now,' Sarah said, still concerned for him. 'Why on earth doesn't he swim for it?'

'He'll have to,' Timothy agreed, 'although if he doesn't get it quickly he's going to have most of his skin removed by the barnacles on those rocks. Look where the ball's going now.'

'Swim, oh swim,' Sarah said below her breath, but the children went on screaming and the man floundered on. Suddenly she understood why.

'He *can't* swim,' she said urgently. 'Look, it's absolutely certain, Timothy. He can't *swim*. We'll have to get it for them.'

'I'll go,' Timothy said without enthusiasm. 'You wanted to sunbathe for at least another hour before going in. I'd better go.'

Touched by his thoughtfulness, she watched him go down the beach with that loping boy's walk that belied his years. As the children cheered him she saw how he shuddered at the first touch of the water, then blessed himself as usual. Before going any further, he bent sensibly and picked up the father's T-shirt which he wrung out and gave to the small girl, pointing at her mother as an indication of what she should do. But the child stood clutching the T-shirt and Timothy waded out, after one expressive gesture in Sarah's direction concerning the coldness of the water. She waved to him and waited for the moment when he would strike out with his powerful crawl and recover the ball in no time. He continued to wade, however, though much more capably than the children's father with whom he was almost abreast.

Sarah saw the red ball bobbing closer and closer to the razor rocks, and at last touch them. She practically cried out in impatience then because Timothy could quite easily have had the ball back by now if he had started to swim at the right time. Instead he began an apparently long conversation with the children's father, gesturing at the rocks, at the ball, shrugging his shoulders, finally pointing to the ball's progress as though it no longer concerned him. They stood together in the sun, in the cold blue water, two middle-aged men in perfect agreement that nothing could be done. The small girl began suddenly to cry and hurled her father's garment further out as both men began to walk back together. Both children ran suddenly back to their mother, who had hardly suspended her knitting during the drama. Incredulous, Sarah watched as the father bent to pick up his soaked shirt and Timothy ran back to her up the beach, still shrugging and laughing. Before he reached her he turned an exuberant cartwheel on the soft sand.

'Golly, what a waste of good time!' he panted. 'Might as well have stayed cosily where I was, mightn't I?'

"Why didn't you swim out for the ball?' she asked, shocked by the contempt that suddenly overcame her.

'Because, my dear girl, you *saw* where it went. Hey, look at it now, firmly wedged between the spikes. Only a maniac would risk his entire coat of skin for a plastic ball whose cost is approximately forty new pence, or free with four washing powder labels.' He was laughing at her now, with all the good white teeth on display, entirely justified to himself.

'There was plenty of time before it got so far,' she said. 'You just stood there, as though it didn't matter.'

'Well, does it?' he said reasonably. 'Do you think that the manager of the new wool factory is too poor to buy his brats another ball on the way home? For heaven's sake, love, what's got into you?' He towelled himself briefly and then lay down beside her, one hand on her warm leg. She shook it off stubbornly.

'It *does* matter,' she said. 'They didn't want another ball. They wanted that one, and you let them depend on you. Would you have been afraid to risk your skin if it had been one of the children? Would you?'

He laughed again, incredulous. "Of course I wouldn't. You can't buy another child as easily as a red plastic ball.'

Sarah said nothing. Inexplicable tears stung her eyelids. She watched the ball as a twist of the tide carried it free of the rocks. The children ran cheering again down to the water's edge, and Timothy turned her face roughly to his. When he saw her eyes he began to laugh nervously again.

'Of all the baffling creatures —' he began, then stopped as he too saw the ball safely swept into clear water. 'So *that's* all it is. Pride. Little girl wanted a gallant princely rescue and was denied. But wait. Just watch this.'

He jumped up and this time raced away down the beach, urged on once more by the children. Sarah put a dress on rapidly over her togs and walked away up the stony track along which they had come. She wondered what on earth she would say to her mother if she arrived home a week early but she felt her young sister might understand.

MARY BECKETT

Heaven

To Hilary in her sixties, heaven was an empty house. She loved to come in from shopping and shut the door behind her knowing that there was nobody in any of the seven neat rooms and that nobody would arrive home until her husband did, shortly after six. A daughter-in-law might wish to call on her for some service but she had insisted from the beginning that they telephone first to arrange a suitable time. She noticed sometimes her opposite neighbour being visited by people who turned the key in the door and walked in. That, to Hilary, would have been intolerable. Occasionally someone said to her that she must be lonely with her four sons grown and gone. She smiled and murmured something about keeping busy and anyway when her sons were healthy and happy that was all that mattered.

She had appeared always as a devoted mother. When she was young her pram had been polished, the pillow immaculate, the blankets fluffy, the baby perfect. The nappies on the line were white and square like a television advertisement. The standard in the district was high except for a few unfortunate backsliders but Hilary was out on her own. Her little boys playing with the other children got dirty in the normal way but it was obviously newly acquired dirt on clean clothes, not general grubbiness. She was fortunate perhaps in that they all had her blonde pink-and-white appearance. None of them had inherited their father's dark hair and shadowed skin although they were tall like him and thin. Hilary often said then that she should slim but instead she dressed in drifty floaty clothes, and before hats went out of fashion she wore black gauzy hats with red cherries, or pink hats with veils or green hats with roses. She dressed up every afternoon to wheel out the pram and do the shopping. Some of the neighbours admired her style, and others criticised that but admitted she had great spirit.

The effort of all this perfectionism drained her each day so that when the children were eventually in bed she sat down by the fire and her husband sat in the opposite chair. She glanced at magazines and ate sweets and sighed or yawned every now and again. He read the papers in their entirety and switched the television from snowy channel to foggy channel and back so that it blared all evening until it closed down for the night. At least then the noise came from one place only. Later, when the boys were in their teens, Hilary had to tolerate transistors in bedrooms and tape recorders as well as the television and record player. So long as she stayed in her kitchen she had some slight refuge but it was there that the younger boys brought their troubles with sums, or spellings to hear or Irish passages to learn, while the older ones brought their complaints about unfair teachers or biased referees.

These worried her. It upset her to see their soft curved mouths drawn down in ugly resentment. She tried to persuade them not to feel aggrieved so readily, that it would become a habit and give them indigestion. She had to laugh them out of it because they would have been very embarrassed if she had confessed that she feared the harm it would do their souls. She never said such things to anyone. The only time she spoke out was at a parents' meeting once in the boys' school. There had been an alarming increase in rugby injuries to boys' spines, not in the school but in the country generally, news of brilliant boys paralysed for life. Some of the parents asked the priests who ran the school how their boys were safeguarded. The priests marshalled reassurances and the parents failed to put forward sensible objections. Hilary said she thought rugby an uncivilised game anyway, and the rivalry between schools concerning rugby and between the priests involved was completely unchristian. There was a murmur of dissent and then several men shouted no, no.

'If anything happens to any of my boys on the rugby field,' Hilary persisted, 'I will go and howl outside the priests' house day and night.'

The other parents laughed but Hilary did not laugh and the priests did not really laugh either and none of her boys made much progress at rugby from that time on.

They did well at everything else, though, much better in their exams than their teachers ever expected going by their class marks and by their judgements to Hilary during parent-teacher meetings. They went to university and there followed years of counting every penny to keep them there, of going without new clothes, of wearing cheap shoes long after they were broken and spread. Her husband had to keep his old car when it was a daily torment of refusing to start in the mornings or even at traffic lights, and people pushing it and looking as if they might get heart attacks. But they did well so that their father often wondered aloud how far he too might have gone in this world if he had had the chances they were getting. Hilary never had such thoughts about herself. She fed them nourishing food morning and night, worried about their not having enough sleep, listened to their panic about exams, and to relieve the terrible feelings of impotence she had about them began going to Mass every morning to pray for their success. Then they were all finished, all with jobs except the youngest who was awarded a grant to do a PhD in an American university and insisted on marrying before he went, to his father's disgust. He fumed and fussed and denounced it as lunatic but Hilary was relieved because she had read novels about American universities and she could hardly believe such depravity existed. A wife would keep him safe.

HEAVEN

Even before the others married she found herself alone in the house for long hours during the day. At first she would stand in the hall with her hands clasped, looking into empty rooms and wondering how she would celebrate. She generally finished up making herself tea and cake or eating a bar of chocolate with a feeling that there was something she was missing. Gradually she realised that this was not an occasional luxury, this solitude, but a routine. So she fixed a time every morning to sit and relish the quiet. As the days passed she grew more intense about it so that frequently the blood surged in her ears and she was whirled into a great cone of silence and stayed there suspended. She had no thoughts, no contemplations. She was not aware of the happiness it induced until she resumed her household activities and found herself smiling. She began hurrying home in the mornings to shut herself in. Only years of discipline insisted that she cleaned, washed and cooked as she always did. Sometimes the silence caught her up out of doors so that she drifted past people without seeing them or speaking to them.

She began thinking of heaven. She imagined deep silence. Innumerable people stood in rapture, no one touching another, backed and divided by pillars and arches as in Renaissance paintings, drawn, she supposed, to God whom she could not imagine, but still and complete in themselves. She was confident she was going there, seeing herself as a middle-aged to elderly ewe in the middle of the flock giving no trouble at all to the shepherd. She had never had any great temptations; she was unlikely, she thought, to have any now. At funeral Masses she happily saw herself as the dead person and arranged in her mind how things should be done about food, flowers and cars. No one would miss her, she had done all that had been asked of her, she could fade out any time.

She did do baby-sitting for the grandchildren whenever she was asked, until her eldest son took his wife off for a holiday to celebrate her getting a job and left their three-year-old boy with

Hilary for a fortnight. By the end of the first week she was consumed by the same desire for perfection in everything to do with this grandson as with her sons more than twenty years before. His hair must shine, his teeth must gleam, his clothes must grace his little straight sturdy body. When she watched him concentrating on a toy she contemplated the possibility of his being lonely at any time in the future or unhappy or unsuccessful and could hardly bear the pain. When her son came to collect him he congratulated her on the child's fine appearance.

'It'll be all right to leave him round on Monday morning when Pauline and I are going to work, won't it?' he asked casually, and Hilary said, 'No, not at all,' sharply, and then made excuses that she was too old, that he'd be better in his own home with someone in to look after him. 'We don't know anybody suitable,' her son protested. 'It's risky to let in someone we don't know. She might not care for him properly.'

'He is your child,' she said tartly. 'He is your responsibility, yours and Pauline's. You cannot shift it on to me. You'll just have to pay somebody well and hope for the best.'

He seized on that. 'But we have every intention of paying you. Of course we had. You mustn't think ...'

'How much would you have thought of? Five pounds a week? No, no, no, money wouldn't make any difference.'

They had actually thought that if there were any question of money they should offer twenty pounds a month — it would be better paid by the month — but that indeed it was unlikely she would take any money. What would she want money for? She never bought anything except just the necessary food. She would be so glad of the child's company during her long empty day. He would give her a fresh interest in life and they'd pick him up most evenings after work.

They did not forgive her. The child was left in a playschool in the mornings and collected by a neighbour who minded him with her own children until his parents came home. It was not satisfactory, really. Hilary, after a week or two of sleepless nights, managed to put him out of her mind most of the time. A year later, tidying a drawer, she came across a silly affectionate birthday card given to her by one of her sons when he was young and felt a pang. It was nice after all when she was of use to them so that they loved her.

One morning her husband opened a letter that made him laugh first and then angered him.

'What is it?' she said with only a polite interest. He hesitated for a minute and then handed it over. It said:

Dear Sir,

You should know your wife is an alcoholic. She is being talked about all over the district. She hurries home in the mornings without talking to her neighbours and shuts herself in the house. Some of these days she will disgrace you.

Signed A Wellwisher

She was alarmed, even though the letter-writer had mistaken the object of her addiction.

'I shouldn't have shown it to you,' he said, looking at her in surprise. 'It's upset you. Sure we all know you drink nothing but coffee and tea, although you drink plenty of them. It's only some crank.' He was watching her, though, and when he came home from work he continued to watch her. He suggested they go for a walk. She refused, murmuring something about tired feet. The next night he thought they should go for a drive. She hadn't been in the car for years except for Sunday Mass or Friday-night shopping.

'What would we do that for?' she asked, embarrassed. 'It's threatening rain.' The attention unnerved her, making it more difficult for her to escape into silence, but she could cope so long as he was there only in the evening.

Then he retired. She had known for years the date of his retirement but refused to face it, as did he.

He would give full attention to the garden, he said, and he tramped in and out of her kitchen, needing water when she was at the sink, wanting her hand to hold a line for beds he was digging. He grunted and groaned and held his hand to the small of his long back. He didn't enjoy it. He had no company. His dark face grew more and more saturnine. Hilary dreaded coming home to him. He had stopped watching her but he continued the recent invitations to walks, drives, meals out. They were no longer a lifeline for her but for himself. She refused, regardless. She had always an excuse; she was tired, she had no clothes. She had never revived her interest in clothes, suppressed while the money was needed for her growing family. She wore black trousers with an elastic waistband and any kind of tunic on top. He urged her to buy something else but she put it off.

One rainy day, when he was sitting in the kitchen rubbing continuously at the threadbare places on the knees of his trousers, he asked, 'Hilary, why did you marry me?'

'Such a thing to ask, out of the blue,' she said, taken aback. 'Have you nothing better to think about than ancient history?'

'It's not ancient history. Whatever there was then surely keeps on now. You don't love me now; you can't stand me around the place. Did you love me ever, that's what I want to know? That's what I have to know.'

'For goodness' sake, it's just that I'm not used to somebody under my feet in the daytime. You're miserable yourself — you should think of something to get you out among other men.'

'You're not answering me.' He kept on so that she snapped at him, 'And I'm not going to answer you. How can I remember what it was like when I was young?'

He said no more but sat there, hunched.

She was uncomfortable, remembering clearly what it was like to see her twenties speeding by, and in spite of her blonde hair and pink cheeks and Ballybunion and Salthill and Tramore and numerous escorts nobody had offered to marry her. She had seized on the prospect of marriage with him as the only way to a real life — her old life had no sense or meaning. They had been well suited, neither until now interested in the other. She had had her children, her house and then her silence. He had had his job and his children to a certain extent. Now he had nothing and, she thought indignantly, he was busy seeing that she'd have nothing either.

While he was about the house she never sat down until night-time. She polished and cleaned things that were already shining. She hovered over the cooker as it cooked their simple meals. He was either in the kitchen reading his paper or in and out of the garden. His breathing banished silence from the house. The smallest sounds impinged on her — the gentle bong of a Venetian blind upstairs at an open window, the click of a thermostat in the bathroom as it turned itself on or off, the ticking of clocks all over the house, unsynchronised.

Before the winter set in she told the priest at her monthly Confession, 'I have feelings of hatred for my husband, murderous feelings. I am afraid I will do him an injury — I have carving knives and heavy casseroles in the kitchen.' The priest told her to pray about it, to see a doctor, to get a hobby for herself or her husband. 'But,' he warned her, 'don't let hatred enter into your soul or you'll be fighting it until your dying day.' She was afraid then of losing her peace in heaven as well as the peace in her home. All the beautiful broad shining avenues of silence would be shut off from her and she would be condemned to some shrieking cacophonous pit.

She urged the buying of a garden shed and a greenhouse to occupy him. He was not enthusiastic about them but he consented after long deliberations on the back mat over where they were to go and then what was to go in them. She tried putting a chair in the shed and bringing out his morning coffee and afternoon tea, but she could not put him out of her mind. Every time she glanced out of the window she could see his shape, stooped. She could even see the sun sparkling on the drip at the end of his nose.

She resigned herself and rang up her daughters-in-law. 'I will mind your children after playschool,' she told them. 'I need my mornings for messages and housework but I'll have them on a regular basis from lunchtime until you come home from work. I don't want any money for it. Their grandfather can collect them. He'll help me with them. I'll not find them too much for me while he is there.'

They were stiff. They were dubious. 'You would need to be sure you're not just using our children to cover your own loneliness,' Pauline said.

'I have never been lonely, Pauline, never in my life,' she answered mildly, so they allowed themselves to be persuaded and every afternoon five children aged between two and six invaded her life.

She had one of her sons go up to the roof-space and bring down all the toys and books stored there since his own childhood, and because there were no girls' playthings she produced her old green and rose-petalled hats so they could dress up. She put a load of builders' sand in the back garden and saw it tramped everywhere. She was vigilant that they didn't rub it into one another's eyes or use the spades as weapons. She hugged them when they cried and loved their hot damp foreheads pressing into her neck. After their tea she sorted them out from the debris, packed them into the car and her husband delivered them to their three separate homes. Apart from collecting and delivering the children he took no interest in them. When the elder son of his eldest son put his hand on his knee and said, 'Come on out and kick football. Grandfather,' he almost blushed but made an excuse and went up to the bathroom, no refuge with five children in the house. One evening he told her that he was tired of the arrangement, too old to suffer all those children. He would still act as chauffeur but he had met another grandfather at the playschool and they had decided to go to a bowling-green not far away on good afternoons and to a quiet pub if it rained. He would not be at home at that time for the foreseeable future. There were plenty of things to do for a retired man still active and alert. Hilary agreed, told him he was perfectly right, and sat down exhausted every evening when she had cleaned up the mess left by the children, far too tired to do anything but leaf through a magazine or glance now and then at her husband's choice of television programmes, six clear channels now, one always blaring.

Now and again, though, she did catch a distant glimpse of calm corridors and vaulted roofs all soundless and it gave her a feeling of great sweetness in anticipation.

LELAND BARDWELL

Out-Patients

'This way. Please. No. Not you dear.' The orderly beckoned to Nina. 'You,' she said. Her voice dropped, not sure whether Nina was next in the queue. Nina held the left elbow in her right fist taking care not to jolt it.

'Have you given your name, dear?'

'No. Not yet.'

'Oh,' the orderly said. 'Then you'd better sit down again.'

Nina sat down on the wooden seat. She could see the nuns bustling around beyond the glass partition; they moved separately from each other, some with papers in their hands, all their faces polished. Behind the partition there was no sound; mute sisters of charity.

Hack away the sleeve as the arm swells! But they're in a hurry and won't notice.

Jesus! the bastard's broken it this time! What can she tell them, these remote women? That she is a lousy wife and gets beaten up every so often?

So she can't admit it? Must she lie, make up a new story each time, each one more improbable than the last in order to maintain the core of the myth that marriage works? So that, as society believes, the woman is, finally, to blame?

Is that it?

Nina was cold, undernourished, too lightly clad; she was trying not to shiver or laugh or annoy the woman beside her; she looked occasionally into the area beyond the glass partition and wondered would the nuns suddenly gather their papers into their arms and stride towards them — the sick, the destitute.

But she did laugh and the woman, or rather girl, beside her crouched low and shook her head; the pale hair rose and fell like cotton on her cheeks.

'They take their time,' she said.

Nina read: NO LOITERING. Like the NO SMOKING notice it had been, always would be, ignored. They hung around and smoked, their hands curled round the cigarettes, wisps of smoke trailing through the fingers. When the nuns came they would stamp the cigarettes and put the stubs in their pockets.

She knew it was lucky it was her left arm, that he had hit for half an hour. Or it had seemed like that. It had been dole day and he had been drinking all afternoon; he was in that sodden destructive mood that came on him every Tuesday and when he saw Frank who had just called in he began.

He'd simply said, 'Go!' and Frank had gone and Brendan had picked up the axe handle. Useless her trying to escape, shielding her face with her forearm which took the punishment. She'd run round the room, ducked under the table, shouting, Stop, please stop!

But it *was* lucky it was her left arm, she thought and thought about the sewing she needed to do; the middle child, poor kid, no button on his coat and off to school in rubber boots.

How did other mothers keep their children neat, spotless? Why couldn't she? That time Frank came and sat beside them on the canal bank she'd been ashamed of their pale grubby faces, the middle one, again holding his coat shut with one hand and fishing for minnows with the other. But a short moment of happiness had come on her when he had put his notebooks on the grass and touched her shoulder.

'You don't say very much,' he had said. 'But you make me feel intelligent.'

'What a strange thing to say,' had she said? Or perhaps, 'But you are, aren't you?' At any rate they had looked into the canal which was clear and still as a photograph till he'd let go her shoulder to stir the water with a stick and splinter their reflections and she thought he must have been embarrassed when he touched her but the touch of his hand on her arm had changed the day, the whole week, even.

The nun had come and was leading the girl beside her down the corridor. It would be her turn soon and she must have her story ready.

Last month it had been a rigmarole about slipping in the wet yard and …

She looked up at the nun who had returned.

'Name?'

A biro was poised over the writing pad.

'Nina Sheridan.'

The few details checked, the nun looked at her arm. A precise glance, 'How did you get this?'

And now the story must run its course. Nina remembered some half-prepared sentences: 'I was diving off a jetty at Seapoint and my arm hit off a rock.'

'Have you children?'

'Four.'

'And where were your children when you were diving into the sea?'

'Playing in the sand.'

'Alone?'

'Yes. They were quite safe. You see …'

Nina stood now before the nun; anger had begun to run down her chest. 'Yes,' she shouted.

'Sit down,' the nun said.

It was all wasted, the anger, the accelerated heart-beat; the nun had walked away and Nina had to sit again, alone this time except for a copy of *The Word* which lay, half open, on the seat beside her.

She would check her fury by reading *The Word*, a magazine which told you facts about people worse off than yourself as opposed to women's magazines which left your mind open to fantasy. She slid her hand over the cover, uneasy, for as yet she was not prepared to admit to the lack of fight that had reduced her own life in essence to the status of some of the women from whom circumstances had removed the last grain of hope. But she was saved from opening it by the return of the nun. She bore upon her with that assertiveness that seemed even worse then, than the anger that had now quite left, or worse, even, than the continuous throbbing of her arm.

'First visit?'

'I was here three months ago with a broken nose.'

The nun looked away.

'I'm accident prone.' Now she could begin to laugh, to ignore.

'I forgot to ask your address.' Nina's arm was picked up and dropped like a stone being quickly replaced on a nest of slugs. The shock of pain lodged under her armpit; tears burnt.

'I'll have to find your file.'

Nina worried about the babies; would Brendan mind them or would he just go out and leave them alone.

'Get up, get up for God's sake, you've broken my arm!' Had she said that with authority? Or, 'I have to go to the hospital. Mind the children!' Please? Hardly!

There were others lined up now, not least an oldish man with all the emblems of the wino — mac stained from nights on the streets, a man who could never be astonished again, an old rag of a bandage on his hand — here for a dressing, a bit of warmth, a secure telling off.

Nina was invaded by coldness. She wished she could afford paper nappies. For how could she wring out pissy blankets with one broken arm?

'You may follow me.' The nun came and went and Nina followed as she strode ahead as though in grand opera. In a small room two patients were already seated. Their expressions laid back, they held charts in their hands. One woman had a plaster cast down her leg which left her five toes bared, inquisitive, impervious to the cold. She wondered how long a fracture would take to heal in her own case? A month? Six weeks? The comedy might continue indefinitely, for how could she take in typing now? Yes, until the fracture knitted they would have to beg Brendan for some of his dole or steal — and not for the first time. She laughed, addressing the woman with the broken leg.

'Have you been here long?'

'I don't know what they're at.'

'Are you an In-patient?'

The woman got painfully up, she had been called to the next stage, the pre-X-ray room, to queue again, presumably. The orderly in charge of her turned to Nina.

'You for X-ray?'

'I think so.'

'Have you got your card?'

'No.'

He herded out the woman on crutches; through the other door, the first nun entered.

'Where's your chart?'

'I haven't got one.'

The nun clicked her heels like a soldier on parade. 'They keep doing that.'

Nina sat on with the second woman who had obscured herself behind a sheet of patience and the nun disappeared once more.

She would give up smoking, save up, buy shoes — those nice Clark's sandals — for the middle child. And walk out to meet Frank on the canal bank, lie in the sun, stir the water, talk of Brendan's cruelty; she became lost in the fraud of fantasy.

'Here's a card!'

The Word tucked under her bad arm, Nina took the card.

118

'I can't find your chart.'

They couldn't take the card away now, she thought. She spoke to the other woman.

'At least I have an identification. Perhaps things will speed up.'

'I doubt it,' the woman spoke undramatically. 'They can change their minds if they like.'

'But they have to X-ray me now.'

'Don't be too sure about that.'

Two nuns entered at last to bring them to the final room.

There the row of patients were mostly in regulation dressing gowns. Their faces were sliced from their bodies by a sly ray of sunshine. Relentless sunshine, showing up the illnesses on each face, making everyone look worse, even, than they were. She counted them — twelve — the radiographer must have gone for her elevenses.

Would Brendan feed the baby, she wondered, looking the length of a TWA poster; the girl, chocolate-faced, sipped a blue drink under the shade of a striped umbrella; she was being watched by a young man, his chunky face animated by lust, his skin a lighter shade than the girl's — the colour of cardboard.

But now they were moving; the queue was diminishing; the radiographer must be back from the coffee break. Had she eaten ginger biscuits?

The patients straightened their features each time a nun passed, but Nina, not knowing why, could not do so; her lies, her self-protection, created an area of secrecy beyond which others could not travel. This she created in herself aware of its lack of value, good sense.

She thought only of the button missing from the child's coat, even forgetting Frank or her husband, Brendan, the man with whom she sometimes felt she had traded her sanity.

The card fell out of her hand, lay at her feet; a discarded bingo card — squares and numbers — Nina Sheridan, upside down and married. Respectable …

'Mrs Sheridan!' How had the room emptied so suddenly? The few magazines sliding from the rep-covered bench; the woman at her typewriter relaxing; a little coffee spilled on the saucer of an empty cup.

'You may go in now.'

She bent for the card to tuck into *The Word*. Careful again not to jolt her arm, aware of the lifting throb as she walked to the door of the X-ray room.

'Did he clout you?'

'Not once, but many times.' No trace of disapproval on the radiographer's face; as she bent, the clean overall swung open over the fresh cotton of her dress. 'Men are beasts!' She smiled, played with her machines. 'I'll try not to hurt you. You had a long wait.'

Now Nina could state: 'Everyone's in the same boat.'

'There's no same boat about it. It's the old formula. Take away people's self-reliance. Tell them nothing. Then we give them the soft sell. Twenty, thirty times a day.'

She brushed Nina's fingers. 'Try to straighten them.'

A half-moon with the hand was crushed back with the effort.

'Sorry.'

'Don't apologise. Just lie there with your arm on the paper. I won't hurt you,' she said again.

The shutters of the machine swished.

'That's great. Fine.'

So she had shut her eyes, she knew, because the face above her swung like a coin in the distance, too far away to touch, for she would have drawn her fingers like a pencil over the contours of the mouth had she been able to reach.

'Perhaps I slept.' The radiographer held out a larger than foolscap envelope. 'Where do I go now?'

'Home.'

The fracture?'

'Don't worry.'

'But the X-rays? May I not see … I mean …'

'I think you are the last this morning. Take your time.'

The radiographer was holding the door open watching the tread of the patient's feet into the empty shoes; *The Word* was on the floor again, cover page folded back. A Somali infant stood naked, navel protruding like a rotten grape.

'I dropped my magazine. Or rather it's not mine. It's a good magazine, isn't it?'

Love is so fleeting, Nina thought. So inadequate.

MAEVE KELLY

Journey Home

The day they arrived it rained. Sean smiled sardonically when he said "We thought we'd left the rainy season behind us." Somehow when Sean smiled it was always sardonically. Josie looked approvingly at him, and agreed. Their two children were hideous. As she packed their things into the boot of her car, Maura thought that she loathed her brother and his wife almost more than she loathed their ghastly children, Nigel and June. It was incredible that her brother, the grandson of a Fenian, could have christened his children so ineptly. But then when you looked at his wife, nothing was incredible. The children whinged and wrangled all the way from the airport. "Don't like this car. It's old and dirty." Little brats. I'd love to whack their bottoms with a thorny cudgel. Her vicious desires surprised even herself. "Shush, dears." Their mother had affected her best colonial accent but could not quite conceal the cockney twang acquired from too long living in lower London society. "You mustn't be naughty now, darlings. We're going to have a lovely holiday and we're all very thankful to Nana that she lets us stay in her lovely old farmhouse." 'Nana!' Maura crashed the car into third gear as she passed an articulated lorry. Sean's knuckles whitened as he gripped the front ledge. "I see you're as good a driver as ever, Morrie." 'Morrie' she snarled silently. 'Nana' makes you want to puke. A Sheanin Ui Duibhir, how much did you sell it for. Next thing he'd be calling himself John Dwyer. "Morrie, how's Nana?" Nana! Et tu, Brute. "Ma," she said deliberately in her flattest

122

accent, "is fine, thank God." Nigel sniggered. "I say," gurgled Josie, "I just love your brogue. People are always telling me I have a lovely brogue, but when I come here, I know I'm only trottttting awfter yoooo." "That right?" said Maura briefly, glancing into the mirror to see if any male driver behind her was about to take advantage of the safe sixty feet she'd left between herself and the oil tanker in front. A fiend with a bald head and a red-headed companion had obvious intention of doing same. She swung out to the middle line, indicator flashing a violent warning. Keep back, you old buzzard, for I'm not about to be pushed off the road. "Aye downt loike Awntie Morrie much," said June. "She dwives awfully fawst." That's right, thought Maura, you pronounce your labials and dentals and you'll do. But not here, by Christ. Not on my bloody farm. My farm, my farm, my farm. Mine it should be, for I've paid for it in sweat and tears. There's my receipt. She shuddered away from the sight of herself in the driving mirror — a grizzly old woman at forty-five. And himself beside her, smooth as a banana skin and almost the same shade now after eight years of tropical living.

"You mustn't say that." Josie's reproof was in a tone which by a subtle cadence on the word 'say', suggested that the child was right not to like her Auntie Maura or her driving, but wrong to express so direct an opinion. "Let her speech away," said Maura. "Honest opinions are hard to come by these days." Josie was determined to agree with everyone. She had a hard job balancing between two stools all the time. A crash on her rump will come sooner or later. Better sooner than later. Oh God, make it soon. Oh Maura, don't appeal to God, that father figure with a beard benignly beaming through rosy clouds, that ascetic man carrying his cross up a hill, that dove fluttering its spirit somewhere else. Oh Lord above, send down a dove, with wings as sharp as razors, to cut the throats of those English dogs, who shot our brave Sinn Feiners. Visitors mean more work. Who'll help me milk the cows? Who'll muck out the yard, scour the churns, feed the calves? Well, Josie can take over mother for a while. Lift her onto the wheel chair with Sean lending a gentlemanly hand. Rub her back to prevent bed sores, clean her toes. Not that I mind doing it, God knows I don't. She's my mother after all. Why do I keep bringing God into it? What was it we used to say up North when we visited greatuncle Tom? 'The dear knows.' Very safe, that. No religious undertones, no expressions of traditional faith. She slammed on the brakes as a lorry pulled out of the side road ahead. She pulled down her window and snarled out at him as he passed, "Bloody nit. You shouldn't be let out on the road."

Sean tut-tutted beside her. "I really don't think you should use such rough language. It's very unbecoming." It becomes me, you nit. Would you prefer louse? Coarse language for coarse people. Me, I'm coarse. Always was. Such a rough child, mother said. Gets it from her father, God rest him. Sean takes after my side, of course. The Hartigans had gentle breeding. Oh Sean won't have any of that pulling and dragging to do. I'll see to that. He'll have a good education and a good job.

I was slow, of course. I don't know why. Not stupid. Slow. Slow to think, slow to act, slow to react. But not anymore. Not anymore. I'm quick, quick, quick. My thoughts are driven by venom. They corrode my mind. They'll burn me away some day, and I'll be led off cursing and people will say I'm a megalomaniac and they'll lock me up. But I'm locked up already. Chained by duty and lack of education to miserable living on rocky Galway land.

"Did you get the flush toilet in yet, Morrie?" Josie's question hung in the drone of the car, dreading the answer 'no' but hoping for 'yes'. "No," said Maura with satisfaction. "Th'auld dry toilet works grand. Thanks be to God," she added for good measure. Sean was displeased. "I especially meant that money to be used for that purpose. Did you spend it?" Oh, on liquor and wild living, brother. "Yes, I spent it. The black Kerry cow got stuck in a drain and died. The money came in handy. Bought a fine strong Friesian heifer. Calved down last month." A lovely calf she had. A beauty. Snow white legs on chequer-board body and a little pink nose where the white hair hadn't grown on the glaze. No trouble to her. Calved out on the paddock there, with the sun shining and the birds singing. Proper order. That's the way things should be. Birth in the sunshine of the day. Death in the sleep of the night. "Well, that's fine. I'm glad the money was useful. But you do need the other thing too." It surprised her again. His refinement. It was so excessive. He couldn't bring himself to say the word. Josie wasn't that bad after all. "I dunno, Mother has to use the chair in the room, and I —" Sean broke in sternly, exercising his great white-master authority, "Morrie, remember the children." What children? Those adult midgets beside me. Call them children? They could buy and sell me. Couldn't buy or sell a good bullock, though. Wouldn't know the difference between a blackface ewe and a mountain goat.

"When I'm gone" — mother had meant dead, of course — "the farm must go to Sean. It's really his place, you know, dear. When he was only a little fellow before your father died, his grandfather put his hand on his head — he had lovely hair too, a mass of black curls, and he said 'This place is to be for this boy.' I always respect the wishes of the dead. I know, dear, that you've worked hard here. But Mick Meany wants to marry you this long time back, and he could give you a good home — when I'm gone, of course — and I'll leave you money for a dowry so you won't go empty-handed to him."

"Yes, ma." Mick Meany. Bald headed old coot. As hard as this stony land. One hundred and twenty years old if he's a day. Think I'd lie in that fellow's bed. I'm not that badly off for a man. Oh for some brawny fellow wider than myself, who could wrap me around with two big strong arms and pull the plough on a windy day, and no bother to him. A fellow who could whistle while he worked, and would gulp his food down in a hurry to be out to his fields. That's the sort of fellow I'd

125

like. Coarse, maybe, but strong. As strong as a horse, and able to tell me bawdy stories that I could laugh at without being ashamed. They don't make fellows like that anymore. Dirty old devils, or sniggery slithers they make in plenty but nothing in between. And who'd have me anyway? A fellow like da. He'd suit me alright. Oh but he was great sport. The jokes he used to tell, and the stories when we'd be bringing up the cows together, Sean inside doing his homework. Da said I was the farmer. He meant me to have the farm. And have it I will, if I have to kill you all for it.

It was twenty miles from the airport to home. Every two years Maura took the car on the same journey. Every two years, during the past eight, Sean came home from British East Africa. Only now it wasn't B. E. Africa. There were new States, new names, new people. Not long down from the trees, Sean said once, emanating his aura of civilised behavior. Maura's fury groped for words in defence of the dignity of man but her educational lack left her inarticulate and twice as angry. Sean was an accountant on an industrial farm. They had a luxury bungalow, their own swimming pool, a car each, a garden boy, and a girl in the house. Josie was always complaining about her domestic help. Every few months she found them so unstable, unreliable and ineducable (all her favourite words) that she dismissed them and hopefully employed more. Ma loved to hear them talk of their life. Casual references to the time they went on safari, boring colour slides, showing elephants trunk view and rump view, antelopes in dainty poses, lions majestical perched on rocks, thrilled her to pride. It seemed a vindication of some sort that a photograph of her son, an Irishman, posing in khaki shorts, a camera slung over his shoulder in lieu of a gun, to a backdrop of flamingoes, could stand on the mantelshelf in the parlour, underneath the pike-head his grandfather had rammed into position many years before. The incongruity of it escaped her completely.

The ancient Irish Castle now in the hands of an ancient Irish-American hotelier lay between them. The rolling green of East Clare changed to the small stone scattered fields of Galway. Maura swung the car off the main road for the last lap home. Beside her, Josie was ecstatic. "Oh, the fuchsia. How lovely it is. And the elderflower is out. Oh and look at the honeysuckle. Let's stop and admire it all." Grudgingly Maura pulled into the scented hedge. The visitors got out, the children grumbling that they were hungry. Maura was impatient. She paced up and down for a few minutes, looked at her watch, and then climbed pointedly back into the driving seat. "Cows have to be milked at five," she said. Sean was apologetic. "Sorry, Morrie." "Watch the lorry," she said, turning on the ignition key. The children chanted it excruciatingly the rest of the way. "Sorry, Morrie, watch the lorry, sorry, Morrie, watch the lorry." "They're quite clever, aren't they?" Sean said amusedly. Oh quite clever. Like you. Clever. Clever. A clever little bastard. Coming in for the visitors in dung-splashed trousers and boots, smiling cheerfully. Isn't he the great little man? He must be a comfort to you now, Mrs O'Dwyer, now that himself is gone. Oh a boy is great on the farm. And he's so good-looking. Look at the head on him, a fine lad. The image of your own father, ma'am. The O'Dwyers were always plain, God help them. Good hardworking people, but not blessed with good looks, you might say. The girl there now, she's an O'Dwyer surely. She has the stamp of them on her. And who but herself with the stamp of an O'Dwyer on her could have milked cows, fed calves, watched the sows farrow all those long years while clever Sean studied. Who but herself with the white fog from the lake thick over the fields could have pulled the calf from the boghole, fixed the slates on the roof, trammed the hay with the help of neighbours. Who but a coarse, rough woman would have lifted and hauled till her muscles bulged and her neck settled into her shoulders. Who but a woman of no breeding could have let tawny hair turn grizzled and dry and white skin run to furrows like a ploughed field.

"I have a letter in my pocket from the convent." She announced the information in the same voice as she would use to say the hens are laying well lately, or the weather is mixed middling. That's the way it is. Thinking about it doesn't change it. "Oh," Sean laughed. "Thinking of taking the veil?" "Yes," said Maura. "Next month with the help of God." Even the children were silenced. "You're not serious of course." Sean had never known whether to take Maura seriously nor not. Maura disdained to reply. "You couldn't leave mother now," said Sean. "Why not?" asked Maura sensibly. "She has yourself and Josie to care for her." In the seat behind, Josie swallowed a gasp. "Well, I know one thing," Sean laughed again, determined to treat it all as a merry joke, "you'll never leave the farm." "Why not?" Maura repeated herself. "It's not my farm. Never has been. I'm only the hired hand. Unpaid. It's time I lived my own life." "Have you discussed it with mother?" asked Sean. "No. Nothing to discuss. I'll leave that to you and Josie. You're the big talker, Sean. You'll be able to put it all into nice convenient words." "But you were never very religious," Josie poked in the ludicrous understatement as a plea for good sense. "You'd be miserable in a convent." "No more miserable than I am now," said Maura. "I've nothing to gain, maybe, but nothing to lose either. Besides, they say a change is as good as a rest."

"It's a funny sort of vocation," said Josie cattily. Maura was pleased. Scratch the veneer ever so slightly and underneath is the same old feline ready to claw to survive. How would she survive on Lough an Eala? She smiled, picturing the crumbling of that polished facade. Sean's banana skin wouldn't stand up to much either. She had them. She had them both. They'd be glad to sign over the place to her. And then let them come home on holidays if they pleased, but she wouldn't be able to take time off from her farm to meet them at the airport.

Sean, Josie and the children were quiet for the next few miles. When Sean spoke it was in the cool tones of a great brain coming out with a carefully considered and irrefutable solution. "As a matter of fact, I'm glad you've decided to live your own life. As you say, it hasn't been much fun for you. And it is, after all, *my* farm. I can't expect you to run it any more. I'll get a good manager in. I can afford one now. Modern methods will do a lot to improve that land. Farmers must be educated now. We can get someone to look after mother. Then when I retire, I can come back myself to Lough an Eala. Josie always loves it. Don't you, Josie? You go into your convent, Morrie, and with God's grace you'll be very happy."

They were coming into a corkscrew road, four miles of humps and hollows, twists and S-bends — as if the road had diligently followed the crazy tracks of a warble-chased calf two hundred years before. Maura put her foot down on the accelerator. A red rage consumed her. She'd never been a match for his cunning and she wasn't now. The old car leapt forward. She was oblivious of Sean's cry, "For God's sake, take it easy," the children whimpering and cowering in the back, Josie's hysterical scream as hedges, grassy banks came flying for them. Her arms ached from wrenching the steering wheel to right and left. She took fierce delight in the screech of brakes as she two-wheeled around the sharpest bends. She blew on the horn ferociously — clear the way everyone — Morrie the great is coming, watch out, accursed world, the killer is on the rampage. She sang loudly and happily —

Is ioma slighe sin do bhios ag daoine
Ag cruinniu pinghinne is ag deanamh oir —

The rowdy drinking song added to the terror of the drive. At last she stopped outside their farm gate. She turned off the ignition key and looked at Sean. His face was contorted.

"You're mad," he said. "I always knew you were crazy." The whimpering of the children and the quiet sobbing of Josie formed a fitting background to his words. "I don't know how mother has survived all these years with you. God knows what she's had to put up with. Josie will care for her from now on."

Maura got out of the car and walked through the side gate to the lake. The sheep dog stopped his excited barking and raced after her. Her mother was calling from the house. "Is that you, Maura dear? Are they here? Did they come? Sean. Sean. Sean. Josie. Are you coming? What's keeping you?" The old querulous voice faded as she neared the lake. The swans were on it. Their grace and beauty made her smile. And they had cold hearts to match. She turned her grizzled head to the field where the cows grazed. Come on, Shep. Hup there, hup there, bring 'em up, bring 'em up.

Josie, she thought. Josie's my trump card. Josie will crack first.

EDNA O'BRIEN

A Journey

February the twenty-second. Not far away was the honking of water fowl in the pond at Battersea Park. The wrong side of London some said, but she liked it and the pale green power station was her landmark, as once upon a time a straggle of blue hills had been. The morning was cold, the ice had clawed at the window and left its tell-tale marks — lines — long jagged lines, criss-cross scrawls, lines at war with one another, lines bent on torment. It was still like twilight in the bedroom and yet she wakened with alertness, and her heart was as warm as a little ball of knitting wool. He was deep in a trough of sleep, impervious to nudging, to hitting, to pounding. He was beautiful. His hair, like a halo, was arced around his head — beautiful hair, not quite brown, not quite red, not quite gold, of the same darkness as gunmetal but with strands of brightness. Oh Christ he'll think he's in his own house with his own woman she thought as his eyelids flickered and he peered through. But he didn't. He knew where he was and said how glad he was to be there, and drawing her towards him he held her and squeezed her out like a bit of old washing. They were off to Scotland, he to deliver a lecture to some students and later to men, fellow unionists who worked on the shipyards.

'We're going a-travelling,' she said almost doubtfully.

'Yes pet.'

At any rate he hadn't changed his mind yet. He was a great vacillator.

She made the coffee while he contemplated getting up, and from the kitchen she kept urging him, saying how they would be late, how he must please bestir himself. For some reason she was reminded of her wedding morning, both mornings had a feeling of unrealness, the same uncertainty plus her anxiety about being late. But that was a long time ago. That was over, and dry in the mouth like a pod or a desiccated cud. This was this. This man upstairs, why do I love him she thought. A working man, shy and moody and inarticulate, a man unaccustomed to a woman like her. They hardly talked. Not that speech was what mattered between people. She learnt that the very day she had accosted him in a train a few weeks before. She saw him and simply had to communicate with him, touched the newspaper he was scanning, flicked it ever so lightly with her finger, and he stared across at her and very quietly admitted her into his presence, but without a word, without even a face-saving hello.   .

'I can't say things,' he had said and then breathed out quickly and nervously as if it had cost him a lot to admit. He was like a hound, a little whippet. It was like crossing the Rubicon. Also daft. Also dicey. A journey of pain. She had no idea then how extensive that journey would be. A good man? Maybe. Maybe not. She was looking for reasons to unlove him. When he came down he almost, but didn't smile. There was such a tentativeness to him. Is it always going to be like this she thought, spilling the coffee, slopping it in the saucer and then nervously dumping the brown granular mass from a strainer onto an ashtray.

'I have no composure,' she said. From him another wan smile. Would her buying the tickets be all right, would he look away while she paid, would it be an auspicious trip? She took his hand, and warmed it and said she never wanted to do aught else, and he said not to say such things, not to say them, but in fact they were only a skimming of the real things she was longing to say. Years divided them, class divided them, position divided them. He wanted to give her a present and couldn't in case it wasn't swish enough. He bought perfume off a hawker in Oxford Circus, offered it to her and then took it back. Probably gave it to his woman, put it down on the table along with his pay packet. Or maybe left it on a dressing table, if they had one. A tender moment? All these unknowns divided them. The morning that she was getting married, he was pruning trees in an English park, earning a smallish sum and living with a woman who had four children. He had always lived with some woman or another, but insisted that he wasn't a philanderer, wasn't. He lived with Madge, now, drank two pints of beer every evening, cuddled his baby and smoked forty cigarettes a day.

In the taxi he whispered to her, to please not look at him like that, and at the airport he spent the bulk of the waiting time in the gents. She wondered if there wasn't a barbers in there, or if perhaps, he hadn't done a disappearing act, like people on their wedding day who do not show up at the altar rails. In fact he had bought a plastic hairbrush to straighten his hair for the journey because it had got tangled in the night. Afterwards he put it in her travel bag. Did she need a travel bag? How long were they to stay? No knowing. They were terribly near and they were not near. No outsider could guess the relationship. In the plane, the hostess tried hard to flirt with him, said she'd seen him on television but he was shy and skirted the subject by asking for a light. He was very active with his union and often appeared on television debates; at private meetings he exhorted the members to rope in new ones. He had made quite a reputation for himself by reading them cases from history and clippings from old newspapers, making them realize how they had been treated for hundreds of years. He was a scaffolder like his father before him, but he left Belfast soon after his parents died. His brothers and sisters were scattered.

When they got to their destination he suddenly suggested that she dump the bag in a safety locker, and she knew then that she shouldn't have brought it, and that possibly they would not be staying overnight. Walking up the street of Edinburgh with a bitter breeze in their faces she pointed to a castle that looked like a dungeon and asked him what he thought of it. Not much. He didn't think much — that was his answer. What did he do — dream, daydream, imagine, forget. The leaves in the municipal flower-bed were blowing and shivering, mere tatters, but the soil was a beautiful flaky black. They happened to be passing a funeral parlour and she asked if he preferred burial or cremation but about that too he was tepid and indifferent. It made no matter. They should still be in bed, under covers, cogitating. She linked him and he jerked his arm saying those who knew him, knew the woman he lived with, and he would not like it to appear otherwise. They were halfway up the hill, and there was between them now, one of those little swords of silence that is always slicing love, or that kind of love.

'If Madge knew about this, she'd be immeasurably hurt,' he said.

'But Madge will know,' she thought, but did not say. She said instead that it was colder up North, that they were not far from the sea, and didn't he detect bits of hail in the wind. He saw the sadness, traced it lightly with his finger, traced the near tears and the little pouch under the lids. He said 'You're a terrible woman altogether,' to which she replied 'You're not a bad bloke,' and they laughed. He was supposed to have travelled by train the night before, the very night when he slept with her and had his hair pulled from the roots. How good a liar was he and how strong a man? He had crossed the street ahead of her and to make amends he waited for her across the road, waited by the lights, and watched her, admiring, as she came across, watched her walk, her lovely legs, her long incongruous skirt and watched the effect she had on others, one of shock as if she was undressed or carrying some sort of invisible torch. He referred to an ancient queen and her carriage.

'It's not that it's not pleasant holding your arm,' he said, and took her elbow feeling the wobble of the funny bone. Then he had to make a phone call, and soon they were going somewhere, in a taxi, and the back streets of Edinburgh were not unlike the back streets of any other town, a bit black, a bit drowsy and pub fronts being washed down.

'He's afraid of me,' she thought. 'And I'm afraid of him,' and fear is corrosive, and she felt certain that the woman he lived with was probably much more adept at living and arguing, would make him bring in the coal, or clean out the ashes or share his last cigarette, would put her cards on the table. For a moment she was seized with longing to see them together, and had a terrible idea that she would call as a travelling sales-woman with a little attaché case, full of cleaning stuffs so as she would have to go in and show her wares. She would see their kitchen and their pram and the baby in it, she would see how tuned they were to one another. But that was not necessary, because he was leaving because it had all gone dry and flaccid, between him and the woman it was all over. When he looked at her then it was a true felt look, and it was laden with sweetness, white, mesmerizing like the blossom that hangs from the cherry trees.

Before addressing the first batch of students he called on some friends. Even that was furtive, he didn't knock, but whistled some sort of code through the letter box. In the big, sparsely furnished room there was a pregnant cat, marmalade, and the leftovers of a breakfast, and a man and a woman who had obviously just tumbled out of their bed. She thought this is how it should be. When, through a crack in the kitchen door, catching a glimpse of their big tossed bed and the dented pillows without pillow-slips, she ached to go in and lie there, and she knew that the sight of it had permeated her consciousness and that it was a longing she would always feel.

That longing was replaced by a stitch in the chest, then a lot of stitches, and then something like a lump in the back of the mouth, something that would not dissolve. Would he live with her like he said? Would he do it? Would he forsake everything, fear, respectability, safeness, the woman, the child? The questions were like pendulums swinging this way and that. The answers would swing too.

The woman she had just met was called Ita and the man was called Jim the Limb. He had some defect in his right arm. They were plump and radiant, what with their night, and their big breakfast and now a fresh pot of tea. They were chain smokers. Ita said her fur coat and the marmalade cat were alike, and he, her lover, said that probably that was a wrong thing to say. But there was no wrong thing as far as she was concerned. She just wanted them to welcome her in, to accept her. When they talked about the union, and the various men, and the weekly meetings, when they discussed a rally that was to take place later in London she thought, 'Let me be one of you, let me put aside my old stupid flitting life, let me take part, let me in.' Her life was not exactly soigné and she too had lived in small rooms and ridden a ridiculous bicycle, and swapped old shoes for other old shoes, but she seemed not to belong, because she had bettered herself, had done it on her own, and now that she was a graphic designer, she designed alone. Also these were townspeople, they all had lived in small steep houses, slept two or three or four to a bed, sparred, lived in and out of one another's pockets, knew familiarity well enough to know that it was the only hope. Ita announced that she was not going to the factory that morning, said dammit, the bloody sweatshop, and told him of two women who were fired because they had gone deaf from the machines and weren't able to hear proper. He said they must fight it. They were a clan. Yet, when he winked at her he seemed to be saying something else, something ambiguous, and saying 'I see you there, I am not forsaking you,' or was he saying, 'Look how influential I am, look at me.' A word he often used was big-shot. Maybe he had dreams of being a big-shot?

Just before the four of them left the house for the college he went for the third time to the lavatory and she believed he had gone to be sick. Yet when he stood on the small ladder platform, holding up a faulty loudspeaker, brandishing it, making jokes about it — calling it Big Brother he seemed to be utterly in his element. He spoke without notes, he spoke freely, telling the crowd of his background in Belfast, his father's work on the shipyards, his having to emigrate, his job in London, the lads, the way this fellow or that fellow had got nabbed, and though what he had to say was about victimization he made it all funny. When questions were put it was clear that he had cajoled them all, except for one dissenter, an aristocratic-looking boy in a dress suit, a boy who seemed to be on the brink of a nervous breakdown. Even with that, he dealt deftly. He replied without any venom and when the dissenter was booed and told to belt up he said 'Aach' to his friends who were heckling. The hat was passed around, a navy college cap into which coins were tossed from all corners of the room. She hesitated; not knowing whether to give a lot, or a little, and wanting only to do the right thing. She gave a pound note, and afterwards in the refectory to where they had all repaired, she saw a girl hand him ten pounds and thought how the collection must have been to foot his expenses.

Ita and Jim decided to accompany them to the next city, where he was conducting the same sort of meeting, in the evening, in a public hall. Getting on the station late as they did, he said 'Let's jump in here,' and ushered them into a first-class carriage. When the ticket collector came, she paid the difference, knowing that he had chosen to go in there because he felt it was where she belonged. At first they couldn't hear one another for the rattle of the train, the shunting of other carriages, and a whipping wind that lashed through a broken window. He dozed, and sometimes coming awake he nudged her with his shoe. The ladies sat on one side, the men opposite, and Ita was whispering to her, in her ear, saying when she met Jim how they went to bed for a week and how she was so sore, and finally had to have stitches. He looked at the women whispering and tittering and he seemed to like that, and there was a satisfaction in the way he rocked and dozed.

They were all hungry.

'Starving you I am,' he said to her as he asked a porter for the name of a restaurant.

'A French joint,' he decided. As they settled themselves in the drab and garish room, Ita tripped over the flex of the table lamp. Jim glowered with embarrassment, said this wasn't home, and to behave herself. They dived into the basket of bread, calling for butter, butter. He made jokes about the wine, sniffed it and asked if for sure it was the best vintage, and knowing that he was shy and awkward with his fingers she fed him her little potato sticks from her plate. He accepted them like they were matches, and then gobbled them down, and the others knew what they had suspected, that this pair were lovers, and Jim said they looked like two people in a picture and they smiled as if they were in a picture and their faces scanned one another as if in a beautiful daze. At the meeting he gave the same speech, except that it had to be shortened, and this he did by omitting one anecdote about a man who was sent to jail for speaking Gaelic in the northern province of his own country. There was a second collection and the amounts subscribed were much higher, because the bulk of the audience were working men, and proud to contribute.

Afterwards they repaired to a big ramshackle room, at the top of a big house in the north side of the city. In the hall there were hundreds of milk bottles, and in the back hall two or three bicycles jumbled together. He had bought a bottle of whiskey, and in the kitchen she heated a kettle to make a hot punch for him because his throat was sore. He came in and told her what a grand person she was, and he kissed her stealthily. The kitchen was a shambles and although at first intending to tidy it a bit, all she did was scald two cups and a tumbler for his punch. Some had hot whiskey, some had cold, whereas she had hers laced in a cup of tea.

In the ramshackle room they all talked, interrupting one another, joking, having inside conversation about meetings they'd been to, and other meetings to which they'd sent hecklers, and demonstrations that they were planning to have and all their supporters in France, Italy and throughout. She looked up at the light shade, crinkled plastic, as big as a beach ball, and with a lot of dots. She felt useless. The designs she made were simple and geometric and somewhat stark, but at that moment they seemed irrelevant. They had no relation to these people, to their conversation, to their curious kind of bantering anger. She remembered nights on end when she had striven to make a shape or a design that would go straight to the quick of someone's being, she had done it alone, and she had gruelled over it but these people would think it a bit of a joke.

The place was slovenly but still it was a place. Several brass rings had come off their hooks and the heavy velvet curtain gaped. He was being witty. Someone had said that there were more ways than one of killing a cat but he had intervened to say that it was 'skinning' a cat. That was the first flicker of cruelty that she saw in him. She was sitting next to him on the divan bed, she leaning back against the wall, slightly out of things, he pressing forward, positing the odd joke. He said that at forty he might find his true vocation in life, which was to be a whizz-kid. There was a rocking chair in which one of the men sat, and several easy chairs with stained and torn upholstery, their springs dipping down, to a variable degree depending on the weight and the colossal pranks of the sitters.

Sometimes a girl with plaits would rush over and sit on her man's knee and pull his beard and then the springs dropped down like the inside of a broken melodion. If only he and she could be that unreserved.

Then he was missing, out on the landing using the phone. She knew they had missed the last plane, and long ago had missed the last train and that they would have to kip down somewhere, and she thought how awful if it had to be on a bench at a station or at a depot. Ita asked her if they were perhaps going to make a touring holiday, and she said no but couldn't add to that, couldn't gloss the reply with some extra little piece of information. When he came in he told her that a taxi was on its way.

'I don't know where we're heading for. Wonderland,' he said, shaking hands with Ita and then he said cheers to the room at large.

The hotel was close to the airport, a modern building made of concrete cubes, like something built by a child, and with vertical slits for windows. They might be turned away. He went in whistling. She waited, one foot on the step of the taxi and one on the footpath and said an involuntary prayer. She saw him handing over money, then beckoning for her to come in. He had signed the register and in the lift, as he fondled her, he told her the false name that he had used. It was a nice name, Egan. In the bedroom they thought of whiskey, and then of milk and then of milk and whiskey, but they were too tired, and shy all over again, and neither of them was impervious enough to give an order, while the other was listening.

'I know you better now,' he said. She wondered at what precise moment in the day had he come to know her better, had he crept in on her like a little invisible camera, and knew that he knew her, and would know her for all time. Maybe some non-moment, when she walked gauchely towards the ladies' room, or when asked her second name she hesitated, in case by giving a name she should compromise him.

She apologized for not talking more, and he said that was what was lovely about her, and he apologized for giving the same lecture twice, and for all the stupid things that got said. Then he trotted around naked, getting his tiny little transistor from his overcoat pocket, studying the hotel clock — a square face laid into the bedside table — trying the various lights. He had never stayed in a hotel before, and it was then he told her that there would be a refund if in the morning they didn't eat breakfast. He had paid. His earnings for the day had been swallowed up by it.

'I'll refund you,' she said, and he said what rot, and in the dark they were together again, together like spare limbs, like rag dolls, or bits of motor car tyre, bits of themselves, together, so effortless, and so fond, and with such harmony, as if they had grown up that way, always were and always would be. But she couldn't ask. It had to come from him. He was thinking of going back home, leaving London, changing jobs. Well, wherever he went, she was going too. He had brought everything to a head, everything she had wanted to feel, love and pity and softness and passion and patience and insatiable jealousy. They went to sleep talking, then half talking, voices trailing away like tendrils, sleepy voices, sleepy brains, sleepy bodies, talking, not talking, dumb.

'I love you, I love you,' he said it the very moment that the hotel clock triggered off, and all the doubts of the previous day and the endless cups of coffee, and the bulging ashtrays were all sweet reminders of a day in which the fates changed. He said he dearly wished that they could lie there for hours on end and have coffee and papers sent up and lie there and let the bloody aeroplanes and the bloody world go by. But why were they hurrying? It was a Saturday and he had no work.

'I'll say goodbye here,' he said, and he kissed her and pulled the lapel of her fur coat up around her neck so that she wouldn't feel the cold.

'But we're going together,' she said. He said yes but they would be in a public place and they would not be able to say good-bye, not intimately. He kissed her.

'We will be together?' she said.

'It will take time,' he said.

'How long?' she asked.

'Months, years …' They were ready to go.

In the plane they talked first about mushrooms and she said how mushrooms were reputed to be magic and then she asked him if he had wanted a son rather than a daughter, and he said no, a daughter, and smiled at the thought of his little one. He read four of the morning papers, read them, re-read them, combed the small news items that were put in at the last minute, and got printing ink all over his hands. The edges of the paper sometimes jutted against her nose, or her eye or her forehead and without turning he would say 'Sorry love'. To live with, he would be all right, silent at times, undemonstrative, then all of a sudden as touching as an infant. Every slight gesture of his, every 'Sorry love' tore at some place in her gut.

A bus was waiting on the tarmac, right next to the landed plane. He said they needn't bother rushing, and as a result they were very nearly not taken at all. In fact the steward looked down the aisle of the bus, put up a finger to say that there was room for one and then in the end grumpily let them both enter. They had to sit separately, with an aisle between them and she began to revert to her cursed superstitions such as if they passed a white gate all would be fortunate between them.

At the terminus he had to make a phone call, and she could see him, although she had meant not to look gesticulating fiercely in the glass booth. When he came out he was biting his thumb.

After a while, he said he was late, that the woman had to stay home from work, that he was in the wrong again. She saw it very clearly, very cruelly, as clear and as cruel as the lines of ice that had claimed the window pane. Claims. Responsibility. Slogans. 'Be here be here.'

They walked up the road towards the underground station. No matter how she carried it the travel bag bumped against her, or when she changed hands, against him. He said she was never to tell anyone. She said she wasn't likely to go spouting it, and he said why the frown, why spoil everything with a frown like that. It went out like a shooting star, the sense of peace, the suffusion, the near-happiness. He asked her to hang on, while he got cigarettes, and then plunging into the dark passage that led to the underground, he saw her hesitate, and said did she always take taxis. They kissed. It was a dark unpropitious passage but a real kiss. Their mouths clung, the skins of their lips would not be parted, she felt that they might fall into a trance in order not to terminate it. He was as helpless then as a schoolboy, and his eyes as pathetic as watered ink. In some indefinable way, and whatever happened, he would be part of her for all time, an essence.

'If I must, if I must talk to you may I,' she said. He looked at her bitterly. He was like a chisel. 'I can't promise anything,' he said, and repeated it. Then he was gone, doing a little hop through the turnstile, and omitting to get a ticket. She walked on, the bag kept bumping off the calf of her leg; soon when she had enough poise she would hail a taxi. Would he go? Would he come back? What would he do? It was like a door that had just come ajar, and anything could happen to it, it could shut tight or open a fraction or fly open in a burst. She thought of the bigness and wonder of destiny, meeting him in a packed train had been a fluke, and this now was a fluke, and things would either convene to shut that door, or open it a little, or open and close it alternately, and they would be together, or not be together as life the gaffer thought fit.

143

JULIA O'FAOLAIN

First Conjugation

She was from Cremona: a patrician creature in her forties, who had followed her refugee husband to our town and taught Italian in our local university. Her colleagues here were peasants' grandsons abandoned by ambition at the top of Ireland's academic tree. Noncoms in an army with nowhere to go, they treated their meek students with weary irony. Among them, the signora's presence was like moonlight in a well. Each glimpse of her was tonic in that tight, cast-concrete arena where the inner walls were painted a washable urine-green.

She alone supplied the hyper-vividness I had expected from college and did so in the first few weeks. In their academic gowns other teachers became moulting crows or funeral mutes. She wore hers like a ball-dress and her green-shadowed Parmigianino neck rose thrillingly from between its gathered billows. Her hair circled her head with the austere vigour of black mountain-streams. Her body moved like channelled water and she had a higher charge of life than anyone I had ever seen.

Her controlled vibrancy enthralled me as did an aloof pity for our simplicity, and the prodigality with which, perhaps for her private amusement, she proposed considerations too fine for our grasp. Had I been a male student I would have been in love with her.

As it was, her beauty set standards towards which, despairingly, I aspired. At night in bed I thought of her, sometimes making up stories in which I won her esteem, sometimes letting myself become her and move through marvellous though shadowy adventures. At sixteen I was pursuing my waking dreams with flagging zest. I longed for something actual to happen and was beginning to think of men. To reconcile my yearnings, I, as the signora, fancied I was courted by a man. 'Oh thou,' he whispered, 'art wondrous as the evening air / In wanton Arethusa's azure arms ...' Who was he? It was hard to give him a face for I did not know any worthy men.

Only students who, if they were not clerics, were pimply, or had necks like plucked quails or faces, as my friend Ita put it, 'like babies' bottoms': a sexual disgrace to any girl they might approach. Not that they approached Ita or me. Or rather only Nick Lucy did, whose sad puffy face appeared with inappropriate suddenness in my dream, staring with his hang-dog look at me-the-signora just as he stared at me-myself every morning in the coffee shop.

Clot! Squirt! How *dare* he disturb my private fancies! I hated him! Maybe he was thinking of me? Telepathically bullying me into thinking of *him*? At the thought that no one but Nick Lucy would do the like I bit the pillow with rage.

'Hold on to Nick,' Ita had recommended that morning when he'd gone to buy us both some doughnuts. 'He'll be useful!'

'He's awful looking!'

'They all are,' said Ita looking round the coffee shop. 'We've no choice.'

'Mike McGillacuddy isn't so bad.' I argued. 'You wouldn't go round with him if he looked like Nick!'

'Mike's ghastly really,' said Ita, 'he's stuck on himself! But he has VV.'

'What's that?'

'Vehicular value. VV! It means he has a car. A fellow with a car can take you places where you meet other fellows. If you stay home you never meet any. No fear of *them* coming looking for us!'

'Well, Nick has no VV — car.'

'One car's enough,' Ita said. 'But we need a man each. Don't you see! Any sort of stooge will do so long as we can go to a dance with him or into a pub. Girls can't go into pubs alone and *that's* where you meet men. When we meet some attractive ones we can drop the stooges. So my sister says. She says Irish fellows don't *like* girls,' Ita explained patiently, 'so it has to be a tough chase with no holds barred.'

Ita's sister was four years older than we and engaged so she, I supposed, must know. I agreed to put up with Nick.

'Though,' I said, 'he gives me the creeps.'

He did. In the last few months my body had become an Aeolian harp, resonant to the slightest breath. If I stirred the down on my arms or the nape of my neck with a pencil tip, pleasure rippled up my spine. When Nick Lucy picked books from my desk, the brush of his sleeve against my cheek had the toad pressure of jellied frogspawn.

'Put down those books, Lucy! I don't want you carrying my books!'

'OK, OK, spitfire!' he said and went off, sauntering and hurt, for he was as moody and torn by yens as myself.

'She's awful to me,' he said to Ita.

'Ah,' Ita said as people do, 'she likes you really.'

I didn't. I was embarrassed by him: a pasty drip whose plight however upset me. For I knew he dreamed of me as I did of Signora Perruzzi and that I had 'led him on'. I knew a gawky face was not the emanation of a gawky soul but that handsome was as handsome did. Or I tried to know. Yes! Yes! But the leaven of my sensuality was stuck deep in the dough of snobbery. I couldn't *make* myself like him, could I? The man who would set my veins foaming was going to have to be spiffing to look at, dream-standard, unlike poor Nick whose plainness seemed somehow contagious.

'Don't follow me to Italian class,' I told him.

I could be kind to him at coffee or, better still, in the leaf-screened alleys of the college grounds where he amused me with stories of his country childhood; but I dreaded being seen with him by the signora. Nick's niceness was not of the sort that met the eye, and I imagined *her* eye as more exacting than my own. Her high-arched brows looked ironic, and I could not imagine her tall neck flexing in pity. Or didn't want to imagine it.

To show he wouldn't be bullied, Nick followed me to Italian class anyhow, and sat in the back row drawing my profile.

I ignored him. It was 'conversation' where the signora gave of her best. She must have been dazzling in the Fascist *salons* of ten years before. Now she exercised her high-powered weapons on three seminarists, four nuns, a few flat-vowelled peasants from the midlands, and myself. I strained towards her. *Why* had she had to leave Italy? Why wound up in this provincial stopping-place from which we all — even the four blue nuns bound eventually to nurse Florentine aristocrats and Prato businessmen — intended to progress? What war crimes were hers that she taught here for a pittance, wasting her coruscations in this pee-green room, under the bare electric light bulb and the painted-over crucifix on the wall? (A Radical professor had insisted on having all crucifixes in the classrooms painted over and now, it was rumoured, objected on political grounds to the signora's being on the staff. The pale patch hung behind her like a reproof.)

'In our patriotic time in Italy,' the signora sighed, 'we used the *voi* not the *Lei*. It is nearer the ancient Roman *tu*.'

She laughed an opulent laugh. Unnecessarily lavish, its throatiness evoked the pile of deep carpets and the fur of snuggly coats in a Lombard winter. She was a gay, not a pitiful exile. 'The Romans,' she said sweetly, 'were democratic. The *Lei* was a subservient Spanish importation.'

147

Nick whose father had been in the British army muttered in the back row.

I turned round. 'Shut up!' I whispered.

When I looked back up the signora's eyes were on me. She frowned. Then her lips formed a brief, tight smile.

'I see,' she cried sprightly. 'You are impatient for conversation! Well, *I* shall converse and you may note my phrases, since your Italian is perhaps not up to replying. What,' she murmured dreamily, 'shall we discuss? I have it: love. Love is the great Italian subject. Or so,' she mocked, 'foreigners think. Who care for it perhaps more than Italians themselves. Well, we have the verb *amare*, first conjugation, regular, *Io amo*, I love. *Tu ami*,' she beamed her attention at a point in the back row, and I stirred apprehensively, 'you love. *Tu ami la ragazza.*' Unbelievably, she was addressing herself to Nick. 'You love the girl,' she told him. '*Egli ama*, he loves.' She turned to the others, and nodded so unmistakably, first in Nick's direction and then in mine, that even the blue nuns giggled and stared from him to me. 'He loves the girl,' said the cruel signora. Oh belle dame sans merci! Dry-mouthed, I listened in horror. She was more beautiful than ever. And bad! Just as I had supposed! But why with me? Why? 'He comes to class because he loves the girl. *Elia ama* or *essa* or we may say *lei ama*,' said Signora Perruzzi with maddening sloth, 'may all mean — for Italian is a rich language — she loves.'

I felt as though she were putting worms on me, as though she were stripping and streaking me with filth. 'If she couples me with him again … If she says …' I could not think what she might say next. Had she X-ray eyes? Did she know I had worshipped her? Was this her way of refusing my devotion? I felt the paralysing embarrassment, the shame I used to feel as a child when I was dreaming out loud and suddenly suspected that my brother had crept under my bed to surprise and deride me. The agony of those few seconds while I used to grope for the electric light switch returned, now realized and suffocating.

'I'll get up,' I thought weakly, 'I'll walk out.' It was Nick I
loathed even while the signora tormented me. 'He's enjoying
this,' I thought with ferocious injustice, 'he's happy at being
connected with me.' *Odiare*, to hate, supplied my grammar:
First Conjugation, regular.

'Does she love him?' pronounced the signora, 'may be
rendered in Italian without any inversion: *Leo lo ama?*' She
stared at me. '*Lo ama?*' she repeated enquiringly, 'which may
also mean "do *you* love him". Do you?' she asked me. 'Do
you?'

I picked up my books and left the room.

As I passed the four nuns, their sleek, blue-veiled heads
bent low over the verbs of the First Conjugation.

That's all: a child's humiliation. Even as 'my most embarrassing
moment' it would hardly rate in competition with men who
lost their trunks on the beach or girls surprised in hair-curlers
by their suitors. Signora Perruzzi, if she remembered her own
teens, may have felt a tiny twinge of compunction. But more
likely not. How could she know on what tumid, thin-skinned
areas she had trodden or that for me the offence was absolute?

I, absorbed in the symmetries of my own taboos, was just
as unaware of her — the real signora. And when I hurt her it
was not a planned *quid pro quo*, but the random flailing
movement of a creature uncertain of its own location.

In the next few weeks she tried to win me round, inviting
me to her flat where she had little Italian evenings with fried
polenta and great moments from Italian opera on records.
Before the pivotal conversation class (BC), nothing would have
given me more joy. Now I refused. Her verve I fancy flagged a
little under my disdain. She could *have* her flat-vowelled
midlanders, seminarists and nuns. I stayed aloof. I did agree to
do a paper on D'Annunzio for the Modern Language Society
but only to deride the poet of 'our patriotic time in Italy'. She

149

gave me good marks. She had not noticed my idolizing of herself and did not seem to care when I attacked her idol.

And then our worlds impinged.

A bachelor friend of my parents begged me to come and make sandwiches for an adult party he was giving and, as a reward, invited me to stay. It was a musical party to celebrate the arrival in our town of a well-known pianist, and among the guests was Signor Perruzzi, my signora's husband. She herself did not come.

He couldn't have been more than half her height.

'Are you sure,' I asked my host, 'that that's he?'

'Yes,' he said, 'that's Signor Perruzzi.'

He was a fat blackbird of a fellow from Rome with all his weight tilted forward so that his evening tails rose a little on his behind, as though he were constantly considering leaning over to kiss someone's hand. He had a lively blackberry eye, a wet mouth, and warm jolly contours to a face which didn't have a single hollow in it. He was altogether astonishingly unlike his wife and kept flinging little candied cherries into his mouth which puffed his cheeks out so that he looked like Tweedledum. And yet it was he, our host told me, who was the cause of their exile. He had been an ardent Fascist, had composed hymns and marching tunes for Mussolini and had even committed imprudences during the days of the Badoglio government.

'Not only political, rather scabrous I gather. Something to do with assaulting a minor,' said the host and then, having looked at me, clearly decided to get off that tack. 'He can't go back,' he told me. 'And he can't get work. He was a well-known conductor you know, but there's a ban against him. His antisemitism …'

'And she?' I asked, thinking of her green-tinged skin, her fine, violent face.

'Oh, she's just a housewife. Nobody has anything against *her*. She adores him and puts up with a lot. He's a bastard to her,' said the host and moved off to welcome someone new.

I was carrying a tray of sandwiches and moved towards Signor Perruzzi. Would he have one, I asked, in careful Italian. He swung round. His hands revolved like a conjuror's. Words flowed with the rush of an open faucet. He was common, a stage Italian, a charm-vendor. He dished out technicolour, cream-topped compliments with the familiar phoney friendlyness of his Irish equivalent. I didn't need to know Rome to know *him*.

'*Ma guarda, guarda che bella signorina!*'

He lengthened the i-i-i of signorina as the Irish uncle-type would have done with that of cailín. ('Isn't she a gorgeous little cailín antirely!')

'And you know Italian? You are studying with my wife? Are all her students as pretty as you? No wonder she keeps them hidden!'

The tone was the same but the look in his fruity eyes was not. Unblinking, cat-like, they changed quality, seemed to change substance as they stared into mine. There was a shameless, peeled excitement in them which I had never seen, never imagined and which contrasted disquietingly with the platitudes which emerged soothingly from his soft lips. 'Is she a good teacher?' he asked. The eyes were black basalt. 'She'll give you a Lombard accent! You should come and have lessons with me. I talk the best Italian. *Lingua toscana in bocca romana!* Do you know what that means? The Tuscan tongue in a Roman mouth!' His own tongue travelled the damp surface of his lips. Suddenly he leaned almost toppled towards me. He was smaller than I was — how much smaller than she? '*Conosce l'amore?*' he asked. 'Do you know love?' I stared at him. What could he mean? One *felt* love. How could one *know* it? And why was he asking *me* such a thing? Remembering how the signora had conjugated the verb to love, I blushed.

He did not smile as an Irishman might. His spearing gaze and my giggle were interrupted by our host who said that my father was leaving and that I should get my coat. I went, but on my way back passed Signor Perruzzi again. 'Going so soon?' he asked. 'Little girls have to get their beauty sleep!' His tone was light and I felt let down as though he had reneged on a promise. But at the door he was there again. 'When,' he whispered swiftly for my father had already gone out to the lift.

'When what?'

'Our conversation lesson?'

'Oh,' I said, 'that was a joke, wasn't it?' and ran out to the landing. 'Goodbye,' I called. 'Give my regards to your wife.' As the lift went down I saw him turn. He was a fat little man.

I thought of him as I sat in Italian class, where the signora now seemed less marvellous to me. Coldly, I noted the wrinkles at the corners of her eyes. The poetry she liked to quote seemed soppy.

'Ecco settembre,' she read, 'O amore mio triste, sogneremo.
In questo ciel l'estramo sogno si dileguera.
D'un pensoso dolore, settembre il ciel riempie,
Gli languon sulle tempoe, le rose dell'esta.'

Was he her amore triste? What had our host meant by his being a bastard to her? Perruzzi's eyes came back to me when I closed my own, imperiously. Black, I thought, like beetles. Round and black like fresh excrement of goats. But that did not send them away.

Then one morning I took a book the signora had lent me and went around to their flat. It was a Saturday and I thought she might be out shopping as my mother often was on Saturday mornings. Signor Perruzzi opened the door.

'Ah,' he said. 'The little signorina!'

Even in my flat-heeled shoes I was taller than he but I knew he had said 'little' to reassure me and exorcise something imminent and furtive in the air.

'I brought back the signora's book,' I said and stood there.

He took it. 'Will you have a coffee?'

'If you're having some,' I said, 'thank you.' And I followed him into the signora's kitchen.

It was an Irish kitchen, rented, with only a few foreign touches: a half-moon shaped meat-chopper, a coffee machine. Signor Perruzzi reached up to the shelf for this. His hand brushed my neck and I trembled. '*Piccola!*' He relinquished the gadget on its shelf, took hold of my shoulders and, pulling them downwards, kissed my neck which he could just reach. He seized my two weakly struggling hands. '*Bambina,*' he whispered and, squashing one hand into his tightly encased stomach, started pushing it determinedly downwards. I jerked it away, then, as he grabbed me, braced my knee against his thigh and, freeing myself with a wrench, fell backwards to collide with someone who had just opened the back door. It was the signora who was arriving, loaded with parcels.

She gave a little scream: 'Eugenio!' then picked up her fallen groceries and put them on the table.

I tried to stand up but my ankle was hurt and shot sharp pains up my leg when I tried to lean on it. I had to sit on a chair, massaging myself and waiting while Signor and Signora Perruzzi quarrelled in rapid Italian. He screamed and she spoke with calm, cold clarity so that anything I did understand came from her. 'Ah no,' she kept saying, 'not again, not any more!' And then: 'I'd rather leave right now!' And later: 'Scandal, I can't stand scandal! This one's only sixteen!' Neither of them paid any attention to me and I had time to make two or three more attempts to stand up and go but each time my leg collapsed under me and I had to sit back on the chair. It was so dreadful to have to sit there listening that the pain was almost a relief. When finally Signor Perruzzi after a particularly shrill

153

crescendo of shouting, paused, bowed to me and walked with slow dignity out the inner door, I began to wonder whether the signora might not assault me physically. Guilt is an isolating feeling and I felt no pity for either of the Perruzzis. Not even wonder at myself. All I wanted was to get home as quickly as possible and forget.

'Are you hurt?' the signora asked quietly. She was probably as eager to get rid of me as I was to go. 'It's probably just a sprain. Lean on my shoulder. See if you can hop as far as the car and I'll give you a lift home.'

We did as she said and she drove me home without saying anything more. I kept looking out the window on my side and only once, when a van braked suddenly on the other side and gave me an excuse, did I glance at her face. It was expressionless but, from close up, the wrinkles were encroaching tendrils of shadows on the apricot lightness.

'This is our gate,' I said. 'Thank you for the lift. I think I can get out myself.' I didn't want her meeting my parents.

She faced me. 'I have to ask you something. It's important to me. You're old enough to understand ...' Suddenly her lips were puckering. The Signora Perruzzi had begun to cry.

Ashamed for both of us, holding my hands tightly in my lap, I waited. I would not have known how to help her if I had still loved her and I did not love her.

'Did he,' she asked, 'did my husband ask you to come to the flat this morning? Did he tell you *I* would be there?'

I looked at her.

'Did he *ask* you to come?' she repeated a little sharply.

I hesitated and then: 'Yes,' I told her, 'yes, he did. He was most insistent,' I said, 'actually. I'm sorry about everything, Signora Perruzzi. Goodbye.'

I hopped out of the car by myself in spite of the pain and dragged myself inside our gate. When I heard the car drive off I called to the maid to come and help me.

'I fell,' I told her, 'getting off the bus.'

FIRST CONJUGATION

It was April, almost the end of the academic year. With the excuse of my ankle I was able to stay home and avoid going to any more Italian classes. In June we had exams. It was during the luncheon break, one examination day, that I ran into Signor Perruzzi in the college grounds. He was feeding the ducks with a little boy of about five, and I would have sneaked by behind their backs but that he caught sight of me and called: 'Signorina!'

'Hullo,' I said, gave him a great gush of a smile and rushed on.

But he ran after me. 'Signorina, wait! I have been wanting to ask ...' He was trotting to keep up with me, dragging the child by the hand so I had to stop.

'Please,' I begged, 'can't we forget ...'

'No, no!' Signor Perruzzi's eyes leaped in all directions. He was no longer bouncy but deflated. Muddy, semi-circular shadows furrowed the flesh at the corners of his eyes and mouth. When he turned round to the child he took the opportunity of checking up on the alley behind us. 'My son,' he explained. 'Say "hullo",' he told the child but turned away from him at once. 'My wife has got the wrong impression,' he told me. 'It is most unfortunate. For reasons you can't know ...' he spoke rapidly and with a vague urgency. 'Most grave. For me. I must ask you to help me ...' His eyes shifted. 'You remember the last time ... we met? It was merely a moment of tenderness,' said Signor Perruzzi while the child pulled out of his arm. 'An impulse. If *you* could tell my wife that. Tell her,' he begged, 'that it was not premeditated ...'

At that moment I saw the signora herself. 'Mama!' yelled the child, running towards her. The signora opened her arms to sweep it up and the black bat-wings of her BA gown closed vengefully around it. She strode towards us. Pitiful and repellent, the wrinkles in her face moved in the sun like the long-jointed legs of agonizing insects. Both she and her husband looked old to me.

155

'So,' she said in English, 'you continue to make app-ointments! My God Eugenio, I cannot sleep, cannot work with worrying about a fresh scandal. If you would even pick on adults ...'

'Maria, I swear,' said her husband. 'There was no appointment. I just met the signorina by chance, two minutes ago. Ask her, I have never given her an appointment. *Ask her!*'

'I asked her the last time,' the signora retorted sourly, 'and she told me then that you *had* made an appointment to meet behind my back! Eugenio, it is too much ...'

This time, unhampered by any twisted ankle, I fled. As I went I could hear the ebb and suspiration of their voices incomprehensibly wrangling. Bitter, painful and obscure, the sounds pursued me across the garden.

I felt guilt of course, remorse which I buried as fast and deeply as I could. What, I argued with myself, could I do anyway? Even if I were to retract my lie, tell the signora that her husband had *not* invited me to their flat that morning or arranged to meet me in the college gardens, she would not believe me. Would she? Besides, wasn't he clearly a bad hat? A weak, lecherous, morally soft creature? I flailed in him my own uncertain shames. She would be well rid of him.

It was October and the start of a new academic year when I heard that she had returned with the child to Italy. She was looking for an annulment it was thought, and he was hanging round town living on expedients. Eventually, I caught sight of him in the street looking no longer like a blackbird but like a mournful thrush in a tweed coat which someone must have given him, for its padded shoulders drooped half-way to his elbow. He did not see me and I cannot remember if I spared him a passing regret.

I had given up Italian and was busy competing with Ita for the attentions of Nick Lucy who had become muscular, tanned and worldly during a summer in the south of France. If we

ever did mention Signora Perruzzi after that, it was to laugh —
happily — at the way she had made fun of us during conversation class.

EMMA COOKE

The Greek Trip

"I'd rather look up than down," Raymond said.

"Out than in," Julia said.

"Forward than back," Paul said.

They turned their gaze from the arch of the Parthenon which, at the end of an avenue of columns, drew their gaze outwards, upwards and on into the burning sky and looked at Dorothy.

"Come on," they said, "it's your turn."

Dorothy stopped rummaging in her duffle bag, pulled out a pomegranate, broke it in two, blinked her blue, blue eyes, and handing one half to Paul said passively, "Right than left, I suppose."

Paul groaned. "Oh God! Politics again."

"Silly," Dorothy said, "let's all move on."

She led them, swinging her bag and jangling her bracelets, across the top of the Acropolis, past the remains of temples once white with marble, now golden in the sun, to the belvedere where they stood gazing down into the city below.

Holiday friendship. Two couples. Raymond and Julia. Paul and Dorothy. They had met on the plane coming from Dublin. Immediately empathy. They fitted. Julia and the two men did most of the talking. Dorothy kept things from getting over-serious. When life blew them apart again they would remember it all as fun.

The minutiae of Athens lay beneath them; behind them the

gods were wrapped in eternal silence. Toy people zigzagged through toy streets. Traffic moved so far down that it was like a silent movie. Steps were swept, trains travelled, baskets filled, dogs kicked, doors opened, plants watered. They could see it all and it had nothing to do with them. A blind shot up in a high building and a pink dot appeared behind glass. Man or woman? No one could tell.

"I feel immortal," Raymond said. He felt sleepy from the sun.

"I suppose some of them have never been up here," Julia said, filling her eyes with the movement, the shimmer, seeing a commotion around a capsized cart, wishing she could hear as well as see, wishing she knew Greek.

Paul turned away from the scenes of life and considered the antiquities and, beyond them, down on the other side of the hill, the sea where their ship was anchored. They had flown from Italy and cruised the rest of the way. A man Paul knew from the ship, a swarthy squat man with white hair and dark sunglasses, sat on a step talking to a boy. The boy looked like a local. He and the man spoke calmly. Then the boy stood up and moved a few steps away from the man and whistled a long, surprised whistle. The man laughed.

"You must live life to the full," Paul said, suddenly bored with the Acropolis.

"Come on, I'm starving!" Dorothy said.

They lunched in a small café down in the heart of the screeching traffic.

"I drink to you, Dorothy, and I love you," Raymond said when they were finished. "If it wasn't for you we would still be up there burning to cinders." He toasted her with his glass of ouzo.

"My tummy was rumbling," Dorothy said.

"That's why I love you. So was mine."

"I love her too," Julia chimed in. "I think she's beautiful."

They had drunk wine before the ouzo. It made her giddy.

"Now, now Julia, don't get kinky on us," Paul said.

Julia laughed. "Don't start that again, Paul. I think you have sex in the head. What I really mean is I love her because I loved my moussaka. I love Dorothy in a most sisterly way, but I do think she is beautiful. Now you tell her you love her. You are her husband."

Paul emptied his glass. He caught Dorothy's chin in his hand and turned her face towards his and kissed her plump, pink, yielding lips. "I love you, pudding," he said. "I love you because you're so sweet."

"And I love you all too," Dorothy said, waving a hand in benediction before shaking pepper into the eyes of the cats that had crept from their corners to cluster beside the table for scraps.

Back on ship in the late afternoon, sailing towards Delphi, they stood on deck watching the sunset.

"I'd love to have been an Oracle sitting on a tripod all day and getting inspiration from underneath," Julia said. She still felt gay and giddy from all the wine. "No wonder their predictions were ambiguous! I predict ..." she closed her eyes and waited, "that ..." she opened them and looked. Dorothy was the only one paying attention. A breeze ruffled her blonde curls into a downy cap and pressed her thin dress against the lines of her body. She looked delicate and soothing, tender as a goddess. "... Dorothy will be pregnant before we get home," Julia finished rapidly.

"Not a chance," Paul said without turning his head. "The bunks are too narrow and there's no room on the floor."

"You're not trying hard enough. Our cabin is just as small and we have all kinds of ways and means," Julia said.

"Julia, take it easy," Raymond said. Sometimes she went too far.

Dorothy sighed. "I'm on the Pill. I have enough children."

"Oh!"

"Two."

They hardly ever talked family in the foursome. It was one of the rules.

"So are we," Julia said, "on the Pill." She had given up telling people how many children she had.

"Both of you?" asked Paul. "Father and mother?"

"Oh, go to hell!" Julia said.

Julia and Dorothy strolled off downstairs to change for dinner. Raymond went into the lounge to read his guide book. Paul remained on the almost deserted deck. He gazed ahead. The sun was hidden by a mountain on an island but its glow still dissolved in the sea, the sky was still molten.

"Beautiful, isn't it?" The voice was American, deep and drawling, Southern. "B-e-e-a-a-u-u-tiful!" The man from the Acropolis came and leaned on the railing.

"Fantastic!" They stood there. "Did you …" Paul had started to ask for the man's impression of Athens but the memory of the boy and his surprised whistle suddenly embarrassed him. Better not. The man would think Paul was spying on him.

The man stared out over the water. "A wonderful place. A wonderful civilisation. It's a good thing that there's something left. Tell me, did you folks enjoy your day?"

"Oh yes, fine."

"Good. I saw you on the hill. Everyone should be happy on holiday," the man nodded and smiled to himself. He looked as if he had had a good time.

"Is your cabin comfortable?" He turned and looked at Paul. He had left off his sunglasses. His eyes were heavy-lidded, watchful.

"Well, it's a bit small."

"Small?" The man raised an eyebrow.

"Small and hot." Paul felt like a schoolboy.

"Small and hot! How interesting." The man laughed.

"I think I had better go. I have to change," Paul said.

"OK," said the man. "My name is George by the way, George Gibson."

"Glad to meet you. I'm Paul Marshall, my wife's name is Dorothy."

"A lovely girl. I've noticed her," the man bowed. "Glad to make your acquaintance, Paul. Congratulations on your charming lady."

"I think that Julia and I will take the bus tour tomorrow," Raymond said at dinner. Tomorrow they would be at Delphi.

"Yes. We don't want to miss anything," Julia said.

"Dorothy and I will take a taxi, it's just as cheap and much more comfortable," Paul said.

"And we won't have to pay in advance so we can change our minds at the last minute if we want to," Dorothy added.

"You must visit Delphi. It's full of significance. You'd be mad to miss it," Raymond said.

"Full of edification," Julia assured them, twirling her glass.

"If it's really warm I think I'll just stay on board and sit in the sun. I'm just beginning to tan nicely. Look!" Dorothy said.

And so she was. They all looked as she pulled back part of the white chiffon top of her dress to show how brown she had become.

"A true worshipper of Apollo," Paul said. "Dorothy doesn't need to visit Delphi. She would consider it a waste of time. Wouldn't you, pet?"

"The sun sets early in October so I can only sunbathe in the morning and anyway we've been to Athens," Dorothy answered.

Paul shrugged. "You see what I mean. She has made up her mind."

"You know," Raymond said, "you should bleach yourself instead of baking yourself brown and then you'd look exactly like a statue of Venus."

"And Paul could put you on a pedestal at home," Julia said. "And come and lay offerings at your feet," she added for good measure.

Dorothy peered down her cleavage and then consulted the men.

"Should I?" she asked.

"Julia should go and jump at herself," Paul said.

Dorothy was not the only one who stayed on board next morning at Ithea. Some of the seasickness victims were attempting to recuperate and people who had overdone things in Athens had given themselves a day off. Postcards of Delphi could be bought on board and sent to friends. The yellow plastic deckchairs were out and piped music drifted over the loudspeaker system. The convalescents closed their eyes and, dozing, thought they were in their own back gardens. Dorothy sat, cloaked in oil, in the middle of a pile of paraphernalia.

"Have a nice time," she called to Raymond and Julia as they moved towards the gangway.

"Where's Paul?" they shouted.

"He went ashore ages ago. You'll probably meet him."

"You look very comfortable. I think I should have opted out too," Julia said.

Raymond caught her arm. "Come on. You'd never forgive yourself." The bus was already honking for latecomers.

On shore Paul walked about looking into shops. They held the usual assortment of souvenirs — probably all rubbish. He avoided the eyes of the vendors at the doors who offered bags, ponchos, and other enticements at ridiculous prices.

"This for the wedding night?" A man with a leering brown face caught the corner of a large fur rug and pulled it out in front of him, almost blocking his way. A silky, voluptuous coverlet. An extreme looking thing.

"What is it made from?" he was forced to ask.

"Fox."

The red furs glistened in the sunshine. It was fashioned so that the animals' tails made a fringe around the edge. Dozens of little foxes. It was the kind of thing that Dorothy would like. Fit for an actress or a bishop. Paul thought it was macabre.

"No thanks." He hurried past to the far end of the shopping place where there was a booth selling coffee. He found a seat and sat down, glad to drop out of the merry-go-round. He wasn't sure what to do with himself. He wanted to go up into the mountains but wished he had someone with him to help him with the bargaining. Taxis were lined up on the other side of the road. One driver, spokesman for the rest, was arranging people into groups for excursions to Delphi. Should he just go over and tag on somewhere? A man slipped out of the throng and came over to him.

"Are you going to Delphi?"

Paul looked up, blinking in the sunshine, at George Gibson in dark glasses and navy tee shirt.

"I think so — yes, I am."

"Are you alone?"

"Yes. Dorothy stayed on board. She's resting."

"Then perhaps we can join up," George Gibson said.

"Well ..." Paul hesitated, wondering — but maybe he was wrong.

"Or do you wish to join your other friends? No? Good! Then perhaps I could arrange a taxi before they are all taken."

He stepped lightly across the road. Paul looked after him, puzzled. It had happened so suddenly. Who was he? He seemed to be quite alone. In his dark clothes and canvas shoes he could be anything, anyone. His tee shirt revealed a suggestion of a paunch, a tendency to over-indulge. Faint traces of dissipation showed in the slight softening of the jawline and a gentle plumpness of face. Nothing more. Just a bird of passage like the rest of us. He came back.

164

"It's all fixed." He showed his strong white American teeth when he smiled. "Let's go."

They got into the car and the driver eased his way into the convoy of cars and buses on the rocky road that veered up through the olive coloured hills. George Gibson sat back and sighed.

"Have you been here before?" Paul asked.

"Many times," George said. "You could call it a pilgrimage. A visit to the ancients." He fell silent and gazed out at the wooded hills.

"Look!" The driver gesticulated backwards and Paul looked back at where the harbour and the ship lay below in the sun. Translated, like the city yesterday from the belvedere, into a stage for puppets.

They drove through a hillside village. One of the tour buses had stopped. People jostled each other off the path as they tried to crowd into the few small shops. Paul saw Raymond leaning against a wall, reading his guide book with an expression of fierce disgust. Julia was pushing in the mêlée. Two embroidered bags hung from her shoulder. Raymond looked up and Paul waved but Raymond gazed blankly at the taxi as if he hated the world.

"Your friend does not look so happy," George said.

"I don't blame him," Paul said.

"But his wife looks satisfied."

"I suppose Julia likes shopping."

"And your Dorothy? What does Dorothy like?" George asked. He asked it simply, as if it was important to know.

"Dorothy?" Paul felt confused. "I don't know. I mean she is unpredictable. She never really bothers much I suppose, just lets things happen."

"A sunny disposition?"

"I suppose so." Yes. That was it.

"Did you just happen to her?"

"I knew her since we were children. Her brother was my best friend." Oh God! Kevin, I'm sorry.

"Was?"

"He died. The year before Dorothy and I were married, as a matter of fact."

Forgive me, Kevin — Paul couldn't help it. He always stopped himself from thinking of that summer. Now it came back and overwhelmed him. And the night he had called up and found Dorothy alone. Sitting together on the sofa, in the dusk, he had put his head on her shoulder and wept. She was the nearest he could get to Kevin. A link — if you could have a link with a dead person. She had rocked him like a baby, and when he had stopped crying she had caressed him, warming his numbed body, making him feel something, something too weak to be called desire but twinges at least of affection or anguish. He did not know which. It was better, anything was better, than the vacuum of the past weeks. Her parents returned just as Dorothy was leaning over him, her eyes enlarged and questioning. She had stopped then and said "Bloody hell!" just the way Kevin used to. He realised then that desire was not out of the question.

Sometimes in bed Paul closed his eyes and tried to relive those early days of courtship. The days when the balm worked. But Dorothy was so easy-going that Paul found it hard to sustain the mood. Nowadays their lovemaking usually petered out in butterfly kisses. He had not entered her for weeks. He had been surprised when she said she was on the Pill. It was probably a safeguard for the holiday. He thought of their cramped, stuffy cabin and felt remorseful. She was gallant. He loved her. He found that he was panting for breath and fighting back tears.

"Delphi," George said as the taxi stopped. They got out. The air was crisp and pure. George took deep breaths, his face upturned to the sky. He seemed oblivious of Paul's distress or maybe he was being kind. "Those boys knew a good thing when they saw it. Just look at that view." He indicated the surrounding hills, then tapped Paul's arm smartly. "But come on, boy. You ain't seen nothin' yet!" He led the way up the winding path.

"How about that?" George Gibson stood, hands in pockets, teetering up and down.

Paul was transfixed, like a moth on a pin. "It's wonderful."

They had entered an upper region. The stadium spread out around them, munificent and peaceful. Stone seats which had once been paved with marble rose tier after tier. Weeds flourished between the cracks. Pools of water from recent rain reflected azure sky. The place was deserted. The tour buses had dallied too long on the way. No other tourists had made it this far. They were still banging about below, looking for bargains. Paul and George were at the zenith of the ancient city.

"If you listen hard you'll hear the cheers of ancient Greece," George said. He hung his head as if at prayer.

Paul closed his eyes and listened. They were suspended between earth and sky in an enormous hush. The indifference of the place frightened him, reducing himself and George to two dots.

"Come on, we'll run a lap in tribute to the dead," George said.

He set off. His short legs travelled surprisingly fast. Paul ran after him. He experienced various sensations. The pure air and light springy ground acted upon him like an elixir. He stopped being afraid. He lengthened his stride and, running easily, overtook George and travelled swiftly around the enclosure. He felt as if he was running through space. He felt himself to be not so much running forward as into himself. His head sang and as he reached the point from which they had started the moment of integration had arrived. His troubles had been located. He was going to be able to cope. He gulped enormous draughts of air and turned to watch George, whose running had slowed to a jog-trot.

"I won," he said. He felt enormously grateful.

George walked the last few paces. He took off his sunglasses and laid them on a stone pedestal. Paul looked into his eyes. His assurance faltered. He remembered the fur rug with its dangling border. He remembered the pecking order, the moment of surrender when the quarry stops and faces the pursuer. It had all happened before, the pain and the relief.

George flexed his muscles, then caught Paul's arm, turned, lightly lifted him and threw him onto his back. He bent over him, his eyes hard as topaz. "I'm a judo expert, would you like to try and beat me at that?" he said.

Paul looked up at him. The fall had not hurt. George seemed to be standing in a nimbus. "Yes," he said.

George looked at him for a moment longer, then he glanced around the stadium. "No. Not now." He caught Paul's hand and pulled him to his feet. They started back down the hillside to where the taxi was waiting. As they passed the Temple of Apollo George stopped and gazed at the tall columns. "Have you ever noticed that when the sun shines everything is more beautiful?" he asked.

"Yes," Paul said. The sun, the pillars, the running and George had combined to give him vertigo. He had to hold onto George's arm.

"You were right, Paul, that bloody bus tour was a fiasco, we should have taken a taxi," Raymond said at lunchtime. He was cross and sulky.

"Oh, come on! It wasn't so bad and there was great value in the shops. We saw enough," Julia chided.

"Our last day in Greece and where do I spend it? Standing outside a shop full of stupid women. I'd prefer to be in my bunk," Raymond said. He felt as if he had been robbed.

"Cheer up. You can always come again and see the sights," Paul said.

"How did *you* get on, Dorothy?" asked Julia to change the subject.

"Can't you see?" Raymond said. "She's bronzed and gorgeous. Sexy. She'll be the envy of the girls when she gets home. Won't you, Dorothy? You can waggle your tan at them. It's a hell of a sight more attractive than a clutch of embroidered bags."

"I went ashore for a while myself," Dorothy said. "Look at what I bought." She had bought a ring. A large turquoise in a gold claw.

"It's lovely," Julia said, thinking how cheap it looked and how flawless Dorothy's nails were. "What do you think of it, Paul?"

"Oh," Paul said dimly, "it's alright I suppose."

"It's right for Dorothy. It's magnificent," Raymond said.

"Everything is right for Dorothy," Julia said, suddenly hating all the bric-a-brac she had piled in her cabin.

Dorothy yawned. "It's not a real jewel of course. It's just for fun." She yawned again. "Who's for a siesta?"

"I am. I'm exhausted," Julia said. She held out her glass to Raymond. "We might as well finish the wine first."

Raymond filled her glass to the brim. Abruptly, as if he was offended or thought she was trying to harass him. He poured the rest into meticulously even measures. A small drop each. He caught Julia's eye as he put down the bottle. She looked at him anxiously but he was still seething. Her thin, freckled face was pale. He refused to feel sorry for her. Alright, she did find the heat trying. Alright, she had not suggested stopping the bus. But she had been there. Then he calmed down. They were on holiday. Why spoil it?

"We could all do with a rest. It was a messy morning," he said.

Paul saw George Gibson pass through the doorway of the dining room that led towards the deck. "You go ahead. I won't bother. I'll catch up on my sleep when I get home," he said.

He watched Dorothy and the others go towards the stairs for the cabins, then he walked stealthily in the other direction.

Up on deck Paul wandered past the people sitting in deck chairs. He barely saw them. He had to steady himself with the deck rail as he walked. They had been travelling for two weeks now. A whole new existence had come into being. A different scale measured the days. He would have found it hard to describe to a stranger what his life at home was like. His children? His colleagues? Nothing but blank discs back there somewhere. He tried to check what he would be doing this time next week. Signing letters? Telephoning? Something useless, no doubt. Keeping alive. Not enjoying himself. Pleasure. Did he get pleasure from it? That was the question you should ask yourself on holiday. An old priest he knew in his schooldays used to ask the same question in confession. He never knew what to answer. He usually said "No". It seemed to mitigate authority. He leaned against the rails and watched the water that was churned up by the passage of the boat. The coastline glided past, grey mountains, dark patches of forest like masses of pubic hair. Murmurs, cries and shrieks from holidaymakers mingled in chorus behind him. It was a balmy afternoon. Pleasure, he thought, I've never experienced it in my life.

"All alone?" George Gibson had come up behind him. His canvas shoes made no sound when he walked.

"All alone," Paul answered. He felt as if a net had fallen over him. And yet, he had known this would happen.

"Where is your wife?"

"Gone to bed for the afternoon."

"And don't you wish to join her?" It was said flatly.

"I find the cabin very warm. Dorothy doesn't mind the heat," Paul said. He had not meant to sound plaintive.

"I see. Small and hot. I remember." George spoke in a low voice. "So she is a sun goddess, not an ice maiden."

"I don't know which she is," Paul answered lightly.

George leaned his elbows on the railings. His arms were strong, muscular, covered with black hairs. A forest of hairs and a gold watch strap. He stared into the distance. Neither of them moved. Paul watched a patch in the water, forcing himself to feel at ease.

George shifted. "I have been searching for you. I had almost given you up," he said. "I wonder if you would care to come to my cabin? It's cool and comfortable. We can drink some good brandy and forget our troubles." He chuckled.

Paul felt tempted to turn and run. It had been years now. Then, quickly, because he was afraid his voice would break, he said, "I'd like that."

He followed George down through the ship to where, at the end of a corridor, George opened the door of a cabin which made their own seem pitiable by contrast. The photographs were all over the place. Young men, younger than he. As young as Kevin had been. All smiling, all happy, all with George posed beside them, behind them or with his arm entwined in theirs. The bunks were side by side and there even was furniture. A table with bottles, an easy chair, a rug made from various patches of leather, an arrangement of dried flowers in a weighted jar. This was one of the luxury cabins. The kind Dorothy had expected them to have.

"Wow!" He turned to George with an uncertain smile. "This is really living!"

George waved him in and, following smartly behind him, softly closed the door and slid the bolt home.

Julia clambered out of her slacks and hung them up. She took some clips from the little shelf over the washbasin and pinned the ends of her hair. Raymond stood behind her. He put his arms around her waist.

"What are you doing that for?" he asked.

"Because if I don't I'll look a mess tonight." She felt tired and grim. "Excuse me." She wriggled from his grasp and put in the last of the clips. She took a book from the wardrobe, squashed the pile of packages on the top bunk into a suitcase and climbed the ladder.

"What are you lying up there for?" Raymond asked.

"The light is better for reading,'" she replied.

Raymond came and stood beside her. His face was level with hers. He felt stupid. "Julia," he raised an arm awkwardly to put around her, "won't you come down here? We'll both fit comfortably."

She glowered at him. "Raymond, I'm tired. I want to rest. Just leave it at that, will you."

He felt as if his face had been slapped. "Very well, if that's the way you want it," he said.

"It is." She opened her book.

He looked at her, amazed at her versatility, the way she could turn from little girl to bitch to manhater in seconds. That was it. She wanted them to be enemies.

"I'll be up on deck," he said. He slammed the door behind him.

Julia lay still for a few minutes, then climbed back down the ladder and bolted the door. She rummaged for a cigarette and, after a moment's hesitation, poured herself a large glass of brandy from the bottle in the wardrobe. She felt as if she would never want to make love again. She resettled herself on the bottom bunk and, smoking and sipping, gazed moodily at the door. After a while she felt better, read a few pages of her book. Then she covered herself with a blanket and slept.

Dorothy came out of the lower deck washrooms as Raymond went along the corridor. Her hair was tied up with a scrap of lace. She wore a short, yellow towelling wrap. Her feet were bare.

"Raymond," she sounded glad and surprised, "I thought you'd be resting."

"No. I'm not," he said.

She looked at him carefully. Her face was scrubbed and shiny like a little girl's. A pleased little girl with a secret. "Do you think you could open our porthole, our cabin is stifling," she asked.

"I'll try," Raymond said.

"Good! It's such a nuisance getting one of the crew down to do it. They make such a fuss."

She led the way back to her cabin. It was more cramped and stuffy than Raymond's. "The ventilator isn't working properly," she explained. Raymond felt embarrassed. The cabin was so tiny that it was impossible to avoid bumping into her if he moved. He closed the door. A jacket of Paul's hung on the back of it. All the rest of the muddle looked like Dorothy's. Bottles and jars, sandals, socks, a packet of washing powder, a magazine, tissues and cottonwool thrown here and there, scarves hanging everywhere. The dress she had worn at lunch hung from the top of the wardrobe, and on the floor beneath it some wisps of underwear. A box of beads and ornaments lay open on a stool. "Sorry about the mess," Dorothy said, "there isn't room for anything." She picked up a bra and dropped it into the washbasin.

It seemed an incredibly intimate moment to Raymond. A tender gesture. "You should see *our* place. It's like a souvenir shop," he said. "Julia goes berserk shopping for the kids."

"Still, you were sensible. You brought slacks and things. Look at me!" She shrugged her shoulders and pouted. She was gorgeous. Like a damp nymph. No wonder Julia was jealous. She was sexy enough to arouse a statue. The anger Raymond had felt on leaving Julia evaporated. All he wanted to do was touch Dorothy. He had been wanting to touch her for days.

"I'll get up on the bunk and hold the porthole steady while you unscrew it," Dorothy said. She climbed up and knelt, waiting for him. He came and stood behind her. Her bare feet were inches from his face. She had small calluses from her sandals. Lumps of translucent amber that made his face throb with desire. He planted a kiss on one of her heels. Dorothy turned her head. He kissed the other one. She turned round and Raymond, holding her by the ankles, pulled her slowly towards him.

So this was what another woman was like! He had often wondered. The difference between her and Julia distracted him at first. She was squashier and slippier. As slippy as a snail. She breathed in a soft hissing way. Julia was bony and tough. Diffident at first, as if she couldn't care less. Then he forgot Julia. And in the end it was good, better than he had believed possible.

Afterwards his forehead ached and his cheeks felt as if they were being pulled from the inside by a piece of string. And then that eased too and his pulses stopped racing and he began to feel a fool. Worse than a fool. How had he let things get so out of hand? He did not believe in infidelity.

Dorothy lay with one arm thrown back over her head. She stroked his chest idly with the other one. The one on which she had put the new gaudy ring. He was surprised that he had admired it. It was not the type of thing he cared for at all. And he didn't like long red nails. He liked short square undecorated ones. But her body was magnificent. Her bikini had left mother-of-pearl patches on bust and crotch. "You're beautiful," he said, remembering his manners.

Dorothy patted his cheek lazily. "Thanks," she said.

He crawled out of the bunk and began to collect his clothes. There seemed to be nothing left to say. Dorothy gave his hair a fond tug as he reached across her for his socks. "I must fix the porthole," he said.

"It doesn't matter. I've changed my mind," she yawned.

"Dorothy ..." He fastened his sandals then looked firmly at her. He wished she would cover herself up.

"Yes?"

He felt awkward. It had just been a trivial aberration.

Nothing to do with Julia. He hoped there would be no fuss. He hoped she saw it that way too.

"I have never … I don't usually … I mean, please, I'd hate Julia to know."

Dorothy sat up, leaning on one elbow. She looked surprised. "Don't be frightened, lover. You don't think I'd tell Paul, do you?"

He shook his head.

"Well then, she can't find out. I'd never say it."

"You don't feel bad?"

She whooped, with merriment. "Bad? I feel great. I always think the less you know people the better it is."

Raymond was horrified. So she was that kind of girl. He could no longer remember why he had ever been attracted by her. All he wanted was Julia, his bookworm, his silly love. "I wouldn't know," he said stiffly.

Dorothy called him back as he was leaving. "Raymond, don't tell Julia," she said. "She's not like me. *She* would take it seriously." He turned away from her nakedness and the kindness of gaze with a heavy heart.

Raymond and Julia went to the dining room early for dinner. The weather had changed. One of those October storms was blowing up. Rain fell steadily. The decks were empty. The boat rocked unpleasantly. People complained about slops on the tables. Waiters mopped up spills in bad-tempered silence and hurled fresh napkins at the disgruntled diners. Julia and Raymond ate in silence. Julia had slept until Raymond came in to dress for dinner. She woke feeling that everything was her fault. She wanted to make amends. Raymond frowned and hummed to himself and pretended not to notice when she stroked the back of his neck.

"We'll be late for dinner," he said, with a most unexpected regard for time. As they ate, gloom, loneliness and resentment crept over Julia.

"Let's order a second bottle of wine," she suggested. She felt like passing beyond this deliberate dullness. She felt like getting drunk. She drained her glass.

"If you want it." Raymond had not touched a drop.

Julia signalled to the wine waiter. He placed a second bottle in front of her. She pushed her plate to one side and pulled it closer. "Here come Paul and Dorothy," she said. Later on I'll sing, she thought, something suitable — a rebel song or a dirge.

"Well!" Paul walked with a stoop as if he was carrying something breakable or had received a kick in the stomach. His voice was shaky. Raymond thought for a moment that Paul had found out but when he looked up at him Paul said, "Did you have a pleasant afternoon?" He seemed absent-minded but polite.

"How's everybody?" Dorothy asked. She was dressed in a fluttery dress. She kept grinning at them all. She had put on earrings the same colour as her new ring.

"Bloody awful," Julia said, "absolutely awful."

"Cheer up," Raymond said, trying to cheer himself up. He was full of pity for himself and Julia. He would spend the rest of his life making it up to her. "We'll be nearly home this time tomorrow."

"If the plane doesn't crash," Paul said. It was his only hope. His despair was so heavy and black that it was as palpable as his aching body.

"You should all have stayed on board this morning instead of killing yourselves over a lot of old ruins," Dorothy said. She picked up her spoon and started to eat her soup. The others sat clutching the arms of their chairs as the boat began to roll. The storm was whipping up. It was going to be a long night.

MARY LELAND

A Way of Life

The hall door shut with a satisfied slam behind her. The rooms empty of children gaped on the landing but the house was warmly ready for her, her sounds and movements animating it as she completed the small rituals of night, the patina of her contentment glazing the waiting air of her bedroom, where books took up the space of another body.

In the chilled mirrors of the bathroom she watched with equanimity the reduction to self, safe here where she was known so well, but not to be feared even elsewhere, when so often as again tonight the texture of her own skin surprised and pleased her, and the thick untinted hair denied years she did not otherwise deny. It was happening: she plucked out a coiled grey hair, and sighed at the trace of blood on the toothbrush.

'I have reached an age,' she reminded herself, 'where it is important that my dentist does not die before I do.' But even this reflection could not dim the glow of tired elation with which she prepared for solitary sleep.

'Don't you just *adore* men?' Peggy had asked her once. They were standing together watching a young and hungry barrister spur the gravel of Peggy's Dublin South avenue as he turned his battered sports-car. 'I do. I just adore them. They're so — *innocent*. So, after everything, so easily pleased.'

Smiling, Anna had wondered again about Peggy. Safe in a marriage which by all Irish standards must be called good, with a wealthy man who didn't drink, didn't smoke, didn't play golf, whose most obvious assertion was his undramatic fondness for Peggy herself, she and her husband were a tanned and thriving couple with a yacht, a house by the sea, children at famous monastic schools, and government ministers to dinner even when their government was no longer in power.

With it all there remained, perhaps essential to Peggy's attractiveness, a trace of raciness, a strange wild flavour to the well-managed life

'No,' Anna said. 'I'm still afraid of them. They own too much, they can do such damage.' Stephanotis arched above its own reflection on the laquered table in the hall where they still stood, still gazing at the shredded gravel before the steps. As Peggy put her hand to the vaulted door, Anna saw the heavy gems on the thin, elegant wrist and recognized Peggy's smile, a smile tinged with remembered satisfactions.

'No,' Anna said again. 'There is nothing that they have that I want. Now.'

Peggy laughed a challenge to the lie. The house made them graceful as they wandered back to the exquisite drawing room, the facets of the chandelier sprinkling light across the pastel ceiling, a green glow coming in from the extravagant city garden beneath the windows. To Anna it looked like an arrival point, and she knew that once they would have sat together in the kitchen, where dark old woods shone against old tiles and cracked ceramics fielded from deputations to the EEC had no comment to make except that of surprised survival.

Even for these conversations, talk about men, they would have sat in the kitchen. They would have wondered what had happened, how it was that they had never thought they would find themselves like this describing to one another the minutiae of love, or at least of love-making, of their lives with men in them. In the drawing room there was no giddy wonderment; the room said it all. This was what had happened, at least to Peggy. Peggy's wealth also gave her an immunity, an equality impossible for others. She could afford, thought Anna meanly, to be generous.

The truth was that Peggy's real practical love was for her husband and family. For the rest it was a matter of emotive energy, cast over anyone who interested her, whom she could help, who attracted her. It was the only thing about her that Anna longed to emulate, that gift of generosity without fear. Admitting it to herself, Anna resorted to one of her stand-by consolations: all this talk about men, she thought, and if I mentioned Henry James she'd wonder where she might meet him!

All the same, Peggy could surprise her.

'How is it we can talk like this,' she said as they curled again into the peacocked armchairs, 'how is it that we, you and I, have no moral anxiety about our sexual lives? About what we want?'

It was nice of her to include herself, technically blameless as she was. But that was Peggy, too. There was something she wanted to say, or to find out, and she could only do it by appearing to talk of something, or someone, else. Look at the time it had taken Anna to realize that Peggy had guessed long before that something was wrong with Anna's own marriage. All those days Anna had spent with her, 'getting a break from the kids'. Those had been getting a break from the husband as well, although Peggy had never hinted at that, treating instead the worried, hurried confidences with a tact and gentleness which had appeased the gnawing anger. And then when it happened that Anna's marriage had become the conversation piece of many people Peggy had offered, characteristically at once, shelter, money, advice, throwing a rope of robust clichés for Anna to clutch, accepting without argument Anna's own imperatives, substituting her own only where Anna could not reach.

In the long calm after that long storm, Anna had redesigned her life, not skilfully, but with growing wonder at how it could all be done, almost easily, once she had accepted that there was no need, any more, to apologize. That dispensation was what made sense of her life now; learning to function without blaming anyone, she less and less blamed herself. The children had become the circumstance of her life, rather than the excuse for its deficiencies. She had grasped what remained to her and added to it, emerging, she felt sure, back where she should have started, had she only known the way.

But when Peggy had wondered, like that, out loud, Anna had been surprised.

'How is it? Peggy — you know how it is! I can talk like this, I can behave like this, because I know I'm going to pay for it. There's no need to feel guilty — retribution is just around the corner!'

She meant it, but they were both laughing. They knew how it was, everything, *everything* was paid for.

'*Everything!*' Anna couldn't stop. 'Look at this weekend — first thing before I leave at all, £19 at the Family Planning Clinic! And then the train, and taxis, and the hotel …'

Peggy didn't prompt her. The hotel.

'Well,' Anna had quietened. 'The hotel. That's it, really. That makes it worth the trouble, not the expense, the secrecy is the trouble, but it's worth it.'

There was a brightness in Peggy's eyes. She knew how it could be worth it, that secret, precious excitement, that breathlessness produced by nothing else at all.

'But you're still afraid of men!' She pounced. 'You don't trust them. You don't trust him.'

Of course Anna didn't trust him. How could she? She was in love with him. She had been almost sick with it, and Peggy had noticed, without saying anything more.

It had been love, hadn't it? That ripening?

This was not a question she could take to sleep with her now. How could she admit it had been love? If she gave that much she would be like a cat crouching before an empty hearth because once it had known warmth there, all the rest of life she would be sitting not before the shrine, but before the source.

It must be that this was what she did not trust, her own sense that in themselves men held a key to a door which would open on an inner life, golden and strong, unthreatened because it was of their own essence. To be in love, if she could look at it now, was to hold the other hand of the hand that held the key, by all one's actions to encourage that key to turn, to open, to bring one in.

She had been right, Anna knew it, in what she had said those years ago to Peggy. Whatever she got, whatever she enjoyed, she would pay for, and had she but known it then, had already begun to pay. Because it had been love, an offering of small perfections which she had disclaimed. She had wanted lightness, ease, the delicacies of sexual rather than any deeper understanding, all kept possible by courtesy. And surely she was only being modern, being careful, in putting herself, politely, first?

Taking those pleasures in a Dublin city with the sun on it, in a London glittering with frost, she had said 'darling' carefully. She had not let him know how surprised she had been that he had found her out, had bothered with her, how every telephone call between them was weighed with wonderment, and if sometimes her voice betrayed her she pretended it was another excitement altogether. Only in bed did she betray her gratitude, where the unspoken love broke to a shouted lovely, where enthusiasm was permitted and could be used as a disguise.

It was good. So good as to be enough, for her. There had been traces of needs to be met which had frightened her, she had seen bleak anxieties behind the gaiety of passion in his eyes. Now that she was secure at last in her womanhood she might have found room for them, but then — then they were auguries of too much, portents which would bring her back, not forward, to before her new beginning. She was living now the new life she had protected then, and here in her own bed, in her own house, there was no longer any need to lie.

'It's not much, though, is it?' he had asked once. 'As a way of life, I mean?'

They were planning, not for the future, but for next week. They had walked a little way downhill from the car to where a brown stream tumbled over stones, and a bank of grass hid them from the road. As the September evening cooled, their serenity broke on the knowledge of parting, coming within an hour or so as the light faded down. They felt the feather of winter brush their skin, and she thought not of the rushing prance against the cold air of the beach, and the casserole in the borrowed kitchen of a friend, and the regular, regulated warmth of hotel bedrooms, but of babysitters, and money, and the lonely, lonely lack of opportunity.

What had he thought of it? Not much, he had said, not much as a way of life. It had not hurt, because he was saying that there was more on offer. Another new start, this time with him. The two children were young enough to take the change, to enjoy it. Could she? The short answer was no. There was no long answer.

'Anna!' Peggy had exclaimed. 'That was too easy! You liked him, you know you did — why not wait a little longer, give it a chance?'

'If I wait it will get harder.'

'But that would mean that you really care for him! That would make the decision for you, you would know what was right!'

'I don't want to need anyone so badly that I would change everything for him, all I have built up in the last few years. I can live without him — and he without me.'

'Yes.' Peggy's voice was subdued. 'I'm sure you can. You can live without him — but do you want to? It will be such a loss to you, Anna, you will always wonder if you could have done things differently.'

'But I wonder about that already.' Anna knew her defences were meagre. 'It's all right for you, Peggy. You're safe. But you want me to feel pain, to do it all properly, to suffer, to put values on things so that they become important to me, too important to lose, even though I know I'm going to lose them. It's a price I won't pay, Peg, I can't afford it.'

When had she decided that the loss was inevitable? It didn't matter now, for it was, it was. The knowledge had governed her life since then, intensifying her relationship with Peggy for they both knew by now that of all friendships, that between themselves as women was the one which would last.

The cat had come in her window and jumped on the bed, kneading the quilt before curling into a complacent ball. The facts of her life settled down again into Anna's mind as she reached to switch off the light, smiling as she thought at last that she could say, like Peggy, that she loved men. And mean it, in almost the same way.

Before she turned into sleep she thought of him, tonight's man. Nice, and nicer because he hadn't really understood from the beginning what she had intended. That their meeting had not been accidental, that she had designed their re-discovery of a mild affection in the past, the cautious flirtatiousness of durable colleagues. As a result she could almost despise him for the ease with which it worked, but although she enjoyed that feeling of mild contempt, a dividend on the perceived disdain on boys' faces long ago at rugby dances, the boat club, although now she could feel she was paying them out, this time, with this one, she didn't.

To meet for a chat was easy, mutual concerns gave plenty of excuses. To prolong that into another drink, a break from the in-house training scheme, on to anxious thoughts about a teenager at home and thence, in a skilful elision, to a sighed reference to the wife, why, that gave room for the touch on the sleeve, the reflection that it was so nice to talk, to really talk, and to the open suggestion that they should do so again.

Lamplit in Kinsale, she had let the silences fill themselves with meaning. There had been, usually there was, a little furtive laughter, a sense of light complicity. On a smile his hand touched hers and as their reminiscing allowed her to mention a lover of the past he grew bolder and his fingers touched her wrist and moved again until they touched the pulse inside her elbow, and she stirred. Then — The Look. And The Question.

Her gaze held his, steady, bright, and sober. Finishing the meal quickly he paid and put her in the car and drove up the hill to the dark pile of the fort where the walls shrouded the cliff with shadows. Unheard beneath them the confident sea pounded against the rocks, and knowing the beat of the waves down there and the surge of the wind blowing their spray against the small cage of the car, she felt again the answering rhythm within herself, the rising response. And she liked to think about it afterwards, the way he had unclasped the seatbelt and taken her authoritatively into his arms.

She looked at him again, showing him that she was deliberately studying his features, that his face mattered to her. He was only a few years older than herself, but at this time in their lives it mattered to be found attractive. He was big, greying, one of those men who become handsome before they fall into age, easily pleasant.

Leaning across to kiss him, she made it gentle, inquisitive but not demanding. The demand must be his, and as their mouths touched he brought his hands up to her head to hold her while he kissed her firmly back and deepened the kiss so that his tongue pushed past her teeth and swelled against the ribs of her throat. So. He meant it. The knowledge gave freedom to the little flick of excitement beneath her stomach and she broke from him, breathless.

'Don't you want to?' Surprise hid the beginnings of anger.

'Yes.' She put her face against his cheek, her voice pitched between a laugh and a groan. This was to be regretful desire. 'I want to. But not here, we'd have to stop. And I want to be with you, really *with* you.'

He understood her, and she knew the next question.

'Where?' Little boy lost.

The second question came as she directed him to the flat she was minding for a friend.

'Do you have something … you know? In case …?'

She had something, he need not worry about that. But she knew there were other moments of worry for him, although the normality of the flat, its casual comforts, the books and stereo, television and telephone, red wine in the kitchen, all these indications of a steady way of life reassured him that the growing feeling of a strangeness to all this could be dismissed.

In the bathroom she wondered, she always did, if he thought about what she might be doing in there, the intimate preparations for his coming. She did not change her clothes, this was to be an honest exchange between adults, not a seduction. There was a contentment in consent, she thought, but when she went back to the living room he looked nervous again. Now what would it be — his wife? Apprehension that his performance would be unmanly or inadequate? The well-founded suspicion that he was here less of his own will than of hers?

This time it was the secrecy problem.

'This will be just between us, Anna, okay?'

It was dangerous to joke about it, so she didn't tell him that she was going to write to the papers. She was willing to draw the plot around her as though accepting his protection, of course it would be just between them. And at least his hesitation meant also that she didn't have to worry about the possibility that he was one of those men who can't accommodate their own peccadilloes, who can't sleep peacefully until their wife knows all, so that she is the one to stay awake night after night.

'Yes, please, just between us,' and she came close to him, raising her arms to his neck, lifting her face so that their coming together began with this purposeful gesture and did not end until they melted away from one another, damply pleased and close with goodwill. The next few moments were often tricky, a time of satisfaction but of separation as well.

'Oh, Jesus, Anna, that was great,' he breathed at last, stirring to the other side of the mattress. He was kind: one hand stretched towards her, his fingers feathering along her side. And he had taken care of her, been diligent once he had forgotten to be amazed. No next time, though. He might want to feel himself in love, and he couldn't afford it.

Gently, absently, kissing his shoulder she whispered that she would have to go soon. She could feel him grow tense with the dilemma: how would he say goodbye without offering another date, but at the same time without appearing to be a louse? It was important to them, men, not to seem to be a louse. And he wasn't. She would do all that for him.

'Friends?' That was the note for the future. Gratefully he took it, and they dressed in accepting compatibility, were easily silent as he drove her home, and the few words at her door allowed him to relax in the knowledge that there was no blame, no expectation, nothing, ever, to disturb his own feeling that he was, after all, a nice guy.

She hoped, now, that she would remember who he was the next time they met, wherever that would be. She was going to have to slow down soon, her stage was small and the cast list was diminishing. Once, only once, Peggy had said: 'Anna, when I see you sometimes, I am afraid of the future.'

'So am I,' Anna had answered. 'And I'm living in it.'

I am, she thought now, lying at her ease. This is my future. My way of life.

For a second the children clung to the edges of her mind, their return tomorrow a thing settled and certain, the spaces they would fill unchallenged by any other claim. But because she still felt, would it always be like this? She still felt some need for an approval beyond theirs, beyond the best that they could ever offer, she led herself to sleep on the remembered choke in his breath when they had first felt, naked, each other's secret skin.

She slept, and dreamed of grief. Through suburbs incandescent with laburnum she walked with long hair, lacings of gold holding a dress with pointed sleeves, a weight of paint on her lips. Trees hung lilac shadows which moved at her step and whispered 'not here, not here'. Hair grew heavy across her shoulders, her feet in thin slippers left patches of silken damp on the cobbles roughening beneath them. The bright tapestry of her gown unravelled, colours slithering as though silent remorseless hands were taking in the threads. The sky lowered, black roofs of empty houses held up the clouds, the air was light and cold, leaves blew brown from the garden walls.

The skin of her mouth cracked, the pain withered into wrinkles, in her thin hands she held a muscle which dripped red on to her bleeding feet. A shadow became a man, it was he, the one whose smile meant life to her, but the shadow turned aside, a cloak shielding his face as in a picture — where? From the flow of his hair, the line of his tunic, the delineation her vision traced of all his form could be, she knew that this was he. A cape of silk eddied against the wall as he stroked past her, so near she held out her hand in trailing rags to touch, but he was gone. In her palm she held a piece of greenish metal, a coin on which her tears fell at last.

She woke to the pain of it. Dawn and bird song, a mist filling the hills across the river.

Her hands clenched the bleached linen of the sheet, clutched grief through the fabric of her life, and she came awake to the gasping sigh with which some recognition, some knowledge of meaning, drifted past her mind.

ITA DALY

Such Good Friends

Although it all happened over two years ago, I still cannot think about Edith without pain. My husband tells me I am being silly and that I should have got over it long ago. He says my attitude is one of self-indulgence and dramatisation and that it is typical of me to over-react in this way. I have told no one but Anthony, and I think that this is a measure of the hurt I suffered, not to be able even to mention it to anyone else. I don't think I am over-reacting — though I admit that I have a tendency to get very excited when I discover a new friend or a potential friend. This may sound as if I am wallowing in permanent adolescence, but even if this were so, the knowledge still wouldn't stop me being overcome with joy if I should meet someone whom I felt to be truly sympathetic.

It may be that I feel like this because I have had so few real friends in my life. I do not say this with any suggestion of self-pity; I am aware that such affinity of spirit is a very rare commodity and so, when there is a possibility of finding it, why, there is every reason to be excited. And it is something I have only ever found with members of my own sex.

Not that I have ever had any shortage of men friends. I have a certain bold physical appeal which seems to attract them, and before I was married, I always had four or five men hovering around, waiting to take me out. I don't deny that this gave me a satisfaction — it was sexually stimulating and very good for one's ego — but I have never felt the possibility of a really close relationship with any of these men. Even Anthony, to whom I have been married for five years, and of whom I am genuinely fond, even he spends half the time not knowing what I am talking about, and indeed, I am the same with him. Men on the whole are unsubtle creatures. You feed them, bed them, and bolster their egoes, and they are quite content. They demand nothing more from a relationship, and for them physical intimacy is the only kind that matters. They don't seem to feel a need for this inner communion, they are happy to jog along as long as their bodies are at ease. I do not bare my soul to men. I tried to once with Anthony in the early days of our marriage, and, poor dear, he became upset and was convinced that I must be pregnant. Pregnant women are known to suffer from all sorts of strange whims.

You may by now think that I do not like men, but you would be quite wrong. I do like them and I am sure that living with one must be so much easier than living with a member of one's own sex. They are easy to please, and easy to deceive, and it is on the whole therapeutic to spend one's days and nights with someone who sees life as an uncomplicated game of golf, with the odd rough moments in the bunker. All I point out are their limitations, and I do so knowing that these views may be nothing more than an eccentricity on my part.

However, to return to Edith. I first met her during a bomb scare when that spate of bomb scares was going on, a little over two years ago. Before my marriage I had been studying law. I passed my first two exams and then I left to get married. About a year later I decided I would try to get a job as a solicitor's clerk, for I found I was bored doing nothing all day long and I thought if might be a good idea to keep my hand in, so to speak. It would make it easier if I ever decided to go back to College and attempt to qualify.

The firm where I got my job had its offices on the top floor of an old house in Westmoreland Street. The offices had a Dickensian air of shabbiness and dust, although I knew the firm to be a thriving one. It consisted of Mr Kelly Senior, Mr

Kelly Junior, and Mr Brown. Along with five typists and myself of course. Mr Brown was a down-trodden man of the people, who was particularly grateful to Mr Kelly Senior for having lifted him from the lowly status of clerk to the heights of a fully fledged solicitor. He spent his days trotting round after the boss, wringing his hands and looking worried, and, as far as I could see, making a general nuisance of himself. Mr Kelly *père et fils* were tall dour Knights of Columbanus. They had crafty grey eyes in emaciated grey faces and they always dressed in clerical grey three-piece suits. One day, Mr Kelly *fils* caused quite a sensation when he ventured in wearing a yellow striped shirt, but this break with tradition must not have met with approval, for next day, and thereafter, he was back to the regulation policeman's blue.

The typists in the office were nice girls. I had little to do with them, as I had my own room, and only saw one of them when I had any work to give to her. In the beginning, as I was the only other female in the office, I did try joining them for morning coffee. However, it was not a success. They were not at their ease, and neither was I. I didn't know what to say to them, and they were obviously waiting for me to leave until they could resume their chatter of boyfriends and dances and pop music. There was only about six years difference in our ages, yet I felt like another generation. It was because of this lack of contact that I hardly noticed Edith's existence, although she had been in the office nearly six weeks. That was, until the day of the bomb scare.

We were cursed with bomb scares that winter and particularly irritated by this one, the third in the same week. We filed out of the building, silently, as people were doing on either side of us. The novelty had worn off and these regular sorties into the winter afternoons were beginning to get under people's skin. It was bitterly cold, and I thought I might as well go and have a drink. It seemed more sensible than standing around in the raw air, making small talk. I crossed over the bridge and turned down towards a little pub that I had discovered on such a previous occasion. I sat sipping a hot whiskey, enjoying the muggy warmth, when I happened to glance across at the girl sitting opposite me. She looked familiar in some vague way, and just as I was wondering if she was from the office, she caught my glance and smiled back at me. Yes, now I remembered, she was one of the typists alright, and now that she had seen me I felt obliged to go over and join her. I hadn't wanted to — I had been looking forward to a nice quiet drink without the effort of conversation. But I couldn't be so obviously rude.

'You're with Kelly and Brown,' I began, sitting down beside her.

Her smile was diffident, almost frightened.

'Yes, that's right. And you're Mrs Herbert. I know because the other girls told me — I haven't been long there myself. My name is Edith Duggan,' she added and held out her hand, rather formally I thought. We sat side by side, both of us ill-at-ease. I was wondering what I could talk about, and then I saw, lying open in front of her, a copy of *The Great Gatsby*. Good — at least this could be a common theme.

'Please call me Helen,' I said. 'Any friend of Gatsby's is a friend of mine. Do you like Scott Fitzgerald?'

'Oh I love him, I think he's great. He's marvellous.'

Her whole face lit up, and it was then I realized what a good-looking girl she was. As I have mentioned before, I have a certain showy attractiveness myself. I know I am not basically good-looking, and I depend heavily for effect on my skilful use of paints. But I have red hair and green eyes, and with a bold make-up I am very much the sort of woman that men stop to look at in the street. I could see now that Helen was not at all like this. She was small and slight, with a tiny face half-hidden under a heavy weight of dark brown hair. You would pass her by and not look at her, but if you did stop to take a second look you would realize that her features, though small, were exquisitely proportioned, that her skin had a translucent sheen and that her eyes — her eyes were deep and soft and tranquil. I was the one getting all the barman's looks, but I could see at a glance that Edith was much the finer of us. She was such a charming girl too, shy and low spoken, yet with none of the gaucherie and bluster that so often accompany shyness.

But though I was pleased by her good looks and her charm, it was not these that excited me. What excited me was a realization that here was someone to whom I could speak. Right from the beginning, from my remark about Fitzgerald, I think we both were aware that we were instantly communicating. We talked that day, long into the afternoon, and the more we talked the more we found we wanted to say. It was not only that we shared values and views and interests, but there was a recognition, on both our parts I thought, of an inner identification, a oneness. I knew that I would never have to pretend to Edith, that she would always understand what I was trying to say. I knew that a bond and a sympathy had been established between us and that I could look forward with joy to the times that we would talk and laugh and cry together. I had found a friend.

Do women love their husbands, I sometimes wonder? Do I love Anthony? I know that I like him, that I am grateful to him, that I feel the constant desire to protect him. But love? How can you love somebody you are so apart from? We live together comfortably, but so distinctly. Anthony wants it so, although if I told him this he would be incredulous. I have come to realise as I lie in bed at night, or at the first light of dawn, with his supple body, wracked by pleasure, lying in my arms, that Anthony is undergoing his most profound experience. His body shudders, and his isolation is complete. Sometimes I am amazed by the exclusivity of his passion, although I know well that this sort of pleasure is something that you cannot share. I know, for I am no stranger to pleasure myself; I have felt a tingling in the loins, a heat in the bowels.

But I have always kept a weather eye out and asked — is there nothing more? Anthony's capitulation to his body is so complete, and his gratitude to me afterwards so overwhelming, that I know that, for him, this is where we touch, this is where he reaches me. And I am left in the cold outside.

But not once I had met Edith. Anthony should have been grateful to Edith, for with her coming I stopped harrassing him. He didn't have to watch me in the evenings, sitting bleakly in our elegant drawing-room, upsetting his innocent enjoyment of the evening papers. I didn't suddenly snap at him for no reason, or complain of being bored, or depressed, or lonely. Edith became my source of pleasure. Soon we were having lunch together every day, and I would drive her home in the evenings after work. She soon confessed to me that she had been unhappy in the office before she met me, for the other girls were as unwilling to accept her as they had been me, although in both instances, to be fair, I think it was a sensible recognition on the typists' part of our essential difference. We just had nothing to share with them.

For a start, she was older than they were. She had been a third-year philosophy student at the University, she told me. A most successful student, apparently, who had hoped to pursue an academic career. She had been working away quite happily, looking forward to her finals, when one day her mother, who had gone quite innocently in search of matches, had found a packet of contraceptive pills in Edith's handbag. It was not, Edith told me, the implication that she was sleeping with a man or men that had so shocked her parents. It was the deliberateness of the act. Young girls did from time to time fall from grace, and it was wrong and they should be punished accordingly. But that anyone, particularly a daughter whom they had reared so carefully, could arm herself with these pills beforehand — that sort of calculation denoted a wickedness and evil of a far more serious order. She was thrown out of the house that very evening and told never to darken the door again.

'The thing I regret most,' Edith said, 'was hurting them. You cannot expect them to understand, the way they were brought up themselves. It's natural that they'd react like that. But I do love them, and I really didn't want to cause them pain. They'll come round, I'm sure. I'll just have to give them a few months, and then everything will be alright I hope. I'll just have to be a lot more careful. But I do miss them, you know — particularly Mammy.'

I had known Edith about six weeks when she introduced me to Declan. She had mentioned him several times, and I gathered that they intended to get married as soon as Declan qualified. He was an engineering student. What a surprise I got the first time I saw him. I couldn't understand, and never did understand afterwards, how someone of Edith's delicacy and intelligence could fall in love with such a slob. And he *was* a slob, a lumbering six-foot-two, with a red face and a slack mouth and a good-humoured, apparently unlimited amount of self-confidence. The night I met him, he had come round after work to collect Edith, and she asked me to stay and have a drink with them. He took us to a rather draughty and gloomy pub, and having bought our drinks, sat opposite me and fixed me with a disapproving eye.

What,' he asked, 'do you think of the situation in South Africa?'

I later discovered that being a swimming champion all through his school days and most of his college days, Declan had come late to the world of ideas. But not at all abashed by his late start, he was now determined, it appeared, to make up for lost time. I found his zeal rather wearying, I must admit, and I resented the off-hand way he dismissed Edith's comm.-ents. I wondered what would happen when he discovered Women's Lib. With a bit of luck he might offer to liberate Edith by refusing to marry her.

In the meantime I realized that Edith would not take kindly to any criticism I might voice and that I had better be careful to simulate some sort of enthusiasm. So next day when she asked me what I thought, I told her I found him very interesting, and that I'd like them both to come to dinner soon and meet Anthony. We decided on the next night, and I said I'd come and collect them as Declan didn't have a car. I planned my dinner carefully and told Anthony to provide an exceptional claret — it was a special occasion. At these times, I'm pleased to be married to a wine merchant, for Anthony can produce the most miraculous bottles, guaranteed to revive any social disaster. I did want Edith to be happy, to like my home and my dinner and my husband. I didn't want to impress her — I knew anyway that the trappings of wealth would leave her unmoved — but I wanted to offer her something, to share whatever I had with her. I was afraid she might be bored.

But I needn't have worried. The evening was a tremendous success and Anthony and Declan seemed to take to one another straight away. Anthony is a most tolerant man, and cannot understand my own violent reactions towards people. I don't think he notices them very much. Once he has had a good meal and with a decent cigar in his hand, he is prepared to listen to all kinds of nonsense all night long. I was amused that evening at the interest he seemed to be showing in Declan's lengthy monologues, nodding his head intelligently and throwing in a 'Really — how interesting' every now and again. Afterwards he told me he thought Declan a 'rather solemn but quite decent chap'.

I blessed his tolerance that night, for I thought it might provide a solution to a problem I saw looming. I had no interest in being lectured to by Declan, and on the other hand, if I saw as much of Edith as I wanted to, if I could take her to films, concerts, even perhaps on holiday, then I knew Declan would begin to resent me and feel perhaps that I was monopolising Edith. But if I could manage to arrange these foursomes, then Anthony would keep Declan happy, and I would have Edith to myself.

And how happy I was at this prospect. The more I saw of Edith, the more I admired and loved her. She had a quietness and repose about her which I found particularly attractive — I am such a strident person myself. I always look for the limelight and though I have tried to cure myself of this fault, I know I am as bad as ever. But Edith actually preferred to listen. And when she listened, you knew that she was actually considering what you were saying, and not simply waiting for an opportunity to get in herself. I talked a lot to Edith, more, I think, than I have ever talked to anyone in my life. The pleasure I got from our conversation was enormous. The world suddenly seemed to be full of things and people and ideas to discuss. I asked for no other stimulant than the excitement generated by our talk, and I looked forward to our meetings with a sense of exhilaration. I loved to buy things for her too. I have always liked giving people gifts, but through being married to Anthony my sense of pleasure had become dulled. Mind you, I don't think it was Anthony, most men would be the same. You can buy a man only a certain number of shirts, and after that — what is there? But with Edith the possibilities were endless. She dressed quite badly — I don't think she ever thought about the way she looked. But I, who saw all the possibilities of her beauty, felt like a creator when I thought of dressing her. A scarf to bring out the purity of her skin, a chiffon blouse to emphasize that fragile line of her neck — the changes I could make in her appearance! Of course I had to be careful not to offend her, as I knew that one so sensitive might be made to feel uncomfortable by all these gifts. So sometimes I would pretend that I had bought something for myself and it didn't fit and she would be doing me a favour by taking it. Or I would accept a pound for a leather bag which had cost me fifteen, saying that I had picked it up cheaply but that the colour wasn't right.

Creating this new Edith re-awoke all my interest in clothes and make-up. I seemed to have been dressing myself and putting on my face for so long that I felt I could do it in my sleep, and I had some time ago grown bored with myself. Besides, presenting my rather obvious persona to the world was a straightforward task, and the subtleties which I used in dressing Edith would have been lost on me. And as Edith saw her new self emerging, she grew interested too. I wondered how this would affect her attitude towards Declan. As she began to realize what a beautiful girl she was, might she not also realize what a slob Declan was, and get rid of him? Not that I thought very much about Declan any more. He was by now busy preparing for his final examinations and when he did have time to go out with Edith he seemed quite happy for them to come and have dinner with us, or at Anthony's club. Anthony had even interested him in wine, and as they sat sniffing their glasses and delicately tasting, we sat giggling over ours, having quaffed too much of the stuff in a most unconnoisseur-like fashion. Edith and I both agreed that we knew little about wine, but knew what we liked. Sometimes, when Declan was studying, I'd go round to Edith's flat for supper, and we'd get through a bottle of plonk enjoying it just as much as any rare burgundy. This formed a bond between us and gave us a nice comfortable sense of vulgarity, of which Declan would have disapproved for intellectual reasons and Anthony for social.

I was happy. It is a state you have to be in to recognise. Before I met Edith, it had never occurred to me that I was unhappy. I knew that I was bored a lot of the time and often lonely. I felt that something was missing from my life and various well-meaning girl friends had told me from time to time that what I wanted was a baby. Instinctively I knew however that this was not so. I have always rebelled at the idea of becoming a mother; I could never see myself, baby at breast, looking out placidly at the world. Now I knew that my reservations had been right: I would probably have made a very bad mother, and I would not have fulfilled myself. All I needed all that time was a friend. A real friend.

But it seems to be a rule of life that, having achieved a measure of happiness, clouds begin to float across one's Eden. I don't know when things started going wrong with Edith and myself, for my state of happiness had begun to blur my perceptions, and I wasn't as conscious as I should have been of all Edith's reactions. Then little by little I noticed changes in her. She started to make excuses about not coming out to the house with me. When I'd ask her to go to a concert or lecture she'd say no thank you, she was doing something else. She grew irritable too, and would cut me off short when I'd begin to talk about something. Then she took to avoiding me in the office or so it seemed to me, and she started bringing sandwiches in at lunch time, saying that she had no time to go out to lunch as she was doing extra work for Mr Kelly.

When I was certain that I had not been imagining Edith's attitude, when I could no longer fool myself that everything was as it had been, I grew very upset. What upset me most, I think, was that I could not offer an explanation for her behaviour. I knew I was not the most tactful person in the world, but I had felt that Edith and I were so close that there was no need for pretence; and anyway I couldn't remember having said anything so awful that she would stop wanting to see me because of it.

One afternoon I became so worried that I burst into tears in the office. Mr Kelly junior was with me at the time, and I think I frightened the poor man out of his wits, for he told me that I looked tired and to go home at once and not to bother coming in the next day, which was Friday. That week-end I did a lot of thinking. Away from the office I grew calm, and I began to think that things would sort themselves out if I could remain calm. Maybe I had been seeing too much of Edith, and if I left her alone for a while she would probably recover her equilibrium and everything would be alright again.

When I returned to the office, I stuck to my resolution. I remained perfectly friendly towards Edith, but I stopped asking her to come places with me, and I began to have my lunch half-an-hour earlier than the rest of the office. It was so difficult, this calm indifference, but I knew it was the only way. Then one morning as I was taking my coat off, one of the typists rushed into my room.

'Isn't it awful, have you heard?' she said.

'No, what is it, what's happened?'

'Edith Duggan's mother was killed last night. Run over by a bus as she was crossing the road. She died instantly. Edith, the poor thing, went to bits, I believe. They couldn't get her to stop crying.'

God, how awful. I felt quite sick. What must Edith be feeling? I knew she had loved her mother ... and that she should have been killed before they could be reconciled ... The guilt she must be feeling, added to the pain. I must go to her, I knew. I put my coat back on and got her home address from one of the girls, and left without even telling Mr Kelly where I was going.

The house was a shabby semi-detached with a few sad flowers struggling for life in the patch of green outside. A man I took to be Edith's father answered the door. He showed me in to the little front room and there I saw Edith, sitting white-faced and stiff, staring at nothing. She looked up and gave me a wintry smile.

'Edith, what can I say —' I began, but she interrupted me with a shake of her head.

'I know. It's alright really. I understand. It was good of you to come.'

The words sounded so small and distant in that front parlour.

'Oh. Edith, my poor, poor Edith.' I ran towards her and put my arms around her, kissing her, kissing her to comfort her. Suddenly she tore at my arms and flung herself from me. She ran behind the sofa and stood there, trembling.

'Get out of here,' she shouted. 'Leave me alone. Go away you — you monster.'

I tried to say something, but she began to scream some incoherent phrases about the girls in the office and how stupid she'd been and how could I have come there then. I could still hear the screams as I made my way down the path.

She didn't come back to the office. Anthony suggested that she had probably been reconciled with her father and was now staying at home to mind the family. I worried about her, for it seemed to me that the shock of her mother's death must have unhinged her mind. How else could I explain the dreadful things she shouted that day in her front room?

Then about a month later, as I was walking down Grafton Street one afternoon, I saw her coming towards me. She saw me too, and as we drew level I put out my hand. She looked at me, directly into my eyes, with a cold hostility.

'Hello Helen,' she said, and she sounded quite calm. 'I'm glad I've met you like this. You see, I want you to realise that I meant what I said that day. I wasn't hysterical or anything like that. I do not wish to see you ever again.' Then she stepped aside and walked on down towards O'Connell Street.

I felt my stomach heave as she walked away. I felt I could never get home, that I would have to stand there, in Grafton Street, rooted to the spot in horror. I twisted and turned, like an animal in a cage, not wanting to face the fact that Edith's shouted obscenities were the result of no temporary derangement. When I did get home and told Anthony, he refused to discuss it. He said that the only thing to do was to put the whole business out of my mind, forget about it completely. But how could I forget? How can I shrug off the pain and the pleasure, as if it had never happened? I can find no way of doing that, no way of wiping out the profound sense of loss I am left with. You see, we were such good friends, Edith and I. Such good friends.

FRANCES MOLLOY

Women Are the Scourge of the Earth

(For Ruth Hooley)

There's some people will try to put the blame for what happened on to me, but I'm not having that. I don't care what that note said. I don't care what the neighbours say. If they think I give a damn, then they're mistaken. That woman was deranged all her life. She was taking tablets for years from the doctor for her nerves. Feared she was to let the wains out to play in case they got shot. Silly cow, I told her to catch herself on. If anybody wanted to shoot the bloody wains, they could come into the house and do it.

I don't care what any of them try to tell you, I never lifted a finger to her in all the years I put up with her. Never mind what that hussy next door tries to make out. The stories I could tell you about her! You should see the odd assortment of characters that comes and goes there when he's out at his work, the poor bugger. There's no telling who or what fathered half that crowd of cross-eyed brats of hers. I must say, it's always the likes of her that does the talking. I can't imagine what kind of an eegit he is to put up with her. She should be run out of the town. Many's a better woman was tarred and feathered for far less. Shooting is too good for the likes of her.

That note my Missus left, made out that I turned her mother and sisters against her, but unbalanced and all as she was, she was still fly enough not to mention why. Well, I'll tell you why, so you'll not be labouring under any illusions about

202

her. She was carrying on with a fancy man. She thought I would never find out when I was at my work, but a friend of mine spotted the same car parked outside my house on the same day every week and gave me the wink. I soon put a stop to it, I can tell you.

I'm not a mug like your man next door. I kicked his teeth right down his throat and let her ladyship know that I would debollocks the bastard on the spot if he ever came snooking round my house again. I'll not be made a laughing stock of.

Her mother was flaming mad when I told her the way her precious daughter was carrying on. She said she was no daughter of hers and she'd never darken her door the longest day she ever lived. To give the woman her dues, she was as good as her word. She never set foot in my house from that day till this. Every one of her sisters backed me at the time too.

The Missus was more deranged than ever after that, eating nothing but these fool tablets from the doctor. Walking through the house in a stupor half the day, never even bothering to change from her night clothes. She was pining for him. You didn't need to be very bright to see that. All the time she kept crying and lamenting about her mother and sisters and trying to get me to go and explain to them that her fancy man was only a friend. I told her I'd see her in hell first. It was her that had got herself into the fix and it was up to herself to get back out of it. I'm not going to be made a fool of.

Never mind your inquest to establish the cause of death. I'm here to defend my good name. The woman was deranged, that's the long, the tall and the short of it. I lived with her for fifteen years and I'm telling you now, she was never in her proper mind. I don't know what I was thinking about, having anything to do with the likes of her in the first place, when I think of some of the women I could have had my pick of. I could have done a lot better for myself and married a good strapping farmer's daughter with a bit of capital behind her.

Indeed, I'll have you all know, I could have had any woman I wanted just for the asking.

And there's another thing I want to draw your attention to, just when I'm at it. A woman is supposed to obey her husband, is she not? She's supposed to do what he bids her, is she not? Isn't that what the law says? Isn't it wrote in the Bible by the hand of the almighty himself? Well, that woman that you're holding your inquest into never done my bidding in her life. Never once in fifteen years did she do a single thing I told her. For example, I warned her to keep away from that woman next door. I didn't want no wife of mine consorting with her likes. But did she heed me? Like hell she did. My friend seen that trollop in having tea with her ladyship whenever I was out at my work. My blood still boils when I think about it. The likes of that trash sitting gossiping in my house and me out breaking my back to earn the money to entertain her. I soon put a stop to that too. I locked the doors to the house and took the keys with me to work every day for a month and let it be known to the madam next door that if she wanted to get into my house, she could try getting in through the window. That put a stop to her visits. I won't be made a fool of.

And there's something else you ought to know too. She turned them five wains of hers against me. Not one of them has a decent word to say to me now. That wee uppity lying bitch Una, went away and told the doctor yarns behind my back. What do you think of that for respect then? Going away behind my back and in defiance of my orders, bringing doctors round the house to see the mother. That woman would be alive today if she'd seen far fewer doctors. It was all the fool tablets that she got from them that made her fall. That's where she got all her bruises from. I never laid a finger on her in my life.

Una is turned into a right snottery wee brat, and she will need to mind her step. She'll not always have the old granny's skirts to hide behind. Just let her wait till all this fuss dies down. A man has a legal right to his own wains. I'll let her know before I'm through, who her boss is. Who does she think puts the shoes on her feet? Who does she think puts the clothes on her back? Who does she think puts the food in her belly? Who does she think's been paying the rent all these years? The beloved fancy man, uncle Harry?

What do you think of that then, uncle Harry? Uncle Harry, if you don't mind. She brought her dear uncle Harry round to her old granny and poisoned her against me. Me and the mother-in-law had always got on well enough. Mine, I'm not saying she wasn't a terrible old battle-axe, for she was, but as the man says, I didn't have to live with her. Now that woman has known me for more than eighteen years, and still, she's prepared to take the word of a total stranger before mine. What do you think of that for loyalty then? I suppose she thinks she's mixing in high-brow society now because he works in an office and wears pansy clothes.

But you haven't heard the best of it yet, no, not by a long shot. Wait till you hear the story the brave fellow is putting about. He's trying to make out that he met me Missus at a meeting of some daft organisation that's for people who has been let out of the funny-farm. What's its name now? Let me think? It's called "Mental" or something. No, that's not right. And it wasn't called "Insane" either for it started with an M, I'm sure of that now. "Mine", that's what it's called. It's for people that's out of their mines. "Mine", that's what its name is. Didn't I say it began with an M? You see, I was right.

He told the mother-in-law that me Missus was suffering from depression and that's why she joined this daft organisation of freaks. He tries to make out that he was suffering from depression too, and that's how the pair of them met. According to him, they were only friends, and it helped them if they came together for a chat and a cup of tea every week. What do you think of that for invention? Isn't it wild touching, wouldn't you say? They were only friends indeed. I'd say he must have been very hard up for a friend if he had to rely on her.

The old granny is doting now, for didn't she swally the whole story, lock, stock and bloody barrel. You should hear her lamenting about how she should never have doubted for a minute, the virtue of her lily-white daughter. All he called for was a chat and a cup of tea! What does he take me for, a real dodo? That's the kind of story nobody but an old doting woman would fall for.

Depressed, indeed, a quare lot she had to be depressed about, I can tell you, with a mug like me out humping bricks on his back all day long to keep her in style. Carpets in every room that woman had. When I think about it yet, my blood still boils. Me out slaving from early morning till late at night to provide grandeur for her to impress her fancy man with.

I'll tell you this now, she's the last woman I'll ever fork out for. Women, they're all the same, after what they can get out of you. There's only one thing a woman is useful for and that's on the broad of her back. Nobody but a fool would marry a woman for that nowadays. There's plenty of it going free and no mistaking. I'm well rid of her. Women are the scourge of the earth. I've learnt my lesson. Once bitten, twice shy, as the man says.

CLARE BOYLAN

The Stolen Child

Women steal other people's husbands so why shouldn't they steal other people's babies? Mothers leave babies everywhere. They abandon them to foreign students while they go out gallivanting, hand them over for years on end to strangers who stuff them with dead languages and computer science. I knew a woman who left her baby on the bus. She was halfway down Grafton Street when she got this funny feeling and she said, 'Oh, my God, I've left my handbag,' and then with a surge of relief she felt the strap of her bag cutting into her wrist and remembered the baby.

I never wanted to steal another woman's husband. Whatever you might make of a man if you got him first-hand, there's no doing anything once some other woman's been at him, started scraping off the first layer of paint to see what's underneath, then decided she didn't like it and left him like that, all scratchy and patchy.

Babies come unpainted. They have their own smell, like new wood has. They've got no barriers. Mothers go at their offspring the way a man goes at a virgin, no shame or mercy. A woman once told me she used to bite her baby's bum when she changed its nappy. Other women have to stand back, but nature's nature.

Sometimes I dream of babies. Once there were two in a wooden cradle high up on a shelf. They had very small dark faces, like Russian icons, and I climbed on a chair to get at them. Then I saw their parents sitting up in bed, watching me.

I have a dream about a little girl, three or four, who runs behind me, trying to catch up. She says nothing but her hand burrows into mine and her fingers stroke my palm. Now and then I have a baby in my sleep, although I don't remember anything about it. It's handed to me, and I know it's mine, and I just gaze into the opaque blueness of the eye that's like the sky, as if everything and nothing lies behind.

It comes over you like a craving. You stand beside a pram and stare the way a woman on a diet might stare at a bar of chocolate in a shop window. You can't say anything. It's taboo, like cannibalism. Your middle goes hollow and you walk away stiff-legged, as if you have to pee.

Or maybe you don't.

It happened just like that. I'd come out of the supermarket. There were three infants left lying out in strollers. I stopped to put on my headscarf and glanced at the babies the way people do. I don't know what did it, but I think it was the texture. There was this chrysalis look. I was wondering what they felt like. To tell the truth my mouth was watering for a touch. Then one of them turned with jerky movements to look at me. 'Hello,' I said. She stirred in her blankets and blew a tiny bubble. She put out a toe to explore the air. She looked so new, so completely new, that I was mad to have her. It's like when you see some dress in a shop window and you have to have it because you think it will definitely change your life. Her skin was rose soft and I had a terrible urge to touch it. *Plenty of time for that*, I thought, as my foot kicked the brake of the pram.

Mothers don't count their blessings. They complain all the time and they resent women without children, as if they've got away with something. They see you as an alien species. Talk about a woman scorned! And it's not men who scorn you. They simply don't notice you at all. It's other women who treat you like the cat daring to look at the king. They don't care for women like me; they don't trust us.

I was at the bus stop one day and this woman came along
with a toddler by the hand and a baby in a push-car. 'Terrible
day!' I said. She gave me a look as if she was about to ask for a
search warrant and then turned away and commenced a
performance of pulling up hoods and shoving on mittens. She
didn't seem to notice the rain. Soaked to the bone she was, hair
stuck to her head like a bag of worms. She had all this
shopping spilling out of plastic bags and she bent down and
began undoing her parcels, arranging them in the tray that's
underneath the baby's seat, as if to say to me, 'This is our
world. We don't heed your sort.' It was a relief when the bus
came and I could get out of gloating range but still she had to
make herself the centre of attention. She hoisted the toddler
onto the platform and then got up herself, leaving the baby all
alone in the rain to register its despair in an ear-splitting
fashion. 'You've forgotten the baby,' I said, and she gave me a
very dirty look. She lunged outward, seized the handle of the
pram and tried to manhandle it up after her, but it was too
heavy. Sullen as mud, she waded back into the rain. This time
the toddler was abandoned on the bus, its little mouth opened
wide and loud. She unstrapped the baby and sort of flung it up
on the bus. Everyone was looking. Back she clambered, leaned
out again and wrestled the pram on board, as if some sort of
battle to the death was involved. I don't think the woman was
in her right mind. Of course, half the groceries fell out into the
gutter and the baby followed. 'You're going about that all
wrong,' I told her, but she took no notice. The driver then
woke up and said he couldn't take her as he already had one
push-car. Do you think she apologised for keeping everyone
waiting? No! She inflicted a most withering parting glance on
us all, as if we were somehow to blame.

Walking away from the supermarket with someone else's
child, I didn't feel guilty. I was cleansed, absolved of the guilt
of not fitting in. I loved that baby. I felt connected to her by all
the parts that unglamorous single women aren't supposed to

have. I believed we were allies. She seemed to understand that I needed her more than her mother did and I experienced a great well of pity for her helplessness. She could do nothing without me and I would do anything in the world for her. I wheeled the pram out through the car park, not too quickly. Once I even stopped to settle her blankets. Oh, she was the sweetest thing. Several people smiled into the pram. When I gave her a little tickle, she laughed. I believe I have a natural talent as a mother. I look at other women with their kids and think, *She hasn't a clue, she doesn't deserve her blessings.* I notice things. The worst mothers are the ones with too many kids. Just like my mum. They bash them and yell at them and then they give them sweets. Just like this woman I saw watching me from the doorway of the supermarket. She seemed completely surrounded by children. There must have been seven of them. One kid was being belted by another and a third was scuttling out under a car. And she watched me intently with this pinched little face and I knew she was envying me my natural maternal gift. I knew a widow once, used to leave her baby in the dog's basket with the dog when she went out to work.

And all this time, while I was pushing and plotting, where was her mother? She might have been in the newsagent's flipping the pages of a magazine, or in the coffee shop giving herself a moustache of cappuccino, or in the supermarket gazing at bloated purple figs and dreaming of a lover. Mothers, who swear that they would die in an instant for you, are never there when you need them. Luckily, there is frequently someone on hand, as for instance myself, who was now wheeling the poor little thing out of harm's way, and not, if you ask me, before time.

I can't remember ever being so happy. There was a sense of purpose, the feeling of being needed. And, you'll laugh now, but for the first time in my life, looking into that dear little face, I felt that I was understood.

When my mum died I got depressed and they sent me along to see a psychiatrist. He said to me, 'You're young. You have to make a life of your own.'

I was furious. 'Hardly anyone makes a life of their own,' I told him. 'They get their lives made for them.'

He asked me about my social life and I said I went to the pictures once in a while. 'You could put an advertisement in the personal columns,' he advised.

'Advertisement for what?' I said.

'A companion,' he said.

'Just like that?' I must say I thought that was a good one. 'You put an advertisement in the paper and you get a companion?' I pictured a fattish little girl of about ten with long plaits.

'People do,' he promised me. 'Or you could go to an introduction agency.'

'And what sort of thing would you say in this advertisement?'

'You could say you were an attractive woman, early thirties, seeking kind gentleman friend, view to matrimony.'

I was far from pleased. I lashed out at him with my handbag. 'You said a companion. You never said anything about a gentleman friend.'

Well, I make out all right. I get a bit of part-time work and I took up a hobby. I became a shoplifter. Many people are compelled in these straitened times to do things that are outside their moral strictures, but personally I took to shoplifting like a duck to water. It gave me a lift and enabled me to sample a lot of interesting things. The trick is, you pay for the bulky items and put away the small ones, settle out for the sliced pan, pinch the kiwi fruit, proffer for the potatoes, stow the sun-dried tomatoes, fork out for the firelighters, filch the fillet steaks. In this way I added a lot of variety to my diet — lumpfish roe and anchovies and spiced olives and smoked salmon, although I also accumulated a lot of sliced loaves. 'Use your imagination,' I told myself. 'There are other bulky items besides sliced bread.'

Perhaps it was the pack of nappies in my trolley that did it. I hate waste. It also just happened that the first sympathetic face I saw that day (in years, in point of fact) was that tiny baby left outside in her pram to wave her toe around in the cold air, so I took her too.

I thought I'd call her Vera. It sounded like the name of a person who'd been around for a long time, or as if I'd called her after my mother. When I got home the first thing I did was pick her up. Oh, she felt just lovely, like nothing at all. I went over to the mirror to see what kind of pair we made. We looked a picture. She took years off my age.

Vera was looking around in a vaguely disgruntled way, as if she could smell burning. *Milk*, I thought. *She wants milk*. I kept her balanced on my arm while I warmed up some milk. It was a nice feeling, although inconvenient, like smoking in the bath. I had to carry her back with the saucepan, and a spoon, and a dishtowel for a bib. Natural mothers don't have to ferret around with saucepans and spoons. They have everything to hand, inside their slip. I tried to feed her off a spoon but she blew at it instead of sucking. There was milk in my hair and on my cardigan and quite a lot of it went on the sofa, which is a kingfisher pattern, blue on cream. After a while she pushed the cup away and her face folded up as if she was going to cry. 'Oh, sorry, sweetheart,' I said. 'Who's a stupid mummy?' She needed her nappy changed.

To tell the truth I had been looking forward to this. Women complain about the plain duties of motherhood but to me she was like a present that was waiting to be unwrapped. I carried her back downstairs and filled a basin with warm water and put a lot of towels over my arm, not forgetting a sponge and all the other bits and pieces. I was proud of myself. I almost wished there was someone to see.

By now Vera was a bit uneasy (perhaps I should have played some music, like women do to babies in the womb, but I don't know much about music). I took off the little pink jacket, the pink romper suit that was like a hot-water bottle cover and then started to unwrap the nappy. A jet of water shot up into my eye. Now that was not nice, Vera! I rubbed my eye and began again, removing all that soggy padding. Then I slammed it shut. The child looked gratified and started to chortle. Incredulous, I peeled the swaddling back once more. My jaw hung off its hinges. Growing out of the bottom of its belly was a wicked little ruddy horn. I found myself looking at balls as big as pomegranates and when I could tear my eyes away from them I had to look into his eye, a man's eye, already calculating and bargaining.

It was a boy. Who the hell wants a boy?

'Hypocrite!' I said to him. 'Going round with that nice little face!'

Imagine the nerve of the mother, dressing him up in pink, palming him off as a girl! Imagine, I could still be taken in by a man.

Now the problem with helping yourself to things, as opposed to coming by them lawfully, is that you have no redress. You have to take what you get. On the other hand, as a general rule, this makes you less particular. I decided to play it cool. 'The thing is, Vera,' (I would change his name later. The shock was too great to adjust all at once) 'I always thought of babies as female. It simply never occurred to me that they came in the potential rapist mode. There are some points in your favour. You do look very nice with all your clothes on. On the other hand, I can't take to your sort as a species.'

I was pleased with that. I thought it moderate and rational.

Vera was looking at me in the strangest way, with a sweet, intent, intelligent look. Clearly he was concentrating. There is something to be said for the intelligent male. Maybe he and I would get along. 'The keynote,' I told him, 'is compromise.

213

We'll have to give each other plenty of space.' Vera smiled. He looked relieved. It was a weight off my mind too. Then I got this smell. It dawned on me with horror the reason for his concentration. 'No!' I moaned. 'My mother's Sanderson!' I swooped on him and swagged him without looking too closely. His blue eyes no longer seemed opaque and new but very old and angry. He opened his mouth and began to bawl. Have you ever known a man who could compromise?

All that afternoon I gazed in wonder on the child who had melted my innards and compelled me to crime. Within the space of half an hour he had been transformed. His face took on the scalded red of a baboon's behind and he bellowed like a bull. His eyes were brilliant chips of ice behind a wall of boiling water. I got the feeling it wasn't even personal. It was just what he did whenever he thought of it. I changed his nappy and bounced him on my knee until his brains must have scrambled. I tried making him a mush of bread and milk and sugar, which he scarcely touched yet still managed to return in great quantity over my shoulder. With rattling hands I strapped him into the stroller and took him for a walk. Out of doors the noise became a metallic booming. People glared at me and crows fell off their perches in the trees. Everything seemed distorted by the sound. I began to feel quite mad. My legs appeared to be melting and when I looked at the sky the clouds had a fizzing, dangerous look. I wanted to lie flat out on the pavement. You can't when you're a mother. Your life's not your own any more. I realised now that the mother and child unit is not the one I imagined but a different kind, in which she exists to keep him alive and he exists to keep her awake.

I hadn't had a cup of tea all day, or a pee. When I got home there was a note on the door. It was from my landlord, asking if I had a child concealed on the premises. I cackled glumly at the concept of concealing Vera and staggered in to turn on the news. By now he would be reported missing. His distraught mother would come on the telly begging whoever had him to please let her have her baby back. It was difficult to hear above the infant shrieks but I could see Bill Clinton's flashing teeth and bodies in the streets in Bosnia and men in suits at EEC summits. I watched until the weatherman had been and gone. Vera and I wept in unison. Was this what they meant by bonding?

Sometime in the night the crying stopped. The crimson faded from my fledgling's cheek and he subsided into rosy sleep. There was a cessation of the hostile shouts and banging on walls from neighbours. I sat over him and stroked his little fluff of hair and his cheek that was like the inside of a flower, and then I must have fallen asleep for I dreamed I was being ripped apart by slash hooks, but I woke up and it was his barking cries slicing through my nerves.

He beamed like a daisy as I wheeled him back to the supermarket. Daylight lapped around me like a great, dangerous, glittering sea. After twenty-four hours I had entered a twilight zone and was both light-headed and depressed so that tears slid down my face as I marvelled at the endurance of the tiny creature in my custody, the dazzling scope of his language of demand, which ranged from heart-rending mews to the kind of frenzied sawing sounds that might have emanated from the corpse stores of Dr Frankenstein. He had broken me. My nerve was gone and even my bones felt loose. I had to concentrate, in the way a drunk does, on setting my feet in front of one another. I parked him carefully outside the supermarket and even did some shopping, snivelling a bit as I tucked away a little tin of white crab meat for comfort. Then I was free. I urged my trembling limbs to haste.

'You've forgotten your baby!' a woman cried out.

My boneless feet tried an ineffectual scarper and the wheels of the push-car squealed in their pursuant haste. Upset by the crisis, the baby began to yell.

There are women who abandon babies in phone booths and lavatories and on the steps of churches but these are stealthy babies, silently complicit in their own desertion. Vera was like a burglar alarm in reverse. Wherever I set him, he went off. I tried cafés, cinemas, police stations. Once, I placed him in a wastepaper basket and he seemed to like that for there wasn't a peep, but when I was scurrying off down the street I remembered that vandals sometimes set fire to refuse bins so I ran back and fished him out. At the end of the day we went home and watched the news in tears. There was no report of a baby missing. Vera's cries seemed to have been slung like paint around the walls so that even in his rare sleeping moments they remained violent and vivid and neighbours still hammered on the walls. Everyone blamed me. It was like being harnessed to a madman. It reminded me of something I had read, how in Victorian almshouses sane paupers were frequently chained to the bed with dangerous lunatics.

By the third day I could think of nothing but rest. Sleep became a fixation. I was weeping and twitching and creeping on hands and knees. I wanted to lie down somewhere dark and peaceful where the glaring cave of my baby's mouth could no more pierce me with its proclamations. Then, with relief, I remembered the river bed. No one would find me there. Feverishly I dressed the child and wheeled him to the bridge. We made our farewells and I was about to hop into oblivion when I noticed a glove left on one of the spikes that ornament the metalwork, so that whoever had lost it would spot it right away. It was an inspiration, a sign from God. I lifted Vera onto the broad ledge of the bridge, hooked his little jumper onto a spike and left him there, peering quite serenely into the water.

At the end of the bridge I turned and looked back. The baby had gone. Someone had taken him. It seemed eerily quiet without that little soul to puncture the ozone with his lungs. It dawned on me just why it was so quiet. There wasn't a someone. There hadn't been anyone since I left him.

'Vera!' I raced back. There was no sound, and when I gazed into the water it offered back a crumpled portrait of the sky.

The child was drowned. This person of dramatic beauty and argument, who could command such audience, make a strange woman fall in love with him and weave out of his infrequent sleep a whole tent of tranquillity, had vanished off the face of the earth.

'Vera!' I mourned.

After a few seconds he surfaced. At first he bounced into view and bobbed in the water, waiting to get waterlogged and go down again. Then he reached out an arm as if there were an object in the murky tide he wanted. He didn't seem frightened. There was something leisurely about that outstretched hand, the fingers slightly curled, like a woman reaching for a cake. He began to show signs of excitement. His little legs started to kick. Out went another arm towards an unseen goal. 'What are you doing?' I peered down into the filthy water in which no other living thing was. Up came the arm again, grabbed the water and withdrew. His feet kicked in delight. His whole body exulted. I moved along the wall, following his progress, trying to see what he saw that made him rejoice. Then I realised; he was swimming. The day was still and there was very little current. He gained confidence with every stroke. 'Wait!' I kept pace along the wall. He took no notice. He had commenced his new life as a fish. 'Wait!' For me, I meant. I wanted to tell him he was wonderful, that I would forgive him all his primary impulses for in that well-defended casement was a creature capable of new beginnings. He did not strike out at the water as adults do but used his curled hands as scoops, his rounded body as a floating ball. He was merely walking on the water like Jesus, or crawling since he had not yet learned to walk. As he bobbed past once again I threw off my raincoat and jumped into the water. I stretched a hand to meet the little waving fingers. A puckish gust strained to sweep him off. At last our hands connected. The simple touch of human warmth restored him to the human world. He began to holler.

I would like to report a happy ending, but then, too, I have always hankered after a sighting of a hog upon the wing. It took five more days to locate the mother. She told the police she had had a lovely holiday at the sea and thought their Clint was being safely looked after by a friend who, like everyone else in her life, had let her down. As it transpired, I knew the mother and she knew me, although we did not refresh our acquaintance. It was the pinched little woman with all the kids who had watched me wheel her child away. She said their Clint was a bawler, she hadn't had a wink since the day he was born. She had no money, couldn't even afford new clothes for the baby and had to dress him in their Darryl's cast-offs. She was only human but she was a mother and would take him back if someone gave her a Walkman to shut out the noise.

No one bothered with me, the heroine of the hour — a woman who had risked her life to save a drowning child. It was the mother who drew the limelight. Thousands of women sent sound equipment. She became a sort of cult figure and mothers everywhere could be seen smiling under earphones, just as a year or two ago they used to waddle about in track-suits. Valium sales slumped as women fondly gazed on infant jaws locked apart in soundless wrath. It was left to us, the childless, to suffer the curdling howls of the nation's unheeded innocents.

Some women don't deserve to have children.

LUCILE REDMOND

Love

The train came out of the tunnel into the light. He sat and looked out. The door at the end of the corridor opened.

"Coley!" He started at his name, but the woman was looking back, calling for a child.

The windows, webbed by marks, carried past the scenes. The seat of hard flock smoothed and sprang back under his fingers. The tabby pattern paled in a trail and regained itself, springing slowly upwards. The woman with the child had taken a seat. She tossed her hair to the side, a smile taking her eyes and her mouth. Her eyes were long, her hair was curled. Watching her he felt a pain of memory pull, and found he was holding his heart. She was so like, though her face was quite different, prettier. She had a high, singing voice. The train ticked over the points. The window showed a country church with old people bundling towards it, and briefly he heard the muffled sound of bells, then the picture was wiped out as the train rushed forward into another dark tunnel.

Coming out, the train slowed, and pulled into the station, brushed by trees. The slam of doors came towards the carriage as the weary stationmaster walked down. "Have you got the staff," he could hear the man calling, and the answer "Aye, but the lever's jammed above," ringing faintly from the nose of the train. The woman jumped on the seat and pulled open the window above her head to talk through it, calling to the stationmaster.

"It's getting warmer."

"It is, and the trees are staying in blossom. Your sister's waiting for you above, miss. She came for the early train, but you weren't on it."

She made some reply, some proverb, and Coley felt suddenly that he could not bear his sadness. She would go on, now, and he would never see her again.

Coley took up his plumber's bag and moved past her. He stepped on to the platform, the woman and the stationmaster watching.

The evening was warm. A bird swung on the telephone line looped between the station house and the gate. He left his ticket on the gate and went into the town. The doors of houses were open, showing halls papered with flowers, carpeted, cats sleeping, caged birds preening in silence. The bough of a tree dipped as he passed, sprinkling him with air. In a high window he saw a girl practising on a trumpet.

He walked along the roads to the hill, passing through the main street with its street lamps and the young estate to the old roads where prosperity thinned. He climbed the hill to her house, and passed it and turned down the lane. At the back of the shed a box had been fitted for testing one of the facilities. The path was broken around it. A convolvulus had grown there, but the white and purple flowers and the leaves were crushed.

He put his foot to the box and leaped to the roof of the garage, swinging the plumber's bag, the tools inside it clanking as it swung. On the roof of the shed a child had left a paper crane.

The kitchen window was open. He felt for the key but it was gone. He put down the bag and moved back. The return sloped, the black cat slept under the hall window on the tar of the roof.

The door was locked, to his surprise. He tried it again, and walked around, looking at the windows. On the second floor a window was open at the top. The roof of the kitchen return was almost below it, and the stems of the clematis covered the house. He climbed up.

A nest of birds was under the window, between the stems of the vine. The birds were fledged and seemed ready to fly. He took one in his palm, resting with an elbow crooked in the vine. It sat in his hand, shivering, and opened its beak for food. He held it to his cheek to feel the heat and hear it cheep, and tipped it back into the hot nest. Its hatch mates set up a hungry yell, and the parent, flying near, gave sharp alarm.

He put his arm through the window and turned the latch, and stepped through. The house was quiet. There was a thump and the cat Henry marched out, clumping along. She gave a chirrup and ran up to the head of the stairs that led down to the kitchen. She stood up, folding her front paws, and rubbed her whiskers against the jamb.

He sat on the top step of the three on the turn and looked out. Outside, the garden with its scented flowers and its herbs was alive, a tree shook its head of leaves in the wind. In the dusty window he saw his own reflection: a thin man with toffee-red hair that hung close to his head in streaks. His skin was fine and thin on his cheeks, hanging close on the bone, freckled, his high nose and round eyes and long mouth giving his face a country look. He sat and watched the tossing tree and his face in the window.

Then: he came sometimes out to this hilly country, a well-off layabout coming into the lives of working people and leaving again. He liked to come in winter, when the hills ran with water, and the sky looked like it was beaded with condensation, the drizzle comforted him. In the hotel he asked whether there was anywhere he could stay a little longer.

They looked at each other and sent him to the house of the singer. He walked up to the highest point in the small town, and there was her house where they had told him, a tree, a garden, heavy, sweet, peppery smells, uncurtained windows, a kitten hunting a butterfly, the doors all open. He walked in and called. There was no answer, but then the door of the kitchen opened and a tall girl came out, wiping hair back off her face with her arm, her hands covered in batter.

"They said you might have a room to let. My name's Coley."

"A room to let? Well, I suppose I could. Are you here for long?" She was putting on the kettle and he was in her long kitchen, looking at the warm flowers, the prints, the open window with the key hung in the frame. She was a strongly built girl with a pale, square face and narrowly set grey eyes, narrow and long in the lid but far apart in her face. There was something a little distant and quiet about her face, her unmoving eyes. She invited him to sit at the wooden table, moving up a green bottle full of scented flowers and making tea for him and her.

"They said you were a singer."

"Yes," she said, "I sing a little for the visitors, in the old style, but really I'm thinking of changing, I like cooking better, I'd like better to be a cook."

He noticed then that she had piles of meat and fish and vegetables on an oilskin on the table and she was slicing them with a small crescent of steel set on a wooden blade.

"What's that?"

"It's an ulu, an Eskimo knife, my brother sent it from Alaska, he's working there on the oil line. They use it for fleshing and skinning — they used to be made of slate, then they made them out of bone."

"It's a dangerous weapon." He handed back to her.

"The only dangerous weapon is here." She pointed to her head and laughed.

"Or here," he said, pointing to his heart.

Outside the kitten still played, making a rush at the tree then running away, its tail fluffed out, through the grass. A blossom fell on it and it leaped in the air. A little wind passed over the grass and the blades bowed in unison.

"This is a spider." She held up a small crab. "You know, in the sea there are the same animals." She swept the blade across the shelled tails of a pile of shrimps. "There are spiders, the crabs, and flies, the shrimps, and mammals, and there are birds, fish are birds in the water, flying just as much as the birds do in the air. Saurian, arachnid, mammal, flowers and grasses. Can you lay the table? I have four people coming, so with you and me that's six places."

Afterwards he went to bed, dazzled with the journey and the talk of these country people who kept glancing at him with wondering looks. In his dreams he was clinking glasses and knives and talking, and he woke in the night with a cry. The cat was by his head, purring and washing its claws. Through the open window he could hear the light rain.

A few days later he said to her as she got ready to go out, "Would you sleep with a fellow?" She went red and ignored him. He followed her down to the hotel and went to drink in the bar. An hour or so later he heard the voice of a woman singing from the writing room, a high, sweet sound. She was singing in the traditional method of the local performers. He asked his neighbour what the song was about.

"It's a lament sung by a young married woman," his neighbour said, a thickset farming man with big red hands, "she's singing about her husband who's been lost in a boating accident. She's saying to his mother, 'I wish that I was in the boat with him when it happened, Mrs Reilly, and I would have gone away with him then.' She's a nice, sonsy little singer, isn't she so?"

He turned away and listened to her high, sweet voice.

When she came home he had tea made for her in the kitchen. She sat with him and drank it, stirring in sugar before she refilled the cup each time. Faintly, from the room upstairs he could hear her two finches calling in their big cage, like a computer touched by quiet fingers.

Asleep in the bed he felt her cold body creep in and curl against him. She cried out, "Coley, Coley," calling his name as if he was far away from her, and fiercely wound her arms around his neck. He laid his cheek on her throat and felt the tapping of her pulse. He knew that it was dangerous to be this happy.

In the corner the kitten played with the wings of a butterfly. The room was square. Outside the vine trembled at the window. A hook of moon glittered through a pane. A fly buzzed and stopped and buzzed again in a web.

The kitchen was different. She had painted it white. There was a white box of growing herbs by the sink. Over the window a plastic basket hung, with a cloud of blue flowers.

The tenderiser hung by the sink, its zinc points glinted in the light, it hung by its wooden handle, its heavy head hung down. The ulu sat in its stand, its crescent blade sharp. The steel cooking chopsticks stood in a cup beside the cooker, near the great-bladed meat knife. Coley lifted the lid of the pot on the hob. Liver and lights. He scattered porridge into the pot. "Now, puss."

She kept her letters in the dresser drawer. "Why am I full of deprivation, desolation?" He swept the ulu blade across the paper, cutting the sandwich of thoughts.

Memories, walking with her, a man shouting, "Get up the yard, you dirt-bird," a box at his feet with the word "harmful" stencilled on it.

There was a distant sense of space in the empty house. He walked from room to room. It was different in ways, in other ways familiar and sad. A serious girl: serious in her work, a serious waitress, a serious singer, now a serious cook with ulu and hand mincer and meat cleaver. The flinch of shame cooled him, his balance gone.

It was a quiet house, set behind its tree on a hill, on a quiet road. The kitchen faced south, the light bathed it. The room with the books was back to back with the kitchen, divided by a tall empty passageway. The cat Henry lay on a chair. She had been called Henry before it became clear she was female. Another of the mistakes that haunt the inefficient in life. Coley rubbed her stomach and waited for the deep purr. She flexed her claws and looked up at him, her pointed pupils slowly opening into an ellipse.

The treads of the stairs were unwaxed wood, the living tongue of light showing through the grain. The edges of the treads were chiselled out by hand and sanded, and the mark of steps dipped the centre of the tread. "Have my steps been here," he thought.

Outside, the summer gave a sigh of warm air. The leaves of the vine that clung to the house trembled again as the warm air passed them by. A nesting bird clasped in its net of crooked stems chirped. Its throaty cluck broke into the room, a bubble of sound scattering.

The room was painted white, with a bed, a metal trunk and a lamp in it. She liked emptiness in rooms as well as in people. The bed had a cover of a woven rug. The wood of the floor was scraped and waxed. He sat on the bed. How quiet it was.

His heart slowed. In the silence he felt the house flex around him. Sounds revealed themselves. Through the walls of Rose's room he heard the finches keep up a quiet meeping. How many times do they utter in a lifespan? A thud joined in their rhythm.

He stood and walked out of the room, touching his fingers to the pimpled wall. Her door was closed. Beyond, the birds played in their big cage. He opened the door to the light. He stood on the grain of the wood, the veins of the tree. The cat Henry was below the window. Her furred lips drew back and a crackling cry of passion broke from her as she crept towards the birds.

The white female was caressing the male, standing close beside him and drawing out the feathers on his head. He leaned his head from her, his eyes closed. She bounced to a higher perch and back, combed out a feather again.

Henry crept across the floor, her black ears pointing forward. The brown finch sprang on to the cage's floor. The white finch flew to the roof and tore a piece of lettuce, watching Coley with one eye, then with the other. Coley sat on the bed, on the white sheet. The brown finch picked up a seed and cracked it in his beak. The white finch cheeped.

The cat whipped a long black arm through the bars and spread her claws on the brown finch. He crouched and screamed, his cries piercing the air. Outside the wild birds took up the cry. It rippled out from the house. Far away, Coley heard a human child cry in fear. The cat lifted her claws. The bird crouched at the side of the cage, its wings spread. It stopped crying as it felt the claws lift, and slowly turned its head, beak gaping, to meet the gaze of the cat. When it saw the cat's open eyes fixed on it, the bird's mouth opened wider, but it made no sound, panting a little with despair. It shrugged its wings, trying to fly. It turned its head to look up to its mate.

She had kept on playing, at first, but when the male began to cry she stopped and watched him with an anxious look. Now, when he turned his open beak up to her, she turned her head, watching again from one eye and then the other the scene below. She was a full three feet above and to the side of the cat and the other bird. How far can birds see, he thought. The birds were silent.

She flew suddenly down, screaming and flapping her wings, and again the birds in the garden cried out. She flew in and out, screaming, and the cat gave a start and slapped her claws down flat at left and right trying to reach her. The cat gave a long, moaning growl.

The male leaped when he heard his mate's voice, and began to creep away under the cat's slamming claws, his movements stiff. Then the white bird came too close and the cat had it. She pulled her claws inwards to the bars with the bird crying, and her nose disappeared in the feathers at the bird's throat. The cat guzzled quietly for a moment and dropped the bird's body. Her eyes returned to her first victim, who stood, now, the membrane of his eyes closing up as he looked towards the cat. The bird and the cat knew what was to follow. The game began.

Coley stood. A light breeze came in the window and ruffled his face, and he saw in his mind the flat red hair lift from his thin skin and fall again. He ran his hands down his jacket, over his ribs. He went out and sat at the top of the stairs and watched the front path through the fanlight of the door.

As the evening drew in the path slowly darkened. For an hour the faint calls of children came in, then the evening traffic passed. The birds flew in, in the centre of town the main street's lights came on.

It was two when she came back. Coley's watch said two. He passed his thumb and middle finger down the sides of his forearm until they touched the watch. She came up the path with a man. The grey moonlight lit them, and the trees as they turned the undersides of their leaves up in the touching breeze.

They stood facing each other. He could see them in black outline, and the underside of Rose's broad chin lit by her white shirt. She was tapping her toe on the ground, her toe pointed to make a straight line to her knee. Her hands were hooked in the back of her belt, throwing the points of her shoulders forwards. The man leaned forwards and their lips took each other for a sad moment. The soft flesh parted and pulled away and she turned and stalked towards the door. Coley smiled. The man put his hand on her shoulder and she turned her head back towards him.

From the night came the hoarse call of an owl, drifting through the dark. All of the leaves of the tree by the gate turned at the same time, showing their pale backs, and turned again so the tree was covered in darkness.

She opened the door.

"Coley?"

She stood in the doorway.

"Coley?" She came forward, looking to the dark kitchen, to the quiet room beside her.

He stood and came down the first two treads.

"Coley? You said you wouldn't come again." Her frown drew down her straight brows. She ducked her hand under the hair falling over her face and flipped it back. She went into the kitchen and started to fill the kettle. He picked up the ulu. "Put that down, Coley."

He sat down and watched her plug the black lead into the kettle.

"We'll make some tea, and then you have to go, Coley." He stood again and walked to the end of the kitchen. He tapped the ulu handle on the cutting board.

The kitchen showed her profession. A line of wooden cupboards was topped by a marble working surface, a double sink and a hob with four rings. Two ovens were set at the end of the row, at waist to eye level. Bunches of herbs and ropes of garlic and onions hung from the walls and shelves. Glass jars and plastic drums full of grains and pulses sat against the walls on the shelves.

Her face was short, and her pale skin gave off a light that was quite joyful, though the slant of her narrow eyes was puzzled and sad. Between the deep lids of her eyes and her thick straight brows the high curve of skin gave her face a childish look, so that it always seemed as if she was looking up into your face.

Now as she frowned over the preparations for tea she gave her crooked little finger a rap against the surface where she worked.

"Don't be angry."

"I am angry. How did you get in here?"

"I got in. This is my place."

Her strong legs carried her to the cupboard and flexed at the knees to drop her to a crouch. She moved her feet apart, right foot forward, left foot back, and gave a gentle stamp with the front foot, balancing her trunk above the heel of her left foot. She rolled back her sleeve from her left hand, and with her left hand took the delft caddy of tea from the low press.

"You've no key."

"This is mine. Who was that man?"

She stood up, the muscles in her thighs and calves shortening to push, her knees flexed straight, her head ducked forward and settled back on to her neck as she settled her balance into her elbows to start the impetus of the walk across the floor.

"Coley, we have not been together now for six years. It's all long since over. You have your own life. Why can't you go and live it?"

She pivoted on her right foot to swing the caddy on to the marble surface with her left hand. With her right hand she dipped the scoop into the caddy of tea.

"I am not as real as you." Coley stood, holding the ulu.

"Coley, it is over. It has been over for a long time. I do not love you. I don't want you here. I want to live the way I live, and it doesn't include you. I know you're lonely, I know you're sad, but I've nothing to give you. If I could call out the feeling for you I would, but it's just not there. I don't love you, Coley."

As the ulu swept down from her shoulder to her waist it laid open her white shirt and her skin together, so that the lips of material parted to show a confiding glimpse of red. She jerked in surprise and the tea sprayed up from the spoon. The fine spots clung to her shirt where the blood was beginning to scatter. She looked down and frowned and looked up, meeting his eyes for the first time. He swept the blade towards her again and she held out the palms of her hands. He felt the crisp snap as the blade passed through a finger. She gave a quick cry and held her left hand in her right, the thin red blood coming through the cradle of her fingers. She pressed her hand to her breast. One finger hung backwards across the wrist. She pressed it to her breast with her right hand.

"Don't be silly, Coley," she said. They were the last words she spoke.

He felt his tongue flicking from his lips. He raised the crescent knife again and she ducked to the floor, holding her bent arms above her. Tears dropped from her wide eyes. Her mouth was open. He cut her across the face, from her brow across the cheek, the knife skipping across the socket of her eye.

Henry mewed. He looked back at the cat washing her paw by the door.

She had stood, on almost bent legs, and was creeping to the door. He ran at her and she staggered, opened the door and swung from it. She ran, on stiff, bent legs, down the path. She was still holding her hand across her cut breast with her right hand, the hand that had left blood on the door. He got the folded cloth from the sink and wiped it. He ran lightly after her.

The night was cool and fresh, the air lightly scented with summer flowers. He heard the quiet step of the rain. She was ahead, but her muscles were pulling her legs slowly as she ran to the lighted street.

The pool she had brought him to when she kissed him first was quite still. He stopped to watch it. A ripple moved across the centre, the elastic frog, stretching and bunching in the night.

In the town's street there were cars parked, but nobody was walking. It was too late. She was knocking on doors, then running, holding one hand in the other against her breast. As he caught her up, John Moriarty, the town policeman, opened the door, a quiet man with a grey-streaked red beard and light blue eyes.

"Ah now. What's going on, now?" He closed the door behind him. She fell on her knees and clasped her arm around his leg. "Rose, Rose go home like a good woman."

Coley pushed him against the wall. He hit him with the hand that held the ulu. His nose broke. "What do you think you're doing?" But the policeman's voice was trembling.

"If you try to do anything about it you'll be quite cut up about it."

"It's a domestic dispute. I can't interfere in a domestic dispute."

Coley swung his arm with all his weight behind it and swept the ulu across Rose's shoulder. The shirt parted under the slice and showed the meat under the glossy skin. Briefly, he saw a secret, the pearly tendons and the shining blue bones they pull, then the hole filled with welling blood. Her face turned and she looked down. She opened her mouth wide and howled, her eyes staring to the bowl of the night, then she jumped up and fled. She ran up the street that she had staggered down, and up past the pool and by the river and the railway tracks. She ran up the path to the house and kicked the door behind her.

He ran to the back and swarmed up the vine on to the return and through the window. She was coming up the stairs, holding the meat tenderiser in her hand, the wooden hammer with its zinc points swinging as she came. He jumped sideways into her room. She came in after him. He looked towards the cage and her glance followed his. Feathers were all around on the floor, one headless bird lay on the floor of the cage, the other had been half pulled through the bars.

Her hand came up to her mouth and left a stain of blood on it. She took her hand away and looked at it. He took the tenderiser from her and struck the first blow to her forehead. It sank in with a crunch. It left the marks of points in a square in the sunken hole. She stood still, her feet firm on the ground, and looked at him. The pupils of her eyes ebbed away into points.

He hit again, on her temple, and the zinc sank in again. She fell. He hit her, and her arms and legs sprang outwards. Her hands stretched at length, clawed and grasped at the floor. He hit again. He hit again. The head's bag of skin was not broken, but the bone was mushing inside, and a drop of blood ran from her ear.

He put the head of the hammer to her ear and turned the head. His heart was beating fast. Her eyes were open, flushed with black, the thin grey iris a rim around the black, but she looked far beyond him to something he did not know.

He went down to the kitchen and turned the kettle off. There was tea everywhere. He got the red hearthbrush and dustpan and brushed some of it up. The water she had put in the teapot to heat it was cold. He threw it out and heated it again, swirling it around, feeling the warmth on his palm, and tossed the water into the sink. Henry the cat came in and smelled the tenderiser and put out her pink tongue to lick it. He swept her away. He put three spoons of tea in the pot and left it for the leaves to uncurl, knocking the kettle on for a second while he got out two mugs and spoons. She still had the cup she'd bought him with the spray of wild roses painted on it. He took out her two-eared pewter sugar bowl. She must take sugar still. He knocked the kettle off and poured water into the pot, starting with the spout low and bringing it up till it was tumbling from two feet above. He sugared her cup, put out biscuits and poured both cups. He put milk in both and took his to the table and started to drink. His left hand hung between his knees.

The kitchen was quiet. The only sound was his breath as his ribs pulled it in and out, puffing with scarcely any noise from his nose. Slugs crossed the long expanse of the concrete floor on their tracks, and raised their faces to drink from the cat's dish.

The kitchen had two doors. There was a series of low wooden cupboards, waxed, not painted, and a series of high

232

shelves. The concrete floor was painted grey. The walls were white. A window stretched across the wall between the shelves, above the sink, looking out on to the garden. The table had two chairs pushed to it. He drank his tea, but her cup went cold. He poured it away and filled another cup for her.

MARY DORCEY

The Husband

They made love then once more because she was leaving him. Sunlight came through the tall, Georgian window. It shone on the blue walls, the yellow paintwork, warming her pale, blonde hair, the white curve of her closed eyelids. He gripped her hands, their fingers interlocked, his feet braced against the wooden footboard. He would have liked to break her from the mould of her body; from its set, delicate lines. His mouth at her shoulder, his eyes were hidden, and he was glad to have his back turned on the room; from the bare dressing table stripped of her belongings, and the suitcase open beside the wardrobe.

Outside other people were going to mass. He heard a bell toll in the distance. A man's voice drifted up: 'I'll see you at O'Brien's later', then the slam of a car door and the clatter of a woman's spiked heels hurrying on the pavement. All the usual sounds of Sunday morning rising distinct and separate for the first time in the silence between them. She lay beneath him passive, magnanimous, as though she were granting him a favour, out of pity or gratitude because she had seen that he was not, after all, going to make it difficult for her at the end. He moved inside her body, conscious only of the sudden escape of his breath, no longer caring what she felt, what motive possessed her. He was tired of thinking, tired of the labour of anticipating her thoughts and concealing his own.

He knew that she was looking past him, over his shoulder towards the window, to the sunlight and noise of the street. He touched a strand of her hair where it lay along the pillow. She did not turn. A tremor passed through his limbs. He felt the sweat grow cold on his back. He rolled off her and lay still, staring at the ceiling where small flakes of whitewash peeled from the moulded corners. The sun had discovered a spider's web above the door; like a square of grey lace, its diamond pattern swayed in a draught from the stairs. He wondered how it had survived the winter and why it was he had not noticed it before. Exhaustion seeped through his flesh bringing a sensation of calm. Now that it was over at last he was glad, now that there was nothing more to be done. He had tried everything and failed. He had lived ten years in the space of one; altered himself by the hour to suit her and she had told him it made no difference, that it was useless, whatever he did, because it had nothing to do with him personally, with individual failing. He could not accept that, could not resign himself to being a mere cog in someone else's political theory. He had done all that he knew to persuade, to understand her. He had been by turns argumentative, patient, skeptical, conciliatory. The night when, finally, she had told him it was over he had wept in her arms, pleaded with her, vulnerable as any woman, and she had remained indifferent, patronising even, seeing only the male he could not cease to be. They said they wanted emotion, honesty, self-exposure but when they got it, they despised you for it. Once, and once only, he had allowed the rage in him to break free; let loose the cold fury that had been festering in his gut since the start of it. She had come home late on Lisa's birthday, and when she told him where she had been, blatantly, flaunting it, he had struck her across the face, harder than he had intended so that a fleck of blood showed on her lip. She had wiped it off with the back of her hand, staring at him, a look of shock and covert satisfaction in her eyes. He knew then in his shame and regret that he had given her the excuse she had been waiting for.

He looked at her now, at the hard pale arch of her cheekbone. He waited for her to say something, but she kept silent and he could not let himself speak the only words that were in his mind. She would see them as weakness. Instead, he heard himself say her name, 'Martina', not wanting to, but finding it form on his lips from force of habit: a sound — a collection of syllables that had once held absolute meaning, and now meant nothing or too much, composed as it was of so many conflicting memories.

She reached a hand past his face to the breakfast cup that stood on the bedside table. A dark, puckered skin had formed on the coffee's surface but she drank it anyway. 'What?' she said without looking at him. He felt that she was preparing her next move, searching for a phrase or gesture that would carry her painlessly out of his bed and from their flat. But when she did speak again there was no attempt at prevarication or tact. 'I need to shower,' she said bluntly, 'can you let me out?' She swung her legs over the side of the bed, pushing back the patterned sheet, and stood up. He watched her walk across the room away from him. A small mark like a circle of chalk dust gleamed on the muscle of her thigh — his seed dried on her skin. The scent and taste of him would be all through her. She would wash meticulously every inch of her body to remove it. He heard her close the bathroom door behind her and, a moment later, the hiss and splatter of water breaking on the shower curtain. Only a few weeks ago she would have run a bath for them both and he would have carried Lisa in to sit between their knees. Yesterday afternoon he had brought Lisa over to her mother's house. Martina had said she thought it was best if Lisa stayed there for a couple of weeks until they could come to some arrangement. Some arrangement! For Lisa! He knew then how crazed she was. Of course, it was an act — a pretence of consideration and fairmindedness, wanting it to appear that she might even debate the merits of leaving their daughter with him. But he knew what she planned, all too well.

THE HUSBAND

He had a vision of himself calling over to Leinster Road on a Saturday afternoon, standing on the front step ringing the bell. She would come to the door and hold it open, staring at him blankly as if he were a stranger while Lisa ran to greet him. Would Helen be there too with that smug, tight, little smile on her mouth? Would they bring him in to the kitchen and make tea and small talk while Lisa got ready, or would they have found some excuse to have her out for the day? He knew every possible permutation, he had seen them all a dozen times on television and Seventies' movies, but he never thought he might be expected to live out these banalities himself. His snort of laughter startled him. He could not remember when he had last laughed aloud. But who would not at the idea that the mother of his child could imagine this cosy Hollywood scenario might become reality? When she had first mentioned it, dropping it casually as a vague suggestion, he had forced himself to hold back the derision that rose to his tongue. He would say nothing. Why should he? Let her learn the hard way. They would all say it for him soon enough: his parents, her mother. The instant they discovered the truth, who and what she had left him for, they would snatch Lisa from her as ruthlessly as they would from quicksand. They would not be shackled by any qualms of conscience. They would have none of his need to show fine feeling. It was extraordinary that she did not seem to realise this herself; unthinkable that she might, and not allow it to influence her.

She came back into the room, her legs bare beneath a shaggy red sweater. The sweater he had bought her for Christmas. Her nipples protruded like two small stones from under the loose wool. She opened the wardrobe and took out a pair of blue jeans and a grey corduroy skirt. He saw that she was on the point of asking him which he preferred. She stood in the unconsciously childish pose she assumed whenever she had a decision to make, however trivial: her feet apart, her head tilted to one side. He lay on his back watching her, his hands interlaced between the pillow and his head. He could feel the blood pulsing behind his ears but he kept his face impassive. She was studying her image in the mirror, eyes wide with anxious vanity. At last she dropped the jeans into the open case and began to pull on the skirt. Why — was that what Helen would have chosen? What kind of look did she go for? Elegant, sexy, casual? But then they were not into looks — oh no, it was all on a higher, spiritual plane. Or was it? What did she admire in her anyway? Was it the same qualities as he, or something quite different, something hidden from him? Was she turned on by some reflection of herself or by some opposite trait, something lacking in her own character? He could not begin to guess. He knew so little about this woman Martina was abandoning him for. He had left it too late to pay her any real attention. He had been struck by her the first night, he had to admit, meeting her in O'Brien's after that conference. He liked her body; the long legs and broad shoulders and something attractive in the sultry line of her mouth. A woman he might have wanted himself in other circumstances. If he had not been told immediately that she was a lesbian. Not that he would have guessed it — at least not at first glance. She was too good-looking for that. But it did not take long to see the coldness in her, the chip on the shoulder, the arrogant, belligerent way she stood at the bar and asked him what he wanted to drink. But then she had every reason for disdain, had she not? She must have known already that his wife was in love with her. It had taken him a year to reach the same conclusion.

She sat on the bed to pull on her stockings, one leg crossed over the other. He heard her breathing — quick little breaths through her mouth. She was nervous then. He stared at the round bone of her ankle as she drew the red mesh over it. He followed her hands as they moved up the length of her calf. Her body was so intimately known to him he felt he might have cast the flesh on her bones with his own fingers. He saw

the stretch marks above her hip. She had lost weight this
winter. She looked well, but he preferred her as she used to be
— voluptuous: the plump roundness of her belly and arms. He
thought of all the days and nights of pleasure that they had had
together. She certainly could not complain that he had not
appreciated her. He would always be grateful for what he had
discovered with her. He would forget none of it. But would
she! Oh no. She pretended to have forgotten already. She
talked now as though she had been playing an elaborate game
all these years — going through ritual actions to please him.
When he refused to let her away with that kind of nonsense,
the deliberate erasure of their past, and forced her to
acknowledge the depth of passion there had been between
them, she said, yes, she did not deny that they had had good
times in bed but it had very little to do with him. He had
laughed in her face. And who was it to do with then? Who else
could take credit for it? She did not dare to answer, but even as
he asked the question he knew the sort of thing she would
come out with. One of Helen's profundities — that straight
women use men as instruments, that they make love to
themselves through a man's eyes, stimulate themselves with his
desire and flattery, but that it is their own sensuality they get
off on. He knew every version of their theories by now.

'Would you like some more coffee?' she asked him when
she had finished dressing. She was never so hurried that she
could go without coffee. He shook his head and she walked
out of the room pulling a leather belt through the loops of her
skirt. He listened to her light footsteps on the stairs. After a
moment he heard her lift the mugs from their hooks on the
wall. He heard her fill the percolator with water, place it on the
gas stove and, after a while, its rising heart beat as the coffee
bubbled through the metal filter. He hung onto each sound,
rooting himself in the routine of it, wanting to hide in the
pictures they evoked. So long as he could hear her moving

about in the kitchen below him, busy with all her familiar actions, it seemed that nothing much could be wrong.

Not that he believed that she would really go through with it. Not all the way. Once it dawned on her finally that indulging this whim would mean giving up Lisa, she would have to come to her senses. Yes, she would be back soon enough with her tail between her legs. He had only to wait. But he would not let her see that he knew this. It would only put her back up — bring out all her woman's pride and obstinacy. He must tread carefully. Follow silently along this crazy pavement she had laid, step by step, until she reached the precipice. And when she was forced back, he would be there, waiting.

If only he had been more cautious from the beginning. If only he had taken it seriously, recognised the danger in time, it would never have reached this stage. But how could he have? How could any normal man have seen it as any more than a joke? He had felt no jealousy at all at the start. She had known it and been incensed. She had accused him of typical male complacency. She had expected scenes, that was evident, wanted them, had tried to goad him into them. But for weeks he had refused to react with anything more threatening than good-humoured sarcasm. He remembered the night she first confessed that Helen and she had become lovers: the anxious, guilty face, expecting God knows what extremes of wrath, and yet underneath it there had been a look of quiet triumph. He had had to keep himself from laughing. He was taken by surprise, undoubtedly, though he should not have been with the way they had been going on — never out of each other's company, the all-night talks and the heroine worship. But frankly he would not have thought Martina was up to it. Oh, she might flirt with the idea of turning on a woman but to commit herself was another thing. She was too fundamentally healthy, and too fond of the admiration of men. Besides, knowing how passionate she was, he could not believe she would settle for the caresses of a woman.

Gradually his amusement had given way to curiosity, a pleasurable stirring of erotic interest. Two women in bed together after all — there was something undeniably exciting in the idea. He had tried to get her to share it with him, to make it something they could both enjoy but, out of embarrassment, or some misplaced sense of loyalty, she had refused. He said to tease her, to draw her out a little, that he would not have picked Helen for the whip and jackboots type. What did he mean by that, she had demanded menacingly. And when he explained that as, obviously, she herself could not be cast as the butch, Helen was the only remaining candidate, she had flown at him, castigating his prejudice and condescension. Clearly it was not a topic amenable to humour! She told him that all that role playing was a creation of men's fantasies. Dominance and submission were models the women had consigned to the rubbish heap. It was all equality and mutual respect in this brave new world. So where did the excitement, the romance, come in, he wanted to ask. If they had dispensed with all the traditional props what was left? But he knew better than to say anything. They were so stiff with analysis and theory the lot of them it was impossible to get a straight-forward answer. Sometimes he had even wondered if they were really lesbians at all. Apart from the fact that they looked perfectly normal, there seemed something overdone about it. It seemed like a public posture, an attitude struck to provoke men — out of spite or envy. Certainly they flaunted the whole business unnecessarily, getting into fights in the street or in pubs because they insisted on their right to self-expression and that the rest of the world should adapt to them. He had even seen one of them at a conference sporting a badge on her lapel that read, 'How dare you presume I'm heterosexual.' Why on earth should anyone presume otherwise unless she was proud of resembling a male impersonator?

And so every time he had attempted to discuss it rationally they had ended by quarrelling. She condemned him of every macho fault in the book and sulked for hours, but afterwards they made it all up in bed. As long as she responded in the old manner, he knew he had not much to worry about. He had even fancied that it might improve their sex life — add a touch of the unknown. He had watched closely to see if any new needs or tastes might creep into her lovemaking.

It was not until the night she had come home in tears that he was forced to re-think his position.

She had arrived in, half drunk at midnight after one of their interminable meetings, and raced straight up to bed without so much as greeting him or going in to kiss Lisa goodnight. He had followed her up, and when he tried to get in beside her to comfort her, she had become hysterical, screamed at him to leave her alone, to keep his hands away from her. It was hours before he managed to calm her down and get the whole story out of her. It seemed that Helen had told her that evening in the pub that she wanted to end the relationship. He was astonished. He had always taken it for granted that Martina would be the first to tire. He was even insulted on her behalf. He soothed and placated her, stroking her hair and murmuring soft words the way he would with Lisa. He told her not to be a fool, that she was far too beautiful to be cast aside by Helen, that she must be the best thing that had ever happened to her. She was sobbing uncontrollably, but she stopped long enough to abuse him when he said that. At last she had fallen asleep in his arms, but for the first time he had stayed awake after her. He had to admit that her hysteria had got to him. He could see then it had become some kind of obsession. Up to then he had imagined it was basically a schoolgirl crush, the sort of thing most girls worked out in their teens. But women were so sentimental. He remembered a student of his saying years ago that men had friendships, women had affairs. He knew exactly what he meant. You had only to watch them, perfectly average housewives sitting in cafes or restaurants together, gazing into each other's eyes in a way that would have embarrassed the most besotted man, the confiding tones they used, the smiles of flattery and sympathy flitting between them, the intimate gestures, touching each other's hand, the little pats and caresses, exasperating waiters while they fought over the right to treat one another.

He had imagined that lesbian lovemaking would have some of this piquant quality. He saw it as gently caressive — tender and solicitous. He began to have fantasies about Martina and Helen together. He allowed himself delicious images of their tentative, childish sensuality. When he and Martina were fucking he had often fantasised lately that Helen was there too, both women exciting each other and then turning to him at the ultimate moment, competing for him. He had thought it was just a matter of time before something of the sort came about. It had not once occurred to him in all that while that they would continue to exclude him, to cut him out mentally and physically, to insist on their self-sufficiency and absorption. Not even that night lying sleepless beside her while she snored, as she always did after too many pints. It did not register with him finally until the afternoon he came home unexpectedly from work and heard them together.

There was no illusion after that, no innocence or humour. He knew it for what it was. Weeks passed before he could rid his mind of the horror of it; it haunted his sleep and fuelled his days with a seething, putrid anger. He saw that he had been seduced, mocked, cheated, systematically, cold-bloodedly by assumptions she had worked carefully to foster; defrauded and betrayed. He had stood at the bottom of the stairs — his stairs — in his own house and listened to them. He could hear it from the hall. He listened transfixed, a heaving in his stomach, until the din from the room above rose to a wail. He had covered his ears. Tender and solicitous had he said? More like cats in heat! As he went out of the house, slamming the door after him, he thought he heard them laughing. Bitches — bloody, fucking bitches! He had made it as far as the pub and ordered whiskey. He sat drinking it, glass after glass, grasping the bowl so hard he might have snapped it in two. He was astounded by the force of rage unleashed in him. He would have liked to put his hands around her bare throat and squeeze it until he'd wrung that noise out of it.

Somehow he had managed to get a grip of himself. He had had enough sense to drink himself stupid, too stupid to do anything about it that night. He had slept on the floor in the sitting room and when he woke at noon she had already left for the day. He was glad. He was not going to humiliate himself by fighting for her over a woman. He was still convinced that it was a temporary delirium, an infection that, left to run its course, would sweat itself out. He had only to wait, to play it cool, to think and to watch until the fever broke.

She came back into the room carrying two mugs of coffee. She set one down beside him giving a little nervous smile. She had forgotten he had said he did not want any.

'Are you getting up?' she asked as she took her dressing gown from the back of the door, 'there's some bread in the oven — will you remember to take it out?'

Jesus! How typical of her to bake bread the morning she was leaving. The dough had been left as usual, of course, to rise overnight and she could not bring herself to waste it. Typical of her sublime insensitivity! He had always been baffled by this trait in her, this attention, in no matter what crisis, to the everyday details of life and this compulsion to make little gestures of practical concern. Was it another trick of hers to forestall criticism? Or did she really have some power to rise above her own and other people's emotions? But most likely it was just straightforward, old fashioned guilt.

'Fuck the bread,' he said and instantly regretted it. She would be in all the more hurry now to leave. She went to the wardrobe and began to lift down her clothes, laying them in the suitcase. He watched her hands as they expertly folded blouses, jerseys, jeans, studying every movement so that he

244

would be able to recapture it precisely when she was gone. It was impossible to believe that he would not be able to watch her like this the next day and the day after. That was what hurt the most. The thought that he would lose the sight of her, just that. That he would no longer look on while she dressed or undressed, prepared a meal, read a book or played with Lisa. Every movement of her body familiar to him, so graceful, so completely feminine. He felt that if he could be allowed to watch her through glass, without speaking, like a child gazing through a shop window, he could have been content. He would not dare express it, needless to say. She would have sneered at him. Objectification she would call it. 'A woman's body is all that ever matters to any one of you, isn't it?' And he would not argue because the thing he really prized would be even less flattering to her — her vulnerability, her need to confide, to ask his advice in every small moment of self-doubt, to share all her secret fears. God how they had talked! Hours of it. At least she could never claim that he had not listened. And in the end he had learned to need it almost as much as she did. To chat in the inconsequential way she had, curled together in bed, sitting over a glass of wine till the small hours, drawing out all the trivia of personal existence: the dark, hidden things that bonded you forever to the one person who would hear them from you. Was that a ploy too? a conscious one? or merely female instinct? to tie him to her by a gradual process of self-exposure so that he could not disentangle himself, even now when he had to, because there was no longer any private place left in him, nowhere to hide from her glance, nowhere that she could not seek out and name the hurt in him. This was what had prompted her, an hour earlier, on waking, to make love with him: this instinct for vulnerability that drew her, like a bee to honey, unerringly to need and pain: this feminine lust to console; so that she had made one last generous offering — handing over her body as she might a towel to someone bleeding. And he had taken it, idiot that he was; accepted gratefully — little fawning lap-dog that she had made of him.

She was sitting at the dressing table brushing her hair with slow, attentive strokes, drawing the brush each time from the crown of her head to the tips of her hair where it lay along her shoulder. Was she deliberately making no show of haste, pretending to be doing everything as normal? It seemed to him there must be something he could say; something an outsider would think of immediately. He searched his mind, but nothing came to him but the one question that had persisted in him for days: 'Why are you doing this? I don't understand why you're doing this.' She opened a bottle of cologne and dabbed it lightly on her wrists and neck. She always took particular care preparing herself to meet Helen. Helen, who herself wore some heavy French scent that clung to everything she touched, that was carried home in Martina's hair and clothing after every one of their sessions. But that was perfectly acceptable and politically correct. Adorning themselves for each other — make-up, perfume, eyebrow plucking, exchanging clothes — all these feminine tricks took on new meaning because neither of them was a man. Helen did not need to flatter, she did not need to patronise or idolise, she did not need to conquer or submit, and her desire would never be exploitative because she was a woman dealing with a woman! Neither of them had institutionalised power behind them. This was the logic he had been taught all that winter. They told one another these faery stories sitting round at their meetings. Everything that had ever gone wrong for any one of them, once discussed in their consciousness-raising groups, could be chalked up as a consequence of male domination. And while they sat about indoctrinating each other with this schoolgirl pap, sounding off on radio and television, composing joint letters to the press, he had stayed at home three nights a week to mind Lisa, clean the house, cook meals, and read his way through the bundles of books she brought home: sentimental novels and half-baked political theses that she had insisted he must look at if he was to claim any understanding at all. And at the finish of it, when he had exhausted himself to satisfy her caprices, she said that he had lost his spontaneity, that their relationship had become stilted, sterile and self-conscious. With Helen, needless to say, all was otherwise — effortless and instinctive. God, he could not wait for their little idyll to meet the adult world, the world of electricity bills, dirty dishes and child minding, and see how far their new roles got them! But he had one pleasure in store before then, a consolation prize he had been saving himself. As soon as she was safely out of the house, he would make a bonfire of them — burn every one — every goddamn book with the word woman on its cover!

She fastened the brown leather suitcase, leaving open the lock on the right hand that had broken the summer two years ago when they had come back from Morocco laden down with blankets and caftans. She carried it across the room, trying to lift it clear of the floor, but it was too heavy for her and dragged along the boards. She went out the door and he heard it knocking on each step as she walked down the stairs. He listened. She was doing something in the kitchen but he could not tell what. There followed a protracted silence. It hit him suddenly that she might try to get out of the flat, leave him and go without saying anything at all. He jumped out of bed, grabbed his trousers from the chair and pulled them on, his fingers so clumsy with haste he caught his hair in the zip. Fuck her! When he rooted under the bed for his shoes, she heard and called up: 'Don't bother getting dressed, I'll take the bus.' She did not think he was going to get the car out and drive her over there surely? He took a shirt from the floor and pulled it on over his head as he took the stairs to the kitchen two at a time. She was standing by the stove holding a cup of coffee. This endless coffee drinking of hers, cups all over the house, little white rings marked on every stick of furniture. At least he would not have that to put up with any longer.

'There's some in the pot if you want it,' she said. He could see the percolator was almost full, the smell of it would be all over the flat now, and the smell of the bloody bread in the oven, for hours after she was gone.

'Didn't you make any tea?'

'No,' she said and gave one of her sidelong, maddening looks of apology as though it was some major oversight, 'but there's water in the kettle.'

'Thanks,' he said, 'I won't bother.'

He was leaning his buttocks against the table, his feet planted wide apart, his hands in his pockets. He looked relaxed and in control at least. He was good at that — years of being on stage before a class of students. He wondered if Helen would come to meet her at the bus stop, or was she going to have to lug the suitcase alone all the way up Leinster Road? He wondered how they would greet each other. With triumph or nervousness? Might there be a sense of anti-climax about it now that she had finally committed herself after so much stalling? Would she tell Helen that she had made love with him before leaving? Would she be ashamed of it and say nothing? But probably Helen would take it for granted as an insignificant gesture to male pride, the necessary price of freedom. And suddenly he wished that he had not been so restrained with her, so much the considerate, respectful friend she had trained him to be. He wished that he had taken his last opportunity and used her body as any other man would have — driven the pleasure out of it until she had screamed as he had heard her that day, in his bed, with her woman lover. He should have forced her to remember him as something more than the tiresome child she thought she had to pacify.

She went to the sink and began to rinse the breakfast things under the tap.

'Leave them,' he said, 'I'll do them,' the words coming out of him too quickly. He was losing his cool. She put the cup down and dried her hands on the tea towel. He struggled to think of something to say. He would have to find something. His mind seethed with ridiculous nervous comments. He tried to pick out a phrase that would sound normal and yet succeed in gaining her attention, in arresting this current of meaningless actions that was sweeping between them. And surely there must be something she wanted to say to him? She was not going to walk out and leave him as if she was off to the pictures? She took her raincoat from the bannister and put it on, but did not fasten it. The belt trailed on one side. She lifted up the suitcase and carried it into the hallway. He followed her. When she opened the door, he saw that it was raining. A gust of wind caught her hair, blowing it into her eyes. He wanted to say, 'Fasten your coat — you're going to get cold.' But he did not and he heard himself ask instead:

'Where can I ring you?' He had not intended that, he knew the answer. He had the phone number by heart.

She held open the door with one hand and set down the case. She stared down at his shoes and then past him along the length of the hallway. Two days ago he had started to sand and stain the floorboards. She looked as if she was estimating how much work remained to be done.

'Don't ring this weekend. We're going away for a while.'

He felt a flash of white heat pass in front of his brain and a popping sound like a light bulb exploding. He felt dizzy and his eyes for a moment seemed to cloud over. Then he realised what had happened. A flood of blind terror had swept through him, unmanning him, because she had said something totally unexpected — something he had not planned for. He repeated the words carefully hoping she would deny them, make sense of them.

'You're going away for a while?'

'Yes.'

'Where to for Godsake?' he almost shrieked.

'Down the country for a bit — to friends.'

He stared at her blankly, his lips trembling, and then the words came out that he had been holding back all morning:

'For how long? When will you be back?'

He could have asked it at any time, he had been on the verge of it a dozen times and had managed to repress it because he had to keep to his resolve not to let her see that he knew what all this was about — a drama, a show of defiance and autonomy. He could not let her guess that he knew full well she would be back. Somewhere in her heart she must recognise that no one would ever care for her as much as he did. No one could appreciate her more, or make more allowances for her. She could not throw away ten years of his life for this — to score a political point — for a theory — for a woman! But he had not said it, all morning. It was too ridiculous — it dignified the thing even to mention it. And now she had tricked him into it, cheated him.

'When will you be back?' he had asked.

'I'll be away for a week, I suppose. You can ring the flat on Monday.'

The rain was blowing into her face, her lips were white. She leaned forward. He felt her hand on his sleeve. He felt the pressure of her ring through the cloth of his shirt. She kissed him on the forehead. Her lips were soft, her breath warm on his skin. He hated her then. He hated her body, her woman's flesh that was still caressive and yielding when the heart inside it was shut like a trap against him.

'Goodbye,' she said. She lifted the case and closed the door after her.

He went back into the kitchen. But not to the window. He did not want to see her walking down the road. He did not want to see her legs in their scarlet stockings, and the raincoat blown back from her skirt. He did not want to see her dragging the stupid case, to see it banging against her knees as she carried it along the street. So he stood in the kitchen that smelled of coffee and bread baking. He stood over the warmth of the stove, his head lowered, his hands clenched in his pockets, his eyes shut.

She would be back anyhow — in a week's time. She had admitted that now. 'In a week,' she had said, 'ring me on Monday.' He would not think about it until then. He would not let himself react to any more of these theatrics. It was absurd, the whole business. She had gone to the country, she was visiting friends. He would not worry about her. He would not think about her at all, until she came back.

ANNE DEVLIN

Five Notes after a Visit

Monday 9 January 1984

I begin to write.

The first note:

'You were born in Belfast?' The security man at the airport said.

'Yes.'

'What is the purpose of your visit there?'

To be with my lover. Well, I didn't say that.

I had written 'research' on the card he was holding in his hand. I remind him of this.

'I would like *you* to answer the questions,' he says.

'I am doing research.'

'Who is your employer?'

'Self.' I stick to my answers on the card.

'Oh! The idle rich,' he says.

'I live on a grant.'

I might have expected this. It happens every time I cross the water. But I will never get used to it.

'Who is paying for your ticket?'

'I am.'

'What a pity.' He smiles. 'And what have you been doing in England all this time?'

'Living.' Trying.

'There was a bomb in Oxford Street yesterday. Some of your countrymen.'

FIVE NOTES AFTER A VISIT

Two feet away some passengers with English accents are saying goodbye to their relatives. A small boy holding his mother's hand is smiling. Two feet between the British and the Irish in the airport lounge; I return the child's smile. Two feet and seven hundred years.

'He's a small man doing a small job!' Stewart says, when he meets me at the other side. 'Forget about him.' I won't. 'Now don't be cross with me. But you could save yourself a lot of trouble if you'd only write British under nationality.'

'I think —' I start to say, but don't finish: next time I'll write 'don't know'.

I come back like a visitor. I always do. And I'm treated like one. On the Black Mountain road from the airport it is getting dark, when the taxi driver says:

'Do you see that orange glow down there? Just beyond the motorway?'

'Yes.'

'Those are the lights of the 'Kesh.'

Like a football stadium to the uninitiated.

'And just up there ahead of us,' he points to a crown of white lights on Divis ridge. 'That's the police observatory station. That's where they keep the computer.'

'Is it?'

'I had to do a run up there once. But I never got past the gates.'

We plunge down Hannastown Hill in the dark towards the lights of a large housing estate.

If I don't speak in this taxi, perhaps he'll think I'm English.

'What road is this?' Stewart asks, as we pass my parents' house. His father is a shipyard worker.

SINN FEIN IS THE POLITICAL WING OF
THE PROVISIONAL IRA

is painted on the gable.

CUTTING THE NIGHT IN TWO

WESTMINSTER IS THE POLITICAL WING OF
THE BRITISH ARMY

'This is Andersonstown,' the taxi driver says.

There is barbed wire on the flower beds in my father's garden. A foot patrol trampled his crocuses last spring. Tomorrow I'll go and tell them I've come home. But not yet. Stewart isn't keen.

'They won't approve of me,' he says. 'I've been married once before. They'll persuade you to go back to England.'

'They won't!' I insist. But I have the same old fear. His first wife lives in East Belfast.

Tuesday 10 January 1984

The second note:

I am looking at the bus that will take me to my mother. Through the gates I can see the others waiting too. I hear myself say: 'Mother, I've come back!'; and I hear her ask me, 'Why?'

I have let him lure me from my undug basement garden in an English town; one egg in the fridge and the dregs of milk; my solitude wrapped around me like a blanket for those six years until he came — and presented me with the only kind of miracle I ever really believed in.

I hear her ask me, 'Why?'

I remember the summer months, our breakfasts at lunch time in my garden, our evening meals on the raft, my bed. When term began again, he said: 'I've got a job in Belfast. Will you come and live with me?'

'Oh, I can't go back,' I said. 'I can't — live without you,' I tell him at the airport when I arrive.

I hear her ask me why?

My house is empty and the blinds are down. The letters slip into the hall unseen. The tanks will still turn on to the Whiteladies Road out of the Territorial Army Barracks and past the BBC. And the black cab driver will drive someone else from the station. 'Where to?' Blackboy Hill.

A For Sale notice stands in the uncut grass ...

I hear her ask me why? I turn away from the stop.

Wednesday 1 February 1984

I have not kept an account of the days in between because I am too tired after work to write. And anyway I go to bed with him at night.

The third note:

It is the third day of the third week of my visit. I am working in the library.

'On the 1st of January 1957 the Bishop of Down and Conner's Relief Fund for Hungarian Refugees amounted to £19,375 0s 6d. Further contributions in a daily newspaper for that morning include: Sleamish Dancing Club, £5; Bon Secours Convent, Falls Road, £10; The John Boscoe Society for the Prevention of Communism, £25; A sinner. Anonymous —'

'Love?'

'£5. Three months later, in April of the same year, the Lord Mayor of Belfast welcomed the first 500 refugees. It was the only issue on which the people of Belfast East and West agreed.'

'Love.'

He is standing at my table.

'Oh, I'm sorry, I didn't see you.'

'Love. My wife's just rung. I'll have to go and see her. She was crying on the phone. She wants to discuss us getting back together. If only you knew how angry this makes me!'

'Will you tell her about me?'

Below the library window, voices reach me from the street. The students are assembling for a march. They shoulder a black coffin: RIP EDUCATION is chalked in on the side.

Maggie. Maggie. Maggie.

Out! Out! Out!

Police in bullet-proof jackets flank the thin demonstration through the square. The wind tosses the voices back and forth; I catch only an odd phrase here and there: 'Our comrades in England ... The trade union movement in this country ...'

'We have to keep a low profile for a while,' he said.

'And don't answer the phone in case it's her.'

When I was young I think, watching the demonstration pass, I must have been without fear. I make a resolution: I will go there after dark.

Thursday 2 February 1984

The Feast of the Purification. And James Joyce's birthday.

I always remember it.

This is the fourth note:

He is scraping barnacles off the mussels when I come back after midnight. 'Where were you?' he asks.

'I went to see my mother.'

'How was it?'

'She asked the usual questions. Did I still go to Mass? She said she'd pray for me.'

'Did you tell her about me?'

'I talked about my research: The Flight of the Hungarian Refugees to Belfast in '57. Can't think why. She said when I was leaving: keep your business to yourself. She was talking about you.'

'My wife cried when I told her. She thinks it's a phase I'm going through — and I'll get over it.'

There are pink and red carnations in a jug on the table, the man-next-door's music is coming through the walls. A trumpet. Beethoven. I'm getting good at that.

'He's obsessive,' Stewart says. 'He's played that piece since ten o'clock.' At the table I make a mistake: I push my soup away, I'm not as hungry as I thought.

'Go back! Go back to England, then! You said you could live with me!'

'I am trying.'

When I wake the smell of garlic reaches me from the bottom of the stairs. It was the mussel soup he lifted off the table. 'Go back! Go back to England! You're not anybody's prisoner!'

'I am trying!'

Mussel shells, garlic, onion, tomato paste, tomatoes and some wine, he threw into the kitchen. But the garlic hangs over everything this morning; and the phone is ringing in a room downstairs.

In some places, he said last night, amid the broken crockery, before a marriage they smash the dishes, they break the plates to frighten off the ghosts. Perhaps this is necessary after all.

When he wakes, I whisper: 'Love, I'll stay.'

'I've found you again,' he says.

The phone is still ringing in a room downstairs. It is 2.30 in the afternoon.

'Send your Fenian girlfriend back where she belongs, or we'll give her the works and then you!'

He is staring at the clock.

'I wonder how they knew?' he says.

'The estate agent has been writing to me from England. It was too much trouble to explain the difficulty of it. The postman would notice a Catholic name in this street. The sorters in the Post Office, too. Or maybe it was the man collecting for the football pools —'

'Football pools?'

'The other night a man came to the door, he asked me to pick four teams or eight, I can't remember now. Then he asked me to sign it.'

'You should have given my name.'

'I did. But I don't know anything about football. And I think I gave myself away when —'

'What?'

'I picked Liverpool! Or it could have happened at the launderette when I left the washing in. They asked: "What name?" And I forgot. Or it could have been the taxi I got last night from here to —'

'I suppose they would have found out some time.'

He is sitting on the bed.

'Could it have been — your wife?'

He looks hurt: 'I never told her that!' he says. 'I suppose they would have found out some time. I think I'd better call the police.'

I get up quickly: 'Do you mind if I get dressed and bathe and make the bed before you do?'

'Why?'

'Because they'll come round and look at everything.'

I am packing a large suitcase in the attic where we sleep when he comes upstairs.

'The police say that anyone who really meant a threat wouldn't ring you up beforehand. They're not coming round.'

'Listen. I want you to take me to the airport. And I want you to pack a bag as well.'

'I'm teaching tomorrow,' he says. 'Please leave something behind, love. That black dress of yours. The one I like you in.'

It is still hanging in the wardrobe. I leave my scent in the bathroom and on his pillow.

'It's just so that I know you'll come back.'

At 3.40 we are ready to leave the house. The street is empty when we open the door. The curtains are drawn.

'We're a bit late,' he tells the driver. 'Can you get us to the airport in half an hour?'

In the car he kisses me and says: 'No one has ever held my hand so tightly before.'

'What will you do?' I ask, as I'm getting on the plane.

'I'll have to give three months' notice.'

'Do it.'

'Teaching jobs are hard to come by,' he says, looking around.

'Whatever this place is — it's my home.'

5.45. Heathrow. Without him I walk from the plane. Who are they watching now? Him or me? Suddenly, a man steps out in front of me. Oh, Jesus!

'Have you any means of identification? What is the purpose of your visit ...?'

Friday 3 February 1984

The fifth note:

A bell is ringing. I go cautiously to the door. I have slept with all the lights on. I see a man through the glass. He is wearing a combat jacket. This is England, I remind myself. The milkman is smiling at me.

'I saw your lights,' he says.

I tell him I've come back and will he please leave one pint every other day.

He tells me his son's in Northern Ireland in the Army.

'No jobs,' he shouts, walking down the path. 'Were you on holiday?'

'No. I was working.'

The bottles clink in the crate.

'It's well for some.'

He is angry, I begin to think, because I do not drive a milk-float.

I am shopping again for one. At closing time I go out to the supermarket. It is just getting dark. There are two hundred people gathered in the road outside the shopping precinct. A busker is playing a love song. The police are turning away at the entrance the ones who haven't noticed.

'What is it?' I ask a young woman who is waiting at a stop.

'A bomb scare. It's the third one this week.'

I should think before I speak.

'There were fourteen people killed in London, in a bomb in a store.'

I am hoping she hasn't noticed. Some of your countrymen?

Then she says:

'Doesn't matter what nationality you are, dear, we all suffer the same.'

The busker is playing a love song. I am shopping again for one.

Noday. Nodate 1984

I keep myself awake all night so I am ready when they come.

MARILYN McLAUGHLIN

Bridie Birdie

I wasn't to speak to Bridie Birdie any more than I needed to, Mother said, Bridie was a bad influence, Bridie had a dark soul. Don't make a friend of her. It would do you no good.

Bridie Birdie lived alone in the little house at the end of the back lane. It was a tiny house, white with a pointy roof, and a little garden of cabbages and spuds beside it. Bridie had her own door through the old high wall, to let her out onto the old road. She kept it always locked and bolted. You wouldn't know from the road that the little house was there, except for the smoke from the chimney.

Sometimes when Daddy took me for a walk and we were caught by the rain on the way back, we'd make a run for Bridie Birdie's gateway in the wall. He'd bang on it and holler. I'd stand all hunch-shouldered in the rain, waiting for the sound of the bolt being pulled back. Bridie Birdie was always slow to open her door, but we'd forgive her at the thought of the shelter we'd get, once inside her little house. And I loved her house.

There were pines let grow tall all around it, so that even before you got into the house, you were already out of the rain and the wind — standing on a carpet of old pine needles while Bridie Birdie rumbled the bolt back into its catch. She locked everything. In her mind burglars were sneaking through every open door, and climbing over walls no matter how high. She had had Daddy set broken glass in a layer of cement all along the top of the high wall beside her house and garden. She must surely have felt safe enough.

'You'll catch your death from the rain,' she'd say and shush us on into the house and then lock and bolt us all safely inside. It was very dark inside because of the trees around. If there was much wind the trees would sing down the chimney and blow smoke down, so that your eyes watered and you coughed.

We weren't often in Bridie Birdie's house, but because of the warning about her dark soul I was especially attentive. I thought that the dark soul had to do with the dark house and tried to learn all I could of it. I tried to puzzle out the shadowy corners, the contents of the high shelves. I would sit on a wooden stool up against the hearth where my coat would dry out, while Bridie Birdie and Daddy talked.

Bridie Birdie would set the black kettle over the fire to boil and put out thick white cups and saucers on the table under the window. There was no cloth on the table, only the bare white boards. On the other side of the hearth from where I sat, on a cushion on the hob, was a black cat, round as the kettle, its paws tucked under its chest and its head up watching us. I would try to outgaze its yellow eyes, but I never succeeded. That cat could outstare the devil.

Once on our way home I asked Daddy why Bridie Birdie was called Birdie.

'It's her name. She was married to a sailor from over the water. He didn't stay long and left her with one child. The child died of tuberculosis. Bridie had a long spell in hospital herself. She's had a hard life.'

'Is that why she has a dark soul, because of the hard life?'

'That's bad talk. Where did you get that from? There's nothing dark about Bridie Birdie. She's as playful as a child, and as innocent.'

But when we got home it was 'I suppose you've been in with Bridie Birdie again. I told you not to take Sally there.'

'It was pelting down, and there's no harm in the old woman.'

Nothing more was said, but my coat was whisked off me so sharply I knew there was harm somewhere.

Bridie's groceries came home along with ours because she couldn't make it to the shops on her own. The cardboard boxes of goods would be left on the kitchen table to be sorted by mother and Mrs Deans. Our stuff would go in the cupboards and larder, and Bridie's into the smallest of the cardboard boxes, and one of the boys would take it up the back lane. Sometimes Daddy would slip in an extra packet or two and Mother would scold. 'What are you doing? She'll only think the worse of you for that.'

'Och, sure it's nothing.' And then he'd leave the room. He couldn't put up with being scolded. The extra packets would stay in the box.

Sometimes when I knew for sure that no one saw me I'd put in a little present of my own — maybe some daisies tied with a thread, or a rose from the garden. Once I put in my red hair ribbon, and another time a brooch with stones missing out of it. Nobody wanted it. I had found it in the button box.

It was very quiet for me at home. The boys were too big to be bothered with me. Anyway, they were boys, going about shouting and kicking off heavy boots that thundered over the floor. So I was on my own most of the time which is why I so very much liked watching and noticing. I was very good at it.

I noticed Mother and Mrs Deans weren't speaking long before Mrs Deans left because of her sciatica. That happened around the same time that her Agnes stopped walking by up the mountainy road. Sometimes our Donnie would go with her. I saw him hide his bike behind the high wall, and climb over it, when he was supposed to be going into town. And I knew that Agnes Deans must have been waiting for him on the other side. I could hear their voices. And once I saw them far away in one of the top fields, dancing and dancing until they fell down together in the long rushy grass. It must have been damp.

When Mrs Deans left, Agnes never walked up the mountain road again, and Donnie went to Scotland, to friends of Daddy's, to learn their ways of working the land. 'Until he settles himself,' Mother said.

On the next Saturday, Mother showed the new girl how to sort the groceries, then went upstairs to lie down. Jack began to yell at Daddy. He said there was too much to do about the place now that Donnie was away, and wasn't it well for Donnie to be out of it. Daddy said he wouldn't be talked to like that, and Jack went out banging the door behind him. So there was nobody to take Bridie Birdie's box over, only Daddy. He looked at his watch and said he had business that couldn't be left, and the goods couldn't wait about or they'd spoil, I'd have to take the box over. He lifted it onto the carrier of Donnie's bike, and though it was too big for me to ride, I could push it — and it was only a short way up the lane.

I was breathless with excitement as I knocked on Bridie Birdie's door. Would she be wearing the red hair ribbon, or the brooch?

'Och, is it you?' she said once she got the door opened. 'Come in, rest yourself.'

As I took my seat by the fire, she lifted the box onto the table, and fastened the three locks on the back of her door.

'Do you keep the door always locked up?'

'Oh yes, you never know what's out there.'

'Sure, there'd be nothing out there. There's never burglars around here, and they'd only go for the well-off sort of people.'

'Well I wasn't talking only about burglars.'

'About what then?"

'Things, just. Now will you take a ginger nut for your trouble?'

I said that I would, and waited for her to find the packet in her box. She was methodical and did not rush. The black cat stared from its cushion on the hob.

'Oh dear,' said Bridie Birdie from the table. 'There's no present from the fairies today. They usually put me in a little something — some wee sort of a thing.'

'What wee sort of a thing?'

'All sorts of wee things. I have them in my tin box. That's where I keep my secret things and I'm not about to show them to the likes of you till I know if you can keep secrets.'

'I know lots of secrets.'

'And you wouldn't be about to tell me any, just to prove it, would you?'

'That would be daft.'

'Well, you've a head on your shoulders at least. We'll see about the secrets as we go on. Will you be back?'

'I don't know.'

Then she gave me a ginger nut and began snapping back the bolts on the door to let me out.

Mother never noticed that I was taking the box to Bridie's. She spent more time resting and would leave the sorting to me and the new girl. The new girl was called Betty and wasn't as good as Mrs Deans. Mother didn't like her being so young, and what about Jack in and out of the kitchen? She wanted no more disasters. But Jack caused no disasters in the kitchen. He was out over the fields every day, or in town with Daddy, learning the ropes.

Sometimes he stayed on late in town, and one morning Betty found his bed hadn't even been slept in. Mother said, 'Give that boy enough rope and he'll hang himself.' One night coming home drunk he fell roaring down the stairs and woke us all up. Mother said he needed the knotted end of a rope across his back, that was how her father had ruled his sons, but it was obvious there was to be no discipline in this house.

There was bad blood in this family with all their go-to-the-devil ways and it wasn't from her they had it and she rued the day she'd crossed the threshold of this house.

Daddy didn't say anything. He got Jack up the stairs and into his room, and then he put me to bed. He tucked me up tight and kissed my forehead, but he looked sad and quiet. He didn't put Mother to bed, because I could hear her slippers going up and down the landing, up and down. And then I went to sleep.

I had a skipping rope with knots on the ends. I knew Daddy wouldn't hit Jack with it, but I hid it the next morning. And because I was angry with Mother I took the lilac gloves she wore on Sundays from the drawer in the hall table.

Bridie Birdie was delighted with them when she found them in her grocery box. 'Would you look at that? Aren't the fairies good to me? Look at the little shape of them.' She laid one of the gloves over the back of her big red hand. The glove looked tiny and reached only halfway down her fingers.

'Sure they'd do you better nor me.'

'I've got gloves,' I said.

'I'll put them in the tin box with all me other things. Aren't they soft and light, and look at the colour of them. Sure I only ever saw flowers that colour.'

'Maybe they're the sort of gloves fairies wear,' I lied.

'Maybe so, to go dancing.'

'Do they dance in our fields?'

'Do they not? They were dancing in your fields before they were your fields. Why do you think I keep the doors locked tight. This is a terrible mischievous area for fairies — it's too close to the mountains.'

'Did you see them dancing ever?'

'No I did not. I'd not be going out in the dark looking for dancing fairies. But I'll tell you where you'd find some.'

'Where?'

'In the field over beyond the beech avenue.'

'Right by the house?'

'The one with the big grey stones in. But here I am, nearly telling you a secret. Away sharp with you.'

And I found myself outside with my ginger biscuit, listening to the bolts of her door shooting home, snap, snap, snap.

I said to Betty about fairies dancing in our fields.

'Where'd you get that from?'

'Bridie Birdie.'

'Sure that's only an oul yarn she's spinning you. That one's away with the fairies herself.'

But that night I did get out of my tightly tucked-in bed to shiver my way over the lino and peep out at the moonlit night. I could see that field from my bedroom, and there was the row of man-sized stones crossing the field. But that's all there was. In the bright moonlight I could see that clearly.

Mother's headaches got worse. She said she had to sleep in a room by herself because of them. Some days she didn't get out of bed at all and Betty had to bring her meals upstairs on trays. When Mother ate upstairs the rest of us ate in the kitchen along with Betty. We didn't bother with the dining room which was always cold, even with a fire lit. I liked eating at the bare kitchen table. It was warm and the dishes made a pleasing thump on the bare wood. Betty never fussed if stuff got spilled, and Jack could tilt his chair back as far as he liked.

Jack said that the dining room was full of ghosts: all the Evanses that had ever eaten there, sitting on each other's laps down all the generations. He said that in his usual dining-room chair he could feel the bones of at least five knobby old ancestors under him. Daddy slapped the boards of the table, and roared laughing. Betty laughed too, but I knew, in the way that I knew all sorts of things, that Betty half-believed Jack and was glad to be out of the dining room. Jack was getting out of his bad moods. That was nice.

The next thing the fairies gave Bridie Birdie was a grey chiffon scarf. It looked like something a fairy would wear, and Bridie Birdie was enchanted by it. Under the yellow gaze of the black cat she held it up by the two corners. 'Would you look at that! Sure what are they thinking of sending me a thing like that. It's as thin as a shadow! There'd be no heat in that! But isn't it just the bee's knees of a gorgeous thing! Looka me!'

She threw it over her head like a veil and hushed. I could see the glint of her eyes behind the transparent grey. I shifted my gaze to the yellow-eyed black cat, because Bridie Birdie in her grey veil was too much of a ghost.

'Hah! Scared you.' She laughed, snatching the scarf from her head.

'I looked in that field,' I said. 'You were wrong. There's no fairies in it.'

'Indeed and there are. Man-big and looking at you. What do you think the stones are?'

'Stones.'

'They're stones now, but they didn't always used to be stones. First they were fairies, dancing fairies.'

'How did they get to be stones?'

'The fairy women danced in the field by moonlight. They were more beautiful than anything you could imagine. There was fairy music too, and when the men heard the music they came to watch the dancing and the women found out and they were jealous as sin. So they ran for blankets and threw them over the dancing fairies to hide the sight of them. And the blankets turned to stone. You go and look at those stones and if the sun's in the right place you'd maybe see a face in the stone, but as if behind a veil, or a knee or a hand, jutting up into the surface of the stone.'

"That's horrible. That's too sad.'

The cat rose, yawned a pink yawn and settled again, blinking its yellow eyes at me. It didn't care about the fairies in the stones.

That night I had terrible dreams and woke screaming, fighting against the tucked-in blankets that held me down in the bed. I woke everyone. For a while I didn't know they were there. I didn't even see the light when they switched it on.

'It's dark. It's dark,' I kept calling. 'The cloth has darkened me.'

'What is this all about?' I heard my mother's voice at last. 'Speak to me. I'm here.' She was holding me tight, very tight. She smelt clean and safe.

'Out there in the hay field. The fairies are in the stones. I can hear them screaming.'

'It's just a dream.'

'It's not, Bridie Birdie told me.'

'It's stupid stories. It's only stones. You'll see by daylight.'

In the morning Daddy said that I was never to go to see Bridie Birdie again. It wasn't allowed. Mother didn't go for her rest that afternoon. 'Headache or no headache, it's clear someone needs to take charge around here.'

Betty was sent to spread the cloth on the dining-room table. We were going to eat there, and we did, with freshly ironed napkins covering our laps.

I had the dream again that night and for many nights. Coping with it seemed to give Mother strength. 'It only proves me right,' she snapped at Daddy. 'I should have kept a better eye on things.'

There were no more headaches. She decided I needed dancing lessons, to civilise me and give me the chance to mix with my own sort. We stood in rows, counting the steps. One two three hop, one two three hop. The dreams stopped after a while. Dullness settled upon me like a blanket of snow. I forgot.

One day a black cat came to the kitchen windowsill. It stared at us with yellow eyes. Betty tried to frighten it away with a flapping tea towel, but it wouldn't go. When Daddy came in from his work and saw it there he said, 'I know that cat,' and he went out again. He was away a long time. When he came back he was weary. He said he had had a hard time breaking in, what with all the bolts. That there was nothing he could do for her, only pull the blanket up over her face. Bridie Birdie had died, bird-alone.

'Well,' Mother said. 'Well …'

ANGELA BOURKE

Deep Down

I told Liam a story last night. His hand was on my stomach under my dress and I thought it might make him stop. It wasn't that I didn't like it. His hand was huge. I couldn't get over the size of it, but it was warm. The eyes were the same as I remembered. Brown eyes that kept on looking at me after I thought he'd look away, so I started to tell him about this thing that happened hundreds of years ago, a story I often think about since I heard it. It's in a manuscript, but it happened not far from my own home — a place called Clonmacnois, on the Shannon. A lot of medieval things happened there.

It was in a church, with a whole crowd of people and a priest saying Mass, just after the Consecration, and the people heard a terrible racket, like something dragging along the roof. They all ran out and looked up, and there was a boat up there in the sky. An ordinary boat, like you'd see on the sea, or on a lake, but it was up above the roof of the church, just hanging in the sky. They were looking at the bottom of it. The light is very clear in Clonmacnois, especially when the river floods.

The anchor was caught in the church door. It was on the end of a long rope coming down through the air, and it was caught in the door they had just come out through. That's what the noise was.

There must have been a terrible commotion. You can imagine them all standing around in the cold with their red faces looking up, but the next thing was a man with no clothes on, just some kind of cloth, swimming down towards them from the boat to get the anchor loose. I have to hold my breath just thinking about it. I'd have been scared stiff.

Some of the men grabbed him and held on to him. He was fighting to get away, but then they had to let him go. He said "You're drowning me", and they could see they were, so they stood back and he flew up away from them.

His own people dragged him into the boat up above, and off they went, away across the sky the way they'd come.

I often wonder if any ancestors of mine were there. They all went back into the church, and the priest finished Mass. They always have to, I believe. It must have been hard for them, coming out at the end, not knowing if the world was changed, or only them.

Liam gave me his jacket getting out of the car because the wind was chilly after the dancehall. It came down to my knees, but it kept me warm. I never knew a leather jacket was so heavy. He made me take off my shoes as well, so I wouldn't ruin them on the beach. But what in the name of God was I doing there? What possessed me?

I'd no idea who he was at the beginning. I don't think I did. Anyone would have noticed him, the way he danced — like a ballet dancer. He reminded me of *West Side Story*, in the tight jeans and the leather jacket — or your man Baryshnikov, the way the hair was flopping onto his forehead. He was taller than the rest of them as well. Longer legs.

A lot of the men around here are good dancers, but they're more heavy-set — their centre of gravity is more in the seat of their trousers. I like dancing with them. I love it when they swing me off the ground and I just go with it, so my feet don't miss a beat when I hit the floor again. I like their strong wrists and the way they laugh a lot. But I don't think I'd ever lust after them, if you know what I mean.

I remembered some of them last night, from when I used to come and stay with Gracie. Men I used to think were old are only five or six years older than me — but then I was only about nineteen. They haven't changed much. Not compared with the women. I got a real shock when I saw some of them — girls that used to be beautiful. Now they're fat and half their teeth are gone and their hair is grey.

It always did me good to come here, I'm ashamed to say. I don't mean the sea air. That'd do anyone good, and all the walking — but the dances, and people fancying me. A suitcase of clean clothes and my hair washed, and off I'd go. I thought I was so glamorous.

Of course at home there were never that many people around. The farms are bigger. I used to feel like an awkward big lump beside the town girls — half asleep and nothing to say, the way you'd see a caterpillar chewing its way through a cabbage leaf. But then I'd come down here and I'd turn into a butterfly, and that's what I was looking for this time too, in spite of what I told Eamonn. I was starting to feel like a fat green lump again. That's not a good sign when you're walking around with fifteen-hundred pounds' worth of diamond engagement ring on your finger.

I didn't say anything to Liam about Eamonn. The ring is back at home where I left it, in the drawer with my Irish dancing medals, and the subject never came up. He didn't even ask me where I was living now. It would have sounded foolish, at that hour of the night. There was so much noise in the hall anyway. Nobody was talking. It's the old-fashioned sort of place. The men all stay on one side and the women are all along the other. They have to walk across the floor to ask you to dance, and there's no such thing as saying no either, unless the man is really footless. When Liam came along he just reached in between two other girls and took hold of my hand, and I just followed him.

His hand was warm, holding on to mine between sets. Dry. He was smiling over my head at the band, but he didn't say anything for ages.

I said nothing either, and now I wonder am I mad? I hardly said a word all evening, to tell the truth, until that time we got back into the car, but that's no excuse.

He did all the talking.

Such a memory! But I should have known better. God almighty — is he even twenty-one?

"Are you Linda Reilly?" he asked me at the end of the third set.

You could have knocked me down.

"Yes," I said. But how did he know? He was young and gorgeous, towering over me, holding onto my hand. You'd think he had to look after me.

"You used to be my babysitter." His teeth were perfect too.

"Oh my God!" It was like opening one of those dolls and finding another one inside. I knew what it was. "Don't tell me. You're not one of the Dunnes?"

"Liam," he said, grinning all over his face, "I knew you the minute I saw you. You came to stay with Gracie Ryan. You minded us when our mother went to hospital."

I used to take them to the beach. Or they used to take me. The same beach we were on last night. Three of them. Liam was the eldest. All the Dunnes were blond, but he was the only one with brown eyes. He used to follow me around. He'd stay sitting with me when the other two were off having adventures. I thought he was worried about his mother.

"I used to dream about you," he said with his arm around me, sitting on the same big rock, after he kissed me the first time. "Did you know that? I was only nine, but I used to go to sleep all excited, thinking about my lovely babysitter."

That smile again. Nobody around here has teeth that good. I could even see them in the dark.

"I couldn't believe it when I walked in there tonight and saw you. You haven't changed a bit, you know."

I nearly choked when he said that, looking at the size of him.

"You have," I said, and we laughed ourselves silly at that. The rock was cold under us, but the sky was warm. And we had his jacket.

All the things you hear about strange men.

Babysitting is different. If kids like you, you feel all strong looking after them. And the funny thing is you feel safe — even after they grow up over six feet and hold your face in their two hands with their two thumbs on the edges of your mouth and their tongue kissing deep into it.

The only thing I worried about was corrupting him, and that made me laugh all over again as soon as I thought of it. I wasn't teaching Liam Dunne anything he didn't know already.

He was the one that started it. He was the one who said it was too cold for me, we should go back to the car.

Something stopped me all the same, in the car. I wasn't cold any more and with his hand on my stomach my whole body felt like some creamy liquid you could pour out of a jug, but then someone's headlights went across the sky. Everyone knows everyone else's car around here. When it's dark you can feel you're the only people for miles, but you never are. Liam's mouth was up against my ear and I could feel his hot whispering, "Trust me," he said, "I'll take care of you. It'll be all right. Just trust me."

I could suddenly see myself in front of a whole crowd of people, holding onto the jug with the last drops dripping out. I was already feeling the relief of warm skin after all the harshness of denim and zips, but I made him stop.

"My mother would love to see you again," Liam said. Maybe that was it. He was sure she'd be delighted, but I could imagine the long cold look she'd give me, the questions about what I'm doing now, am I married yet? Oh, engaged? And what does he do? And where's your ring? Another long hard look, with Liam looking hurt and young, his face up near the low ceiling, not understanding.

I opened the window on my side to let the sound of the waves in. The wind came clean and salty, cooling our skin. That was when I told him about the boat in Clonmacnois.

"I was never there," he said, tucking his shirt in, "but I heard about it. All the monks. It was a big city, I believe."

"Was it?" I said, "I didn't know that."

"And you living beside it?" He sat back in his seat and took a packet of sweets out of somewhere, the way Eamonn would reach for his cigarettes.

"We had a teacher at the Tech that told us about it. I used to love all them stories. I never heard that one before though."

"Could we go now, do you think?" I asked him. It was nearly three in the morning. He turned the key to start the engine, and I wound up my window.

"You mightn't believe what I'm going to tell you," he said, coming up over the rise past the first houses. His voice was grim, "but something like that happened my grandfather back out there."

"Out where?"

"In the bay there, a bit off the Head."

I sucked on my sweet. He must eat them all the time. They tasted like his kisses.

"He was out with three other fellows, fishing for cod. They're all dead now. The last of them went Christmas last year."

I waited, looking at the small haystacks and the fuchsia hedges appearing and disappearing in front of us when the headlights hit them.

"One of the other fellows was at the helm, and my granda had a line out. He felt a heavy sort of weight, and when he pulled it in, what do you think was on it?"

"What?"

"A baby."

I felt an awful lurching. The sweet was in my mouth, but I didn't know what it was doing there. Why was he telling me this? And on a line. Hooked. A baby on a hook — not even in a net.

When I was about fifteen someone buried a dead baby in the corner of a field near us. Nobody let on they knew anything about it. The guards came around all the houses, but the girl was already gone to England.

I opened the window and Liam looked around at me. "It wasn't dead," he said quickly. He put his hand on my knee. Warm again. "That's what I'm telling you. It was a live baby, fit and well, with clothes on it."

"How could it be alive?" I laughed with the relief.

"That's what I don't know. All I know is my grandfather was one of the best fishermen around here, and he wasn't making it up."

"They don't fish here any more, do they?"

"Not since 1968."

"Is that when the drownings were?"

"Two boat-loads of men in one night. My granda was one of them."

Liam was stopping the car. My guesthouse was in on our left, but I wanted to hear more.

"I didn't know that. You must have only been a baby then."

He turned off the engine, then the lights.

"I wasn't even born. My mother was carrying me. I have all his things above in the house. She kept them for me. I'm called after him."

"Did she tell you the story too?"

"She did. And she made me promise I'd never go fishing for a living."

"It's a dangerous life all right."

"There was another bit to the story too," he said slowly, "only it wasn't from my mother I heard it."

"What was that?" I felt like his babysitter again. Careful. Maybe it was the houses around, or the paved road.

"One of the other old fellows that was out that day used to say they had to throw the child back."

"Back into the water?" Funny I never even asked him what they did with it.

The car was very quiet with the engine off. I could see Liam's face in the light from the sky. He was looking straight ahead, leaning on the steering wheel, not touching me.

"I don't know," he said quickly, "but that's what they did. He said a woman came up beside the boat in the water and cursed them up and down for hooking the child out of its cradle down below."

I didn't laugh. He wasn't laughing. I saw his hand go to the key and come back. His mother was on her own in the house, I suppose. He'd told me his two brothers were in Boston, and I knew his father was dead years ago. She'd probably lie awake till she heard the car.

"I'll go in," I said. "Thanks for the lift"

He started the engine. The lights flashed a screen of stone wall and fuchsia hedge up in front of us.

"Sure I might see you tomorrow." A bit of a smile at last.

"Sure you might, I suppose," I said, smiling back. This was the usual chat, visitors flirting with locals. Harmless really.

I walked up to the front door, but I didn't go in. I stood there on my own in the quiet night, watching the car's headlights cut through the dark sky until I couldn't see them anymore.

EVELYN CONLON

Park-Going Days

They took their chairs and children, of whom they were terribly proud today, to the park on the first day of summer, relieved that the darkness was over and repeating again and again 'Great day', so that maybe such sun worship would bring them a summer. You would never have believed that in those few houses there could be so many children — you could easily have forgotten Kathleen's fifth or that Bridie, during the winter, had had another, because, naturally, you never saw it, Bridie's new one, due to the freezing conditions. If you did, Bridie was a bad mother and there were no good or bad mothers around here (even the ones whose sons were inside) — just mothers. It was a Thursday after lunch — the one man who had a job nearby had been fed. No one would have gone to the park before that happened, not in deference to Jack eating, but because Jack's wife wouldn't be free until then, and there was nothing to make a woman feel housebound like all the other women trooping up to the park before her, and there was nothing worse than feeling housebound on a sunny day.

The park-going days of sunshine were truly numbered in this country — fifteen last year, two the year before, ten the year before that and forty on the year that God was otherwise occupied and forgot to switch off the heat, or else decided to tease everyone and make them mournful for the next five years. No woman in this country had any doubt but that God was a man — is a man. There's no was about that fellow unfortunately. Some had the view that the man himself was intrinsically all right and that it was the ones who took over after him who mucked the whole thing up. Could be true — he may have been all right. Perhaps. But it's a hard thing to believe, in a country that only once had forty days of sunshine.

It's amazing the amount of preparations women used to mothering can put into a trip to the park. One folded-up light deck chair, suntan oil, face cloth, sandwiches (which will avoid having to make a children's tea at six), rug to put sandwiches and children on, sunglasses, small lightish jumpers in case it turns cold suddenly, drinks, the antibiotics that the child is on, some toys for the baby — for the ones who were pregnant last summer — the baby's bottle, one nappy and *all* that baby stuff, *and* ice-cream money.

At ten past two all the doors opened and out they poured, nearly invisible behind all the paraphernalia, calling around them the children who had been dreamy and inside and the ones who had already been outside getting burned and thirsty and cranky. And dirty.

'Look at the face of her. Come here to me until I give you a wipe. Disgracing me.' She dug the face cloth into the child's face, disgracing it in front of friends who hadn't noticed at all.

They went, and Rita went after them. She didn't go to the park but she passed it on the way to the shops, half hoping that if there was a summer next year, or if this one lasted beyond the day, they would ask her to join them, knowing that it would be better if they didn't, because if they ran out of steam — which they would when they realised the sort of her and why — there could be no more casual comments passed between them as strangers. They and she could whistle pleasantries back and forth at the moment; they, prepared to waste their sweet words on her because of curiosity — a new resident — she, to make them less curious, and failing.

The more she said, 'Nice day', the more they wanted to know. The more she felt their sniffing, the more frightened she got. That sneaky-faced woman in the nylon housecoat, too old to walk to the park, polishing her brasses again. Who did she think she was fooling! Of course, she was lonelier than if she was dead, but Rita couldn't be expected to be built of sympathy.

Rita walked after them, aggravated at the bits and pieces of garages built at the ends of gardens, as if thrown together in shapeless anger. In winter she could escape them by looking down at her feet, which she did, but today the sun threw their shadow across the street under her eyes. A bulldozer was needed badly. Knock down the whole lot of them. She had no soft spots for old farm barns, mudwall byres or extended hen houses, so she couldn't see anything for the garages but the bulldozer. Her husband would not have agreed. But then he came from places where fields lay companionably beside other fields that ran casually into more and more fields, flat and hilly, offering space grudgingly to the occasional house, which was then forced to use rickety outhouses as protection against the ever approaching grass. She was from a geometrician's dream, where back gardens were only concessions to the superior needs of houses.

She passed the park and saw them. They belonged to a time before the time of one earring. Two ears, two earrings. Fingers were the only single part of them that divided into ones. They put rings on them. Most importantly, they put one ring on one finger, sometimes along with another, varying in degrees of vulgarity and awfulness. The rings marked stages in their self-denial and destruction. Rita saw the rings glistening in the sun, picking out unreachable baubles in the sky. The women saw her and thought different things, none of them actually about her, more about her type.

'You couldn't satisfy *him*. If it's not the smog, it's the dirt or the accents. Jayzus, would yeh listen to whose talkin' about an accent.'

'How *does* she put up with him? An' it's made her odd.'

'There's somethin' else odd about her but I can't put me finger on it.'

'Ah well.'

In the end they knew in their hearts that the only thing funny about her was that they didn't know her and that she was married to a culchie. Not much of a gap to be got over.

They settled in their chairs and watched their collective new generation, comparing it favourably with the other groups in the park, conscious that they were all part of even more park groups, between them accounting for hundreds of miles of discarded umbilical cords. They uttered unconnected sentences at random. Conversation was organised only when there was tragedy or scandal to be related. But the silence was never silent, it was just a space of time between words of explanation and words of exasperation.

Bridie watched hers out of the corner of her eye. Sean always dirty. As a baby he sucked the ends of his Babygro and got a red wrist in his fat little cracks from wet aggravation. Now he sucked his jumper and pulled at his waist all the time, ending up each evening with hand marks branded in frustration on his clothes. His pores seemed to suck in every bit of street dirt going. His cuts usually went septic. Anne. Wise. Precocious and clean. She would have children too — it didn't bear thinking about. She played with her older brothers in a superior bossy way, as if she knew.

'She'll be coming out of school at half two when she makes her communion, please God.' That would be another step passed in the sending off of her to the Lord.

'It took me all day to get out of town yesterday. Pickets outside the Dail. They should put that buildin' down the country somewhere and not be stoppin' people tryin' to get home. They wouldn't be so quick to picket it if it was down there.'

They shifted their fat bodies around on the deck chairs. They had suffered from the usual disappointments being married to their husbands. Kathleen's man had been mortified one day when she was nearly due and she'd sat down on the steps of the bank in town, not fit to move another inch. It was a Saturday and the bank was closed — what could he have been going on about?

In her early marriage before having any children, Molly used to call on her husband at work. She thought it was a nice thing to do and she was lonely on her own — she'd been getting eleven pounds before the wedding, now with tax it was only five, so there wasn't much point in her going to work for the short while; the bus fare was two pounds. One day he said that she'd have to stop calling and get used to their new house for both their sakes. The men at work would start talking.

'But I don't know anyone.'

'You'll get to know some mothers later.'

He smiled. She smiled. It was a small subtle exclusion, preparation for the major ones — the tapping on the shoulder as women walked absentmindedly, not deliberately, not provokingly, into supermarkets pushing prams. She never called again.

Bridie's man, when he was young, had kept running from one country to the other, filling himself up with experience, pouring himself all over the Continent and still he hadn't one word to say for himself. He'd only once said 'I love you'. He was a consumer of cultures — he had a few words of French, which gave him an edge on the other men on the street but that was no help to Bridie.

Deirdre's man — the drinker — did his bit for his children. He talked about them occasionally in pubs in the serious way that drunk men do, once getting first-day issue stamps for them from a man who worked in the P & T, who happened, just happened, to be drinking beside him. Now that was more than a woman could do.

Kathleen had broken her mother's heart — 'Ma, I wasn't going to tell you this but seeing we're out for the day and that it's on my mind and I have been keeping it to myself and all that and it's no good for me or anything and all that and no good for you either and I'm pregnant.'

Kathleen sighed. Bridie put her varicose veins on the wheel of the pram. These — the fat, the veins, the sighs — were the shapes of the backbone of the country. You'd never think it to see the corkscrew, frown-free pictures that poured from the ad men's anorexic fantasies.

'Great day.'

'A doctor said to my mother once that there are two terrible bad things for a woman — ironing and not dropping everything to run outside when she sees the first blink of sun.'

'Yeah, it's a great day.'

'I'd love a cigarette. Funny the way you feel like it some-times and not at others.'

'I didn't know you smoked, Molly.'

Molly raised her voice to panic pitch. 'Smoke. Smoke is it? I was a chain-smoker. What! I had meself burnt. Me lips, me skirts, me bras, me slips. One match would do me the whole day. Lit one off the other.'

'What did you smoke?' It was neither a question nor a statement after Molly's emotion.

'Albany.'

'Were they a special cigarette, I don't remember them? I used to smoke Woodbine. No one ever died that smoked Woodbine.'

'It's near tea time.'

That was a grand day. No one had got cut or desperately badly hurt. There had been the odd row but not enough to deserve a beating. One woman, not belonging to their group, had set her child up for a battering. She hit her because she wanted to go on the swings too often. The child kicked her back. The women nodded a sort of ungrudging, serve-you-right nod. The mother hit her more. The incident might have spiralled into murder but the floating disapproval, the soul sympathy, and the take-it-easy-it'll-get-better thoughts made the mother acknowledge defeat. Yes, a great day.

They were gathering up their stuff when Rita walked past, on her way home. They delayed, to let her go on. They were sick of her kind, really — never any children, coming to live in that rented house, teasing their curiosity and staying aloof.

'You wouldn't mind so much marrying a culchie but getting *used* to him.'

They laughed. They could have remarked that she was unhappy but they denied her that status, in the mean way that city people can, surrounded as they are by so many, some of whom, precisely because of the number, are dispensable. They turned their noses up and pulled their curtains down an inch from their faces like country ones could never do. (Perhaps you might need your neighbour in twenty years when all the rest would be gone, to America, or Dublin.)

As they struggled nearer their doors, exhausted from heat, children whingeing when *they* saw the prospect of home looming closer, that they hadn't stayed long enough in the park, only three hours, Mammy, they each withdrew themselves from collective experience and concentrated on their individual problems. Parks were all right — open-air sum totals of lives that were normally lived in box rooms with thick enough doors and walls to shut out obscenities — but all the same, you wouldn't want to live in a park all your life and you wouldn't want to behave in your own house as if you were in a park. After a while people get on your nerves, even on sunny days — that was why the tenants in the rented house were always handy. Everyone on the street could take their mutual spite out on them and so avoid major street fights.

Rita knew what they were thinking. Sometimes at four in the morning — she often woke at four — she would look out and see reflections of their lights and she would feel like forgiving them because who couldn't forgive a woman anything when they saw her struggling at that unearthly hour to

285

silence a crying, hungry baby? Rita had had a child of her own. The child had died and she wasn't allowed to think about it. What had happened was anyone's guess — it just died. But Rita was fine now. Fine. The street would have gushed with sympathy if it had known. One thing Rita regretted not having was park days with mothers. She'd noticed the way mothers made up to the children on park days. Made up to them for all sorts of troubles, things like concentrated, compressed family violences that emptied onto children's backsides when men and women decided at the same moment that they would have to put manners on the offspring who was at that second holding their nerves to ransom. They could do that because they knew that mothers would make it up sometime soon — certainly in a park if it was a sunny day. Rita would have liked the making-up bits.

It was Bridie in the end who asked Rita if she wanted to sit down with them in the park, just for a few minutes, for a little rest. Rita stretched her legs out in front of her and said to herself, now I'll have to leave. They talked busily as they watched the replay of yesterday and yesterday, Rita not thinking all the time of her own because she wasn't allowed to; each of the other women remarking to herself how nice she was really. The next day it rained. Clouds stalked over the bit of sunshine they'd had and Rita started packing. She said goodbye before herself and her culchie husband left, knocked on the single doors and got away before they learned anything about her. A week later if you could have cut bits out of the walls, you would have seen them cleaning noses, swiping at bare legs, sneaking off for a rest and drying clothes, bending over babies in the way that causes bad backs, again, again, as the tenants moved in and the rain poured on them all.

RITA KELLY

Soundtracks

The heat, the vacuity. The smeared sleepers, the dull series of them summed to an infinity, a good yard apart, battened down in an ooze of broken stone, cushioning the steel which bears the glitter of journeys, wheels, steel wearing steel to a stasis, a screeching stop.

A voice cries close to one. 'Chickens for Attymon, -ymon, -ymon.'

Answering echoes only. No one. Nothing, only the old placename, a comic name, even on the name-board it seems full of grinning faces and laughter, some bitterness, transmuted in one's mind into the sharp tang of elderblossom.

One sits like a daylight ghost, broad sweep of hat, sunglasses, they hide nothing really. It is all there, waiting, the little bits of glitter in the broken stone. Panicles of elderblossom push in over the railings, a few rusted wagons stand to one side, their foolish buffers, tensed, defensive, pushing an emptiness.

Ruth was accused of intelligence. The word bright but heavy. It was an acceptable understatement to those who admired her, a compromise to those who did not. To the scatter-brained, dodging girls in the class it was the solution: they worshipped it, feared it, made bargains with it, and treated it generally as they treated the statues and other pious objects in their experience. Intelligence to them was knowing, without effort, the past participle of the verb *voir*, the coefficient of x in any given situation, the excretory habits of the watersnail, and who in hell was Beelzebub.

One saw Ruth secure her bicycle in the empty shed, in before anyone, and come out of the dawn's indistinction with her breath hanging on the air. One felt the spikelets which she shook from her hat to melt upon the cloakroom floor.

Then those, to whom a liberal education was an unexplained burden, an earthly purgatory, would stumble into the classroom, blinded by sleep and the night's expenditure of physical energy. Ruth made many attempts to elicit interest in the particular subject, to awaken delight even, and to capture for the mind some of the energy of those throbbing bodies. They laughed or groaned — it was often difficult to decide which — until Ruth, with a lost look, would hand over her exercise books to be copied, exposing in determined handwriting her night's trance. The problems, the verbal creations, methodically solved. The intrinsic delight. All that, she gave to be pawed, pulled, and tattered by mindless fingers.

Or at evening, one saw her as she rode into the vacuous countryside, flushed, the whirring spokes, the unavoidable shadow.

One could not befriend Ruth, she had everything, pencils, specimens of the phylum Platyhelminthes, period pills, and in the proper order. Her generosity was disturbing, reckless, and annoyingly self-destructive. It even seemed to destroy the recipient. One could say: 'Poor Ruth', but only in some illogical, some subnormal mood. The utterance dissipated the feeling, and one thought of Ruth's intelligence, such a girl could not need sympathy.

Quite suddenly she abandoned her bicycle and travelled the six miles to school by train.

Her train-schedules allowed her two hours after class for study, for recreation; but mainly for sitting pensive in the empty classroom. Some unease took hold of her. She would rush to the station an hour before it was necessary, and one saw her drop her satchel on the platform-seat and walk back and forth, a slim figure in the school uniform — it was slate grey, one remembers, cool and virginal — but one sees the figure now almost black against the sun. Abstractedly, she would finger the cut limestone of the windowsills, walls, and door-surrounds. Sensing the compacted skeletons, the powered calcium, the teeming life petrified; the joints, the frame of life only, and all a memory pulling at the mind. She looked with pity upon the remains of a Victorian incongruity, because it seemed as if the stone were made molten and squeezed out of pipes, like water-icing, and left to set into its hideous shapes. An insult to the material.

Her trains pounded in from places far distant, whose names were burdened with myth and mystery. Ruth boarded her train, then a signal, a shrill in the air, and she was gone. The withdrawing rumble allowing the silence to settle back, swathing the station, the isolation, the pathetic insignificance — left like a toy in a field, suffering the child's forgetfulness, the dusk and the dewdrops, rusting a little, disturbing really, a persistent memory, unrecognized.

Ruth would be a doctor, and no one was surprised. Having satisfied the scattered curiosity of the class by 'doctor', she did not elaborate, and paid no heed as they surmised the number of scholarships which she must unquestionably win.

Her train-journeys terminated, and she became a remembered face, a name, in the general dispersal. And even those who envied her were glad to see her take an eminent place at the university.

With time came tidings. Ruth was seen balancing in the early hours of morning, on the main bridge of the university city. Her hair dishevelled, her singing voice more inane than all the inanities of that gin-and-scruffy set. She repeatedly failed her examinations. Her incoherent behaviour was a surprise even to the scatter-brained who found themselves in her vicinity; what would be orgies in them, in her were oddly shocking. Repellent even. Their cheerful chattering voices, one can still distinctly hear them, delighted to hear reports, savouring the sumptuous details. They were quite explicit in describing the symptoms of the malaise, which they could only explain as some kind of late-development, because they themselves were now veterans of that kind of thing, and bore the fruits of it within the bonds of respectability.

Ruth avoided all the old faces, and if accidentally thrown into their company she would meticulously cut short any reiteration of time past. This was the greatest shock of all, as the scatter-brained idea of oral communication and social intercourse is a giggling regurgitation of narrow-escapes; the *obiter dicta* of indeterminate people in undefined situations; their evolving insights into reproductive systems in general, their own in particular.

Then Ruth disappeared. It might be said that Ruth had already disappeared — at least the Ruth one knew. The sense of place receded, the scent of mornings, the drive and the urge, what were once sharplit images were rusted into the background, as the dull years mercifully obliterate the lifelike image of oneself.

Until one May afternoon, one was aware of a young woman in an elegant blue coat, cut precisely to the figure, standing on the platform-edge. Ruth. And by her side a little girl, the eyes unmistakable. Ruth in miniature, the little features not yet moulded into that cool distinction of the young woman.

She walked up and down, taking the child by the hand along with her, at times almost dragging the little thing. What was the impatience, the consuming annoyance, that drove her up and down the edge of the platform? To look back down along the tracks losing themselves in a wilderness of furze. The interminable journeys, the grinding wheel. And forward, there was no distinction, again the meticulous parallels melted into each other in a distance, a pseudo-distance, there is never anything but the isolated self.

SOUNDTRACKS

Was this really Ruth? The chic cut of coat, in its own way as ridiculous as the Victorian wedding-cakery and mock turrets of the station. Defunct purposes. Defunct pasts. Her days of utter isolation embodied in the very limestone, in the pathetic buildings clinging to the line of steel, timber, and ballast of broken stone. The fecundating boglands waiting to infiltrate, undo the precision. Rust and the rotting timber.

She found herself standing stock-still. The child at a distance, on tiptoe, fingering a hording. Huge lettering. Anywhere. Anytime.

'Ruth', she called, 'come here, Ruth.'

The command was released mechanically, it hung in the gap between them, sounding and strangely not sounding. The childish figure turned its head, the fingers lingered under the words. Oddly at a distance, alien. Sharp chin, glint of dark hair, looking at one out of grey intelligent eyes.

Intelligence. Of course. They had accused her of intelligence. A word to goad the memory in all its possible tones. The chattering crowd, the hare-brained exercises, the frosty mornings, clamouring for Ruth to do their work for them, then the figure left alone in the empty classroom as the light dwindled in the windowscape. Intelligence. One felt the idea now like a frostbite.

Presentations, concerts, operas, ballgames, prize-giving, it was always Ruth. The swell of applause, the hand-clappings, the inciting fragments of phrases. 'Extremely intelligent' — if one could but wipe that word, that cool figure, from the memory. And ladies in furs, tired women really, surveying her — 'So this is Ruth?' — and passing some inane remark as if they too might have been intelligent, or could have produced intelligence, were it not for the inevitable old hysterectomy which prevented them from passing genius into the world. Genius — another word one would like to strangle.

A thrumming in one's ears. One is involved in a mounting terror. Nothing ahead but the huge letters looming. Anywhere.

Anytime. All one's youth one long interminable, intelligent mistake.

Suddenly she is there, the demure figure in the slate grey skirt, the neat school satchel, just beside her on the brink of the platform. Ruth at seventeen, just as one remembered her, yet smaller somehow, more fragile. She was turned away looking up the line, yet one knew that the eyes which looked out from under the brim of the felt hat were one's own eyes.

The thrum and trundle was almost upon them, the susurration of steel on steel. Firmly, one placed one's hand between the thin shoulder-blades and pushed, banishing the image.

But they will not stay still, the chattering voices, the roar, and the applause. A rising tide of handclaps, an iron clatter, out of which one screams to wake up. Then a rift of silence, one is left on the brink, looking down at the little teeth on the tracks.

ÉILÍS NÍ DHUIBHNE

Summer Pudding

We camped at Caer Gybi for three days waiting for Father Toban. Two tinkers we'd met in Llanfair told us he was on his way there from Bangor. But although we'd kept an eye out for him on the road we had not seen him, and we had not heard tell of him either. When we asked about him people laughed, or gave a useless answer or no answer.

We camped on a patch of ground above the beach, close to the harbour, where we could see the packet sailing in and out. The weather was dry and calm, and the tides were quiet for April. We'd missed three sailings in the three days.

'We should go,' I said, 'without him. We can say our own prayers.'

Naoise did not believe this and neither did I. The truth was, I did not want to say prayers at all any more. But he did. He would not go. He had it in his head that Father Toban would come and that was that. I was getting to know him, and already I knew that he was stubborn as an ass. He had told me that anyway, proudly, and warning at the same time. I was proud, too, when he told me, and I knew that his stubbornness was good for me, a gift for me. Now I could see it could have another side.

There is sharp marram grass on the ground and it is not comfortable to lie on, or to love on. It is dry, however. The dunes are alive with rabbits and we have had a good stew every day — I have onions that I lifted from an old one in the town. I go in during the day for a few hours and sell tin cans. The

293

Welsh here are not as bad as in other parts, being used to us, I suppose, by now. They should be.

Father Toban. Who is he? I have heard him talked about ever since I came but I haven't seen him and everything I have heard about him has a hollow ring to it. Maybe he is an old *piseog*, like the banshee.

'Do you believe in the banshee, Naoise?' I asked him.

He did.

'She must have been busy during the last couple of years. Or does she have helpers?'

'Go away out of that,' he said. He didn't like it.

I didn't tell him that I thought Father Toban was like the banshee. Somebody only your friend's friend has ever laid eyes on.

In July I came over with my sister Mary and a band of people from Kildare. Dunnes and Connors mostly, who had been on the road for years and already knew the tinsmith's trade, as we, of course, did not. Our father was a farmer outside Kilkenny and had just died a few months before we came over. Our mother had died the year before that and all our brothers. We pledged their clothes in a pawnshop in Naas, where we were not known. We had been told we should burn them because of the fever but we needed money and the clothes were good — trousers with no patches, two good frieze coats, a pair of leather shoes and two pairs of wooden brogues. I washed them in the river and dried them two days in the sun and I do not think there could have been any fever left on them. With the money we got for them and for some pots and pans and the blankets from our beds, and the one week's wages our father had got on the Relief, we had enough money for the two tickets. The tinkers we met at the docks and took up with there.

Mary did not like them. 'They are wild animals,' she said. Not 'they are like wild animals', which is what I thought at first.

Long scrawny things, with loose arms and legs — loose tongues, loose other things as well. They have bushes of frizzy red hair or fair hair, never combed, sticking up on top of their heads or just tumbling down any old way around their shoulders. The strangest thing is their eyes. The men have mad eyes, that don't seem to blink, like the eyes of cats or foxes. Maybe it is from the *poitín*, which they drink whenever they can — they carry a still with them, on a handcart, so they can make more whenever they camp anywhere for any length of time. The women throw their bodies along the road rather than carry them like Mary does and, I suppose, me as well, as if we were jugs of milk that might spill if we didn't take care. They spread their legs when they sit by the fire and suck in the heat of the flames. Right in. No underpants. They laughed at the way we looked and at our dresses.

'What have you your hair pulled out of the roots like that for?' they said, pulling it down. 'Who do you think you are anyway?'

We have flat black hair, which falls lank down the sides of our faces when the bands are off. Our dresses are plain grey calico.

'You are a sight,' they said, 'for sore eyes.'

They did not ask where we had come from or why we had joined them. They could guess. The surprising thing was that they let us stay with them, and they gave us some of their food.

'I want to leave them as soon as we land,' Mary said. 'I can't stand them.'

We were eating half a loaf of bread we'd got from them. We had not had bread in months.

'How can we do that? We don't know our way around. We don't know the language.'

'Do you think that lot of eejits know any language apart from their own Paddy bad language?'

They did, some of them, speak Welsh and English, because they had been over before. More importantly, they could get

295

food wherever they went. They could snare rabbits and hares. grouse and pheasants, they could make whiskey and tin cans. And they could beg and sell, they could steal and frighten people into giving them things. They could erect a tent that kept out the rain. We couldn't do even one of these things.

We soon learned.

'Into the town and come home with your dinner,' Molly Dunne, the one who talked to us most said. She had grey hair, curled like carrageen moss, down to her waist nearly, and a huge beak of a nose.

'Will we sell something?'

'What have you to sell?'

'Well …'

'You can sell yourselves if you like but I don't think you'll get much of a price with the cut of you. Do what you see the rest of them doing.'

We went off down the road from the camp with nine or ten of them, women and a few men. The women all had their striped cotton dresses on and big blue cloaks flying around them, and their red hair flying, and the men had white shirts and black coats and carried thick sticks on their shoulders. They moved in a strung-out group along the thin road from the sea to the marketplace, and we were among them. I thought they must look like the wind, blowing into the place. People scattered before them as if they were — the wind, or a band of bad mischievous fairies. The little Welsh women in their black clothes, with their little white lace bonnets close to their faces, fled.

Not all of them saw us, or got away in time. The tinkers cornered any who stayed on the street.

'Ma'am, will you buy a pot from me? A good little pot?'

The Welsh women looked terrified and said in their sing-song voices, '*Dim Sasenig*', although the tinkers were speaking Irish. The men stood close by, staring at the frightened women with their cat eyes, rubbing their sticks thoughtfully. All the women bought a pot or a pan or a mug and then ran into some shop. I heard the word '*Gwydellion*' for the first time. '*Gwydellion Gwydellion Gwydellion.*' It was a whisper, a whimper and a curse. Also a warning and a plea for help. I knew what it meant without asking.

I stole a loaf, not from a stall or a shop, but from a woman's basket. She put her basket down on the grey slabs while she tested some apples on a stall. In the basket were eggs. butter and something I did not recognise, a thick wedge of red stuff, like butter, as well as the loaf of bread. I pretended to be looking at the apples and pears which were heaped on the stall. The woman behind the stall looked suspiciously at me and muttered '*Gwydellion*' under her breath but not aloud. She wasn't sure, maybe. I did not look quite like the other Gwydellion, with my black hair, which I had tied back again behind my neck, and my plain dress.

It was easy to snatch the bread and then I ran away like the hammers of hell.

'Good girl yourself,' Molly Dunne said. 'I didn't think you had it in you.'

Neither did I. I was as proud as punch, and Mary was as downhearted and disapproving as you would expect her to be, a girl who had spent a year studying with the nuns and who might have been some sort of a kitchen nun herself, if things had gone different.

When we camped near a town we were often attacked. People came and tried to set fire to our tents. Often fights broke out because the tinkers were quick to defend themselves. The Welsh men were smaller than ours but they were strong; they had plenty to eat and did not drink whiskey, only their own sweet ale. Once, one of our lads was killed in one of these battles. What Molly said was, 'Just as well it was not the other way round, or we'd all be on the way to Van Diemen's Land, if not worse.'

That was the first time I heard about Father Toban. It was actually the first time I heard about religion from the band, but now it turned out that they wanted Father Toban to bury the dead boy, one of the Connors. They wanted him to get a Christian burial and Father Toban was their only chance of that. 'He is the only Catholic priest in all Wales,' they said.

'Where is his church?' This was Mary. She'd want to know, so she could visit it and get Mass. That she had not got Mass in weeks and weeks was a great heart's scald to her.

'Oh, be quiet, you fool! Do you think he'd have a church in this place?'

'I see a lot of churches.'

'Not one Catholic church.'

'What is their religion, then?'

'They are Protestant, and worse than that.'

'What is worse?'

'They are heathens like the blacks of Africa or the wild men of America.'

'They look like Protestants to me,' I said. And they did. I had never in Ireland seen anyone that looked half as Protestant as the Welsh women, not even in Dublin or Kingstown.

'They are Centers. The Centers is what they call themselves, they are worse than the Protestants.'

We did not find Father Toban and Tadg was buried in a bog on the slopes of the mountain called Wydfa, where we camped after the fight that killed him. It was a remote place, not too close to any town, and there we felt safe. Some villages, Llanberis and Beddgelert, were about an hour or two's walk away, and during the day we could visit them, sell tin cans or steal. I never begged. I couldn't, although Mary became quite good at that. I stole all before me, preferring that, even though I knew what would happen if I got caught. I stole from farms as well as from towns — eggs and milk, bread sitting out to cool on windowsills. I took the red stuff called, I knew now, cheese. Once, I lifted a lamb from under the nose of a boy on the side of Wydfa. Naoise, whom I had got to know by then, killed it for me and we all ate it, roasted over the fire, for supper.

We were at Wydfa for a long time, for months. The tents bleached in the sunshine as the summer wore on, and I lay on the short grass, smelling thyme and gorse, and all the summer smells, and felt happy. There were hares and rabbits in the mountains, carrots and even potatoes on the farms, everything you could think of in the shops of the village. I felt my face getting plumper, browner, and saw this happening to Mary, too, although she was very thin otherwise. I liked, as well as all this, living in a tent. I liked to feel the sun heating the canvas in the morning when I woke up, or even to hear the rain pounding against it, as if it would wear it away with its beating. I liked to know that I could pull it up in a few minutes and pack it on my back and move. Although we did not move, once we found the valley near Wydfa, and the band stayed there for a long long time, so long that the Welsh people came to know it and to call it the Valley of the Gwydellion.

Mary met the Ladies of Llangollen. Of course she did. She had heard about them at home. For weeks she had been trying to drag me to Llangollen to meet them. She hated the Gwydellion with a vengeance, hated them as much as the Welsh did, if not even more. And they hated her, too, because they were not stupid and could see her hatred. She was above them all, always thinking of her convent and our father's house and our family. She could not forget. If it had not been for me they would have thrown her out, or they would have starved her or maybe killed her.

She met one of the Ladies on the main street of the town less than an hour after we had arrived there. How did she know who it was? She knew because the lady was the richest-looking old woman walking along the main street on her own, and also because she was wearing trousers. A black coat, black trousers, a high stiff white collar. A man's black hat. Everyone knew that that's what the Ladies wore as soon as they got away from their families (before, in Ireland, they wore silk dresses, pink and yellow, ball gowns, lovely hats, just like all other fine ladies).

Was the Lady of Llangollen delighted to meet a sister Irishwoman? She was not. The country was crawling with them. 'Here is a halfpenny for you now,' she said to Mary, and turned away from her.

'I am not begging, yer hanner,' said Mary, speaking English. 'I am not a tinker at all but a respectable Irish girl looking for a place, yer hanner. I have read the Sixth Reader and was a monitor in my own school in Kilkenny.'

Mary said that because she knew the Ladies of Llangollen were from Kilkenny. She thought it would arouse some neighbourly sympathy, although we hadn't been neighbours, exactly, with the Butlers of Ormonde. Still, it worked. The lady in the black trousers invited Mary up to her house the next day. I went with her, at her insistence.

It was the strangest house I ever saw. It was perched like a bird's nest set on the side of a hill, shaded by big oak trees. The roof was thatched, high and pointed like a cock of hay, and it had tiny black windows set into it, like shiny black eyes. The doors were also black, and when you came close to them you could see they were carved all over with angels and devils and mermaids and foxes and birds and fishes. The walls of the house were white stone, crossed with thick oak beams like the cross on Calvary. Inside, the house was packed with things: furniture, books, ornaments, musical instruments, brass flowerpots. The walls were so thick with pictures that you could not see any wall at all. The furniture was made of the same kind of wood as the front door: black oak, heavy as lead, knotted and curled all over with engravings. Everything was as cluttered up as it possibly could be.

We sat in the kitchen, of course, and talked to the cook, in Welsh — we had learned enough now to have a little conversation. The lady in the trousers came and talked to us in English and then we ate scones and jam and drank some coffee.

Naoise looked different from the others. All the other men looked the same to me, with their wild eyes and skin that looked as if a fine sack cloth had been draped across it, their hair sticking up like straw on their heads, or like bushes of gorse. Naoise had tidy hair, and his skin was clean and glossy, like an ordinary Irishman's, except that on the side of his face he had a birthmark. It was a small purple patch, between his cheekbone and his ear, shaped like a potato, a port wine stain.

The mark was small and you would hardly notice it but it is that that made him quiet and good. Even when he got drunk, as they all did, from the Welsh beer, stolen from farms, as often as from their *poitín*, he did not shout or swear or fight with his stick, but looked contented and became sleepy. Maybe he did not drink quite as much as most of them. He didn't beat his wife, not that I could see, but sat with her and talked to her, and sometimes he played with their baby, counting her toes and singing, 'This little piggy went to market', or carrying her on his shoulders as he walked about, showing her things.

When I needed pots I went to him rather than to anyone else, because he was the only man in the band I wasn't afraid of. He didn't mind helping me — I gave him some of the money I made, and bits of anything I got. I gave his wife some blue ribbons I stole from a stall in Betws-y-Coed once, and she took them, although she had not much to say to me. Jealous. Naoise and I were fond of one another, we all three knew it.

One night I caught him alone, behind the encampment, where I was fetching water from the stream. He stood still beside me while I filled the pandy and when I stood up he was right in front of me, his face close to my face, his stomach to my stomach. I put my free hand on his face and caressed it. I couldn't stop my hand going up to his face, he was so close to me, it was dark and silent in the middle of the mountains, so that I felt everything in the world had stopped moving. We kissed.

After that he didn't speak to me for a few weeks and made a show of being fond of his wife, putting his arm around her when I was near them. I let on I didn't care. His wife was pregnant again, yellow-skinned and dirty, with her domes hanging off her, and smelly and old-looking. She was the way the tinker women are as soon as they are married any length of time at all. Scrap.

Poor thing, poor thing, poor scrap. He had kissed me for three minutes, hard, and his heat and his man's smells had gone right into me and stayed there.

We were scullery maids. They had a scullery maid already, a little Welsh girl called Gwynn, and they did not really need us but took us out of pity for Mary, who begged. Mary is a good begger. We were to get our keep but no wages at all. Our bedroom was in a hayshed in the garden.

'It's better than that tinker camp,' Mary said, stretching in the straw.

Old dry dust tickled my nose and the straw scratched my skin. 'Oh yes indeed,' I said.

All day long we worked in the kitchen. Mary washed up, standing over the sink, scrubbing pots and dishes, glasses, cups and plates. I got up at six in the morning to light the fire and make the early morning tea for the cook and for the ladies. I scrubbed the front steps and the nagged floor of the kitchen. I brought the rubbish to the dump around the back and I emptied chamber pots from the bedrooms and I hung washing out to dry and brought it in. I gathered vegetables from the garden.

Most of the things I did were hard and unpleasant, the things none of the others wanted to do. But after a while I learned how to cook some things. I learned how to brew beer.

I learned to spin flax and wool, and at night in the winter I sat by the fire with a candle burning and hemmed the linen sheets.

The scullery maid hadn't much work left. She peeled vegetables, she brought stuff in from the garden. Sometimes she went off to the town to market. We never did. Never left the house at all. In eight months we never walked outside the gate.

The scullery maid did not talk to us much. None of the maids did. The kitchen maids were Welsh and the upper maid was English. The English maid never talked to the Welsh ones, not because she did not know their language, but because she felt so high and mighty. And now the Welsh maids had someone to look down upon themselves. Us. It impressed them not a bit that we could speak some Welsh, as well as English and Irish. But it did impress the Ladies, a little.

'Why did you not go to the workhouse?'

'We tried to get into it but it was full. Hundreds of people were turned away, not just us.'

'You did not think of going to America?'

'We had not the price of the ticket. Maybe …?'

But we would not get the price of the ticket from here either, since we never got a penny.

'Did your family die?'

'They all died.'

'Of the fever?'

'The fever, yes.'

'It is the fever that kills people, not the hunger, isn't it?'

'Yes, ma'am.'

We were hungry and that is why the fever got us. It would not have got us if we had had enough to eat. When we cut through the lumpy potatoes in July, through their browny-purple, warty skins, and saw them black and sticky inside, soft and sweet, we saw the fever. Their sweet sickening smell was the smell of the fever. The hunger and the fever were the same thing, although people like to think they were different.

Mary had let on we had had a good farm.

'The hunger was not bad in our village,' I said to the lady. 'Everyone had enough. There were a lot of fish in the river, and we had bread and milk, butter. We had corn. The people worked hard and had enough to eat. It was not like other places, in our village. It was the fever that killed people, not the hunger.'

She nodded, her blue eyes sparkling, her little glasses sparkling. 'Yes, yes, the fever is the tragedy. We sent what we could.'

The girls in the kitchen thought this was a joke. They thought the Ladies were a joke. You could tell this from the way they called them the Ladies of Llangollen when it was not necessary to do so.

'Ellen, go and empty the Ladies of Llangollen's pots,' the cook would say.

'The Ladies of Llangollen like their beef rare,' she laughed. 'Oh yes, they do. Rarer than any man, rare as rarebit.'

Mary got cross when this sort of thing went on. She got so cross that she cried, because she was so grateful to them for rescuing her from the tinkers. 'We could be dead,' she said. 'They have saved our lives.'

'Yes,' I said.

'Look at the food we get.'

'Yes.'

'And the dry place we have to live.'

'Yes.'

Mary thought she would be rewarded for her hard work by being promoted and getting paid. She thought she would become a lady's maid here in the cottage, and then become a lady's maid somewhere else, and live in a big house, with her own bedroom and her own sitting room. That was her dream. The cups and the plates gleamed, she polished them so much. They were like lakes in the summer sunshine, each white china plate, or like valleys full of hard snow. Every saucer shone on its shelf, shiny as a new dream.

The scullery maid told us the Ladies were not from Ireland at all. They were not the real Ladies of Llangollen.

'Who are they, then?' we asked.

'They are Englishwomen, queer Englishwomen, who have bought their house and wear their clothes. And carry on in the same way. The Irish ladies died long ago.'

We did not believe them. We thought they were saying it to annoy us, because we were Irish like the Ladies.

'And we are ladies, too,' Mary said. She said it when we were alone.

'Ladies, but not like them.'

'Why not?' she said, pretending not to know.

I blushed, inside anyway. The thought of what the Ladies did confused me completely. They had one bed in their dark, lovely, oaky room, where there was plenty of room for two.

'They are kind. They love one another. What's wrong with that?' Mary said.

At the back of the house was an orchard, with apples, pears, greengages and plums, and there were many fruit bushes and vegetables. I had never been near so much food, even in the convent. Every day we had chops or boiled mutton, bread and cheese, apples, plums, sweet cake, beer.

One day soon after we arrived the cook made summer pudding. I watched her doing it, because I had brought in the berries from the garden and because I wanted to see how she made something with a name like that. She put slices of bread into a bowl, then filled the bowl with blackcurrants, redcurrants, blackberries. Then she put more bread across the top of the bowl and weighed it down with a pound weight from the scales. She carried it to the coldest place in the house, the dairy, and left it there to cool, beside a basin of silent cream.

The next day she carried in the pudding to the big wooden table in the kitchen. When it was turned out on a plate it looked funny, white with red-purple blotches. She cut into the skin with a knife. Inside, it was black and purple, soft, sticky, sweet. She gave us each a slice and poured yellow cream over it from the blue jug.

It tasted like the sun on the white wall in the garden. It tasted like the smell of white cotton that has dried on the line. It tasted like Naoise. Not like his mouth, which was soft and salty, like all men's mouths, but like his name and like his face.

I closed my eyes and said to myself, 'Please, Naoise. Please.' I wished I had a salt herring to eat, so that I could dream of him. But there were no salt herrings in the house. I dreamt of him anyhow.

One of my jobs was to help the washerwoman who came on Mondays to boil the clothes. I helped her wring, in the hot steamy washroom, and I hung the clothes out for her. When they were dry I carried them into the kitchen and put them on the table and then someone from upstairs came and took them away.

I liked to be out in the yard where long lines were strung between trees, and I liked the feel of the clean cotton against my face. All the lovely white clothes, the nightgowns and frilly blouses, the aprons, the sheets and pillowslips, smelled of the wind, and of something else, grass maybe, or leaves. I let my nose into the heaps of white cloth, and let the sheets flap around me like clouds.

I was there in April. We had spent many months in Llangollen, autumn and winter, dark days in the hot kitchen. Mary was still washing up. Her hands were big and red, and the skin on her arms permanently puckered. I was still in the scullery, doing everything.

The garden was full of daffodils. They had thousands, all along the stone wall, under every tree. The sun danced. Soon it would be Easter. My arms were full of white clothes and I had a white apron on and a white cap.

Someone was standing by the wall, beside the green door leading onto the lane outside. A man, taller than a Welshman. He had a black soft hat, a black coat with tails, and a thick stick. He was standing very still and quietly, looking at me. I knew he had been there for a while, because I had heard nothing at all except the wind rustling in the clothes on the line.

I put my heap of clothes on the damp grass and went over to him.

'I thought you were a goose,' he said, opening the gate. I went out with him onto the road.

A man with grey curly hair and a tweed jacket, a gentleman, passed close to our tent.

"That is Father Toban,' Naoise said. This was the fourth day in Caer Gybi.

'How do you know?'

'I know by the cut of him. He wears that sort of coat. I will speak to him and see.'

Naoise spoke to him in Irish and he answered in Irish. He said: 'I am not Father Toban.'

'You are,' Naoise said. 'I know you are Father Toban. You will give us a blessing now before we sail for Ireland, since we do not know what is in store for us.'

'If I said I was not a priest but a Protestant and an Englishman, would you believe me?'

'I would not, Father.'

'If I said I could not bless you, would you hit me?'

'I might, Father.'

'If I said I would not give you my blessing, would you kill me with your big shillelagh?'

'I would, Father.'

'Kneel down there the three of you.'

I would not kneel for him. The little girl could not kneel, but Naoise held her in front of him so the blessing would land on her. I watched him, bowing his head and closing his eyes, to the man he believed was the priest.

My father said to me and Mary, the only ones left, after he, and everyone else in our parish, had lost their work on the Relief: 'Kill me and eat me. I will die soon enough anyway.'

It was the beginning of July, hungry July, the beginning of summer. We had dug the first potatoes early. He knew it would be hungry July, hungry August, hungry winter. Again. Half the people in the village were dead. The landlord had sent others to Canada on a ship from Cork but we had heard terrible things about that journey, and about Canada.

'Get a passage to America,' he said, 'as soon as you can.'

I said yes. I knew I would not go to America, because I would never get the money for the fare together. I knew if I had half a crown I would get to Wales and the poorhouse there would feed me.

'*In nomine Patris et Filii et Spiritus Sancti. Vade in pace. Amen,*' the man in the tweed coat said.

We sailed that afternoon for home.

MARY O'DONNELL

Come In — I've Hanged Myself

The social worker had described him as fairly typical of his age group. "You know the sort of thing I mean," he drawled casually over the phone, "a bit mixed-up, needs somebody patient to take an interest." And Lorna, eager to appear cooperative and parental, had replied, "I know, I can imagine," when she could do neither. Missing his parents. Father in England. Mother in a psychiatric ward. She made a point of not tidying the house on the day of his arrival. An air of spit-and-polish would inhibit him, she thought. He'd want to relax, feel at home, as if he belonged. No point in creating a formal sanctuary, a sacramental atmosphere. Feeling slightly apprehensive she left the previous day's papers tossed on the floor of the sitting room and decided not to arrange fresh flowers in a vase in place of wilting carnations.

When they opened the hall door, the social worker was hearty. He grinned, pulling on his beard as he introduced his charge. "And this bod here is our Martin!" he enthused with a flourish of the hand. "Go on shake hands with Lorna and Luke like a good man," he intoned encouragingly. They shook hands. Lorna heard herself respond brightly, cheerfully, to the mumbled greeting. Her head, unexpectedly alarmed and unsettled, whirred with attentiveness. He was pathetically ugly. It had nothing to do with dress or build. He wore black and grey, the current A-bomb garb of despair and redundancy: black trousers which ended mid-calf, a grey shirt under a black tunic. A chain belt hung round his narrow hips. He was much what they'd expected. "Come on in," Luke beckoned, sounding hospitable and easy-going. Fatherly. "The fire's just on — it'll only take a wee minute to warm up."

They chatted, the first awkward moments mitigated by mugs of coffee. Mugs, not cups. Deliberately chosen for the occasion. One part of her responded superficially. Another wrestled with uncertain feelings. The boy looked around aimlessly. He could only be described as unfortunate looking: his hair was wiry and short, neither brown nor blond but pale and neutral. His face was ravaged with acne, the skin waxy, the cheeks and chin pocked with volcanic swellings, angry pimples, and the scars of half-healed eruptions. His jaw showing the primitive angularity of a young male. Here and there, wisps of hair sprouted. His eyes were pale blue, ringed with a pig-like pinkness.

They'd painted the walls of his room a plain buff, in case he wanted to put up posters. He shuffled from one foot to the other, sheepish and tongue-tied.

"D'you think you'll be OK here, Martin?" she asked.

"Yeh."

"If there's anything you need you'll let us know, won't you?"

"Where's the jacks?"

"Oh of course, nearly forgot," Luke half-apologised. "This way." The chain belt clanked all the way across the landing.

All young people liked chips. Burgers and chips, Luke had suggested. So Lorna chopped onions, minced round steak, added herbs and bound the lot with egg in big juicy mounds.

The chips were home-made. They sat down together, feeling awkward.

"Are you hungry, Martin?" she asked, certain of culinary success.

"Yeh."

"Oh — you can wash your hands at the sink before you begin, if you want," Luke interjected. They'd agreed on this in advance. No direct requests yet. Certainly no orders. You achieved more by example.

"I washed them half an hour ago."

"Fine. Fine," Lorna said quickly, her look meeting Luke's. She handed the boy a plate. He eyed it uncertainly.

"I don't eat chips."

"Oh?" she queried, surprised. Waiting for him to say more. He didn't. Began to pick at the burger.

"I don't like pepper in things."

"Oh well, we'll get you something else then." She made to remove the plate. He stopped her.

"It's all right. I'll eat it this time." He sounded almost aggressive with his deep and half-broken croak.

"Are you sure? It's no trouble." She laughed uneasily. She was uncharacteristically nervous. He poked at the burger, cut it finally and ate a mouthful, looking straight ahead. This had to be what a blind date was like. No inkling of what was in the other person's head. No clue to their wants. And natural parents could imagine things. Could trace things, mistakenly or not, to genetics. But this was *tabula rasa*. He lifted his fork solemnly. "I'll eat this today. The chips make me skin worse. I like them. But that's why I don't eat them."

It was as if a light had gone on. She found herself admiring his blithe reference to his skin, to the distorted plumage of his face. He had declared his cards, in a manner of speaking. Or some of them. Had told them something about the sort of person he was. She was flooded with curiosity. All things in time. The rest of the meal passed easily. She and Luke tried to tell him about their friends and their friends' children. Their relatives and the Sunday visit in a few weeks time.

He liked toad-in-the-hole, he told Lorna suddenly, one Friday. "And shepherd's pie. Me Ma used to make things like that when she was feelin' up to it," he remarked.

"I'll do shepherd's pie tomorrow," she said, delighted at this reference to his mother. Things were shaping up.

"No. Do whatever ya were goin' to do," he said hastily, in a wavering baritone voice. Of course, she thought. How stupid. How insensitive not to realise that to cook a favourite meal would perhaps make him lonely.

She knocked on his door that night. To say goodnight, even though they'd already done that. "Yeh," he called express-ionlessly. She pushed the door. He lay on the bed, arms behind his head, staring at the ceiling. The radio was on. They'd get him a better one, with headphones. And tapes perhaps. He liked AC/DC and Cindy Lauper. "Good-night," she mouthed, unwilling to disturb him. Unwilling also perhaps, to deal with the uneasiness he aroused in her each time they attempted communication. It was apparently simpler for Luke. No complications. A bland directness. Mutual. Devoid of complexities. What could they really say about what went on behind that face? That pock-marked face. Sometimes, it seemed as if he wasn't really with them. Like a strange bird, an alien creature moulding itself to an existence where everything was cruelly unfamiliar, where the other denizens were made of paper. Hollow where he was full. Useless at meeting his wants. Or perhaps *they* were the aliens.

He grew sullen. More truculent in manner. Determined seemingly to thwart their efforts. He despised routine. The night before the Sunday visitors arrived, he stayed awake, listening to music. That did not disturb them. More the notion of a wakeful and slightly hostile presence stalking around downstairs. The next morning, Lorna asked him if he did that often.

"What?" he muttered blankly, staring into space.

"Stay up all night."

"Yeh."

She would be patient. This was the sort of thing you got.

"Can't you sleep then?" she continued casually, pretending to be more interested in the cookery book she held in her hand.

The boy was silent. Just when she'd decided that he was going to be perverse, he stirred.

"I can think better."

"Oh. I see."

Don't tell me we're going to have four months of nocturnal philosophising, she thought. In the summer too. He should be out and about during the day, getting some air. Still. Fairly typical behaviour, when you thought about it. Attention. He probably did lots of things for attention. They'd have to ignore the exhibitionism. Make him feel important in other ways. Build up his self-esteem. Life makes you what you are.

Later that morning, she tried to involve him in the dinner preparations. But he dawdled uninterestedly, arms folded. Watching her. She had to admit that he was tiresome. The old understanding between herself and Luke vanished in his presence, so bent were they on pleasing him. Nothing pleased him. He was a gigantic puzzle, brooding and mysterious, who foiled their anxious attempts to find the missing piece — some anodyne to a mutual and mounting chagrin. Her patience was dwindling steadily. He'd been with them two weeks.

"Right Martin," she announced briskly, trying a new approach, "you can set the table — you'll find cutlery in that drawer and the crockery's here beside you." She smiled matter-of-factly. He didn't smile back. Just looked. Instantly seeing through her facile adult psychology. But he went to the drawer and got out the cutlery.

Dinner was a disaster. The vegetables were passed around while Luke sliced the lamb. The boy stared at his plate, pale-eyed. Somebody — Luke's father, she thought — started grumbling about unemployment. It was an easy topic, the sort of thing about which everybody could rave, feel hard done by. They bantered agreeably for a few minutes over the clink of plates and cutlery. "What do you think, Martin?" Luke's mother asked gently.

"About what?" he muttered, not looking at her.

"Well," she hesitated, "about unemployment and that, all those young people like yourself who'll be leaving school in a few years and no jobs for them — what do you think's going to happen?" He put down his knife and fork as if about to make a statement of policy.

"I don't know and I don't give a damn," he spat.

There was a brief, uneasy silence. Lorna cut in.

"Right, you don't give a damn. Very original, Martin," she smiled.

"I'm not tryin' to be *original*," he scowled, mimicking her.

Her face flared. "More lamb please," Luke's father said, clearing his throat.

"The streets are going to run red." They all looked up startled by the sudden announcement made five minutes later.

"What you were askin'," he gestured at Luke's mother with his knife.

"It's going to be a blood-bath in ten years." He helped himself to another piece of meat.

"However do you mean?" Luke's mother asked quizzically.

"Don't have to explain, streets are goin' to run red — I don't have to justify that to anybody," he growled, head swaggering in the glow of their acute attention. Somebody — Luke more than likely — sighed.

They talked in low voices as they did the dishes.

"A lot of it's for attention," Luke reasoned. "If we ignore it he'll stop eventually." Lorna disagreed.

"We have ignored it and there's no change," she fumed.

"He's still acting as if he were doing us a favour by being here — it's as if we're idiots — can you imagine him when he goes back to school?" She paused to pull the plug, and dried her hands angrily. "Carrying on about us: how we behave, imitating us!"

When they went into the sitting-room, he was rolling his own cigarettes. As if he were alone. She watched him, fascinated. Totally self-engrossed. Oblivious to their presence as he fiddled with the flimsy paper, his shoulders hunched, head and neck protruding forwards. Sixteen. She reminded herself of their obvious advantages. And his disadvantages. Insecurity, fear, immaturity, no experience of a loving home. And an appalling appearance. Pity was the last thing he needed. She felt so little affinity with him. Because he gave nothing. Went through the motions of being cooperative. If he enjoyed anything, he never said. Presumably he'd never been shown how to express pleasure. Maybe there'd been none to express in the first place. No. It was up to her and Luke to make the effort. Go farther than half-way. Beyond the median line of compromise. Possibly nobody had ever gone beyond what was necessary on his account.

"Don't flick ash on to the carpet, love — there's an ashtray beside you." He glared at her. The family left early. They departed quietly. Luke's mother would probably phone the following day.

No doubt he saw them as set in their ways, committing over and over the mortal sin of middle-class adulthood. Dinosaurs with pea-brains, who knew nothing about pain, loneliness, anguish, who were eternally sure of themselves. Yet his own behaviour was so familiar. Predictable. The very thing he objected to continuously. *Come In — I've Hanged Myself* proclaimed a sign on his door. Another, on the bedroom wall, read: *Life Is Like A Shit Sandwich*. Everything about him was an indication of internal furies, an unsubtle display of nihilism and youthful ennui.

It came to a head the next day. Luke had gone shopping, unable to persuade the boy to accompany him.

"That's wimin's stuff," he announced to Lorna.

"In this house it's everybody's stuff," she replied firmly. "You can go next week, Martin — we all take turns here."

He rolled his eyes heavenwards, curled his pale lips down defiantly, helped himself to one of her cigarettes.

"Are you out of pocket-money already?" she asked. He lit up, contemplating the smoke. "Nope," he muttered.

"What would you have done if I'd said you couldn't have one?"

"I'd have taken it anyway."

The little shite. He knew how to rise her.

"Look," she began reasonably, "we've tried to make life pleasant for you but all you do is throw everything back at us … as if … as if …"

"I don't owe you anything," he shouted, hammering the table with his fist. A hint of violence that made her stomach curdle. She studied him carefully, lighting a cigarette herself. Distant and assessing. He was hateful-looking when he was angry. He returned her gaze, challengingly.

"Martin, the one thing you do owe us," she began softly, determined not to raise her voice, "is consideration." She gesticulated with the lit cigarette, "And that means making an effort — some attempt at playing your part — and none of this 'I-don't-give-a-damn' nonsense. We only want you to feel at home …"

Suddenly he rose, pushing the chair back noisily, stubbing the cigarette so roughly that it broke in two.

"Nobody could be at home in this … *kip!*" he bellowed. He might as well have hit her. "Well, if that's how you feel Martin you've only to say the word; we don't want to hold you against your will if you're not happy; if you can do better elsewhere …" Echoes of her own mother, years ago, when faced with mutiny. Her voice was even, controlled, in spite of the hurt. To her surprise, his face flooded pinkly.

"You don't really want me here at all," he croaked. Her face dropped.

"Ya couldn't have yer own kids so ya got me on trial, like y'can hand me back when me time's up, forget all about me."

He paused momentarily, like a hurricane building up to its peak of destruction, the veins on his neck bulging.

"I don't want to be stuck with a pair of cranks who couldn't have their own; you're batty, that's what you are, with your books and music," he goaded effectively. Despising. Determined to stab where it hurt most.

"Anybody that listens to operas, ah — whatever ya call it — has to be up the creek. A header. That's what you are," he hissed maliciously, pointing at her.

There had to be some redemption. Something positive had to come out of this. A reason she could connect with, some moment of salvation that would heal them both. She would ignore most of it. She would. She would. She tried to control the nervous tremor in her voice. But she could not let him see her reduced. Perceptive boy. She'd call his bluff. "You're right, Martin," she tried to sound blasé, unshockable. "We couldn't have our own kids. And you're right again. You are second-best. In fact, come to think of it, you're third-best, because we couldn't adopt either." He shrank visibly. But she couldn't stop. Knew she was hitting back. Meeting him with even greater maliciousness. And she didn't want to stop. "That's if you go around measuring things. We don't. It's nothing to do with third-best. You're you. You're nearly grown up. You're not a child even if you behave like one. We thought we'd like to have somebody like you live with us. We have lots of space. It could be handy for a fellow … and we're not trying to be your parents." Her voice jerked. He started to shriek at her. "But y'are, y'are!"

The perversity of it dawned. The real want. But, by then, she could not relent. "Look honey, I wouldn't want to be your Ma for all the tea in China. Don't delude yourself," her voice hard.

Luke came in then. Looked expectantly from one to the other, sensing an airing of emotion on the normally neutral domestic channels. "I hate you, *bitch*!", he roared, kicking the chair as he made for his room. Crying. She was crying too.

It was fifteen minutes before she could say anything comprehensible. It poured down her face. They couldn't get this right either. Came across to the boy as a pair of stuffed shirts. Tied up in reproductive tensions and what they had transmitted to him as "culture". Antiques who knew nothing about anything that mattered. Who would soon be extinct. Acting Mr and Mrs Bountiful and *understanding*. In reality, they understood nothing. They had nothing. He'd stripped them, bared the hoarded pain of years, the mask she wore to conceal it. Like some wild thing tearing at flesh. And she was no better. Had kicked back every bit as hungry. As defiant. Had re-affirmed the image of self-loathing and repulsion which he harboured towards himself.

Unforgivable.

They decided not to disturb him when he didn't appear for tea. Let him cool off. She began to think of the sign on the door. Supposing? Would he realise they cared? Before they went to bed, she knocked on his door. Silence. She tried again. A rustling sound. Then silence. She knocked a third time.

"It's open," rasped a half-fledged voice.

He didn't look at her. Lying on the bed, smoking, the air curling grey-blue. Flat out, locked up in himself, impenetrable as a piece of steel. Wrap the tender part up. Bury it like a broken bone. Let it fester.

"Martin?" Silence. He exhaled.

"I'm sorry. Just called in to say ... that I really didn't mean ... never let the sun set on your anger ..." She was incoherent. Touched his shoulder. He flinched.

"There's food in the fridge ... if you're hungry ..." She left quietly.

Went to bed, doomed and impotent. They were a right pair. Clueless. And the boy hated her. Clearly. The venom he packed. The blind energy of something unexploded, which could shred their civilised masks to ribbons, expose the raw nerve of need. Headers. That's what he'd called them. Called *her.*

She wanted to crawl away. Anywhere. To find peace. Somewhere safe. Where the effort of doing the right thing wouldn't always backfire in her face like a badly primed pistol. A place of reason and salvation. Some people had it easy. She drifted towards sleep. So easy. All fell into place. Two point five: average family.

MARY MORRISSY

A Lazy Eye

Bella Carmichael woke in a pool of blood. Startled she lay rigid, afraid to move in case she would exacerbate the wound. She was surprised she felt no pain but the shock was probably acting as an anaesthetic. The sheet, blue in the moonlight, felt clammy around her loins. At first she thought it was the heat. It was a sticky night. Clouds raced across the moon in a thunderous flurry. The room juddered suddenly; the first breaking of the storm? Then it heaved again and she felt a rumbling beneath the floor. An earthquake. I have slept through the first great upheavals, she thought. The heaviness in my limbs is because I am pinned under some vast piece of fallen masonry. I should have stood under a door lintel, she thought. Only after several minutes when the wheels set up a clangour and there was a soft screech of brakes did she remember where she was. She was on a train, on the top bunk of a sleeper. Somewhere in Europe. Beneath her, a travelling companion who had boarded late the night before, groaned and turned over. Bella reached up and turned on the overhead light. There seemed to be blood everywhere — a huge stain beneath her, a clotted pattern on the top sheet, smears on her thighs. Damn it to hell, she cursed, my period.

Bella's trip had been dogged by small misfortunes and large disappointments — waking on a bus journey having dribbled on the lap of a nun, ousted by an attendant who caught her washing her armpits in the ladies' room of a motorway cafe, hissed at in the street by men in Naples. There was the dismal business of tourist offices where she had queued for hours, the crowded hostel rooms with ragged underwear and socks hanging to dry on the bed ends. It was not as she had expected. Setting out she had envisaged being caught up in revolution, swept up in some large-scale catastrophe, baton charges by police, a bombing in a public place — only these things, she felt, would give her stature. Instead here she was — in one of the two Germanys, was it? — with no tampons.

Bella's preoccupation with other people's tragedies had started years before with the death of President Kennedy. She remembered the newspaper pictures of Caroline Kennedy, a little freckled girl in a swing coat and ankle socks, clutching her mother's hand at Arlington Cemetery. Bella had been envious of her. She had been singled out, given the chance to be heroic, the small solemnity of her mourning emphasising the enormity of the offence. What could Bella point to in her own life that was of such epic proportion?

The Carmichaels went to school with their hems hanging and sugar sandwiches in their satchels. They slept two to a bed on sheets with a floral sprig pattern that had long since faded into faint track marks as if some tiny insect had laboured across the snowy wastes of the material. They played on a green in front of the house, scorched in the summer, a mire in the winter. They ate their meals in relays because the kitchen wasn't big enough to accommodate them all at once. From the scullery there would be the hissing sound of frying, a plate of potato cakes would nosedive to the table and there would be a spasm of outstretched arms. There were never any leftovers in the Carmichael household. The hot press, wedged between the lavatory and the bathroom on the cramped landing, was a common store of smocked dresses, woollens — pale and shrunken — odd socks balled up like snail shells. You closed your eyes and fished something out; it became yours for the day. Meanwhile, Granny Carmichael dozed in the sunken settee in the living room among crumpled newspapers and flayed LPs out of their sleeves. Above her on the mantelpiece — since this was the good room — was a proud Manhattan of football trophies.

Bella searched in vain for some singularity in all of this. Her homely mother with the soft, embarrassed look of a woman who has just given birth — well, in fact, she usually had. There were eleven of them, after all. Her sister, Phyllis, was already a grandmother. All of them had been rudely healthy; none had succumbed to wasting diseases; the next generation was ruddy and bold. And who would have assassinated Bella's father? He worked as a bank porter, standing to attention in a marbled lobby, his gold buttons gleaming, holding the door for customers. The only way he was likely to meet a violent, public death was at the hands of men in balaclavas with sawn-off shotguns. And even then, he was too comical and biddable a man to be killed thus. If a gang had held up the bank, Bella knew that he would have been the first to drop to the floor roaring 'Merciful hour!'

Bella had inherited her father's lazy eye. His gaze veered shiftily to the right as if something very lewd was going on behind other people's backs. As a child, Bella had thought of it as the evil eye, all-seeing, masterful. Until, that is, this congenital weakness of her father's emerged in her. Then it did not seem nearly dramatic enough. If it had been her choice Bella would have opted to be an albino like Deborah who lived two doors up — a short, white-headed girl with light, snowy lashes and pink, pained eyes. The other children regarded Deborah's short-sightedness as stupidity; they imitated her anguished grimace; they mimicked her dazed way of walking. But Bella saw her as saint-like, a precious, luminous creature, so sensitive that she could not bear the light of the world. She often speculated on how Deborah had come to be this way. Perhaps, at the moment of birth, a careless nurse had turned the full glare of the delivery room lamp on her and had scorched all the pigment from her skin and hair. Or, alternatively — an explanation which satisfied Bella more — Deborah had witnessed something as a baby that had been so frightful it had left her permanently pink with shame. What was a lazy eye in comparison to that?

Nevertheless, for one glorious year, Bella too was marked out. She had to wear a pair of glasses with the right lens patched over with sticking plaster. It gave her a lopsided, partial view of the world — a huge, pinkish blur before her and a sensation of an obstruction looming ahead which was never encountered but yet never went away. She sometimes feared that this flesh-coloured wall that met her gaze was, in fact, a fresh layer of skin growing over the unused eye. Frequently she had to take the glasses off to reassure herself that her walled-up eye was still there, and still worked.

'Is it sore?' her schoolfriends asked about the eclipsed eye, associating sticking plaster with pain. Some were convinced that Bella did not have a second eye; others that she had been badly scarred and it was too unsightly to expose. Her good eye languishing in its pink prison elicited a mixture of pity and regret. Bella was exempted from rough games; in the playground she was allowed to stand in at skipping in case a crack of the rope might send her glasses flying. Behind her back she knew they called her specky two-eyes but it was better than being 'just one of those Carmichaels'.

Even among the Carmichaels, Bella's spectacles were treated with a solicitude that was rarely shown to her. 'Where are Bella's glasses?' her mother would demand before each mealtime sitting as if they had a life independent of their owner. And Granny Carmichael was never allowed to reverse into the sofa or a fireside chair before the cushions were first checked for Bella's specs. Bella had always been a poor reader, besieged at school by hissing prompters as the gap between each of her blurted-out words yawned. But that year she was never once asked to read aloud. She discovered that the glasses with the patch were a protection behind which she could lazily daydream. And, in time, she grew to regard the unexposed part of her face as something magical, an obvious but secret wound, an area of deep mystery unclaimed by the world. And when the plaster was eventually removed the skin around her right eye had a pale, sickly look like the papery relic of a saint. Alas, the treatment worked. The lazy eye had righted itself and within six months, Bella didn't even have to wear glasses anymore.

Dawn crept into the compartment. Bella eased the blind up and watched as the night disappeared in long streaks of indigo cloud and a weak sun rose in the huge, bleached, watery sky. The train shuttled past dark, wooden-framed farmhouses huddled together like beasts averting their eyes from something ancient and frightening. Bella hung over the edge of her bunk and watched as the countryside passed like a speckled scarf drawn over her features — a toss of angry trees in her hair, the steep rise of pasture on her cheeks, a pair of boulders for her eyes. Fleeing through the early morning the train made hardly an impression on the landscape; it could not even boast of a shadow, Bella thought. She roused herself from her vacant-eyed stupor. What was she going to do about the mess in the bed? Her predicament reminded her of Franny, her next sister up, with whom she had shared a bed through her girlhood. Franny had been a bed-wetter. She slept so heavily that she never woke in time to make it to the toilet. She was a fat, indolent girl and the family considered this just another manifestation of her laziness. Bella would wake to the stench of pee and a sensation of hot seepage around her arse and Franny sitting on the side of the bed, head hanging, shoulders hunched, shivering and, Bella realised now, ashamed. But then she was convinced that Franny did it on purpose. And once her nocturnal crime was committed, Franny seemed incapable of remedying it. It was Bella who would have to get up and strip the bed while Franny stood listlessly to one side clutching her soaked nightie. Afterwards they would climb back into bed silently, carefully avoiding the damp spot in the middle covered now by the top sheet, and pulling the blankets up to their chins, they would turn away from one another resolutely and sleep back to back. In the morning, though, when Mrs Carmichael came to rouse them, it was Bella who would call out — 'Franny's done it again!'

Bella eased herself out of the sodden bunk and down the stepladder. Throwing on her dressing-gown she slipped into the deserted passageway and fled to the lavatory at the end of the carriage. If, at that moment, she could have leapt from the train without injuring herself, she would have done it. When she returned, the mystery occupant of the lower bunk was brushing her teeth at the tiny basin in the compartment. She was a large-boned young woman of about Bella's own age, with a fringe of heavy fair hair and a scrubbed complexion. She wore oversized, white pyjamas with navy piping on the collar. She stopped brushing as Bella came in. She had a rather fierce air, stooped thus, her teeth bared and little gobbets of toothpaste foaming at the corners of her mouth.

'Hello,' Bella said cautiously.

The girl nodded amiably. She spat noisily into the basin and wiped her mouth with a towel. Then she uncapped a bottle of breath freshener and with the exuberance of a schnapps drinker she tossed it back and gargled noisily, her throat rippling, her eyes rolling in the back of her head. Bella waited. She might as well have been in the back bedroom with Franny; travel might broaden the mind but it forced the body into the most narrow confines of intimacy with strangers. A jet of peppermint-coloured liquid was spewed into the basin, the tap was turned on to wash it away and then the girl turned and extended a hand.

'How do you do?'

She said this with the careful enunciation of one tackling a second language.

325

'My name is Irma. Good morning!'

Bella smiled tightly, her mind racing. She did not want to get trapped into pleasantries knowing what she had to ask this woman and the longer the pleasantries persisted the harder it would be to broach the subject.

'May I ask you something?'

'Ja! Sure!' Irma nodded enthusiastically.

'You wouldn't have any ... tampons?' She said the last word with emphasis.

Irma knitted her brow.

'Sanitary towels?' Bella ventured.

'Ah, towel!' Irma plucked from the basin the towel she had been using and proffered it.

'No, no ... sanitary pads.'

Irma shook her head quizzically.

'Period,' Bella said pointing extravagantly to herself. 'Blood.'

'Blood?' Irma looked alarmed.

If she didn't make herself clear soon, this girl would think she was a nutcase, Bella thought. She reached up and grabbed a fistful of bloody sheet from her bed.

'Ah, ja!' Irma smiled broadly. 'It's Auntie Jane, ja?'

Bella's father had financed her trip. Enda Carmichael, door-opener. He had left money. Not much, but they had all been surprised that he had any at all. Bella imagined him picking up and saving every dropped coin in the bank for forty years and putting them by. For what? For her, it had turned out. For Bella, my youngest daughter, the proceeds of my savings account. She was, along with her mother, the only one to be named. She wondered why. Granted, she had seen him through his final months — she was the only one of the brood now at home. Maybe her name was the only one of the eleven that came to mind. (He often got the girls mixed up. Their names were tradeable.) Or perhaps he had intended it this way all along? While she had longed for a father other than him, and a glamorous, dead version at that, he had been, in his way, singling her out for special attention.

Had Bella Carmichael and Irma Kalinin become friends they might, in years to come, have laughed about that early morning introduction, exaggerating the gulf of misunderstanding between them with each retelling. As it was, they smiled shyly about it over breakfast in the dining car and engaged in the small talk of low-budget travellers. That hostel in Vienna — eyes turned heavenward. How their paths had crossed unknowingly in Berlin. There was a beer hall in Munich Bella simply had to see; a cathedral in Budapest Irma mustn't miss. It struck Bella that at any given time Europe was being traversed by thousands of people plodding dutifully after one another on a sort of dull crusade, following the same route and using the same guidebook. It certainly convinced her that independent travel was neither spontaneous nor anonymous. Rather, she had felt like a piece of luggage abandoned on an airport carousel, going endlessly round and round. And as for anonymity, there was a letter from her mother at each *poste restante*. Of course, she needn't have collected any of them but it made her feel anchored in a new city to know that somewhere in a pigeon-hole in a gloomy post office a letter lay with her name on it. Through these letters the Carmichaels travelled with her. Across the seas the primacy of *their* news echoed — Johnny's new apprentice, Peggy's wedding plans, little Ivor's first words. This plaintive incantation of domestic news seemed more concrete than any of Bella's own experiences. If she had written back she would have been reduced to describing the grandeur of Rome. And what would they have made of that?

As Bella and Irma made their way back to their compartment, the train attendant who usually sat in a little cabin at the end of the carriage brushed past them. He was a small man with large brown eyes and a curiously aristocratic-looking moustache. There were nicotine stains on his fingers. He had appeared after they had crossed the Polish frontier, replacing the large Russian woman who wore a tight black pencil skirt and her blonded hair up. She would gratuitously lock the door of the toilet between stations and retreat to her little den where, Bella suspected, she grappled with passengers in a crumb-ridden bed or napped fully-clothed. She responded to any entreaty with a stony 'Niet!' This man, in comparison, had seemed almost pleadingly friendly. He always left the door of the cabin open. From outside it looked warm and dishevelled like an animal's lair. He kept the blind drawn so the light inside was brown and mottled. He brewed tea on a stove in the corner and made sandwiches with large beef tomatoes which he kept in a muslin bag under his bunk.

Now he strode purposefully by them, looking cross. He had been busy in their absence. There were great mounds of bed linen all along the corridors; he had stripped the beds. Bella was relieved. They were about to enter their compartment when he came up behind them again. He was accompanied by a ticket collector, a tall, stern-looking man with a pocked face and large hands, a bulky book of timetables tucked under his arm. The attendant pointed at Bella and expostulated in a rush of French.

'What's he saying?' Bella asked Irma.

'He is asking is this your compartment,' Irma repeated after the attendant. Bella nodded.

The attendant stooped and lifted one of her sheets from the floor. In the full glare of morning, the blood- stains looked deliberate, sinister. There was another rush of words from the attendant — agitation turning to anger.

'He asks what has been going on here,' Irma intoned.

Several passengers, hearing the commotion, came to the doors of their compartments. The attendant pointed to the sheet again and spat out another sentence.

'Animals. You are animals. What is going on here? Animals.' Out of Irma's cool mouth the words seemed disconnected like a soundtrack out of synch with the film.

The attendant poked a finger at Bella's breast.

'He is saying you should be ashamed of yourself.' Irma persisted dutifully with the translation. '*Never* in all his life has he ...'

He peered around the door of the compartment. His eyes narrowed. Some new accusation was about to be levelled. Bella held her breath.

'What perversions have you indulged in?' Bella felt she was now being directly accused by Irma. 'There has been evil-doing here.'

Irma delivered this with an air of finality. For the first time she met Bella's eye.

'Tell him,' Bella pleaded, 'for God's sake, tell him.'

'*Elle a ses règles,*' Irma said.

'Tell him I will pay for the sheets. How much? How much?'

'*Elle a ses règles,*' Irma repeated. '*Mon amie paiera.*'

The attendant shouted back, spittle on his lips, and pointed to the ticket collector.

'They do not want your money,' Irma said regretfully. 'They want you to leave the train.'

It was somewhere in Belgium; that was all she knew. A small town; a two-minute stop. The ticket collector, on whose authority she had been banished, helped her with her bags. The other passengers crowded into the gangway, murmuring quietly to one another. There was a shocked, subdued atmosphere as in the moments after news of a great tragedy has been received. They stood back to let her by, recoiling as she passed in case they might be contaminated. She wondered if afterwards they would fall upon the bloodied sheets and tear them into pieces for souvenirs. Irma was nowhere to be seen, skulking in the compartment, no doubt. Bella did not know what she had expected of her. Some outrage, perhaps.

'Don't they understand?' she had asked Irma. 'I didn't do it on purpose, it just happened. I wasn't expecting it. Don't they know that women bleed?'

Irma shrugged and stuffed a pair of shoes into Bella's bag. She helped Bella pack with the same glassy indifference with which she had translated the attendant's French. Perhaps she, too, thought there was something unnatural about it, though quite what Bella couldn't figure out. What was she being accused of?

She stepped off the train. It was a glorious day, a blue sky woolly with cloud. The sun felt warm on her cheeks or perhaps she was just flushed. The ticket collector slung her last bag out after her. It landed in a heap at her feet; this, she felt, was what he wished to do with *her*. She sensed the gaze of many eyes upon her as the door wheezed shut and the train lurched once before slowly chugging away. She stared defiantly after it; she was determined to be dignified. She had, after all, been waiting for this moment all of her life.

She waited until the train was out of sight before sitting dejectedly on her bags. She sighed and looked around her at the uncaring landscape, flat and treeless. Across the tracks stood a small stone station house. The rails hummed in the heat. She felt curiously deflated. She had expected there to be more exhilaration. Instead, she felt merely punished.

It was no different from all the other reversals on her travels — and in her life before that. She thought about home — the ramshackle house on Vandeleur Green, the crowded bedrooms, the lack of privacy and space, the pans of white bread and the cheap cuts of meat. The sum of all these small humiliations, *these* were what had marked her out. There would be no large, singular event to validate her existence. There would only be more of this — official retribution for bleeding in public. She felt as she did when the doctor had first taken the glasses with the eye patch off; her vision unobscured, her lazy eye finally cured.

BLÁNAID McKINNEY

Please

Now this thing had its beginning in the car park. He was a young man, around twenty-four, distressingly handsome, and he sat in his car loading his gun. This was new to him, and awkward. He had none of the authentic bloodlessness of a man who is comfortable handling a gun. It felt like a melon in his hands, which were calloused. The black dirt, or perhaps oil, under his fingernails, had a true, terminal kind of blackness. He looked like a man who could fix things. Loaded, the gun was too heavy. He removed the bullets and shook them from his fist into the glove compartment, then he put the gun in his jacket pocket and got out of the car, stooping, as if he carried the weight of the world. He began to walk slowly towards the hospital entrance. He had a nice walk, a slightly rolling gait, but his bowed head gave him the look of a man with elderly heels and a broken heart, a man with some antique injury.

At the entrance, he gripped the railing and looked up at the hospital's structure, shielding his eyes from the glare. It was a beautiful, white, Modern Movement building, a cool, redemptive place he had been to so often that its smells had become as familiar as those of his own kitchen. A decent, optimistically menacing place, where he had stayed overnight many times. He hauled himself up the dozen steps or so and walked inside. In his pocket, it seemed to weigh a ton. The Reception was a noisy, brazen place and he loved it. Cascades of nurses stalking about with important pieces of paper; white coats and metallic tannoy voices, and the diffident wounded, the shy, injured patients just waiting around, bored and grateful at the same time — this slovenly place was his sanctuary and his bedroom, and it teemed with shuddering, rough people, each intent on his or her own purpose. He recognised most of the staff as he walked slowly through the lobby; he wobbled slightly and thought that perhaps their nerveless calm, the sheer velocity of their vocation, as they helped people, and healed and soothed and murmured, might shame him from his own purpose, might cause him to turn round and walk back to his car, dropping the gun in a litter bin as he walked. He caught sight of himself in a mirror. He was twenty-four and he looked like an old man. He had dark circles under his eyes and the guilty frown of someone who had only one small thing left to lose. He looked into those eyes and then, because he was afraid that he might cry, right there in the reception, he shook himself and headed for Paediatrics.

There was a blonde nurse, young and very beautiful, who looked after the day-to-day running of the unit. Sometimes she felt more like an electrician, or a plumber, than a nurse. They were so tiny, so ugly. She believed with a terrifying fierceness, but once in a while they made her flinch, and occasionally she disliked the softly implosive delicacy with which they had to be handled, and the brightness of the place. She worked off her energy in the gym, and escaped the bullet beams in bars where darkness and mystery had not yet been made casualties. She was tending to one baby on life support. The baby was two months old and had not been expected to last as long as that. Her veins were still visible. She was hooked up to a plastic forest of tubes and electrical wires. She was utterly still, apart from the small sucking, fluttering of her heart, which made the waxy skin on her chest shine and anxiously recede.

The doctor came in and leaned over the incubator with her. He came by several times a day, every day, just to look at the nurse, and the baby, and listen to the quiet hum of the unit. Time, it seemed to him, slowed down here. There was no real activity. It was just a matter of watching and waiting and being careful. He was thirty-two and sometimes the tiredness made him want to curl up and die. It was the carelessness that got to him more than anything. The unkind word that could so easily be bravely ignored, but led instead to a glamorous knife wound, the husband whose wife's evening class on assertiveness drove him so crazy with a rage he didn't even understand, and could only deal with by using his fists, the uncomprehending drunks, the thoughtful revenges, the blurred Chaplinesque gang fights, the little ladies who thought that varicose veins for fifteen years was nothing serious and besides, they were busy living their lives, bringing up families … Sometimes he just liked to come here and feast his eyes on the beautiful nurse's pale face and watch the babies hanging on like grim myths, for dear life, and listen to their faint, faint breath. This child in particular. There was no hope. She shouldn't even be here. Another week. Two at the most. It had arrived with her and they couldn't fix it. He was irritated by that. And he was irritated by the fact that she still had a presence in this place, a pained, struggling insult.

He climbed the second flight, his hand in his pocket. Even without the bullets, it still weighed him down on one side. He was walking so slowly now. He would have welcomed a hand slapped on his shoulder, a stern, authoritarian face asking him where he thought he was going and what was that in his pocket. A soft capture, an easy end to this, that was all he wanted. He passed the janitor cleaning the stairs.

The janitor had been working at the hospital for twenty years. He really had been there, done that, bought the T-shirt and he wasn't fearing a damn thing. Even when his wife got cancer, all it did was set up a grainy, adrenal response in his heart and he just got on with it. That's all you can do. Sure, there were times when the things he saw in this place almost took his breath away, with their horror and cruelty, but he had a daughter who was smart and ambitious, and when he got too old to do this any more, she would look after him. He smacked his broom as noisily as he could against the underside of the wall radiator, sending up dust like a swarm of fruit flies, and smiled at the pale gent passing him on the stairs, his fists bunched in his pockets.

This murderous climb might beat him yet. He felt as weak as a kitten and his heart was pounding. His life seemed to be flashing in front of his eyes, fleshed out by the worn progress of his heels. He kept thinking of the future that would not be. Daughters in swarms of glee, talking nonsense, swatting his face with their small, complicated fingers. He had had the future whipped into shape. And then the viscous tragedy of her birth had damn near killed them both. Two apprehensive months, at best. He'd had a mental picture of her as an infant in the polite grasses of their garden, knees buckled, collapsed in padded safety, arms hovering, the dog not quite knowing what to make of this creature. Right now, he envied its ignorance. He felt as if one more flight would be more than he was capable of. The relatives were the worst part of this nightmare. Their distilled, flabby sorrow did not help. It made it worse. He knew it wasn't his fault, it wasn't some sneaky, disreputable gene of his. He knew it wasn't anybody's fault. He just hadn't wanted to be in the glare of their overheated sympathy. He wanted cool, quiet, charitable shadows, where he could think this thing through. And he had. And he had come to a decision that would end nobody's suffering. But it would give their suffering a kinder colour. He wanted a witchcraft solution. This was the best he could do.

The doctor looked at the nurse while she checked the feeds. She was roughly tactile in what she did, as if she was checking fresh vegetables in a supermarket. He liked that. All the nurses scared him with the businesslike hardness of their charity. Sentimentality had no place here, so the hell with it. If you crumble with what used to be called 'fellowfeel', then you're no use to anyone. No place for it in a place like this. But he had never acquired the knack of being genuinely, usefully detached. He just acted that way. He hadn't felt involved with a patient for years, he was too tired for that. But some guilty impulse in the back of his mind and in the back of his heart injected his voice with an elaborate, persuasive concern that his patients knew was false. They were more comfortable with the nurses.

The janitor worked his way slowly up the stairs towards Paediatrics. He would stop by and talk to the beautiful nurse with the pale skin, and see if that dying rag of a baby was still there. Pausing, he took out a Kleenex. He spat on it and cleaned his glasses, humming to himself. He was in a good mood. He felt strong today. He felt like he could sweep all day. He was going to retire soon and, on that day, he would begin to live for ever.

The doctor and the nurse were still leaning over the cot when he approached, like two friends in a bar on their third drink. She turned and saw his face, and smiled. He had been here so many times and she had grown to like his looks. Her smile became a redundant, frozen thing and slowly faded as she stared at the gun that was pointing directly at her heart. The doctor, hearing her gasp, turned and saw the young father he'd got to know quite well. His face was grey and exhausted, and the gun trembled in his hand. His whole arm shook as he gestured them to move away from the child. No one spoke. They stared silently at the gun, fear freezing their lungs, and they forgot to breathe. Then the doctor moved dreamily to one side and pulled the nurse gently with him, still staring at the young father with the pining eyes and the gun in his hand. He felt the resistance in her body. She didn't want to leave the child. She knew what he was going to do. She knew what he was going to do. They moved to the far side of the room.

Still pointing the gun at them, the father began with his left hand delicately to pluck the tubes and wires and the mask from

PLEASE

his daughter's mottled body. It was so hushed in here. The
nurse began to sob quietly. The doctor's throat hurt and tears
scalded his eyes. When the young man had removed all the life-
support feeds and monitors, he slid his palm under her spine
and scooped her to his chest in one movement. She wasn't
much bigger than his hand and hardly weighed anything. He
walked the couple of steps to the wall and sat down heavily in a
chair beside them. He bent his head silently and wanted to
crush the child to his chest, he loved her so, but he was afraid
she would break. The gun was pointing at no one in particular
and his face had the look of a blind man. All he had to do was
wait. The nurse cried in distress and begged him, with a
bruised, wet sign language, not to do this terrible thing, not to
commit this sin. She pleaded with her eyes and said one word,
over and over again — 'Please'. He could barely hear her. He
felt as if he was very far away, as if his spirit had floated away
from this hugely nervous place, and was alone and far away, in
some vast reservoir of solitude.

He did not understand this thing, he could not get a smart
enough grasp on the vocabulary of our ascent, how one life
avoids catastrophe for ever while another crashes hopelessly at
a sigh. He knew every colossal detail of this tiny bundle in his
hand and he could feel the burden of breathing begin to fall
away from her. And under his jewelled scrutiny she died.

The janitor opened the stairwell door and strolled towards
the unit. A small semicircle of people had gathered around the
door and were murmuring quietly to each other. A young man
was sitting beside the wall, holding his dead child, weeping
bitterly. And the janitor saw that the young doctor and the
pretty nurse were staring, vacant and red-eyed at the dead
child, as if they couldn't quite believe any of this. The gun was
lying on the floor and the young man was clutching the child's
body with both arms. Thin, terrifying curses rose in the
janitor's heart but he said nothing. He strode forward and
picked up the gun. He didn't have to check to know that it

337

wasn't loaded. He knew enough about guns. He looked around him at the doctor and the nurse, and the few others, a brood bereft of purpose, and he looked at the broken youngster. For a moment he felt that he might strike him. He raised his hand and his rage made him the strongest man on earth. But there was nothing to be done. There was nothing to be done. To repair this thing, to patch decently would be next to enough. He lowered his hand and stroked the young man's trembling head, and made soothing noises and wiped his tears, the way he would comfort a wounded animal.

Somebody called the police.

ANNE ENRIGHT

Luck Be A Lady

The bingo coach (VZE 26) stopped at the top of the road and Mrs Maguire (no. 18), Mrs Power (no. 9) and Mrs Hanratty (no. 27) climbed on board and took their places with the 33 other women and 0 men who made up the Tuesday run.

'If nothing happens tonight ...' said Mrs Maguire and the way she looked at Mrs Hanratty made it seem like a question.

'I am crucified,' said Mrs Hanratty, 'by these shoes. 'I'll never buy plastic again.'

'You didn't,' said Mrs Power, wiping the window with unconcern.

'I know,' said Mrs Hanratty. 'There's something astray in my head. I wouldn't let the kids do it.'

Nothing in her tone of voice betrayed the fact that Mrs Hanratty knew she was the most unpopular woman in the coach. She twisted 1 foot precisely and ground her cigarette into the plastic mica floor.

When Mrs Hanratty was 7 and called Maeve, she had thrown her Clarks solid leather, solid heeled, T-bar Straps under a moving car and they had survived intact. The completion of this act of rebellion took place at the age of 55, with fake patent and a heel that made her varicose veins run blue. They pulsed at the back of her knee, disappeared into the fat of her thigh, ebbed past her caesarian scars and trickled into her hardening heart, that sat forgotten behind two large breasts, each the size of her head. She still had beautiful feet.

She kept herself well. Her silver hair was thin and stiff with invisible curlers and there was *diamanté* in her ears. She was the kind of woman who squeezed into fitting rooms with her daughters, to persuade them to buy the cream skirt, even though it would stain. She made her husband laugh once a day, on principle, and her sons were either virgins or had the excuse of a good job.

Maeve Hanratty was generous, modest and witty. Her children succeeded and failed in unassuming proportions and she took the occasional drink. She was an enjoyable woman who regretted the fact that the neighbours (except perhaps, Mrs Power) disliked her so much. 'It will pass,' she said to her husband. 'With a bit of luck, my luck will run out.'

At the age of 54 she had achieved fame in a 5-minute interview on the radio when she tried to dismiss the rumour that she was the luckiest woman in Dublin. 'You'll get me banned from the hall,' she said.

'And is it just the bingo?'

'Just the bingo.'

'No horses?'

'My father did the horses,' she said, 'I wouldn't touch them.'

'And tell me, do you always know?'

'Sure, how could I know?' she lied — and diverted 126,578 people's attention with the 3 liquidisers, 14 coal-scuttles, 7 weekends away, 6,725 paper pounds, and 111 teddy bears that she had won in the last 4 years.

'If you ever want a teddy bear!'

'Maeve …' she said, as she put down the phone. 'Oh Maeve.' Mrs Power had run across over the road in her dressing gown and was knocking on the kitchen door and waving through the glass. There was nothing in her face to say that Mrs (Maeve) Hanratty had made a fool of herself, that she had exposed her illness to the world. Somehow no one seemed surprised that she had numbered and remembered all those lovely things. She was supposed to count her blessings.

There were other statistics she could have used, not out of anger, but because she was so ashamed. She could have said 'Do you know something — I have had sexual intercourse 1,332 times my life. Is that a lot? 65% of the occasions took place in the first 8 years of my marriage, and I was pregnant for 48 months out of those 96. Is that a lot? I have been married for 33 years and a bit, that's 12,140 days, which means an average of once every 9.09 days. I stopped at 1,332 for no reason except that I am scared beyond reason of the number 1,333. Perhaps this is sad.' It was not, of course, the kind of thing she told anyone, not even her priest, although she felt a slight sin in all that counting. Mrs Hanratty knew how many seconds she had been alive. That was why she was lucky with numbers.

It was not that they had a colour or a smell, but numbers had a feel like people had when you sense them in a room. Mrs Hanratty thought that if she had been in Auschwitz she would have known who would survive and who would die just by looking at their forearms. It was a gift that hurt and she tried to stop winning teddy bears, but things kept on adding up too well and she was driven out of the house in a sweat to the monotonous comfort of the bingo call and another bloody coal-scuttle.

She was 11th out of the coach, which was nice. The car parked in front had 779 on its number plate. It was going to be a big night.

She played Patience when she was agitated and on Monday afternoons, even if she was not. She wouldn't touch the Tarot. The cards held the memory of wet days by the sea, with sand trapped in the cracks of the table that made them hiss and slide as she laid them down. Their holiday house was an old double-decker bus washed up on the edge of the beach with a concrete block where the wheels should have been and a gas stove waiting to blow up by the driver's seat. They were numberless days with clouds drifting one into the other and a million waves dying on the beach. The children hid in the sea all day or played in the ferns and Jim came up from Dublin for the weekend.

'This is being happy,' she thought, scattering the contents of the night bucket over the scutch grass or trekking to the shop. She started counting the waves in order to get to sleep.

She knew before she realised it. She knew without visitation, without a slant of light cutting into the sea. There was no awakening, no manifestation, no pause in the angle of the stairs. There may have been a smile as she took the clothes pegs out of her mouth and the wind blew the washing towards her, but it was forgotten before it happened. She just played Patience all day on the fold-down table in a derelict bus and watched the cards making sense.

By the age of 55 she had left the cards behind. She found them obvious and untrustworthy — they tried to tell you too much and in the wrong way. The Jack of Spades sat on the Queen of Hearts, the clubs hammered away in a row. Work, love, money, pain; clubs, hearts, diamonds, spades, all making promises too big to keep. The way numbers spoke to her was much more bewildering and ordinary. Even the bingo didn't excite or let her down, it soothed her. It let her know in advance.

> 5 roses: the same as
> 5 handshakes at a railway station: the same as
> 5 women turning to look when a bottle of milk smashes in the shop: the same as
> 5 children: the same as
> 5 odd socks in the basket
> 5 tomatoes on the window-sill
> 5 times she goes to the toilet before she can get to sleep.
> and all different from

4 roses, 4 shakes of the hand, 4 women turning, 4 children, 4 odd socks, 4 tomatoes in the sun, 4 times she goes to the toilet and lies awake thinking about the 5th.

The numbers rushed by her in strings and verification came before the end of any given day. They had a party all around her, talking, splitting, reproducing, sitting by themselves in a corner of the room. She smoked them, she hung them out on the line to dry, they chattered to her out from the TV. They drummed on the table-top and laughed in their intimate, syncopated way. They were music.

She told no one and did the cards for people if they asked. It was very accurate if she was loose enough on the day, but her husband didn't like it. He didn't like the bingo either and who could blame him.

'When's it going to stop?' he would say, or 'the money's fine, I don't mind the money.'

'With a bit of luck,' she said, 'my luck will run out.'

On Wednesday nights she went with Mrs Power to the local pub, because there was no bingo. They sat in the upstairs lounge where the regulars went, away from the people who were too young to be there at all. Mr Finn took the corner stool, Mr Byrne was centre-forward. In the right-hand corner Mr Slevin sat and gave his commentary on the football match that was being played out in his head. The other women sat in their places around the walls. No one let on to be drunk. Pat the barman knew their orders and which team were going to get to the final. At the end of the bar, Pauline made a quiet disgrace of herself, out on her own and chatty.

'His days are numbered ...' said a voice at the bar, and Mrs Hanratty's listened to her blood quicken. 'That fella's days are numbered.' There was a middle-aged man standing to order like a returned Yank in a shabby suit with a fat wallet. He was drunk and proud of it.

'I've seen his kind before,' he counted out the change in his pocket carefully in 10s and 2s and 5s, and the barman scooped all the coins into one mess and scattered them into the till. Mrs Hanratty took more than her usual sip of vodka and orange.

'None of us, of course,' he commented, though the barman had moved to the other end of the counter, 'are exempt.'

It was 2 weeks before he made his way over to their table, parked his drink and would not sit until he was asked. 'I've been all over,' he told them. 'You name it, I've done it. All over,' and he started to sing something about Alaska. It had to be a lie.

'Canada,' he started. 'There's a town in the Rockies called Hope. Just like that. And a more miserable stretch of hamburger joints and shacks you've never seen. Lift your eyes 30 degrees and you have the dawn coming over the mountains and air so thin it makes you feel the world is full of … well what? I was going to say "lovely ladies" but look at the two I have at my side.' She could feel Mrs Power's desire to leave as big and physical as a horse standing beside her on the carpet.

He rubbed his thigh with his hand and, as if reminded, slapped the tables with 3 extended fingers. There was no 4th. 'Look at that,' he said, and Mrs Power gave a small whinny. 'There should be a story there about how I lost it, but do you know something? It was the simplest thing in the County Meath where I was as a boy. The simplest thing. A dirty cut and it swelled so bad I was lucky I kept the hand. Isn't that a good one? I worked a combine harvester on the great plains in Iowa and you wouldn't believe the fights I got into as a young fella as far away as … Singapore — believe that or not. But a dirty cut in the County Meath.' And he wrapped the 3 fingers around his glass and toasted them silently. That night, for the first time in her life, Maeve Hanratty lost count of the vodkas she drank.

She wanted him. It was as simple as that. A woman of 55, a woman with 5 children and 1 husband, who had had sexual intercourse 1,332 times in her life and was in possession of 14 coal-scuttles, wanted the 3-fingered man, because he had 3 fingers and not 4.

It was a commonplace sickness and one she did not indulge. Her daughter came in crying from the dance-hall, her husband (and not her father) spent the bingo money on the horses. The house was full of torn betting slips and the stubs of old lipstick. Mrs Hanratty went to bingo and won and won and won.

Although she had done nothing, she said to him silently, 'Well it's your move now, I'm through with all that,' and for 3 weeks in a row he sat at the end of the bar and talked to Pauline, who laughed too much. 'If that's what he wants, he can have it,' said Mrs Hanratty, who believed in dignity, as well as numbers.

The numbers were letting her down. Her daily walk to the shops became a confusion of damaged registration plates, the digits swung sideways or strokes were lopped off. 6 became 0, 7 turned into 1. She added up what was left, 555, 666, 616, 707, 906, 888, the numbers for parting, for grief, for the beginning of grief, forgetting, for accidents and for the hate that comes from money.

On the next Wednesday night he was wide open and roaring. He talked about his luck, that had abandoned him one day in Ottawa when he promised everything to a widow in the timber trade. The whole bar listened and Mrs Hanratty felt their knowledge of her as keen as a son on drugs or the front of the house in a state. He went to the box of plastic plants and ransacked it for violets which were presented to her with a mock bow. How many were there? 3 perhaps, or 4 — but the bunch loosened out before her and all Mrs Hanratty could see were the purple plastic shapes and his smile.

She took to her bed with shame, while a zillion a trillion a billion a million numbers opened up before her and wouldn't be pinned down at 6 or 7 or 8. She felt how fragile the world was with so much in it and confined herself to Primes, that were out on their own except for 1.

'The great thing about bingo is that no one loses,' Mrs Power had told him about their Tuesday and Thursday nights. Mrs Hanratty felt flayed in the corner, listening to him and his pride. Her luck was leaking into the seat as he invited himself along, to keep himself away from the drink, he said. He had nothing else to do.

The number of the coach was NIE 133. Mrs Maguire, Mrs Power and Mrs Hanratty climbed on board and took their places with the 33 women and 1 man who made up this Thursday run. He sat at the back and shouted for them to come and join him, and there was hooting from the gang at the front. He came up the aisle instead and fell into the seat beside Mrs Hanratty with a bend in the road. She was squeezed over double, paddling her hand on the floor in search of 1 ear-ring which she may have lost before she got on at all.

He crossed his arms with great ceremony, and not even the violence with which the coach turned corners could convince Mrs Hanratty that he was not rubbing her hand, strangely, with his 3 fingers, around and around.

'I am a 55-year-old woman who has had sex 1,332 times in my life and I am being molested by a man I should never have spoken to in the first place.' The action of his hand was polite and undemanding and Mrs Hanratty resented beyond anger the assurance of its tone.

All the numbers were broken off the car parked outside the hall, except 0, which was fine — it was the only 1 she knew anymore. Mrs Hanratty felt the justice of it, though it made her feel so lonely. She had betrayed her own mind and her friends were strange to her. Her luck was gone.

The 3-fingered man was last out of the coach and he called her back. 'I have your ear-ring! Maeve!' She listened. She let the others walk through. She turned.

His face was a jumble of numbers as he brought his hand up in mock salute. Out of the mess she took: his 3 fingers; the arching 3 of his eyebrows, which was laughing; the tender 3 of his upper lip and the 1 of his mouth, which opened into 0 as he spoke.

'You thought you'd lost it!' and he dropped the *diamanté* into her hand.

'I thought I had.'

He smiled and the numbers of his face scattered and disappeared. His laughter multiplied out around her like a net.

'So what are you going to win tonight then?'

'Nothing. You.'

'0'

SARA BERKELEY

Thin Ice

Perhaps, at eleven, it was Christopher I feared most in the world, and I suspect that, at forty-two, he feared me. That Christmas we went down to grandfather's in Sussex. The south of England sat patiently under heavy snow. The beach looked odd beside snow, and the dogs loved it, rushing through the woods, setting off small avalanches from the still branches with their barking. Ian said, as he saw the ice begin to thaw between myself and my new father:

"Good. Let it all be over now. Let the two of you be friends."

Ian chose his words carefully. He steered away from words that would topple me into a mute resistance as skilfully as he drew the dogs away from the ice.

I was learning a lot of things that Christmas, but I thought I already knew a great deal. I knew there was a god who had my death written down on his calendar, and who knew when it would happen and, more importantly, how. I knew it wouldn't be for a long time: not, say, until after I was seventeen and had been to a disco. It could be lung cancer, I reckoned, because Frank Kelly had taught me to smoke cigarettes in the henhouse in his father's garden — how to hold them and suck in carefully so you didn't cough up and set off a cloud of chicken feathers. God was very real to me then. I thought he needed a lot more space than most people seemed to give him. Ian thought so too and when he found me clearing all the surfaces in my bedroom he knew I was making space and he left me alone. He did not point out, like Christopher did, that having your books and pencils and photograph albums all in the wardrobe when there were perfectly good shelves made no sense. I cannot say whether I was scared of the man my mother had married because he was only learning to be a father and I knew it, or whether it was because he shouted and sometimes broke things, when he was angry. I know I began to like him the day he brought his hand down on a vase that had been my grandmother's and cracked it so he cut his finger badly and had to sit in silence while my mother dressed it. That day I realised that you could be grown up and still do things you had to suffer for. Still, the streak of restless resentment in me caused me to say the kind of things that provoked him into these rages. It was long after this day that I first allowed feelings of affection, even of acceptance, to be admitted. Before this happened there had to be a lot of shouting and a lot of bringing down of hands. They even tried to send me away to school but I could not sleep in a room that was not next to the room where Ian slept and I only stayed in that school for a week. My mother took me home then because I was ill.

In grandfather's house there was a piano. We had no piano where we lived in London but some of my friends had pianos and I knew that Virginia Cole had first kissed a boy under a piano. It was at a birthday party but nobody ever explained to me that there were two different types of piano — one that stood up and one that lay sort of propped on its elbow. My grandfather's piano stood up and I stared at it for a long time wondering how Virginia got all that kissing done in such a small space. She was a very active girl and I knew kissing involved quite a bit of moving about.

The day after Christmas I climbed a tree to see how far off France was. People said it wasn't too far off the coast of England and if they dug a tunnel under the channel you could make a train get there in less than an hour. I couldn't see it and, in the most petulant moment of my disappointment, I misjudged how high off the ground a branch can be when it has taken you four different footholds to get to it. I suppose it was jumping out of that tree that really ensured a lifelong friendship with my new father; but at that moment, the awful sickening jarring moment when I realised that I had landed on my feet but they had slipped from under me, I simply screamed as any hurt eleven-year-old would have. Something inside me that hadn't wanted to come apart was forced to do so and I could only think through all that pain of Katy in *What Katy Did*, who had fallen off a swing and hurt her back and how, for some reason I couldn't recall, she had to cook the dinner for her whole family for a long time. When Christopher found me, all the tears were gone and I was crying a dryness that hurt my throat even more than it hurt my back. I had to let the pain do anything it wanted. I had to sob in arid croaks into Christopher's shoulder all the way back up to the house, and I couldn't help repeating over and over "I don't want to cook the dinner! Don't make me cook the dinner!" In spite of this, there was still part of my mind that bitterly resented being caught sobbing like a baby. So I was mildly surprised when, through the fog of being undressed and put to bed, I heard Christopher explaining reasonably that Katy only had to *decide* what everyone should have for dinner, and tell the cook; and this was because her mummy was dead, so she had to act mummy; and even though I still had a mummy, who was perfectly alive and loved me very much, I could, if I wished, decide what everyone should have for dinner for as long as I liked, and he would try and make sure they got it.

After I had lain in bed for a bit and Christopher had phoned the doctor and the friends whom my mother and Ian and grandfather were visiting, he came and sat on the bed and held my hand and I felt the bandage on his finger and pretty soon I forgot that he had married my mother to try and make a stranger of her, and I remembered instead how still and quietly he had sat while she was bandaging the finger. Suddenly it seemed clear to me that if I was frightened of him, he might also be frightened of me, and since the pain in my back was making spots before my eyes, I let a fresh wave of tears carry me into a jumble of murmured confessions to which he listened with a grave, but not unkind expression on his face. When he thought I was asleep he smoothed the covers a little and just before he turned the light out I felt his lips brush softly against my hair.

I woke from a sullen, heavy sleep and the room was lit by a green lamp, spreading light like a pale, watery, green sun.

"You fell. You hurt your back," my mother told me firmly. "Does it still hurt?"

Ian was there, and when I tried to sit up and fell back with a louder cry than was really necessary, he winced. Ian felt other people's pain as though his own was not enough. Christopher was not in the room.

"Who made the light green?"

"We've put green lenses in your eyes," Ian said. "Look at me, I'm G-R-E-E-N!" he leered over the bed, and then ruffled my hair. "Who told you the ground was bouncy?"

"I didn't bounce," I muttered thickly, caught between a laugh and tears. I was exploring the possibilities of the occasion. My mother moved about the room, doing things I couldn't see.

"Can we have jam doughnuts for dinner?" I said. "And clam soup?"

She stopped. "Together? Or separately? Or perhaps you'd like clam doughnuts and jam soup?" she smiled. "Go ahead. Tell us what we'll have for dinner. It saves your grandfather a lot of trouble."

I ordered mushroom omelette and peanut butter, doughnuts and ribena. Everyone had to drink ribena, from the plastic tumblers we used on the beach in the summer for picnics.

Later in the evening I asked for paper and a pencil and wrote down a painful list of my favourite foods.

"How d'you spell chocolate mousse? How d'you spell toasted cheese sandwiches with pickle and tomato ketchup?"

And the next day while mother was shopping and grandfather had taken Ian out with the dogs, I told Christopher that the only way I could really be at peace would be if my bed were brought into the library. I even used that phrase, 'at peace'. Somewhere in my head I had a picture of being laid out in the library, the white sheet turned back and my hands folded restfully over it. There would be a slight smile on my face and when the people saw me, they would cry, with white handkerchiefs, and murmur 'at peace'.

Christopher moved my bed. The library was down a narrow polished landing from my room. It was filled with an accumulation — forty, fifty years of books, maps, models, glass, bits and pieces. It was a wealthy room. Astronomical instruments of brass and models of bronze stood on the shelves; books lined the walls, floor to ceiling. A figure of a woman hung poised from the ceiling and grandfather had once had to point out to me how one of her feet was attached to a solid wood book-mark on the top shelf. And there were photographs, black-and-white ones, pictures of the serious, lovely girl who was my grandmother: looking downwards out of a window, wearing a broad-brimmed hat, the lack of colour highlighting the structure of her face.

"I knew a woman lovely in her bones," murmured Christopher. He was looking at the photographs while I was clambering slowly into my bed and he did not know whether to go or to stay. It seemed to be very awkward for him. I had had a dream of him before I woke to the green light, and after this dream I thought a lot more of how he had brought me in his arms back to the house, and of how he had looked as he put me on the bed, and of his bandaged finger — and I wondered if it hurt him.

"You can tell me a story if you like." My voice surprised even myself when it came out. I had meant to say it nicely. It came out like a bark.

"I don't know stories." He kept looking at the photographs.

"Well … tell me … tell me about times you were in foreign places then."

"In where?"

"Spain," I said promptly, sensing the bait taken.

Christopher was not very used to telling stories. You could see it sat ill with him, to settle into a story-telling frame of mind, even to find the correct position on the side of my bed. I was afraid to help him out, to make even the smallest gesture that might indicate I was no longer feeling exactly the way I had been feeling towards him. I didn't snuggle down a little in the bed and assume an expression of dreamy attention. I didn't give a funny sigh that would indicate I was all settled down and ready for some stories. I didn't put my hand down near his. I thought of doing it, and it sent a shiver over me.

"Once," he began, and paused so long I became aware of every breath I took, "I saw a man get on a trolley bus with no money. When the conductor came to him he explained he had no money, and he offered to write a note promising to pay the money to the trolley bus company."

"Was he poor? Did he wear raggedy clothes?"

"No. No — he was quite well dressed. He wrote the note carefully on a page of his notebook with a fountain pen. And the conductor took it and folded it and put it in his breast pocket. And that was that."

"Wasn't it all jiggling in the bus? I mean, how could he write?"

"I expect," Christopher answered gravely, "it was pretty difficult to write in a trolleybus, yes."

"And … and why didn't everyone else try the same thing?"

"I don't know. But nobody did."

I thought for a while about the man sitting on the trolleybus, writing out this note with his fountain pen and Christopher thought about it too. After a while I said:

"Are there any more stories?"

My voice sounded very small in the room full of books and maps and astrological instruments. Christopher thought some more.

'There was once a room," he said at last, "that was thirty feet across and circular. The ceiling was made of stone and if a person stood against the wall and whispered very quietly, close into the wall, another person standing on the other side of the room, if he put his ear very close up to his bit of wall, could hear the whisper. Clear as if it were right — in — his — ear."

I rolled this story round my mouth for a little and when I had got my tongue around it I asked:

"What would the person whisper?" with a sense as I said it of the stories ending.

"He would whisper," Christopher said slowly and bent down close to my ear, "sleep now and dream sweetly."

There was a lot of trouble about my move to the library, but I stayed there for a week until I was well, inventing menus and reading the titles of the books as far as I could make them out from my bed. Ian entertained me a great deal and in the evenings I was allowed downstairs to sit by the fire in the sitting room; but during the mornings when everyone was out, Christopher would come and sit by my bed. Sometimes he would read his paper or smoke a pipe. Sometimes he told me stories about Spain or about the time he lived in Africa. Sometimes he just sat in silence. My mother protested about draughts and about the inconvenience; my grandfather plodded in and out, fetching books and carrying them downstairs to read in the kitchen porch. My mother said you couldn't sleep in a library; she said you read in a library, that there was no room there for beds, that that was what bedrooms were for. She pointed out to Christopher the marks made by dragging the bed on the polished wooden floor of the landing and she wondered aloud what on earth he had been thinking of. Christopher would wink at me and keep quiet. I don't think he ever told my mother just what he had been thinking of.

CLARE KEEGAN

Men and Women

My father takes me places. He has artificial hips, so he needs
me to open gates. To reach our house you must drive up a long
lane through a wood, open two sets of gates and close them
behind you so the sheep won't escape to the road. I'm handy. I
get out, open the gates, my father free-wheels the Volkswagen
through, I close the gates behind him and hop back into the
passenger seat. To save petrol he starts the car on the run,
gathering speed on the slope before the road, and then we're
off to wherever my father is going on that particular day.

Sometimes it's the scrapyard, where he's looking for a spare
part, or, scenting a bargain in some classified ad, we wind up in
a farmer's mucky field, pulling cabbage plants or picking seed
potatoes in a dusty shed. Sometimes we drive to the forge,
where I stare into the water-barrel, whose surface reflects
patches of the milky skies that drift past, sluggish, until the
blacksmith plunges the red-hot metal down and scorches away
the clouds. On Saturdays my father goes to the mart and
examines sheep in the pens, feeling their backbones, looking
into their mouths. If he buys just a few sheep, he doesn't
bother going home for the trailer but puts them in the back of
the car, and it is my job to sit between the front seats to keep
them there. They shit small pebbles and say baaaah, the
Suffolks' tongues dark as the raw liver we cook on Mondays. I
keep them back until we get to whichever house Da stops at
for a feed on the way home. Usually it's Bridie Knox's, because
Bridie kills her own stock and there's always meat. The

handbrake doesn't work, so when Da parks in her yard I get out and put the stone behind the wheel.

I am the girl of a thousand uses.

'Be the holy, missus, what way are ya?'

'Dan!' Bridie says, like she didn't hear the splutter of the car.

Bridie lives in a smoky little house without a husband, but she has sons who drive tractors around the fields. They're small, deeply unattractive men who patch their Wellingtons. Bridie wears red lipstick and face powder, but her hands are like a man's hands. I think her head is wrong for her body, the way my dolls look when I swap their heads.

'Have you aer a bit for the child, missus? She's hungry at home,' Da says, looking at me like I'm one of those African children we give up sugar for during Lent.

'Ah now,' says Bridie, smiling at his old joke. 'That girl looks fed to me. Sit down there and I'll put the kettle on.'

'To tell you the truth, missus, I wouldn't fall out with a drop of something. I'm after being in at the mart and the price of sheep is a holy scandal.'

He talks about sheep and cattle and the weather and how this little country of ours is in a woeful state while Bridie sets the table, puts out the Chef sauce and the Colman's mustard and cuts big, thick slices off a flitch of beef or boiled ham. I sit by the window and keep an eye on the sheep who stare, bewildered, from the car. Da eats everything in sight while I build a little tower of biscuits and lick the chocolate off and give the rest to the sheepdog under the table.

When we get home, I find the fire shovel and collect the sheep-droppings from the car and roll barley on the loft.

'Where did you go?' Mammy asks.

I tell her all about our travels while we carry buckets of calf-nuts and beet-pulp across the yard. Da sits in under the shorthorn cow and milks her into a bucket. My brother sits in the sitting room beside the fire and pretends he's studying. He will do the Inter-cert next year. My brother is going to be somebody, so he doesn't open gates or clean up shite or carry buckets. All he does is read and write and draw triangles with special pencils Da buys him for mechanical drawing. He is the brains in the family. He stays in there until he is called to dinner.

'Go down and tell Seamus his dinner is on the table,' Da says.

I have to take off my Wellingtons before I go down.

'Come up and get it, you lazy fucker', I say.

'I'll tell,' he says.

'You won't,' I say, and go back up to the kitchen, where I spoon garden peas on to his plate because he won't eat turnip or cabbage like the rest of us.

Evenings, I get my school-bag and do homework on the kitchen table while Ma watches the television we hire for winter. On Tuesdays she makes a big pot of tea before eight o'clock and sits at the range and glues herself to the programme where a man teaches a woman how to drive a car. How to change gears, to let the clutch out and give her the juice. Except for a rough woman up behind the hill who drives a tractor and a Protestant woman in the town, no woman we know drives. During the break her eyes leave the screen and travel with longing to the top shelf of the dresser, where she has hidden the spare key to the Volkswagen in the old cracked teapot. I am not supposed to know this. I sigh and continue tracing the course of the River Shannon through a piece of greaseproof paper.

On Christmas Eve I put up signs. I cut up a cardboard box and in red marker I write THIS WAY SANTA and arrows, pointing the way. I am always afraid he will get lost or not bother coming because the gates are too much trouble. I staple them on to the paling at the end of the lane and on the timber gates and one inside the door leading down to the parlour where the tree is. I put a glass of stout and a piece of cake on the coffee table for him and conclude that Santa must be drunk by Christmas morning.

Daddy takes his good hat out of the press and looks at himself in the mirror. It's a fancy hat with a stiff feather stuck down in the brim. He tightens it well down on his head to hide his bald patch.

'And where are you going on Christmas Eve?' Mammy asks.

'Going off to see a man about a pup,' he says, and bangs the door.

I go to bed and have trouble sleeping. I am the only person in my class Santa Claus still visits. I know this because the master asked, 'Who does Santa Claus still come to?' and mine was the only hand raised. I'm different, but every year I feel there is a greater chance that he will not come, that I will become like the others.

I wake at dawn and Mammy is already lighting the fire, kneeling on the hearth, ripping up newspaper, smiling. There is a terrible moment when I think maybe Santa didn't come because I said 'Come and get it, you lazy fucker,' but he does come. He leaves me the Tiny Tears doll I asked for, wrapped in the same wrapping paper we have, and I think how the postal system is like magic, how I can send a letter two days before Christmas and it reaches the North Pole overnight, even though it takes a week for a letter to reach England. Santa does not come to Seamus any more. I suspect he knows what Seamus is really doing all those evenings in the sitting room, reading *Hit 'n' Run* magazines and drinking the red lemonade out of the sideboard, not using his brains at all.

Nobody's up except Mammy and me. We are the early birds. We make tea, eat toast and chocolate fingers for breakfast. Then she puts on her best apron, the one with all the strawberries, and turns on the radio, chops onions and parsley while I grate a plain loaf into crumbs. We stuff the turkey and waltz around the kitchen. Seamus and Da come down and investigate the parcels under the tree. Seamus gets a dartboard for Christmas. He hangs it on the back door and himself and Da throw darts and chalk up scores while Mammy and me put on our anoraks and feed the pigs and cattle and sheep and let the hens out.

'How come they do nothing?' I ask her. I am reaching into warm straw, feeling for eggs. The hens lay less in winter.

'They're men,' she says, as if this explains everything. Because it is Christmas morning, I say nothing. I come inside and duck when a dart flies past my head.

'Ha! Ha!' says Seamus.

'Bulls-eye,' says Da.

On New Year's Eve it snows. Snowflakes land and melt on the window ledges. It is the end of another year. I eat a bowl of sherry trifle for breakfast and fall asleep watching Lassie on TV. I play with my dolls after dinner but get fed up filling Tiny Tears with water and squeezing it out through the hole in her backside, so I take her head off, but her neck is too thick to fit into my other dolls' bodies. I start playing darts with Seamus. He chalks two marks on the lino, one for him and another, closer to the board, for me. When I get a treble nineteen, Seamus says, 'Fluke.'

'Eighty-seven,' I say, totting up my score.

'Fluke,' he says.

'You don't know what fluke is,' I say, 'Fluke and worms. Look it up in the dictionary.'

'Exactly,' he says.

I am fed up being treated like a child. I wish I was big. I wish I could sit beside the fire and be called up to dinner and draw triangles, lick the nibs of special pencils, sit behind the wheel of a car and have someone open gates that I could drive through. Vrum! Vrum! I'd give her the holly, make a bumpersticker that would read: CAUTION, SHEEP ON BOARD.

That night we get dressed up. Mammy wears a dark-red dress, the colour of the shorthorn cow. Her skin is freckled like somebody dipped a toothbrush in paint and splattered her. She asks me to fasten the catch on her string of pearls. I used to stand on the bed doing this, but now I'm tall, the tallest girl in my class; the master measured us. Mammy is tall and thin, but the skin on her hands is hard. I wonder if someday she will look like Bridie Knox, become part man, part woman.

Da does not do himself up. I have never known him to take a bath or wash his hair; he just changes his hat and shoes. Now he clamps his good hat down on his head and puts his shoes on. They are big black shoes he bought when he sold the Suffolk ram. He has trouble with the laces, as he finds it hard to stoop. Seamus wears a green jumper with elbow-patches, black trousers with legs like tubes and cowboy boots to make him taller.

'You'll trip up in your high heels,' I say.

We get into the Volkswagen, me and Seamus in the back and Mammy and Da up front. Even though I washed the car out, I can smell sheep-shite, a faint, pungent odour that always drags us back to where we come from. I resent this deeply. Da turns on the windscreen wiper; there's only one, and it screeches as it wipes the snow away. Crows rise from the trees, releasing shrill, hungry sounds. Because there are no doors in the back, it is Mammy who gets out to open the gates. I think she is beautiful with her pearls around her throat and her red skirt flaring out when she swings round. I wish my father would get out, that the snow would be falling on him, not on my mother in her good clothes. I've seen other fathers holding their wives' coats, holding doors open, asking if they'd like anything at the shop, bringing home bars of chocolate and ripe pears even when they say no. But Da's not like that.

Spellman Hall stands in the middle of a car park, an arch of bare, multi-coloured bulbs surrounding a crooked 'Merry Christmas' sign above the door. Inside is big as a warehouse with a slippy wooden floor and benches at the walls. Strange lights make every white garment dazzle. It's amazing. I can see the newsagent's bra through her blouse, fluff like snow on the auctioneer's trousers. The accountant has a black eye and a jumper made of grey and white wool diamonds. Overhead a globe of shattered mirror shimmers and spins slowly. At the top of the ballroom a Formica-topped table is stacked with bottles of lemonade and orange, custard-cream biscuits and cheese-and-onion Tayto. The butcher's wife stands behind, handing out the straws and taking in the money. Several of the women I know from my trips around the country are there: Bridie with her haw-red lipstick; Sarah Combs, who only last week urged my father to have a glass of sherry and gave me stale cake while she took him into the sitting room to show him her new suite of furniture; Miss Emma Jenkins, who always makes a fry and drinks coffee instead of tea and never has a sweet thing in the house because of her gastric juices.

On the stage men in red blazers and candy-striped bow-ties play drums, guitars, blow horns, and The Nerves Moran is out front, singing 'My Lovely Leitrim'. Mammy and I are first out on the floor for the cuckoo waltz, and when the music stops, she dances with Seamus. My father dances with the women from the roads. I wonder how he can dance like that and not open gates. Seamus jives with teenage girls he knows from the vocational school, hand up, arse out, and the girls spinning like blazes. Old men in their thirties ask me out.

'Will ya chance a quickstep?' they say. Or: 'How's about a half-set?'

They tell me I'm light on my feet.

'Christ, you're like a feather,' they say, and put me through my paces.

In the Paul Jones the music stops and I get stuck with a farmer who smells sour like the whiskey we make sick lambs drink in springtime, but the young fella who hushes the cattle around the ring in the mart butts in and rescues me.

'Don't mind him,' he says. 'He thinks he's the bee's knees.'
He smells of ropes, new galvanise, Jeyes Fluid.

After the half-set I get thirsty and Mammy gives me a fifty-
pence piece for lemonade and raffle tickets. A slow waltz
begins and Da walks across to Sarah Combs, who rises from
the bench and takes her jacket off. Her shoulders are bare; I
can see the top of her breasts. Mammy is sitting with her
handbag on her lap, watching. There is something sad about
Mammy tonight; it is all around her like when a cow dies and
the truck comes to take it away. Something I don't fully
understand is happening, as if a black cloud has drifted in and
could burst and cause havoc. I go over and offer her my
lemonade, but she just takes a little dainty sip and thanks me. I
give her half my raffle tickets, but she doesn't care. My father
has his arms around Sarah Combs, dancing slow like slowness
is what he wants. Seamus is leaning against the far wall with his
hands in his pockets, smiling down at the blonde who hogs the
mirror in the Ladies.

'Cut in on Da.'

'What?' he says.

'Cut in on Da.'

'What would I do that for?' he says.

'And you're supposed to be the one with all the brains,' I
say. 'Gobshite.'

I walk across the floor and tap Sarah Combs on the back. I
tap a rib. She turns, her wide patent belt gleaming in the light
that is spilling from the globe above our heads.

'Excuse me,' I say, like I'm going to ask her the time.

'Tee-hee,' she says, looking down at me. Her eyeballs are
cracked like the teapot on our dresser.

'I want to dance with Daddy.'

At the word 'Daddy' her face changes and she loosens her
grip on my father. I take over. The man on the stage is blowing
his trumpet now. My father holds my hand tight, like a
punishment. I can see my mother on the bench, reaching into

her bag for a hanky. Then she goes to the Ladies. There's a feeling like hatred all around Da. I get the feeling he's helpless, but I don't care. For the first time in my life I have some power. I can butt in and take over, rescue and be rescued.

There's a general hullabaloo towards midnight. Everybody's out on the floor, knees buckling, handbags swinging. The Nerves Moran counts down the seconds to the New Year and then there's kissing and hugging. Strange men squeeze me, kiss me like they're thirsty and I'm water.

My parents do not kiss. In all my life, back as far as I remember, I have never seen them touch. Once I took a friend upstairs to show her the house.

'This is Mammy's room, and this is Daddy's room,' I said.

'Your parents don't sleep in the same bed?' she said in a voice of pure amazement. And that was when I suspected that our family wasn't normal.

The band picks up the pace. Oh hokey, hokey, pokey!

'Work off them turkey dinners, shake off them plum puddings!' shouts The Nerves Moran and even the ballroom show-offs give up on their figures of eight and do the twist and jive around, and I shimmy around and knock my backside against the mart fella's backside and wind up swinging with a stranger.

Everybody stands for the national anthem. Da is wiping his forehead with a handkerchief and Seamus is panting because he's not used to the exercise. The lights come up and nothing is the same. People are red-faced and sweaty; everything's back to normal. The auctioneer takes over the microphone and thanks a whole lot of different people, and then they auction off a Charolais calf and a goat and batches of tea and sugar and buns and jam, plum puddings and mince pies. There's pebbles where the goat stood and I wonder who'll clean it up. Not until the very last does the raffle take place. The auctioneer holds out the cardboard box of stubs to the blonde.

'Dig deep,' he says. 'No peeping. First prize a bottle of whiskey.'

She takes her time, lapping up the attention.

'Come on,' he says, 'good girl, it's not the sweepstakes.'

She hands him the ticket.

'It's a — What colour is that would ya say, Jimmy? It's a salmon-coloured ticket, number seven hundred and twenty-five. Seven two five. Serial number 3X429H. I'll give ye that again.'

It's not mine, but I'm close. I don't want the whiskey anyhow; it'd be kept for the pet lambs. I'd rather the box of Afternoon Tea biscuits that's coming up next. There's a general shuffle, a search in handbags, arse pockets. The auctioneer calls out the numbers a few times and it looks like he'll have to draw again when Mammy rises from her seat. Head held high, she walks in a straight line across the floor. A space opens in the crowd; people step aside to let her pass. Her new high-heeled shoes say clippety-clippety on the slippy floor and her red skirt is flaring. I have never seen her do this. Usually she's too shy, gives me the tickets, and I run up and collect the prize.

'Do ya like a drop of the booze, do ya, missus?' The Nerves Moran asks, reading her ticket. 'Sure wouldn't it keep ya warm on a night like tonight. No woman needs a man if she has a drop of Power's. Isn't that right? Seven twenty-five, that's the one.'

My mother is standing there in her elegant clothes and it's all wrong. She doesn't belong up there.

'Let's check the serial numbers now,' he says, drawing it out. 'I'm sorry, missus, wrong serial number. The hubby may keep you warm again tonight. Back to the old reliable.'

My mother turns and walks clippety-clippety back down the slippy floor, with everybody knowing she thought she'd won when she didn't win. And suddenly she is no longer walking, but running, running down in the bright white light, past the cloakroom, towards the door, her hair flailing out like a horse's tail behind her.

Out in the car park snow has accumulated on the trampled grass, the evergreen shelter beds, but the tarmac is wet and shiny in the headlights of cars leaving. Thick, unwavering moonlight shines steadily down on the earth. Ma, Seamus and me sit into the car, shivering, waiting for Da. We can't turn on the engine to heat the car because Da has the keys. My feet are cold as stones. A cloud of greasy steam rises from the open hatch of the chip van, a fat brown sausage painted on the chrome. All around us people are leaving, waving, calling out 'Goodnight!' and 'Happy New Year!' They're collecting their chips and driving off.

The chip van has closed its hatch and the car park is empty when Da comes out. He gets into the driver's seat, the ignition catches, a splutter, and then we're off, climbing the hill outside the village, winding around the narrow roads towards home.

'That wasn't a bad band,' Da says.

Mammy says nothing.

'I said, there was a bit of life in that band.' Louder this time.

Still Mammy says nothing.

My father begins to sing 'Far Away in Australia'. He always sings when he's angry, lets on he's in a good humour when he's raging. The lights of the town are behind us now. These roads are dark. We pass houses with lighted candles in the windows, bulbs blinking on Christmas trees, sheets of newspaper held down on the windscreens of parked cars. Da stops singing before the end of the song.

'Did you see aer a nice little thing in the hall, Seamus?'

'Nothing I'd be mad about.'

'That blonde was a nice bit of stuff.'

I think about the mart, all the men at the rails bidding for heifers and ewes. I think about Sarah Combs and how she always smells of grassy perfume when we go to her house.

The chestnut tree's boughs at the end of our lane are caked with snow. Da stops the car and we roll back a bit until he puts his foot on the brake. He is waiting for Mammy to get out and open the gates.

Mammy doesn't move.

'Have you got a pain?' he says to her.

She looks straight ahead.

'Is that door stuck or what?' he says.

'Open it yourself.'

He reaches across her and opens her door, but she slams it shut.

'Get out there and open that gate!' he barks at me.

Something tells me I should not move.

'Seamus!' he shouts. 'Seamus!'

There's not a budge out of any of us.

'By Jeeesus!' he says.

I am afraid. Outside, one corner of my THIS WAY SANTA sign has come loose; the soggy cardboard flaps in the wind. Da turns to my mother, his voice filled with venom.

'And you walking up in your finery in front of all the neighbours, thinking you won first prize in the raffle.' He laughs and opens his door. 'Running like a tinker out of the hall.'

He gets out and there's rage in his walk, as if he's walking on hot coals. He sings: 'Far Away in Australia!' He is reaching up, taking the wire off the gate, when a gust of wind blows his hat off. The gates swing open. He stoops to retrieve his hat, but the wind nudges it further from his reach. He takes another few steps and stoops again to retrieve it, but again it is blown just out of his reach. I think of Santa Claus using the same wrapping paper as us, and suddenly I understand. There is only one obvious explanation.

My father is getting smaller. It feels as if the trees are moving, the chestnut tree whose green hands shelter us in summer is backing away. Then I realise it's the car. We are rolling, sliding backwards. No handbrake and I am not out there putting the stone behind the wheel. And that is when Mammy gets behind the wheel. She slides over into my father's seat, the driver's seat, and puts her foot on the brake. We stop going backwards. She revs up the engine and puts the car in gear. The gear-box grinds — she hasn't the clutch in far enough — but then there's a splutter and we're moving. Mammy is taking us forward, past the Santa sign, past my father, who has stopped singing, through the open gates. She drives us through the snow-covered woods. I can smell the pines. When I look back, my father is standing there watching our tail-lights. The snow is falling on him, on his bare head, on the hat that he is holding in his hands.

ELIZABETH CULLINAN

Life After Death

Yesterday evening I passed one of President Kennedy's sisters in the street again. They must live in New York — and in this neighborhood — the sister I saw and one of the others. They're good-looking women with a subdued, possibly unconscious air of importance that catches your attention. Then you recognize them. I react to them in the flesh the way I've reacted over the years to their pictures in the papers. I feel called on to account for what they do with their time, as if it were my business as well as theirs. I find myself captioning these moments when our paths cross. *Sister of the late President looks in shop window. Sister of slain leader buys magazine. Kennedy kin hails taxi on Madison Avenue.* And yesterday: *Kennedy sister and friend wait for light to change at Sixty-eighth and Lexington.* That was the new picture I added to the spread that opens out in my mind under the headline "LIFE AFTER DEATH".

It was beautifully cold and clear yesterday, and sunny and windless, so you could enjoy the cold without having to fight it, but I was dressed for the worst, thanks to my mother. At three o'clock she called to tell me it was bitter out, and though her idea of bitter and mine aren't the same, when I went outside I wore boots and put on a heavy sweater under my coat. I used to be overwhelmed by my mother's love; now it fills me with admiration. I've learned what it means to keep on loving in the face of resistance, though the resistance my two sisters and I offered wasn't to the love itself but to its superabundance, too much for our reasonable natures to cope with. My mother should have had simple, good-hearted daughters, girls who'd tell her everything, seated at the kitchen table, walking arm in arm with her in and out of department stores. But Grace and Rosemary and I aren't like that, not simple at all, and what goodness of heart we possess is qualified by the disposition we inherited from our father. We have a sense of irony that my mother with the purity of instinct and the passion of innocence sees as a threat to our happiness and thus to hers. Not one of us is someone she has complete confidence in.

Grace, the oldest of us, is married and has six children and lives in another city. Grace is a vivid person — vivid-looking with her black hair and high color, vivid in her strong opinions, her definite tastes. And Grace is a perfectionist who day after day must face the facts — that her son, Jimmy, never opens a book unless he has to and not always then; that her daughter Carolyn has plenty of boyfriends but no close girlfriends; that just when she gets a new refrigerator the washing machine will break down, then the dryer, then the house will need to be painted. My mother tells Grace that what can't be cured must be endured, but any such attitude would be a betrayal of Grace's ideals.

My middle sister, Rosemary, is about to marry a man of another religion. Rosemary is forty and has lived in Brussels and Stuttgart and Rome and had a wonderful time everywhere. No one thought she'd ever settle down, and my mother is torn between relief at the coming marriage and a new anxiety — just as she's torn, when Rosemary cooks Christmas dinner, between pleasure and irritation. Rosemary rubs the turkey with butter, she whips the potatoes with heavy cream; before Rosemary is through, every pot in the kitchen will have been used. This is virtue carried to extremes and no virtue at all in the eyes of my mother, whose knowledge of life springs from the same homely frame of reference as my sister's but has led to a different sort of conclusion: Rubbed with margarine the turkey will brown perfectly well; to bring the unbeliever into the fold, you needn't go so far as to marry him.

Every so often I have a certain kind of dream about Mother — a dream that's like a work of art in the way it reveals character and throws light on situations. In one of these dreams she's just died — within minutes. We're in the house where I grew up, which was my grandmother's house. There are things to be done, and Grace and Rosemary and I are doing them, but the scene is one of lethargy, of a reluctance to get moving that belongs to adolescence, though in the dream, as in reality, my sisters and I are grown women. Suddenly I realize that Mother, though still dead, has got up and taken charge. There's immense weariness but no reproach in this act. It's simply that she's been through it all before, has helped bury her own mother and father and three of her brothers. She knows what has to be done but she's kept this grim knowledge from Grace and Rosemary and me. She's always tried to spare the three of us, with the result that we lack her sheer competence, her strength, her powers of endurance, her devotedness. In another dream Mother is being held captive in a house the rest of us have escaped from and can't get back into. We stand in the street, helpless, while inside she's being beaten for no reason. The anguish I feel, the tears that wake me are not so much for the pain she's suffering as for the fact that this should be happening to her of all people, someone so ill-equipped to make sense of it. Harshness of various kinds and degrees has been a continuing presence and yet a continuing mystery to her, the enemy she's fought blindly all her life. "I don't think that gray coat of yours is warm enough," she said to me yesterday.

"Sure it is," I said.

"It isn't roomy enough." As she spoke, she'd have been throwing her shoulders back in some great imaginary blanket of a coat she was picturing on me.

"It fits so close, the wind can't get in," I explained. "That's its great virtue."

"Let me give you a new coat," she said.

When I was four years old I had nephrosis, a kidney disease that was almost unheard of and nearly always fatal then. It singled me out. I became a drama, then a miracle, then my mother's special cause in life. From this it of course follows that I should be living the life she'd have liked for herself — a life of comfort — but desire has always struck me as closer to the truth of things than comfort could ever be. "I don't really want a new coat," I told her yesterday. "I like my gray one."

"Dress warmly when you go out," she said. "It's bitter cold."

As I was hanging up there was an explosion — down the street from me, half a block on either side of Lexington Avenue is being reconstructed. The School for the Deaf and the local Social Services Office were torn down, and now in place of those old, ugly buildings, battered into likenesses of the trouble they'd tried to mend, there are two huge pits where men drill and break rocks and drain water, yelling to each other like industrious children in some innovative playground. And all day long there are these explosions. There was another; then the phone rang again. It was Francis, for the second time that day. "Constance," he said. "What a halfwit I am."

I said, "You are?"

He gave the flat, quick, automatic laugh I hate, knowing it to be false. When Francis truly finds something funny, he silently shakes his head. "Yes, I am," he said. "I'm a halfwit. Here I made an appointment with you for tomorrow afternoon and I just turned the page of my calendar and found I've got some sort of affair to go to."

"What sort of affair?" I asked. It could have been anything from a school play to a war. Francis produces documentaries for television. He's also married and has four sons, two of them grown. He's a popular man, a man everyone loves, and when I think of why, I think of his face, his expression, which is of someone whose prevailing mood is both buoyant and sorrowful. He has bright brown eyes. His mouth is practically a straight line, bold and pessimistic. He has a long nose and a high forehead and these give his face severity, but his thick, curly, untidy gray-blond hair softens the effect.

"I'm down for some sort of cocktail party," he said. "This stupid, busy life of mine," he added.

This life of his, in which I figure only marginally, is an epic of obligation and entertainment. Work, eat, drink, and be merry is one way of putting it. It could also be put, as Francis might, this way: Talent, beauty, charm, taste, money, art, love — these are the real good in life, and each of these goods borrows from the others. Beauty is the talent of the body. Charm and taste must sooner or later come down to money. Art is an aspect of love, and love is a variable. And all this being, to Francis's way of thinking, so — our gifts being contingents — we can do nothing better than pool them. Use me, use each other, he all but demands. I say, no — we're none of us unique, but neither are we interchangeable. "Well, if you've got something else to do, Francis," I said to him yesterday, "I guess you'd better do it."

He said, "Why don't I come by the day after tomorrow instead?"

I said, "I'm not sure."

"Not sure you're free or not sure you want to?"

"Both." I wasn't exactly angry or hurt. I have no designs on Francis Hughes, no claim on him. It would be laughable if I thought I did.

"Ah," he said, "Inconstance."

I said, "No, indefinite."

He said, "Well, I'm going to put Thursday down on my calendar and I'll call you in the morning and see how you feel about it."

"All right," I said, but on Thursday morning I won't be here — if people aren't interchangeable, how much less so are people and events.

"Tell me you love me," said Francis.

I said, "I do."

He said, "I'll talk to you Thursday."

"Goodbye, Francis," I said, and I hung up and put on my boots and my heavy sweater and my gray coat and went out.

The college I went to is a few blocks from this brownstone where I have an apartment. It's a nice school, and I was happy there and I can feel that happiness still, as though these well-kept streets, these beautiful houses are an account that was held open for me here. But New York has closed out certain other accounts of mine, such as the one over in the West Fifties. Down one of those streets is the building where I used to work and where I first knew Francis. His office was across the hall from mine. His life was an open book, a big, busy novel in several different styles — part French romance, part character study, part stylish avant-garde, part nineteenth-century storytelling, all plot and manners, part Russian blockbuster, crammed with characters. His phone rang constantly. He had streams of visitors. People sent him presents — plants, books, cheeses, bottles of wine, boxes of English crackers. I was twenty-two or three at the time, but I saw quite clearly that the man didn't need more love, that he needed to spend some of what he'd accumulated, and being twenty-two or three I saw no reason why I shouldn't be the one to make that point. Or rather, what should have put me off struck me as reason for going ahead — for the truth is I'm not Francis's type. The girls who came to see him were more or less voluptuous, more or less blonde, girls who looked as if they were ready to run any risk, whereas I'm thin, and my hair is brown, and the risks I run with Francis are calculated, based on the fact that the love of someone like me can matter to someone like him only by virtue of its being in doubt. And having, as I say, no designs, I find myself able to be as hard on him as if he meant very little to me when, in fact, he means the world. I try now to avoid the West Fifties. Whenever I'm in that part of the city, the present seems lifeless, drained of all intensity in relation to that lost time when my days were full of Francis, when for hours on end he was close by.

I also try to avoid Thirty-fourth Street, where my father's brother-in-law used to own a restaurant, over toward Third Avenue. Flynn's was the name of it, and when I was twelve my father left the insurance business to become manager of Flynn's. He's an intelligent man, a man who again and again redeems himself with a word, the right word he's hit on effortlessly. His new raincoat, he told me the other day, "creaks". I asked if there was much snow left after a recent storm, and he said only a "batch" here and there. Sometimes he hits on the wrong word and only partly accidentally. "Pompadour", he was always calling French Premier Pompidou. He also has a perfect ear and a loathing for the current cliché. He likes to speak, with cheery sarcasm, of his "life-style". He also likes to throw out the vapid "Have a good day!" "No way" is an expression that simply drives him crazy.

The other night I dreamed a work of art about my father. He was in prison, about to be executed for some crime having to do with money. Rosemary and my mother and I had tried everything, but we failed to save him. At the end we were allowed — or obliged — to sit with him in his cell, sharing his terror and his misery and his amazing pluck. For it turned out that he'd arranged to have his last meal not at night but in the morning — so he'd have it to look forward to, he said. I woke up in despair. My father's spirit is something I love, as I love his sense of language, but common sense is more to the point in fathers, and mine has hardly any. As for business sense — after eight months at Flynn's, it was found that he'd been tampering with the books; six thousand dollars was unaccounted for. No charges were pressed, but my father went back to the insurance business, and from then on we didn't meet his family at Christmas and Easter, they didn't come to any more graduations or to Grace's wedding, Rosemary no longer got a birthday check from Aunt Kay Flynn, her godmother. You could say those people disappeared from our lives except that they didn't, at least not from mine. Once, when I was shopping with some friends in a department store, I spotted my Aunt Dorothy, another of my father's sisters. She was looking at skirts with my cousins Joan and Patricia, who are Grace's age — I must have been about sixteen at the time. A couple of summers later I had a job at an advertising agency where my cousin Bobby Norris turned out to be a copywriter. He was a tall, skinny, good-natured fellow, and he used to come and talk to me, and once or twice he took me out to lunch. He never showed any hard feelings toward our family, and neither did he seem to suspect how ashamed of us I was. Around this time I began running into my cousin Paul Halloran, who was my own age. At school dances and at the Biltmore, where everybody used to meet, he'd turn up with his friends and I with mine. Then one Christmas I got a part-time job as a salesgirl at Altman's. A boy I knew worked in the stockroom, and sometimes we went for coffee after work, and once he asked me to have a drink. We were walking down Thirty-fourth Street when he told me where we were going — a bar that he passed every day and that he wanted me to inspect with him. Too late to back out, I realized he was taking me to Flynn's. As soon as I walked in, I saw my father's brother-in-law sitting at a table, talking to one of the waiters. He didn't recognize me, but I couldn't believe he wouldn't. I'm the image of my mother and I was convinced this would have to dawn on him, and that he'd come over and demand to know if I was who he thought I was, and so I drank my whiskey sour sitting sideways in the booth, one hand shielding my face, like a fugitive from justice. Or like the character in a movie who, when shot, will keep on going, finish the business at hand, and then keel over, dead.

It's three blocks north and three blocks east from the house where I live to the building where I went to college. Sometimes, of an afternoon, I work there now, in the Admissions Office, and yesterday I had to pick up a check that was due me. The Admissions Office is in a brownstone. The school has expanded. Times have changed. On the way in I met Sister Catherine, who once taught me a little biology. "Is it going to snow?" she asked.

I said, "It doesn't look like snow to me."

In the old days these nuns wore habits with diamond-shaped headpieces that made them resemble figures on playing cards, always looking askance. Yesterday Sister Catherine had on a pants suit and an imitation-fur jacket with a matching hat on her short, curly gray hair, and it was I who gave the sidelong glance, abashed in the face of this flowering of self where self had for so long been denied.

"It's cold enough for snow," Sister Catherine said.

I said, "It certainly is," and fled inside.

The house was adapted rather than converted into offices, which is to say the job was only half-done. Outside Admissions there's a pullman kitchen — stove, sink, cabinets, refrigerator, dishes draining on a rack. Food plays an important part in the life of this office, probably because the clerical staff is made up of students who, at any given moment, may get the urge for a carton of yogurt, or a cup of soup, or an apple, or a can of diet soda. I went and stood in the doorway of the room where they sit: Delia, Yeshi, Eileen, Maggie. They knew someone was there, but no one looked up. They always wait to make a move until they must, and then they wait to see who'll take the initiative. One reason they like it when I'm in the office is that I can be counted on to reach for the phone on the first ring, to ask at once if I can help the visitor. But the routine of

Admissions is complicated; every applicant seems to be a special case, and I work there on such an irregular basis that I can also be counted on not to be able to answer the simplest questions, and this makes the students laugh, which is another reason they like having me around. That someone like me, someone who's past their own inherently subordinate phase of life, should come in and stuff promotional material into envelopes, take down telephone requests for information, type up lists and labels — and do none of this particularly well — cheers them. I stepped into the office and said, "Hello, everybody." They stopped everything. I said, "Guess what I want."

"You want your check," said Yeshi, who comes from Ethiopia — the cradle of mankind. Lately I've been studying history. A friend of mine who's an Egyptologist lent me the text of a survey course, and now there are these facts lodged in my mind among the heaps of miscellaneous information accumulating there. "Where is Constance's check?" asked Yeshi. She speaks with a quaver of a French accent. Her hands are tiny, her deft brown fingers as thin as pencils. She has enormous eyes. "Who made out Constance's time sheet?" she asked.

Maggie said, "I did." She wheeled her chair over to the file cabinet where the checks are kept. "It should be here. I'm sure I saw it this morning with the others." Maggie is Haitian. Her hair is cut close and to the shape of her head. She has a quick temper, a need to be listened to, and a need, every bit as great, to receive inspiration. "Uh-oh," she said.

"Not there?" I asked.

"It's got to be. I made out that time sheet myself," said Maggie. "I remember it was on Thursday — I'm not in on Wednesdays, and Friday would have been too late."

I said, "Well, I don't suppose anyone ran off with it. It was only for a few dollars."

"Money is money around here." This came from Delia, a pre-med student and the brightest of the girls. Her wavy light-brown hair hangs below her waist. She has prominent features — large hazel eyes, an almost exaggeratedly curved mouth, and a nose that manages to be both thin and full; but there's a black-haired, black-eyed sister, the beauty of the family, and so Delia must make fun of her own looks. She's Puerto Rican and must also make fun of that. She speaks in sagas of self-deprecation that now and again register, with perfect pitch, some truth of her existence. "There's no poor like the student poor," she said yesterday.

"That's a fact, Delia," I said. "But I don't plan on contributing my wages to the relief of the Student Poor."

Maggie began pounding the file cabinet. "I made out that time sheet *myself*. I brought it in *myself* and had Mrs Keene sign it; then I took it right over to the business office and handed it to feeble-minded Freddy. He gave me a hard time because it wasn't with the others. I hate that guy." She pounded the cabinet again.

Yeshi said, "Maybe Mrs Keene has it."

"Is she in her office?" I could see for myself by stepping back; Olivia was at her desk.

"Come on in," she called.

I said to the students, "I'll be back," and I went to talk to my friend.

"You're just in time for tea and strumpets," she said.

Olivia was in school with me here, but her name then was McGrath. She's been married and divorced and has two sons, and I say to myself, almost seriously, that the troubled course of her life must be the right course since it's given her the name Keene, which describes her perfectly. She's clever, capable, resilient, dresses well, wears good jewelry, leads a busy life. Except for the divorce, Olivia is an example of what my mother would like me to be, though her own mother continually finds fault. "I wonder what it's like to be proud of your children," Mrs McGrath will say.

Olivia reached for the teapot on her desk and said, "Have a cup."

"No thanks," I said. "I only came by to pick up my check, but it doesn't seem to be outside."

She opened her desk drawer, fished around, and came up with a brown envelope. "Someone must have put it here for safest keeping." She handed me the envelope and said, "Come on, sit down for a minute. Hear the latest outrage."

I sat down in the blue canvas chair beside the desk. I love offices and in particular that office, where the person I am has very little fault to find with the person I was. I begin to wonder, when I'm there, whether the movement of all things isn't toward reconciliation, not division. I'm half-convinced that time is on our side, that nothing is ever lost, that we need only have a little more faith, we need only believe a little more and the endings will be happy. Grace's children will be a credit to her. Rosemary will find herself living in a style in keeping with her generous nature. My mother will come to trust the three of us. Olivia's mother will learn to appreciate Olivia. Francis will see how truly I love him. I'll be able to walk down Thirty-fourth Street and not give it a thought. "All right," I said to Olivia, "let's hear the latest outrage."

"Yesterday was High School Day."

"How many came?" I asked.

"A record hundred and seventy, of whom one had her gloves stolen, five got stuck in the elevator, and twelve sat in on a psychology class where the visiting lecturer was a transsexual."

"Oh God," I said.

"Tomorrow I get twelve letters from twelve mothers and dads."

"Maybe they won't tell their parents." I never told mine about seeing Aunt Dorothy shopping for skirts, or about the time I went to Flynn's for a drink, or how my first boyfriend, Gene Kirk, tried to get me to go to bed with him. To this day, I tell people nothing. No one knows about Francis.

Olivia said, "Nowadays kids tell all. Last week Barney came home and announced that his teacher doesn't wear a bra."

I looked at the two little boys in the picture on Olivia's desk. "How old is Barney?" I asked.

"Ten."

He has blond hair that covers his ears, and light-brown eyes with a faraway look. He calls the office and says, "Can I speak to Mrs Keene? It's me." His brother, Bartholomew, is a couple of years older. Like Olivia, Bart has small, neat features and an astute expression. He sometimes does the grocery shopping after school. He'll call the office and discuss steaks and lamb chops with his mother, and I remember how when I was a little older than he I used to have to cook supper most evenings. The job fell to me because Grace wasn't at home — she'd won a board-and-tuition scholarship to college — and Rosemary was studying piano, which kept her late most evenings, practicing or at her lessons. And after my father's trouble at Flynn's my mother had to go back to teaching music herself. She's a good — a born — musician, but the circumstances that made her take it up again also made her resent it. I resented it, too, because of what it did to my life. After school, I'd hang around till the last minute at the coffee shop where everyone went; then I'd rush home and peel the potatoes, shove the leftover roast in the oven or make the ground beef into hamburgers, heat the gravy, set the table — all grudgingly. But Bartholomew Keene takes pride in his shopping and so does Olivia. In our time, people have made trouble manageable. I sat forward and said, "I'd better get going."

"Think of it," said Olivia. "A transsexual."

I said, "Put it out of your mind."

In the main office, the students were in a semi-demoralized state. Their feelings are in constant flux; anything can set them up or down, and though they work hard, they work in spurts. My turning up was an excuse to come to a halt. I showed them my pay envelope. Maggie pounded the desk and said, "I knew it had to be around here somewhere."

"And I believed in you, Maggie," I said.

" 'I be-lieve for ev-ry drop of rain that falls,' " sang Delia, " 'a flower grows.' " They love to sing — when they're tired, when they're fresh, when they're bored or happy or upset.

" 'I be-lieve in mu-sic!' " Maggie snapped her fingers, switching to the rock beat that comes naturally to them. Eileen got up and went into her dance — she's a thin, pretty blonde with a sweet disposition and the soul of a stripper.

" 'I be-lieve in mu-sic!' " they all yelled — all except Yeshi, who only smiled. Yeshi is as quiet as the others are noisy but she loves their noise. Noise gives me eyestrain. I began backing off.

"When are you coming in again?" asked Delia.

I said, "Next week, I think."

Yeshi laughed. Her full name is Yeshimebet. Her sisters are named Astair, Neghist, Azeb, Selamawit, and Etsegenet. Ethiopia lies between Somalia and the Sudan on the Red Sea, whose parting for Moses may have been the effect of winds on its shallow waters.

After I left the office yesterday, I went to evening Mass. I often do. I love that calm at the end of the day. I love the routine, the prayers, the ranks of monks in their white habits, who sit in choir stalls on the altar — I go to a Dominican church, all gray stone and vaulting and blue stained glass. Since it's a city parish, my companions at Mass are diverse — businessmen and students and women in beautiful fur coats side by side with nuns and pious old people, the backbone of congregations. I identify myself among them as someone who must be hard to place — sometimes properly dressed, sometimes in jeans, not so much devout as serious, good-looking but in some undefined way. It's a true picture of me but not, of course, the whole truth. There's no such thing as the whole truth with respect to the living, which is why history appeals to me. I like the finality. Whatever new finds the archeologists may make for scholars to dispute, the facts stand. Battles have been won or lost, civilizations born or laid waste, and the labor and sacrifice entailed are over, can perhaps even be viewed as necessary or at least inevitable. The reasons I love the Mass are somewhat the same. During those twenty or so minutes, I feel my own past to be not quite coherent but capable of eventually proving to be that. And if my life, like every other, contains elements of the outrageous, that ceremony of death and transfiguration is a means of reckoning with the out-rageousness, as work and study are means of reckoning with time.

Yesterday Father Henshaw said the five-o'clock Mass. He doesn't linger over the prayers — out of consideration, you can tell, for these people who've come to church at the end of a day's work — but he's a conscientious priest and he places his voice firmly on each syllable of each word as he addresses God on behalf of us all, begging for pardon, mercy, pity, under-standing, protection, love. By the time Mass was over yesterday, the sun had set, and as I stepped onto the sidewalk I had the feeling I was leaving one of the side chapels for the body of the church. The buildings were like huge, lighted altars. The sky was streaked with color — a magnificent fresco, too distant for the figures to be identified. The rush hour had started. The street was crowded with people — flesh-and-blood images, living tableaux representing virtue and temptation: greed on one face, faith on another, on another charity, or sloth, fortitude, or purity. And there, straight out of Ecclesiastes, I thought — vanity of vanities, all is vanity. Then I realized I was looking at President Kennedy's sister. She was with a dark-haired man in a navy-blue overcoat. I had the impression at first that he was one of the Irish cousins, but I changed my mind as she smiled at him. It was a full and formal smile, too full and formal for a cousin and for that drab stretch of Lexington Avenue. It was a smile better given at official receptions to heads of state, and I got a sense, as I walked behind the couple, of how events leave people stranded, how from a certain point in our lives on — a different point for each life — we seem only to be passing time. I thought of the Kennedys in Washington, the Kennedys in London, the Kennedys in Boston and Hyannis Port. Which were the important days? The days in the White House? The days at the Court of St James's? Or had everything that mattered taken place long before, on the beaches of Cape Cod where we saw them sailing and swimming and playing games with one another?

We reached the corner of Sixty-eighth and had to wait for the light to change. It's a busy corner, with a subway station, a newsstand, a hot-dog stand, and a flower stand operated by a man and his wife. The flower sellers are relative newcomers to the corner. I began noticing them last summer, when they were there all day, but when winter came they took to setting up shop in late afternoon. For the cold they dress alike in parkas, and boots, and trousers, and gloves with the fingers cut out. They have the dark features of the Mediterranean countries and they speak to each other in a foreign language. They have a little boy who's almost always with them. I'd guess he's about five, though he's big for five, but at the same time he also seems young for whatever age he may be, possibly because he appears to be so contented on that street corner. A more sophisticated child might sulk or whine or get into trouble, but not that little boy. Sometimes he has a toy with him — a truck or an airplane or a jump rope. He also has a tricycle that he rides when the weather is good. If it's very cold he may shelter in the warmth of the garage a few doors down from the corner, or he'll sit in his parents' old car, surrounded by flowers that will replenish the stock as it runs out. In hot weather, he sometimes stretches out on the side walk, but that's the closest I've ever seen him come to being at loose ends. He's a resourceful little boy, and he's independent like his parents, who work hard and for the most part silently. I've never seen them talking with the owner of the hot-dog stand or the newsdealer. Business is business on that corner, and not much of it comes from me. I never buy hot dogs, flowers only once in a blue moon, and newspapers not as a rule but on impulse. Yesterday, I put my hand in my pocket and found a dollar bill there and I decided to get a paper. I picked up a *Post* and put my money in the dealer's hand. As he felt through his pockets full of coins, the flower sellers' little boy suddenly appeared, dashed over to his parents' cart, seized a daisy, and put his nose to the yellow center. The newsdealer gave me three quarters back. The traffic lights changed. President Kennedy's sister started across the street. The flower seller's wife grabbed the daisy from her son, and he ran off. I put the quarters in my pocket and moved on.

Yesterday's headlines told of trouble in the Middle East — Israel of the two kingdoms, Israel and Judah; Iran that was Alexander's Persia; Egypt of the Pharaohs and the Ptolemies. I love those ancient peoples. I know them. They form a frieze, a band of images carved in thought across my mind — emperors, princesses, slaves, scribes, farmers, soldiers, musicians, priests. I see them hunting, harvesting, dancing, embracing, fighting, eating, praying. The attitudes are all familiar. The figures are noble and beautiful and still.

M. J. HYLAND

My Father's Pyjamas

He usually wore pyjamas during the day. If he dressed it was only in case of an emergency, such as a fire or the arrival of an attacker. He was afraid of daylight and believed his nose was growing.

He asked me, 'Did you ever see a proboscis so humungous?' He looked at his reflection in the stainless steel kettle. 'What's the use of it? I'm going out for a beer.' Using his freckled forearm he pushed the kettle against the wall. The lid flew off and hit his toe. 'Pick that up for me, sweetheart, I'm afraid to bend just now.' I picked the lid up and put it on the bench.

'Your nose looks the same to me,' I said.

'You're sucking up to your father. I'll have you know that this nose is casting shadows on the bedroom wall that wake me while I sleep. I often think there's a Concorde about to land on the bed.'

He tousled my hair and tugged at the cord that held up his pyjama bottoms. He went into the bathroom. He splashed water on his face. He squeezed toothpaste onto his tongue. He used his index finger to smear the paste around his mouth, then spat.

'That stings,' he said. I stood on the edge of the bath.

'What are you gawking at?' he asked.

'Are you going on my bike?'

'I bought it,' he said. 'I believe that gives me the right to borrow it.' I got down from the edge of the bath.

'Don't you feel embarrassed riding a bike in your pyjamas?' I asked.

'No. I'd feel more embarrassed dressing up just so some fool in a tie behind the bottle shop counter doesn't look too hard at me.'

He hitched up his pyjama bottoms and headed for the door.

'I'd feel more embarrassed paying for a taxi that slows down at orange lights when I can get there on two perfectly good wheels.'

I went after him. He stopped in the hallway to get money out of his jacket pocket. I ran to the door and stood in front of it to block his way.

'That won't work,' he said. 'Move aside and let the dog see the rabbit.'

He opened the front door and stood on the scratchy mat that said Bless This House.

He had been drinking most of the afternoon. When the porch light came on he yelled, 'Hey wake up you boring good-for-nothing eejits. Come and see a drunk get on his little girl's bike.' He screamed hard and fell forward. He turned his fall into a jig. Just as when he fell in the house he would convert the fall into a forward roll and laugh. Now he danced in circles, throwing out his arms and legs with sharp flicks as though warding off a swarm of insects. I'd seen him dance this way before, usually at night. His loud music would wake me and I'd go into the kitchen and see him spinning in circles.

'Don't be ashamed,' he hollered. 'Show your ugly wormy good-for-nothing faces.' He danced on the wet grass. I stepped back onto the doorstep. He took his pyjama top off over his head. He had the chest and arms of a boy.

'Come and dance with me,' he said.

'No,' I said. 'Stop it.' I didn't want him to wake the Edelmans who lived across the road. Mr Edelman had a good vocabulary. Together we looked up new words in a dictionary.

He'd won a car on Sale of the Century. Kids at school called him 'That Jew Who Looks Like a Turtle'.

My dad span in circles, coming closer to me. 'Scream with me,' he said, 'it'll do you good. Come on, don't stand there like a coward. Let it all hang out.' He came at me. He pulled the sleeve of my cardigan.

'Can't you just stop?' I said.

Mr Edelman took me to the Jewish Holocaust Centre on my tenth birthday. We looked at photographs of pits filled with starved, white, naked bodies, with chests like greyhound dogs. After the rows of photos along the shining white walls, we followed the tour guide into a small projection room to watch a short film about gas chambers. When the people went into these chambers to be gassed they seemed not to know that they would die. They looked around with curiosity at the windowless walls and the nozzles in the ceiling. They looked at each other blankly; they didn't touch each other.

As we left the dark auditorium I vomited. Mr Edelman crouched down and used his handkerchief to wipe my vomit from the floorboards.

'You will become a beautiful human being,' he said. 'You will lead people.' He smiled. I held my breath so I would not smell the sick. He wiped the corners of my mouth. I was too preoccupied with shame and stink and the unpredictability of him to feel his warmth. I wanted to get away. I asked him, 'Can I have some water?'

'You can have the world,' he said.

My dad paced on the lawn.

'Stop,' I said.

'Stop dancing. Stop dancing,' he mocked in a high pitched voice. He undid the cord around his waist, took off his pyjama bottoms and flung them at me. He was thinner than I had known; his thighs no thicker than his calves. He danced in circles. He fell over and crawled on the grass.

'I'm a fly in a sticky ointment,' he said. 'Watch me crawl out of the sticky fly-catching ointment. Here I go. Out I climb. Oh, will my sticky wings dry in time?'

'Dad!' I wanted to slam the door and bolt it. I wanted to lock him out. I also knew what he meant about having sticky wings, about not being able to fly, about feeling stuck when you knew you should be able to float, to hover, to feel less heavy, to lift from the ground.

'Come out, come out wherever you are,' he screamed. 'I am the Queen of the Dance said she.'

His dick leapt between his legs like a rubbery creature, freshly hatched and jumping on a nest of fur and twigs. His arms snapped at the clouds. He danced faster.

'Go. Get your Jewball friends out here for a celebration. This is the genocide of polite civilisation.'

'You're being stupid,' I said. It was cold. I couldn't breathe properly. My neck was expanding.

Mr Meadows screamed over the fence, 'Shut the fuck up!'

Mr Meadows called the police the day my dad lit a fire on our front lawn and went knocking on doors. We piled bookshelves and broken chairs on the lawn and then set them alight. We started at the top of the street and knocked on doors. My dad was having a bonfire of the inanities. He asked for donations and sacrifices.

'Give me your inanities and I'll burn them like marsh-mallows on my fire,' he said. It was my job to hold an ice-cream container to take the donations.

'I'll ask people to write on our pieces of paper. I'll ask them to write down the most common things they say to their husbands or wives, like: We've run out of milk, honey.' They were also requested to write down the thing they thought about most. 'We'll see what junk their heads are full of,' said my dad. Everybody slammed their doors. Everybody said, 'Go away.'

'Write that down,' my dad ordered me. 'Write down *go away* on those bits of paper. We'll burn them all.'

My dad was taken away by the police that night. Two policeman shoved him into the back seat of the police car. He hit his head on the door frame. He slouched against the window and rubbed his head with handcuffed hands.

I stayed at my teacher's house that night. She stroked my forehead until I slept. She drove me to school in her car which smelt of eucalyptus. She wrote a message for me on a religious card: The Chinese ideogram for crisis is made up of two separate characters — fear and opportunity.

After school she wanted to come inside and speak to my dad but I wouldn't let her. 'He's asleep,' I said. 'In the cells they make you stay up all night and drink the policemen's urine.'

'Come and stay with me for a few days,' she said.

'No way,' I said. She said things like: hang on in there; chin up, be brave — and then she said she'd pray for me. I snapped at her. I told her that God was gone. I told her God had run away. He'd run away during World War II because he had run out of ideas and he knew that everybody had misunderstood. It's like, I said, when you write something really interesting on the blackboard and you ask a question and everybody just stares at their feet or out the window or they just want to eat the chips or chocolate hidden in their desks and you say to the class. Oh, I give up. That's what God said, I told her. It's obvious, I said, God gave up.

I didn't want my dad to be taken to the police station again. I held his wet pyjama bottoms up to my face. I sniffed them. Hot urine. I threw them onto the lawn. 'You better get dressed,' I said.

'Clever girl. Saves the old Jews from the party ... but does she really save them?' He ran out to the street and screamed again. 'What have you cunts really learnt?' He stood on the small brick wall at the front of our garden. 'What have any of you arseholes really learnt? Watch your fucking televisions then. Huddle together in front of your microwaves. Mourn the rise of crime but don't let a man scream on his goddamn front lawn.' He fell again.

'Stop it, dad,' I yelled.

He got dressed in his wet pyjamas and went to the garage to get my bike. He rode to the corner and onto the main road. I closed the door and waited. I wanted to see him in the bottle shop. I wanted to hear what he said to the man who served him. I didn't like being in the house without him. I went to the kitchen and got a glass of water. In front of the mirror in my room I poured some of it in my eyes. Water ran down my face. But to cry properly you need somebody watching. I went to my room and got the holy picture my teacher had given me. I sat on my bed with pillows behind my head. Mary Mother of God was holding baby Jesus. I held the picture in front of my face.

'Look at me,' I said to her.

'Look at me,' I said. Mary was smug. Her face was perfect. She couldn't care less. I opened the card and read about the Chinese ideogram. Fear and opportunity. My top was damp. I got into my nightdress and waited.

When my dad came back I was asleep. He rang the bell. I got up and let him in.

'The bottle shop was closed,' he said. 'I went down to the pub but the pervert wouldn't let me in. I'm very bloody thirsty.'

I tried to make myself look more tired than I was. I yawned.

'Hey, would you do your dad a favour and go and ask the old Jew across the road for a bottle of something. He won't mind, sweetheart.'

No drink and he'd make me sit with him until the morning. He'd rock back and forth in the kitchen chair listening to John Denver and make me sing along.

'I don't want to,' I said.

'Why the bloody hell not? I'm your father aren't I?'

The front door was still open. I walked out in my bare feet. Fear and opportunity, I said. Fear and opportunity. I knocked on the door. The lights were out.

Mrs Edelman came to the door in her nightie.

'Can I come inside?' I asked.

'Of course, dear, of course.'

Mr Edelman came out of the bedroom in his brown and blue checked dressing gown. 'I'll heat some milk,' he said.

'What's wrong, dear?' Mrs Edelman asked.

'My dad wants something to drink. He really needs it. If he doesn't get it he won't sleep.'

Mrs Edelman pulled the chain across the front door. We went into the living room. She told me to sit on the couch. She left and came back with a pair of woolly socks and the picnic rug I always used. The room was warm. I sat on the couch.

'Can I bring him a bottle of something?' I asked.

'No, dear, I don't think that's a good idea. He'll be okay.' She turned the lamp on and turned off the main light. She walked with a limp I hadn't noticed before.

'He won't be okay,' I said.

Mr Edelman came in from the kitchen with a mug of milo. He put it on a coaster on the small table next to me.

'Your father is a very sick man, child.'

I pushed the rug away. 'That's not true,' I said. They were standing in front of me. Mrs Edelman picked the rug up from the floor and wrapped it around my shoulders.

'I'm too hot,' I said.

Mr Edelman crouched down in front of me. 'You love your father. We understand that. But he isn't a good man.'

'Drink your milk, love,' said Mr Edelman. He put his hand on the nape of my neck and held the mug of milo to my mouth. 'Drink, love.'

'No thank you,' I said.

'Well I can't force you, but you need to calm down.'

'No I don't,' I said. I pushed the rug away again.

He stood. 'You can sleep in the spare room,' he said. There's an electric blanket. You're going to be fine.'

'No. My dad's waiting. I said I'd get him something to drink. I want to go back. I don't want to stay here.'

Mr Edelman went to the back door and turned the key. He went to the front door and turned the key to deadlock. He went to the bedroom and came back in with a long brown gun. He came and stood in the centre of the room, leant on the gun, one finger wriggling inside the barrel. 'You'll be safe here. You're safe now. He won't get to you here.'

'What are you going to do with that gun?' I asked.

'It will be a warning when he comes, that's all.'

I stood up to go.

'Sit down, child,' said Mr Edelman. 'You're confused. You don't know what's best. Your father screams in the street. He is full of mad poetry and nonsense and booze. You need your rest.'

'Let me go,' I said. 'I'll go and tell him you don't have anything to drink and then I'll come back. I promise.'

'No, love,' said Mrs Edelman. 'You're better off here.'

I didn't like the musty smell of them; the smell coming off Mrs Edelman's nightgown, the smell of their house. The polish and air freshener. Dark paintings on the walls.

'Drink your milk, child,' said Mr Edelman. 'It's time to forget about your father. It's time to think about your future. Drink and get some rest.'

He picked the mug up and put it to my lips.

'Drink. Try to relax.'

'No. It's cold now. I really don't want it.'

Mr and Mrs Edelman went into the kitchen down the hall. My feet were sweating in the woolly socks.

I imagined my father in his pyjamas rocking back and forth in his kitchen chair. I imagined him going to the window to look out for me. Getting up and sitting down. Pacing and sweating and turning the music up louder to stop his pain. I saw him singing; his neck arched back, singing at the ceiling.

I drank some milk. They came back into the room.

'I'll stay,' I said. 'I'm fine.'

'Good. We'll be in the kitchen,' said Mrs Edelman. 'We'll do a few chores while you relax, then we'll make up your bed. Call out if you need anything.'

I sat and listened. I heard Mrs Edelman say that I could stay with her sister. They began to wash dishes.

I said to myself — I moved my lips and I said to my dad — and I said to myself, Cry dad. You can cry. If you cry I will. I saw him with his head in his hands. I saw tears fall onto the kitchen table. I scooped them up and put them on my face, rubbed them on my face and then let him take my tears and put them in his mouth. I called out to him in my head, through the throbbing in my temples. You can scream if you like, I said to him, I talked to him along the line that connected our brains. I know why you scream. I want to do it too. Next time I will. Next time I'll scream with you. I saw him walk to his bed and lie across it, head in one corner, legs in the other. I saw him take a pillow and bring it into his chest. I heard him say, 'What have you learnt? What have any of you learnt?'

The Edelmans stacked clean plates and glasses in their cupboards. I lay face down on the couch and put my face into a cushion. I brought the cushion tightly up around my mouth and I screamed. I screamed hard and loud with my nose rammed so hard into the cushion that it felt bruised. I coughed when I'd finished. I drank some milk to soften the pain in my throat.

I went to the lounge-room window and opened the curtains. I stared into the dark street. The curtains opened in my dad's bedroom window. My dad pressed his face up against the glass. I stared across the street at him. 'Dad, I have learnt to scream. I know what you mean.' He waved and I waved. We waved for a stupidly long time, neither of us wanting to close the curtains and draw away. I waved and smiled but somebody had to stop. I had to sleep. I waved and I mouthed the words, I will scream with you. I believe that he heard me. His face left the window and the curtains fell together. I believe that he felt a little better. Before Mr and Mrs Edelman came back into the room, I lay on my back, pulled the picnic rug up under my chin, closed my eyes and pretended to sleep.

BRIDGET O'CONNOR

Bones

The hospital frightened them into it. They went the whole hog: relatives from America, an open car, church service with white dress, with white invitations, a singer (her sister). Simone arranged all of it, up on one elbow (a portophone, a sketch pad) during her convalescence. He didn't have to arrange any of it. He just had to be there. He really did think someone else would be there for him. Donna would stand up in the congregation and shout out for him. At the altar, he thought, like a kid, run, I can still run, his heart was sweating just holding her hand.

The consultant said, 'Both of you, calm down.'
    Simone was lucky. They were lucky. Everyone told them they were lucky: there were complications but the growth was benign. The important thing was the growth was benign. Why? How did it get there, why? The consultant lit the X-ray screen. Nobody knows *why*; sometimes cells just find a place to grow. He tapped his pen at the cloud, clicked his tongue. It certainly was a beauty. He said, 'Both of you, calm down, let's get this into proportion.' He peeled a nail. 'Think of it like a giant moth husk.' Simone became hysterical. That was the second blow. Euan looked at her and saw her crack. He didn't know it was over then but it was. Weight fell off her. First, her skin bagged, then it went all the way down to bone.
    They did the operation.

They called it an 'investigation'. After the investigation, after they'd cut it all out, he rushed to the hospital. He pumped his horn in traffic jams, the front of his brain went. Hunched over the wheel, his lips began to chatter, soon get back to normal, soon get back. He looked in the mirror and saw his eyes were rapidly receding ... dots. He screeched up the high street, the back of his brain screeched. He got to the hospital. Everywhere — red. His family, hers, had to force him to visit after that. But he visited in dreams. The same dream: a war in casualty, some kind of pile-up, rag dolls on stretchers, everywhere blood. He never could stand the sight, the tin-rusting smell, of blood. Through it, somehow, and in a lift, the further he went, the quieter and darker, his footsteps crashed, he held the bunch of flowers upside down, he tugged the petals off, he shredded the stalks. Her mum's shock looped on the intercom. '... had the stuffing knocked out of her, the stuffing ...' Following arrows, he found her, in a crowded ward. He couldn't believe it was someone he knew; she was wired up like an amplifier. Her eyes were clenched, her bottom lip was all tooth marks. He saw her empty; dead. He thought he should find a chair, hold her hand but he couldn't touch her. He dropped the flowers, ran to the corridor, one hand on the cold wall and threw his guts up.

He started to talk about it in the pub. 'It weighed four pounds, that's two bags of sugar, that's this big.' He made a gesture like he was lying about a fish. 'Behind her ovaries, *behind her ovaries.* This scar, you'd think a fucking shark had got her.' He looked from his pint to his short, choosing. Hours. Then, into Frank's eyes. 'The stitches went septic. She had tubes stuck *in* her.' 'Gross me out,' Frank said, pretending to puke, 'gutted.'

She was so frightened her lips shook. She said, 'Look at this!' She should have warned him, she pulled the hospital rag up, 'Look what they've done to me Euan.' It was so disgusting he proposed. She clung to his hand, all knuckle, bone.

She said, 'Oh Euan, come closer.' He bent his ear to her mouth, the delicate hairs there iced, 'You do still fancy me Euan, you won't leave me Euan?' She cried like he'd seen nobody cry. To make her stop, to get out of there he said, 'Silly, we're getting married aren't we? Silly. I don't want anyone else Simone. I only want you.' But it was no longer true. He looked at her cadaverous face on the pumped-up pillows. He smelt her warmed insides coming through the scar.

He rang Donna from a pub.

Why her? He didn't know why. He hardly knew her. She fancied him though, obvious. He made rapid progress, got half a leg short of legless. She drove him home.

Why her? It was obvious. She arrived outside the pub within the hour, climbing out of her Mini in the noisy rain, the rain pelted her shell jacket and her too-tight jeans, her spiral perm, the smile she gave him full of dimples, pretty teeth. He told himself he just wanted to talk to a girl. He couldn't talk to his mates. You can't talk to mates. He just wanted to talk to her. He never told himself the truth. Sometimes they all — his mates, Simone's — went bowling together: Donna, Terry, Sandra, Dave, Tina, Frank, Simone. Donna was Simone's friend's friend. Funny, acting the goat, her plump rump, plump rump, the words were made for her, holding the bowl as if it would pull her down, her upside-down head between her legs. When she heard it was him on the line she giggled. She always giggled at all his jokes, made him feel good. She giggled when he wasn't joking. He made happy rapid progress. A fake tapas bar, fake Spanish waiters yelled at them. He drank straights. She would look after him, drive him home, drink up. She said, 'Oh you poor thing.' She was dead good. He felt how good she was. He said she must go to the doctor's. He made her promise. He told her pink blinking face about the growth behind Simone's ovaries. Simone's routine visit to the doctor, the internal (he looked at her to see how she took the word), *internal* examination. She took his hand. He felt tears. He let them go, felt himself come totally undone. In the Mini, on the way to the flat, he said, 'The weight fell off her.' On the way up the stairs he turned and hugged her head. He said, in her springy hair, 'You know it's funny I can't eat eggs.' The top of his head whirled round. He said, 'Am I boring you?' In the flat, he fell backwards on the bed, drifted. She drifted beside him. He heard her struggling out of her clothes. From far away he heard her say, 'Euan, don't let me sleep in my contact lenses.' He said, 'It weighed four pounds, can you believe ... four fucking pounds. I don't know ... don't know ... did they weigh or ... estimate?'

He started to drink. He'd drunk before but now he needed it. He showed his face at work in the mornings, at the furniture store, had a lot of mileage there, got through it, delegated responsibilities (made his assistants floor-walk, dust), then a bunk off to an old boy's pub he'd found where he knew no one, that was still good after the fifth pint, so extremely beautiful after the sixth: becalmed bar staff; a bit of still-life at the bar. A wave of fading pink lino. Days, weeks, months, and they still didn't greet him, not a nod. Brilliant. He seriously and slowly drank, fish-eyes steady, steady with his pint. Drinking there or lying in bed during her convalescence, hands holding his prick for comfort or, double betrayal, with Donna under his arm, he'd live their pretty, glittery life.

He'd see her striding across the Bolton Road. He'd watch her in her big girl's blouse, it's blue-white sucked in all the light. Her classy black bob, her bank skirt and bank briefcase, he'd squint from his shop doorway at the plastic name tag swinging on her breast: Simone. Wonderful, foreign-sounding name. Simone. He rolled it around in his mouth all day.

Simone and Euan, Euan and Simone: double income, no kids, two cars (a boy racer and something roofless), exercise bikes, matching mountain bikes, a Perpetual Year Planner over the fridge; trawl of magnetic arrows over the three years of their true love. He choked. Life was so good.

He'd see her … Her dark grey shadow parted cars. They met. She strode in looking for a bed base. He was bored, filling out an order, sucking on his shirt. He looked up and there she was. Simone.

She took him up, boxed him into shape, streamlined his blokiness, made him sharp and lean and neat. She talked — 'direction', 'getting on'; her Seven Year Plans. She made graphs of their future: felt-tip peaks; her thick white nails tapped in row upon row of green-lit accounts. This flat: the house after that. He was so bloody happy the store was a laugh. People liked being there. Coffee percolated all day, Danish pastries in the microwave, bit of piped-out muzak, not too much piped-out crap. It all went down brilliant with the bosses. They didn't know what it was but it worked. He laughed a rich, easy, happy-man's laugh. Their cheek-to-cheek beamed off his desk all day.

All smashed now like a plate, all bloody smug.

His colour changed. If Simone didn't see it, they did. His skin went from sun-lamp brown to beige to yellow to palest blue. Simone's mum came to stay in the flat, then his. He hunched over the TV set. His eyes slid away from theirs. All day they cooked and stocked the freezer up, ran up to the hospital with their small temptations wrapped like gifts in silver foil. They forced him into the car, made him stand over Simone, prompted him to chat. Christmas was coming. Christmas went. Simone stayed in hospital, one month, two. She had tinsel still hanging off her tubes. Her eyes were huge and black against the pillows. He heard Frank's voice laughing, chafing her along, '… like pissholes in snow, girl, eat that up, c'mon …' He braced himself and strode in. He never mentioned the wedding, a date, he was trying to find a way to retract, keep it dateless, laugh the whole thing off. Simone looked up at him. She looked at him. When he left the ward he heard her cry all the way down in the lift.

Back from a wet lunch ratted. He was so easy-going the staff laughed. They knew it all anyway, Simone this, Simone that, every stitch. The first time it was funny. Funny Euan. He knocked over a shelf unit posing like a plant. His assistant's assistant, the lovely Jenny, very young, bossy, he liked that, he *really* liked that, rushed at him. 'Euan? Oh dear Euan, go home.' He sobbed, 'Do you know what they put in Weetabix fuck's sake, Riboflavin, Thia … Thiamin, fortified …' He stumbled over a bedside lamp, pulled off the machine-lace cover simultaneously with his tie, and burrowed down the four-poster 'star attraction' bed. He belched distinct bubbles: whiskey, ginger, lager … gin. He heard someone, Gary, snigger. He'd get Gary. He'd bloody *sack* … The lovely Jenny tugged his shoulder. He peeled back a lid, her clean eyes, it was urgent he tell her, go to the Doctor. He said, 'Go …' and passed out.

'Euan, come here.' Her mother sobbed. Her mother fell apart, took him by the shoulder, shook, 'You make her eat Euan, make her.' Her whole family suspected him, he knew, of causing it, making *it* grow. He nodded. Now he suspected himself. His mum watched him. When she found the bottles under his bed she slapped him round the face. He let her beat and berate, throw names from his past … what he did to Sandy, Rose, Nicole, names he didn't know she knew. She didn't know Donna's. He wanted her to know Donna's. He was going to tell her so she could smash it up for him. 'I know you,' she hissed, 'you're just like your father, weak. You're going to stay with that girl, so help …'

What was left of him?

What was left of him crumpled under her will. The families ganged up, sat him down, extracted a guest list, a date in June. Then everyone went away. He lay on the couch. The ansaphone whirred with instructions, the dust fell heavily on the exercise bike, on the mountain bikes in the hall, on the empty breakfast bar.

Simone began to eat. The tubes were taken away, the drips. She was so happy about the wedding, she told everyone just how happy she was. She started to eat. He couldn't eat. He looked at his own gut, the water bag of it over his jeans. He heard it gurgling. The thought of defrosting something cooked, he couldn't ... stuff rotted in the fridge, colours revolted him, putrid: red, yellow greens. He went routinely, then not at all, to the supermarket. He read the lists of food additives, preservatives on packets, poisons. He wheeled his empty shopping cart down the wide aisles, the bright white lights pressed on the tender part of his crown. He wanted to get out of it, run. But he felt so weak.

Out of hospital for the New Year: wheeled out, Simone talking non-stop, waving her bone arms and bone legs. Now they both looked very sick; him back to gut, red-eyed, her so thin and yellow he could have lifted her and carried her for miles. If he could bear to touch her; which he could not. Simone did not seem to see him, how he looked, how he did not touch her. She could not see herself. She *liked* her new shape, he couldn't believe it, he could not. She stood up sideways from him, like a line. At the party, the Welcome Home Simone, she talked about the wedding. She went on and on: relatives from America, an open car, church service with white dress, engraved invitations ... Her cake fork waved in the air. As the last relative left she was still talking; the bridesmaids' slippers, ballet shoes, what did he think? He got so pissed on sparkly he couldn't think; he passed out cold, in a curl, on the couch. In the morning she laughed at him, at his 'partying'; he could not move his neck. She was packing to go to Kent, remember? To convalesce? They couldn't sleep together anyway, her infected stitches, they wouldn't be able to lie down together, do it. She might as well get looked after. She laughed — get fed up. Her sister Annie's idea. He was so glad it wasn't his idea he couldn't look her in the face. He couldn't look her in the face. She went on. She packed clothes into a suitcase. She was bones. To get strong again. She would be fine for the wedding, they could save it all up (she squeezed him) for the wedding night. She would stay with Annie and Mike, plan a dream wedding, get a portophone, ring, write ... send sketches of her wedding dress, the bridesmaids'. Time would pass. Get back to normal. Get back. At the train station she kissed him, licked inside his mouth. The back of his knees went. He saw her on to the train, watched its tail-end recede in a tight yellow space. A long sit down. Drink.

Then, Donna's pretty piglet face, blinking pink at him in a pub, then in her car, then in his flat. Feel her chatter break on his forehead. Her pink chewing-gum tongue peeped. Feel her complete body, stroke her plump boneless soft flower-scented skin, can't do anything else but hold on, stroke, hold on, too pissed anyway; but hold on, swiped by surprise every time, the deep soft deep falling down comfort of her cushion-covered skin.

Drum roll for him on the tables. Friday nights like old times, before Simone, with Frank and his mates. He'd get in their local gut first. They'd beat a drum roll for him on the table with their glasses. The count down. The wedding this, the wedding that. They'd yell, 'the yuppies come home!' Shiny rolled-up faces. They drank to 'the noose', the 'wedding ring' to 'boys on top'. They all laughed at that one, they all knew Simone was boss. But they wouldn't let him talk about it, the growth, bored with that joke. It was all like a joke. Keep your pecker up. Look at him letting himself go already, frog neck. Frank clucked his disappearing chin, said, 'You don't know how lucky you are Euan. The lovely Simone. You've got it made!' He felt his throat close. The words were there caught; 'I can't touch her, I can't stand ...' Drink drowned them.

He'd drink his gold pint down in one, seized by his, seized by his great swelling love for Simone. Simone! Outside the curry house his mates hugged him, hung on to him, slapped his back. Their sweat-wet running cheeks. Time to get home. He'd need to be home *now*. Outside, signal taxis in the middle of the road, swear ferociously as they sped past, empty himself out like a machine gun on somebody's garden, on their petrified rose trees, serve them right. Whee! Bang! His mood swung. He was so bloody happy. Sober himself up outside his door, giggling, fall straight for the couch. 'I'm too dra-unck to touch you, my lovely, my lovely ...' Simone wasn't even there. Ha ha, what a joke. A man comes home ... He kept on forgetting, Kent, Annie's, dust. He swallowed the relief. Messages on the ansaphone. Donna's: 'How are you Huey? Call me.' He winced from it. Simone's. Her voice was strong and big, she sent kisses. She said, 'Love, only another week to go.' Kisses. She blew them down the line. He hugged his head with a pillow.

And dreamt he followed arrows. He was behind thick glass in an operating theatre, a sweating doctor, a sweating nurse. Donna sat in the congregation. Under the spinning disk of her hat she jumped up. He was making love with Simone. He was moving on her, inside her. He heard — snapping, but he couldn't stop, losing his way. He started to bang on the glass. He screamed, back climbing the wall. Simone was standing before him. She opened her rib cage like a shirt and threw knife after knife ...

By his stag night he was so oiled he could drink himself right through vertigo. Didn't see the growth then. A row of drinks in front of him, more lined up at the bar, his mates were spiking everything. Then, it was all he saw. The strippagram did her stuff — recited a ditty. His mates ringed them, yelling. She unhinged her bra, her breasts fell out. Under the club lights her skin had the glimmer of lard. He fixed his eye on her stomach, her plugged belly-button. He thought: in there, four pounds, that's my two hands put together.

Everything cracked, fell apart.

Train journeys on Sunday after Sunday at Annie and Mike's. On the last Sunday he told himself; get off the train ... *get off the train*. He was pale blue and his hands shook from drink and not drinking that morning so his breath would be sweet. He was only fooling Simone. Annie saw, Mike saw, how far he had gone. The light knifed his sight, he wavered for a moment, punch drunk, then crunched up the gravel chips — a box of fancy cakes, sweets for the kids, so many presents. He walked in on them through smoke, dim shapes, a telly-lit room. Simone was saying, "Ah Mike, stop, it *hurts*.' Mike was laughing, 'Well he can't — Richard Gere can't kiss.' They all laughed. They were all laughing. The kids grabbed the sweets. He touched Simone on the cheek, merged the touch with settling himself down on the gritty carpet for a day of it.

He watched Richard Gere kiss on the rewind.

Her breathing. Her hand on his head played with his curls, his whole skin crawled away from her touch, his whole skin crawled. He felt drops … one drop, two … run under his arms. In the blue telly gloom sweat stood out on his face like rain. And there she was. There — the image of her former great shape on the television screen: the swing of her big black hair, her glossy bank blouse. He saw cars swerve around her. In the stainless steel of their beams, he saw their life together in a shine behind her. Their life together a wide silver shine in front: all of it, gone.

'All turn round and greet Simone.' Cameras flashed. A white shadow, bone white, a drip of flowers, her big black hair swathed in lace. The organ squeaked. The priest meandered through the service. Then, it was done. They were out in the rushing light for photographs: air kisses for her, for him bitter-tasting powdered cheeks. He held pose after pose with her. Euan and Simone. Simone and Euan. Inside he was creased. He could not believe it, he still could not … Simone took his hand. He breathed quickly, quietly, but she heard. She put her lips on his ear. He could not move. He heard her smile, her whisper, 'Oh Euan love, soon.'

Notes on the Authors

Leland Bardwell, born in India in 1928 of Irish parents, returned to Ireland at the age of two. From 1970 she began to publish collections of poems, novels and stories as well as plays for the stage and for radio. She also wrote a musical about Edith Piaf. *Different Kinds of Love* (1987) is a collection of short stories. Her novels are *Girl on a Bicycle* (1977), *That London Winter* (1981), *The House* (1984) and *There We Have Been* (1989), and her poetry collections include *The Mad Cyclist* (1970), *The Fly and the Bed Bug* (1984), *Dostoevsky's Grave* (1991), *The White Beach* (1998) and *Pagan at the Table* (1998). She is co-editor of the literary magazine *Cyphers* and winner of the 1992 Martin Toonder Award for Literature. A member of Aosdána, she lives in Sligo.

Mary Beckett, born in Belfast in 1926, worked as a primary school teacher in Ardoyne until 1956, when she moved to Dublin. In the 1950s her stories were published in *The Bell* and other literary journals. She has published two collections of short stories, *A Belfast Woman* (1980) and *A Literary Woman* (1990), and the novel *Give Them Stones* (1987). The author of several books for children, she received the Bisto Merit Award in 1995.

Sara Berkeley, born in Dublin in 1967, read English and German at Trinity College, Dublin and published her first volume of poetry, *Penn* (1986), as a nineteen-year-old student. Other collections include *Home Movie Nights* (1989) and and *Facts about Water* (1994). She is the author of a collection of short stories, *The Swimmer in the Deep Blue Dream* (1991), and of the novel *Shadowing Hannah* (1999). Having spent a year at the University of California, Berkeley, she obtained an M.Sc. in Technical Writing at South Bank Polytechnic, London and currently lives and works in San Francisco.

Angela Bourke, born in Dublin in 1952, is Senior Lecturer in Irish at University College, Dublin, specialising in Irish oral tradition and literature, and has been a Visiting Professor at Harvard University and the University of Minnesota. Her stories have appeared in Ireland and in the US where she was the 1992 winner of the Frank O'Connor Award for Short Fiction. *By Salt Water* (1996) is her first short story collection. In 1999 she published *The Burning of Bridget Cleary: A True Story*. She is co-editor of the forthcoming *Field Day Anthology of Irish Writing*, vols. 4 and 5: *Irish Women's Writing and Traditions*.

Elizabeth Bowen, born in Dublin in 1899, spent her childhood in Dublin and at Bowen's Court, Kildorrery, Co. Cork. She studied at Trinity College, Dublin and in Oxford. In 1918 she moved to London where she joined the Bloomsbury group. During World War II she worked for the British Ministry of Information. In 1949 she returned to Bowen's Court. After selling the estate in 1960, she went back to Oxford and Kent. Among her many short story collections are *Encounters* (1923), *Ann Lee's* (1926), *Joining Charles* (1929), *The Cat Jumps* (1934), *Look at All Those Roses* (1941), *The Demon Lover* (1945) and *A Day in the Dark* (1965). She is the author of ten novels, among them *The Last September* (1929), *The House in Paris* (1935), *The Death of the Heart* (1938), *The Heat of the Day* (1949) and *Eva Trout* (1969). Bowen died in 1973 in London.

Claire Boylan, born in Dublin in 1948, worked as a journalist before she became, in 1983, a full-time writer. She was feature writer with the *Evening Press* (Benson & Hedges Journalist of the Year Award 1974) and editor of *Young Woman* and *Image*. She has published four books of short stories: *A Nail on the Head* (1983), *Concerning Virgins* (1989), *That Bad Woman* (1995) and *Another Family Christmas* (1997), and her *Collected Short Stories* appeared in 2000. Her novels include *Holy Pictures* (1983), *Last Resorts* (1984), *Black Baby* (1988), *Home Rule* (1992), *The Stolen Child* (1996), *Room for a Single Lady* (1997) and *Beloved Stranger* (1999). She is a member of PEN and of Aosdána. In 1997 she received the Spirit of Life Arts Award.

Juanita Casey, born in England in 1925, the daughter of an Irish travelling woman who died in childbirth, was abandoned by her English Romany father as a one-year-old and brought up by benefactors on a farm. She left school at thirteen, married at sixteen and led a nomadic life as a horsemaster in a circus. Largely self-taught, she has published short stories: *Hath the Rain a Father?* (1966); poetry collections: *Horse by the River* (1968) and *Eternity Smith* (1985); and novels: *The Horse of Selene* (1971) and *The Circus* (1974).

Evelyn Conlon, born in Rockcorry, Co Monaghan in 1952, was educated at St Patrick's College, Maynooth. She lived for a number of years in Australia and has travelled extensively in Asia. She was active in Irishwomen United and a founder member of the Dublin Rape Crisis Centre. While writer-in-residence in Limerick, she edited *An Cloigeann is a Luach.* Her novels are *Stars in the Daytime* (1989) and *A Glassful of Letters* (1998), her short story collections *My Head is Opening* (1987), *Taking Scarlet as a Real Colour* (1993), the title story of which was performed at the Edinburgh Theatre Festival, and *Telling* (2000). She lives in Dublin.

Emma Cooke, born in Portarlington, Co Laois in 1934, was christened Enid Blanc. The Blancs, descendants of the Hugenots, are mentioned in Joyce's *Finnegan's Wake* as 'Blong's best from Portarlinton's Butchery'. She received her education at Alexandra College, Dublin and Mary Immaculate College, Limerick. A mother of nine, she was active in cultural community affairs for many years. She published her short stories in the collection *Female Forms* (1980). Her novels are *A Single Sensation* (1979), *Eve's Apple* (1985) and *Wedlocked* (1994). For her short story 'An International Incident' she won the Francis MacManus Award. She lives in Co Limerick.

Elizabeth Cullinan was born in New York in 1933 and, after graduating from college, went to work at *The New Yorker*. From 1960 to 1963 she lived in Dublin. She is the author of two collections of short stories, *The Time of Adam* (1971) and *Yellow Roses* (1977). Many of these stories were first published in *The New Yorker*. Her novel *House of Gold* (1969) received the Houghton-Mifflin Literary Fellowship Award in 1970. In 1982 she published *A Change of Scene*. She teaches at Fordham University and lives in New York City.

Ita Daly, born in Drumshanbo, Co Leitrim in 1945, studied English and Spanish at University College, Dublin and worked for some years as a teacher. Her short stories, for which she won two Hennessy Awards, were published as *The Lady with the Red Shoes* (1980). Her novels include *Ellen* (1986), *A Singular Attraction* (1987), *Dangerous*

Fictions (1991), *All Fall Down* (1992) and *Unholy Ghosts* (1997). She has published a number of children's books, including *Candy on the Dart* (1989) and *Candy and Sharon Ole* (1991), as well as *Irish Myths & Legends* (2000). She lives in Dublin.

Anne Devlin, born in Belfast in 1951, studied English in Coleraine. In 1984 she settled in Birmingham where she lectures in drama. Her short stories are collected in *The Way-Paver* (1986). Her plays for theatre, television and radio include *A Woman Calling* (1984), *The Long March* (1982/1984), *Ourselves Alone* (1985), *Naming the Names* (1987), *The Venus De Milo Instead* (1987), *Heartlanders* (1989) and *After Easter* (1994). In 1998 she published *Titanic Town*, a play based on a novel by Mary Costello. Devlin has received many awards, including the Samuel Beckett Award in 1984 and the Susan Smith Blackburn Prize in 1986.

Mary Dorcey, born in Co Dublin in 1950. An active feminist, she was founder member of Women for Radical Change, Irishwomen United and the Irish Gay Rights Movement. She has lived and worked in England, France, the US and Japan. Her poems have been published in numerous anthologies and were collected in *Kindling* (1982), *Moving into the Space Cleared by Our Mothers* (1991) and *The River That Carries Me* (1995); her short stories were collected in *A Noise from the Woodshed* (1989), for which she was awarded the Rooney Prize for Literature. 1997 saw the publication of her début novel *Biography of Desire*. She is currently a lecturer at Trinity College, Dublin.

Anne Enright, born in Dublin in 1962, was educated at Trinity College, Dublin and the University of East Anglia, Norwich. She worked as a television producer with Radio Telefís Éireann. Her collection of short stories, *The Portable Virgin* (1991), which won the Rooney Prize for Literature, was followed by the novels *The Wig My Father Wore* (1995) and *What Are You Like?* (2000). She lives in Bray, Co Wicklow.

Lilian Roberts Finlay, born in Malta in 1915, studied acting at the Abbey Theatre School and submitted many plays to the Abbey, all rejected on moral grounds. While bringing up ten children, she wrote and published a number of short stories collected as *A Bona Fide*

Husband (1991). She is the author of the bestselling novel *Always in My Mind* (1988) and its sequel *Forever in the Past* (1993). Other novels are *Stella* (1992) and *Cassa* (1998).

Nora Hoult, born in Dublin in 1898, died in 1984 in Greystones, Co Wicklow. Orphaned as a child, she attended English schools and returned to Ireland in 1931. From 1937 to 1939 she lived in the US. Her short story collections are *Poor Women* (1928) and *Cocktail Bar* (1950). In almost two dozen novels she conducted detailed sociological and psychological studies of women belonging to different social strata. Her Irish novels are *Holy Ireland* (1935), *Coming from the Fair* (1937), *Father and Daughter* (1957) and *Husband and Wife* (1959). Other novels include *Augusta Steps Out* (1942), *Frozen Ground* (1952), *Last Days of Miss Jenkinson* (1962), *Not for Our Sins Alone* (1972) and *Two Girls in the Big Smoke* (1977).

M. J. Hyland, born in London to Irish parents in 1968, spent her early childhood living in Dublin. In 1980 her family migrated to Melbourne, Australia, where she now works as a lawyer. She has been published in Australia, Ireland and the US and is a recipient of an Arts Victoria scholarship for the writing of her first novel.

Claire Keegan was born in Clonegal, Co Wicklow in 1968, where she grew up on a farm. She completed her undergraduate studies in English and Political Science at Loyola University, New Orleans and received a Master's degree in Writing from the University of Wales. *Antarctica* (1999), a collection of short stories, for which she won numerous awards, is her first book publication. She is currently writer-in-residence at Dublin City University.

Maeve Kelly, born in Dundalk, Co Louth in 1930, trained as a nurse in London and Oxford. She was a founding member of the Limerick Federation of Women's Organisations and of Adapt. Her publications include two novels, *Necessary Treasons* (1985) and *Florrie's Girls* (1991), two collections of short stories, *A Life of Her Own* (1976) and *Orange Horses* (1990), a collection of poetry, *Resolution* (1986), and a feminist fairy tale, *Alice in Thunderland* (1993). She won a Hennessy Award in 1972 for the title story of *A Life of Her Own*. Having farmed in Co. Clare for many years, she now lives outside Limerick.

NOTES ON THE AUTHORS

Rita Kelly, born in Galway in 1953 and educated in Ballinsloe, Co Galway, writes poetry, fiction, criticism and drama in English and Irish. Her poetry has been collected as *An Bealach Éadóigh* (1984) and the bi-lingual *Fare Well: Beir Beannacht* (1990). Her short stories have been collected as *The Whispering Arch* (1986), and she wrote a play called *Frau Luther* (1984). With her late husband, the Irish language poet Eoghan Ó Tuairisc, she published *Dialann sa Díseart* (1981). More recently, she published *From Here to the Horizon: Laois Anthology* (1999) and *Travelling West* (2000). She won the Merriman Poetry Award in 1975 and the Seán Ó Ríordáin Memorial Prize for Poetry in 1980.

Mary Lavin, born in 1912 in East Walpole, Massachusetts, the daughter of Irish emigrants, moved at the age of ten with her mother to Athenry, Co Galway, later to Dublin and to an estate in Bective, Co Meath where her father worked as a steward. She attended Loreto Convent School, Dublin and studied English at University College, Dublin. Later she lived for part of the year at Abbey Farm, her farmhouse in Bective. 1964-65 she was President of Irish PEN, 1971-73 of the Irish Academy of Letters. She was awarded many honours, among them her elevation to Saoi in 1992. In addition to children's books and the novels *The House in Clewe Street* (1945) and *Mary O'Grady* (1950), she published nineteen collections of short stories, among them *Tales from Bective Bridge* (1942), *The Long Ago* (1944), *The Becker Wives* (1946), *At Sallygap* (1947), *A Single Lady* (1951), *The Patriot Son* (1956), *The Great Wave* (1961), *In the Middle of the Fields* (1967), *Happiness* (1969), *A Memory* (1972), *The Shrine* (1977) and *A Family Likeness* (1985). She died in 1996 in Dublin.

Mary Leland, born in Cork in 1941, has worked as a journalist and feature writer with the *Cork* (now *Irish*) *Examiner*, the *Irish Times* and other newspapers. She has published the novels *The Killeen* (1985) and *Approaching Priests* (1991), a collection of short stories, *The Little Galloway Girls* (1997), and *The Lie of the Land: Journeys through Literary Cork* (1999). She lives in Cork.

Blánaid McKinney, born in Co. Fermanagh in 1961, graduated in Politics from Queen's University, Belfast and worked first at the DTI in London, then for the European Unit of Aberdeenshire Council in

Scotland. She is now working for the Greenwich Waterfront Development Partnership in South London. *Big Mouth* (2000) is her first short story collection.

Marilyn McLaughlin, born in Derry in 1951, read English and German at Trinity College, Dublin and spent a year in Germany researching fairy tales. From 1975 she worked in Derry as a teacher, researcher on BBC Radio Foyle, and an illustrator and graphic designer. In 1996 she won the Brian Moore Short Story Award. *A Dream Woke Me* (1999) is her first short story collection, *Fierce Milly* (1999) a children's book.

Frances Molloy, born in 1947 in Derry, left school at fifteen to work in a local pyjama factory. In 1965 she spent some time in a convent and in 1970 she emigrated to Lancashire to return eighteen years later. Her novel *No Mate for the Magpie* (1985) is written in Ulster dialect. After her death in 1991 the children's book *Black Bootie and the Beer Can Trap* (1997) was published, and 1998 saw the posthumous publication of a volume of short stories, *Women Are the Scourge of the Earth*.

Mary Morrissy, born in Dublin in 1957, works for the *Irish Times*. She has published one collection of short stories, *A Lazy Eye* (1993) and the novels *Mother of Pearl* (1996) and *The Pretender* (2000). She won a Hennessy Award in 1984, a Lannan Literary Prize in 1995, and was shortlisted for the Whitbread Prize in 1996. She lives in Dublin.

Val Mulkerns, born in Dublin in 1925, was educated at Dominican College, Dublin and from 1945 to 1949 worked as a civil servant. After a sojourn in London she was Associate Editor of *The Bell* (1952-54) under Peadar O'Donnell. From 1968 to 1983 she contributed as a weekly columnist to the *Evening Press*. After her novels *A Time Outworn* and *A Peacock Cry* appeared in 1951 and 1954 respectively, there was a break of more than twenty years before she re-entered the literary world. She has published the short story collections *Antiquities* (1978), *An Idle Woman* (1980) and *A Friend of Don Juan* (1988) and has written two more novels, *The Summerhouse* (1984) and *Very Like A Whale* (1986). Together with Peadar O'Donnell, she was awarded the Allied

Irish Bank Prize for Literature. A member of Aosdána, she lives in Dublin.

Éilís Ní Dhuibhne, born in Dublin in 1954, studied at University College, Dublin and the University of Denmark, Copenhagen, was awarded a doctorate on Irish folklore and works as a keeper at the National Library of Ireland. Her first volume of short stories, *Blood and Water* (1988), was followed by the novel *The Bray House* (1990). Other works include the short story collections *Eating Women Is Not Recommended* (1991), *The Inland Ice* (1997) and *The Pale Gold of Alaska* (2000), the novel *The Dancers Dancing* (1999), historical novels for children and a play in the Irish language.

Edna O'Brien, born in 1930 in Tuamgraney, Co Clare, was educated at the Sisters of Mercy Convent School Loughrea and studied at the Pharmaceutical College, Dublin. In 1959 she moved to London, where she still lives most of the time. With her "Country Girls Trilogy" *The Country Girls* (1960), *The Lonely Girl* (1962; 1964 as *Girl with Green Eyes*) and *Girls in Their Married Bliss* (1964) she achieved a *succès de scandale*. She has published six volumes of short stories: *The Love Object* (1968), *A Scandalous Woman* (1974), *A Fanatic Heart* (1976), *Mrs Reinhardt* (1978), *Returning* (1982) and *Lantern Slides* (1988). Among her other novels are *August Is a Wicked Month* (1964), *Casualties of Peace* (1966), *A Pagan Place* (1971), *Johnny I Hardly Knew You* (1977), *The High Road* (1988), *Time and Tide* (1992), *House of Splendid Isolation* (1995), *Down by the River* (1996) and, most recently, *Wild Decembers* (1999). She has lectured in English Literature at City College, New York and at the John Hopkins University, Baltimore and received numerous awards, among them the Aristeion European Literature Prize in 1995 and the Irish PEN / A. T. Cross Literary Award in 2001. Her prolific and varied output comprises numerous plays for the stage and for television, filmscripts, children's books, travel books and biographies.

Bridget O'Connor, born in London in 1961, read English at Lancaster University and works in adult education. In 1990 she was awarded the *Time Out* Literature Prize. She has published the short story collections *Here Comes John* (1993) and *Tell Her You Love Her* (1997).

NOTES ON THE AUTHORS

Mary O'Donnell, born in Monaghan in 1954, studied at St Patrick's College, Maynooth. Along with three volumes of poetry, *Reading the Sunflowers in September* (1990), *Spiderwoman's Third Avenue Rhapsody* (1993) and *Unlegendary Heroes* (1998), she has published a short story collection, *Strong Pagans* (1991) and the novels *The Light Makers* (1992), *Virgin and the Boy* (1996) and *The Elysium Testament* (1999). A contributor to newspapers and arts programmes, she was awarded the 2001 James Joyce Suspended Sentence Residency in Australia. She lives in Maynooth.

Julia O'Faolain, born in London in 1932, the daughter of writers Sean and Eileen O'Faolain, was educated at universities in Dublin, Rome and Paris. She worked as a language teacher and translator in Florence. O'Faolain is the author of novels such as *Godded and Codded* (1970), *Women in the Wall* (1975), *No Country for Young Men* (1980), *The Obedient Wife* (1982), *The Irish Signorina* (1984) and *The Judas Cloth* (1992), and has published the short story collections *We Might See Sights!* (1968), *Man in the Cellar* (1974), *Melancholy Baby* (1978) and *Daughters of Passion* (1982). In 1973 she co-edited *Not in God's Image: Women in History from the Greeks to the Victorians.*

Lucile Redmond, born in Dublin 1949, was educated in Ireland, England and the US. She has published a volume of short stories, *Who Breaks Up the Old Moons to Make New Stars* (1978) and has been awarded the Hennessy and the Allied Irish Bank Awards.

Eithne Strong, born in Glensharrold, Co Limerick in 1923, entered the civil service for a year. In 1943 she married the poet and psychoanalyst Rupert Strong with whom she had nine children and co-founded Runa Press. Having attended Trinity College, Dublin as a mature student, she worked as a teacher in Dublin from 1973 to 1988. Apart from her short story collection *Patterns* (1981), she wrote the novels *Degrees of Kindred* (1979) and *The Love Riddle* (1993) as well as several poetry collections in both English and Irish, among them *An Gor* (1942), *Songs of Living* (1961), *Sarah, in Passing* (1974), *Cirt Óibre* (1980), *Flesh — the Greatest Sin* (1980), *Fúil agus Fallaí* (1983), *My Darling Neighbour* (1985), *Let Live* (1990), *Aoife Faoi Ghlas* (1990), *An Sagart Pinc* (1990) and *Spatial Nosing* (1993). A member of Aosdána, she died in Dublin in 1999.

Acknowledgements
(in order of appearance)

Nora **Hoult**: 'Nine Years Is A Long Time' reprinted from *Selected Stories*, London / Dublin: Maurice Fridberg, 1946. Elizabeth **Bowen**: 'Unwelcome Idea' reprinted from *The Collected Stories*, Harmondsworth: Penguin, 1983. Mary **Lavin**: 'Lilacs' reprinted from *Tales from Bective Bridge*, Dublin: Town and Country House, 1996. Lilian **Roberts Finlay**: 'A Bona Fide Husband' reprinted from *A Bona Fide Husband and Other Stories*, Swords: Poolbeg Press, 1991. Eithne **Strong**: 'Thursday to Wednesday' reprinted from *Patterns and Other Stories*, Swords: Poolbeg Press, 1981. Juanita **Casey**: 'One Word' reprinted from *Territories of the Voice*, Boston: Beacon Press, 1989. Val **Mulkerns**: 'Away From It All' reprinted from *An Idle Woman*, Swords: Poolbeg Press, 1980. Mary **Beckett**: 'Heaven' reprinted from *A Literary Woman*, London: Bloomsbury, 1990. Leland **Bardwell**: 'Out-Patients' reprinted from *Different Kinds of Love*, Dublin, Attic Press, 1987. Maeve **Kelly**: 'Journey Home' reprinted from *A Life of Her Own*, Swords: Poolbeg Press, 1976. Edna **O'Brien**: 'A Journey' reprinted from *A Scandalous Woman and Other Stories*, Harmondsworth: Penguin, 1976. Julia **O'Faolain**: 'First Conjugation' reprinted from *Melancholy Baby and Other Stories*, Swords: Poolbeg Press, 1978. Emma **Cooke**: 'The Greek Trip' reprinted from *Female Forms and Other Stories*, Swords: Poolbeg Press, 1980. Mary **Leland**: A Way of Life' reprinted *from The Little Galloway Girls*, London: Black Swan, 1988. Ita **Daly**: 'Such Good Friends' reprinted from *The Lady with the Red Shoes*, Swords: Poolbeg Press, 1980. Frances **Molloy**: 'Women Are the Scourge of the Earth' reprinted from *Women Are the Scourge of the Earth*, Belfast: White Row Press, 1998. Claire **Boylan**: 'The Stolen Child' reprinted from *That Bad Woman: Short Stories*, London: Little, Brown, 1995. Lucile **Redmond**: 'Love' reprinted from *Modern Irish Short Stories*, Dublin: Irish Times, 1985. Mary **Dorcey**: 'The Husband' reprinted from *A Noise from the Woodshed: Short Stories*, London: Only Women Press, 1989. Anne **Devlin**: 'Five Notes after a Visit' reprinted from *The Way-Paver*, London: Faber and Faber, 1986. Marilyn **McLaughlin**: 'Bridie Birdie' reprinted from *A Dream Woke Me and Other Stories*, Belfast: The Blackstaff Press, 1999. Angela **Bourke**: 'Deep Down' reprinted from *By Salt Water: Stories*, Dublin: New

Island Books, 1996. Evelyn **Conlon**: 'Park-Going Days' reprinted from *My Head Is Opening*, Dublin: Attic Press, 1987. Rita **Kelly**: 'Soundtracks' reprinted from *The Whispering Arch*, Dublin: Arlen House, 1986. Éilís **Ní Dhuibhne**: 'Summer Pudding' reprinted from *The Inland Ice*, Belfast: Blackstaff Press, 1997. Mary **O'Donnell**: 'Come In — I've Hanged Myself' reprinted from *Strong Pagans and Other Stories*, Swords: Poolbeg Press, 1991. Mary **Morrissy**: 'A Lazy Eye' reprinted from *A Lazy Eye*, London: Jonathan Cape, 1993. Blánaid **McKinney**: 'Please' reprinted from *Big Mouth*, London: Weidenfeld & Nicolson, 2000. Anne **Enright**: 'Luck Be A Lady' reprinted from *The Portable Virgin*, London: Secker & Warburg, 1991. Sarah **Berkeley**: 'Thin Ice' reprinted from *The Swimmer in the Deep Blue Dream*, Dublin: The Raven Arts Press, 1991. Claire **Keegan**: 'Men and Women' reprinted from *Antarctica*, London: Faber and Faber, 1999. Elizabeth **Cullinan**: 'Life after Death' reprinted from *Cabbage and Bones: An Anthology of Irish American Women's Fiction*, New York: Henry Holt, 1997. M. J. **Hyland**: 'My Father's Pyjamas' reprinted from *Nocturnal Submissions*, Melbourne: M. J. Hyland, 1995. Bridget **O'Connor**: 'Bones' reprinted from *Here Comes John*, London: Joanathan Cape, 1993.